D0044698

ASK NOT

BOOKS BY MAX ALLAN COLLINS

The Memoirs of Nathan Heller

*Ask Not**
*Target Lancer**
Triple Play (novellas)
Chicago Lightning (short stories)
*Bye Bye, Baby**
Chicago Confidential
Angel in Black
Majic Man
Flying Blind
Damned in Paradise
Blood and Thunder
Carnal Hours
Stolen Away
Neon Mirage
The Million-Dollar Wound
True Crime
True Detective

The Road to Perdition Saga

Return to Perdition (graphic novel)
Road to Paradise
Road to Purgatory
Road to Perdition 2: On the Road (graphic novel)
Road to Perdition (graphic novel)

With Mickey Spillane

Complex 90
Lady, Go Die!
Kiss Her Goodbye
The Big Bang
The Goliath Bone
The Consummata

With Barbara Collins (as Barbara Allan)

Antiques Chop
Antiques Disposal
Antiques Knock-off
Antiques Bizarre
Antiques Flee Market
Antiques Maul
Antiques Roadkill

Quarry Novels

The Wrong Quarry
Quarry's Ex
Quarry in the Middle
The First Quarry
The Last Quarry
Quarry's Vote (aka *Primary Target*)
Quarry's Cut (aka *The Slasher*)
Quarry's Deal (aka *The Dealer*)
Quarry's List (aka *The Broker's Wife*)
Quarry (aka *The Broker*)

Writing as Patrick Culhane

Red Sky in Morning
Black Hats

With Matthew Clemens

No One Will Hear You
You Can't Stop Me

*A Forge Book

ASK NOT

MAX ALLAN COLLINS

A Tom Doherty Associates Book
New York

ASK NOT

Edited by James Frenkel

A Forge Book
Published by Tom Doherty Associates, LLC
175 Fifth Avenue
New York, NY 10010

www.tor-forge.com

Library of Congress Cataloging-in-Publication Data

Collins, Max Allan.
Ask not : Nathan Heller Mystery / Max Allan Collins. — First Edition.
p. cm.—(Nathan Heller mysteries ; 14)
ISBN 978-0-7653-3626-2 (hardcover)
ISBN 978-1-4668-2745-5 (e-book)
1. Heller, Nathan (Fictitious character)—Fiction. 2. Private investigators—Fiction. I. Title.
PS3553.O4753A85 2013
813'.54—dc23

2013018440

Forge books may be purchased for educational, business, or promotional use. For information on bulk purchases, please contact Macmillan Corporate and Premium Sales Department at 1-800-221-7945, extension 5442, or write specialmarkets@macmillan.com.

First Edition: October 2013

Printed in the United States of America

0 9 8 7 6 5 4 3 2 1

For Nate and Abby—
who will make their own history

Although the historical incidents in this novel are portrayed as accurately as the passage of time and contradictory source material will allow, fact, speculation, and fiction are freely mixed here; historical personages exist side by side with composite characters and wholly fictional ones—all of whom act and speak at the author's whim.

The promoters of the systemic evil involved in killing President Kennedy counted on our repression and denial of its reality.

—James W. Douglass,
JFK and the Unspeakable

That little Kennedy . . . he thought he was a god.

—Allen Dulles

We'll take out insurance by setting up some nut to take the fall for the job, just like they do in Sicily.

—Carlos Marcello

One out of every four presidents has died in office.

—Lyndon Baines Johnson

We're all mad here.

—Lewis Carroll

ASK NOT

CHAPTER 1

September 1964

My son's generation will always remember two key events of their teenage years—where they were when news came of President Kennedy's assassination, and seeing the Beatles on Ed Sullivan.

I learned of the former in a guest room at Hugh Hefner's Playboy Mansion in Chicago—in the company of Miss November, fittingly enough. Soon, amid beauties with their mascara running, she and I had hunkered around a portable television with a little gray picture in a big shiny white kitchen. The latter broadcast I somehow missed, but Sam has made it abundantly clear over the years that the February 9 appearance of those four Liverpool lads on *The Ed Sullivan Show* was right in there with JFK getting it.

My son once told me that that joyful noise had signaled a rebirth for his generation, the Baby Boomers, granting them permission to smile and have fun and be silly again. But it also signaled the end of barbershops as we knew them and extended the fad called rock 'n' roll through the rest of the century and beyond.

Unlike many of my contemporaries—I was a successful businessman in my well-preserved late fifties—I did not have disdain for the Beatles. They were a pretty fair combo, better than most of the little bands that had made the Twist a very big deal on Rush Street, and they seemed to have a sense of humor. Earlier this year,

Sam had convinced me to take in their flick *A Hard Day's Night,* and I'd liked it. More importantly, Miss November—who you may have calculated was younger than me—loved it.

The Beatles, through no fault of their own, had created a problem for me with Sam. He lived with his mother and my ex-wife (that's one person) in Hollywood with her husband, a fitfully successful film producer. Normally Sam spent summers with me in Chicago, but he had begged off of June and July because his combo—yes, the Beatle bug had bit him hard—had a weekly pool party gig at a Bel Air country club that paid "incredible money" ($100).

"So what about August?" I'd asked him over the phone.

"August is cool. August is groovy. Everybody's going on vacation with family, so we can't take gigs anyway. Dad, are you okay with this?"

"It's cool. Maybe not groovy, but cool." I had maintained a strong relationship with my son by not insisting on having my own way. That's right. I spoiled his ass. Divorced dads get to do that.

Have to do that.

And August had been swell. At a second-run theater in Evanston, we took in *From Russia with Love,* and before the film began I bragged about having met James Bond's papa during the war.

"I doubt Ian Fleming was on Guadalcanal, Dad," Sam had said skeptically over his popcorn.

"It was on Nassau," I said. "He was doing spy stuff."

"The stories you tell! How am I supposed to know when you're bullshitting me?"

Another way I spoiled Sam was to let him swear around me. His mother hated it. Which I loved.

I sipped too-sweet Coke. "Someday you'll appreciate your old man."

"Hey, as dads go, you're one of the cooler ones."

Not cool, just one of the cooler ones. I'd settle.

Sam—actually Nathan Samuel Heller, Jr., but his mother and I decided one Nate around the house was plenty (more than enough, as it turned out)—had caught up with my six feet now. He had my late mother's Irish good looks, the Jewish half of my heritage nowhere to be seen in either of us, and we looked enough alike to be brothers. If he had a really old brother.

Oh, and he had his mother's brown hair, not my reddish variety. Cut in that Moe Howard bowl haircut the Beatles had bestowed on American males. Once upon a time I'd wished he would let that dumb crew cut grow out. Careful what you wish for.

"Listen, uh, Dad . . . I need to talk to you about college. I'm thinking about liberal arts."

"Not business?"

"No. I want to be able to take music courses."

Like the Beatles had ever studied music!

Sam was my only son. My only kid period. I had no desire to reshape him into Nathan Heller, Jr., even if that was his name. But I did have a successful business—the A-1 Detective Agency, here in Chicago and with branches in Los Angeles, New York, and more recently Las Vegas—and I hoped he'd eventually take it over.

Not as a detective—private eye days were long gone. Hell, they'd even canceled *Peter Gunn.* But the agency was a very profitable business indeed, and Sam would make a great executive—he was smart and personable and already pretty darn savvy.

"Music, huh?" I said lightly. "You'll teach, then. What, marching band? Chorus? What's the starting salary, thirty-five hundred a year?"

"Money isn't everything, Dad."

Said the kid with two well-off parents.

"Anyway," he went on, "I don't wanna teach. I don't know what I want to do, maybe keep playing my music . . ."

His music. The last time I looked, "his" music was the Beach Boys, Beatles, Chuck Berry, and, what was that instrumental group? The Adventures? Surf music. Jesus God.

". . . or something else, maybe, but not . . . *business.*"

He said the word the way a Republican says Democrat.

"You know I'll support you any way you want to go, son. But you might, I'm just saying *might,* want to—"

"It's starting," Sam said, meaning the movie, or anyway the previews.

And it was starting. The first major struggle between father and son, at least since back when he wanted to stay up and watch Johnny Carson on school nights.

So August flew by, and we went to the fights and to ball games and more movies and had plenty of great food with an emphasis on Gino's pizza. We loafed around my Old Town bachelor pad and watched my color TV with its impressive 21-inch screen. I even arranged for an afternoon tour of Hef's mansion, just to give Sam a little hint of what being a successful businessman might bring.

Anyway, it was September now. This was Saturday and Labor Day was Monday. Back in Beverly Hills, school had been in session a couple days already, but I'd arranged for Sam to stick around so I could give him his seventeenth birthday present.

The Beatles were performing tonight at Chicago's International Amphitheater. This was the hottest ticket in town, the latest stop on a twenty-four-city, thirty-two-day tour. Tickets were going for $2.50, $3.50, and $4.50. A really great dad, with just the right connections, might be able to score his kid one of those tickets. But I could top that.

Just like the Beatles could top Elvis Presley, whose first Amphitheater appearance had required two hundred policemen, for security—*three hundred fifty* cops were being put on for John, Paul, George, and Ringo, plus a couple hundred firemen with half a dozen ambulances standing at the ready. But celebrities like these required personal security as well, for their Midway Airport arrival, their Stock Yard Inn press conference, and the concert itself.

And that was where the A-1 Detective Agency came in. Alan Edelson, who was handling press arrangements in Chicago, said Brian Epstein himself had requested me. I pretended to be impressed, and later really was, when my son informed me that Epstein was the boy wonder who had discovered and signed the Beatles. Mr. Epstein had apparently read of me across the pond in a *News of the World* story about Hollywood's "Private Eye to the Stars."

In reality I remained Chicago's private eye to anybody with a fat wallet, and spent at most maybe three months in California spread out over an average year. But *Life* and *Look* magazine articles, focusing on star clients like Frank Sinatra, Bobby Darin, and the late Marilyn Monroe, had made a minor celebrity out of me.

Normally as president of the A-1, I would have left this job to my staff and whatever add-ons from other agencies we might require. Sure, I'd likely stop around, shake a famous hand to provide the celebrity reassurance (and the A-1 a photograph), then go on my merry way.

But attending to the Beatles personally gave me an opportunity to maybe be a hero to my son.

We skipped the madhouse at Midway Airport because I knew the best opportunity for Sam to meet his real heroes was at the Saddle and Sirloin Club, the Stock Yard Inn's restaurant. The medium-sized Tudor-style hotel itself was at Forty-second and Halsted, adjacent to the amphitheater. Sam and I were already there—half a dozen of my agents were doing the actual security work—when the Beatles arrived in a phalanx of blue uniforms.

The dining room—a replica of an old English inn with oaken paneling arrayed with hunting prints—was jammed with linen-covered tables at which only invited reporters whose credentials had been checked were allowed. Screaming teenagers outside held back by sawhorses made a kind of muffled jet roar. Blue cigarette smoke drifted lazily in contrast to a general air of tension. Every table had a photographer on his feet with flash camera ready.

They were so young, these four superstars who took chairs at a microphone-strewn banquet table on a modest platform. With the exception of Ringo Starr, who was maybe five seven, the others were around six feet, slender, smiling, amused. They wore sharp unmatching suits in the mod British style, Paul and Ringo in ties, John with his collar buttoned, George unbuttoned. A row of cops, their caps with badges on, were lined up behind them, as if not sure whether to protect or arrest.

Sam was in a suit similar to what the Beatles were wearing, but it was a Maxwell Street knockoff I bought him, not a Carnaby Street original; like George, he wore no tie and his collar was open. His shoes were something called Beatle boots that a lesbian might have worn to an S & M party. Not that anyone cared, I was in a dark-gray suit by Raleigh with a black-and-gray diamond-pattern silk tie. And Florsheims, not Beatle boots.

Before the questioning could begin, I approached the raised table with Sam at my side, and introduced myself to McCartney.

"You're the private eye," he said, pleasant if not overly impressed. He was smoking. They all were. My God, they were young. Not far past twenty. Just four years or so older than Sam.

I handed him my card. "These are my private numbers, if you need anything or there's any problem at the hotel."

After the concert, they would be staying, briefly, at the O'Hare Sahara awaiting their Detroit flight later tonight.

"Obliged," McCartney said.

I took a shot. "This is my son—Sam. You mind signing something for him?"

They were all agreeable, signing a cocktail napkin. Sam was frozen, so I mentioned he was in a band himself.

"Watch what you sign, man," Lennon said, as he was autographing the napkin. He winked at Sam, who took the flimsy paper square and nodded and said thanks to all of them. They had forgotten him already, but I will always remember that they were nice to my son.

"Have you fellas given any thought to what you're going to do when the bubble breaks?"

"Well," Lennon said, "we're gonna have a good time."

"We never plan ahead," Harrison said.

"How about your retirement, or buying into a big business?"

"We already are a big business," Lennon said, "so we don't have to buy into one."

That was a smart-ass reply, which the reporter well deserved, but Lennon's lilting accent took the edge off. Americans were suckers for a British accent; there was something seductive about it. I'd been with a couple BOAC stewardesses myself.

"What do you think of Chicago?"

Gesturing as he spoke, McCartney said, "I'm looking forward to seeing the gangsters with their broad-brimmed hats and wide ties."

I'm sure the cute Beatle considered that a gag, but the day before, a restaurant got blown up on Mannheim Road for resisting the protection racket, and two mob factions were currently shooting at each other over control of gambling on the North Side.

Anyway, the lads were funny and made monkeys out of any number of smug reporters. Sam wore a big grin throughout, holding onto that cocktail napkin with both hands.

The concert started at 8:30, but the Beatles didn't come on right away. The vast high-ceilinged chamber was packed with fifteen thousand audience members, most of them teenagers, chiefly girls, often with beehive hairdos. They didn't scream much during the four opening acts—a couple of nondescript combos, an out-of-place R & B singer, and a long-haired blonde who looked like she belonged in the audience—and I started to wonder what all the fuss was.

I'd been told the audience would scream so loud, you couldn't hear a damn thing. I was hearing these opening acts much better than I cared to. When the blond girl wrapped up her short set, meaning the headliners were next, the screaming kicked in, the sound like a burning building with flames eating away.

Finally at 9:20, the Beatles emerged, led onto the stage by Chicago cops, coming down stairs off to one side. Grinning and waving, the three front men strapped on their guitars—Ringo getting behind his drums on a little stage-on-the-stage—and the place went wild. Stark raving mad. Like the Playboy mansion the day JFK was shot, lots of mascara was running. The shrieking was unbelievable. That muffled jet roar wasn't muffled now—the damn jet was flying around in circles in the place, which was almost possible, since they held indoor drag races in here. There were six hundred thousand square feet of it, after all, currently filled by thousands of girls having a nervous breakdown.

We had front-row seats and could almost hear the music. Well, Sam seemed to hear it just fine—he was singing along to "I Saw Her Standing There" and "Twist and Shout" and all the rest.

I officially joined the older generation by covering my ears. Oddly I could hear the music better that way, particularly the bass guitar and drums. The damn thing seemed to go on forever. I thought I might weep. Finally it was over—thirty minutes that had earned these four twenty-year-olds a grand a minute.

When the Beatles fled the stage, I took advantage of my security status to enlist a cop to lead Sam and me out a side exit while the audience was still on its feet screaming and crying. As for me, my ears were ringing. It was like I had a seashell up to either ear and could hear waves pounding the shore.

We came around to an ocean of cars—the lot held four thousand and was at capacity—but the kids hadn't started to stream out yet, lingering inside in the afterglow of Beatle hysteria. All across the lot, parents were standing by cars, waiting, smoking, the little red tips bobbing like fireflies in the night.

A fairly short walk away, my car was parked across from the Stock Yard Inn on South Halsted. Short walk or not, I was well aware that this was the South Side, an area tougher than a nickel steak, not that the Saddle and Sirloin Club had served up any nickel steaks lately.

The nearby stockyards consumed a sprawling area between Pershing Road on the north, Halsted on the east, Forty-seventh on the South, and Ashland Avenue on the west—close to five hundred acres. Still, you could neither hear nor smell those thousands of doomed cattle, unless you counted the fragrant aroma wafting from the Saddle and Sirloin.

"You want me to get that napkin framed up for you?" I asked Sam.

"You won't lose it or anything, will you?"

"No. I can be trusted with evidence."

"That would be fab."

Engines starting up, mechanical coughs in the night, indicated the teenagers were finally exiting the amphitheater for their rides. The wide street was still largely empty, though, as we jaywalked across, making no effort at speed.

We paused mid-street for a car to go by in either direction. Across from us, my dark-blue Jaguar X waited patiently, with its hubcaps and everything—not bad for this part of town.

"I'll just hold on to it for now," he said, meaning the napkin. It was still in his hands like the biggest, luckiest four-leaf clover any kid ever found.

He would be seventeen later this month, but I had that same surge of feeling for him I'd first experienced holding him in my arms at the hospital. I was studying him, trying to memorize the moment, slipping an arm around his shoulders, and he tightened, hearing the engine before I did.

It came roaring up from our left, where somebody had been parked on the Stock Yard Inn side, a light-blue Pontiac Bonneville, screaming down the street like those girls at the amphitheater. The vehicle, even at this stupid speed, was no danger to us, but we began to move a little quicker across our lane.

"Dad!"

Headlights were bearing down on us. The Pontiac had swerved—not swerved, *swung* into our lane, as if we were its targets.

Maybe we were.

The damn beast was right on us and it clipped me a little but it would have been much worse if Sam hadn't tackled me and shoved me out of harm's way. I glimpsed a blur of a dark-complected face in the window of the Pontiac as it whipped by, dark eyes glaring at me as if I were the one who'd hit him. Well, I had, a little.

Sam and I both landed hard on the pavement, and I had taken some impact, a glancing blow but still painful, on my left hip.

I was on my other side and Sam was hovering, saying, "Dad, Dad" over and over, as I managed to sit up, pointing.

"Son! Get that license number! Can you see it?"

I was too dazed—all I could see were red halos around taillights.

But Sam was nodding. He stared after the receding vehicle. It had disappeared by the time he got a pencil out of somewhere and jotted the number down on the back of his precious cocktail napkin, which was already rumpled and wadded from when he'd clutched his fists and tackled me to safety.

He had tears in his eyes. I'll never know if it was out of fear for himself or concern for me or sorrow over his ruined Beatlemania artifact.

But I'd lay odds on the latter.

He helped me up and drunk-walked me the few steps to the Jag. Another car went by, slow, the driver giving us a dirty look. We were just a couple of lushes lurching across the street.

Nobody had seen the incident, at least nobody who bothered to come help or anything. I told Sam to drive, fishing out the keys for him, and he helped me into the rider's side. Now the stream of amphitheater traffic was picking up, slowed by traffic cops. Like they say, where was a cop when you needed one?

"I'm going to get you to a hospital," Sam said over the purr of the Jag. "What one should I go to? I don't know this part of town."

"Just get us back to Old Town. I didn't get hit that bad."

"Dad, no!"

"Son, I'll be bruised up, and my chiropractor will make a small windfall out of me. But I'm fine. Drive."

We'd gone about half a block when he said, "Shouldn't we call the cops? We should go back to that Stock Yard hotel and call the cops."

"No."

"What was *wrong* with that guy? Was he drunk?"

"Don't know."

"It was almost like he was *trying* to hit us!"

More likely me. Sam hadn't been on the planet long enough to make my kind of enemy.

We stopped at an all-night drugstore to pick up some Anacin, four pills of which I popped, chasing them with a Coke. Despite all that caffeine, I was asleep when Sam pulled behind my brick three-story on Eugenie Street, one block north of North Avenue. I woke up just as he was pulling the Jag into my stable-turned-garage. The main building, par for this side street, was narrow and deep with not much of a backyard.

I lived on the upper two floors, the ground level a furnished apartment the A-1 used for visiting clients and as a safe house. Sam was still helping me walk as we entered in back through the kitchen and across the dining room into the living room, an open space with off-white wall-to-wall carpet and a wrought-iron spiral staircase. The plaster walls, painted a rust orange, had select framed modern artwork, and one wall was a bookcase with as many LPs as books. Furnishings ran to overstuffed couches and chairs, some brown, some green.

I settled into my brown-leather recliner and used the phone on the table where the *TV Guide* and remote control also lived.

"You know, old married people like me," my longtime partner Lou Sapperstein said gruffly, "aren't necessarily up at this hour."

"It's not even midnight. You still got friends in Motor Vehicles?"

"I have friends everywhere, Nate. Even in Old Town."

"Do you have friends in Motor Vehicles who work night shift?"

"Are you okay? You sound funny."

"Yeah, I'm a riot. Rowan and Martin got nothing on me. I'm going to give you a license plate to have your friend run. And I want to know right now. Not tomorrow."

"Okay," Lou said, no more kidding around. "I got a pencil. Go."

I gave him the number.

Twenty minutes and two glasses of rum later, I picked the phone up on first ring.

"Pontiac Bonneville," Lou said. "'61. Light blue."

"That's the one."

"Stolen earlier this evening."

"Big surprise."

"Found abandoned within the last half hour on the South Side."

"Within, say, half a mile of the International Amphitheater?"

"You are a true detective, Nathan Heller. What's this about?"

"Maybe nothing. Maybe something."

I'd already gotten the nine millimeter from the front closet and rested it on the *TV Guide.*

Lou was saying, "If there are any prints on that vehicle, we'll know tomorrow."

"Tomorrow's Sunday."

"I have friends who work Sundays. I have all sorts of friends."

"This is where I came in," I said, thanked him, and hung up.

Sam was sitting on the nearby couch, leaning forward, hands clasped. He looked worried. A little afraid. He'd watched me go to the shelf to fetch the Browning automatic and its presence in the room, near my reach, was palpable.

"What's this about, Dad?"

"I don't know. Maybe nothing. Maybe a joyrider. Or a drunk. Or a husband who didn't like the art-study photos I took of him for his wife."

Sam was well aware of what I did for a living, though we both knew it had been a long, long time since I had shot pictures through motel windows. Although my agents still did.

"Dad, are you *sure* you're all right? I think we should get you to an emergency room."

"An emergency room at a Chicago hospital on a Saturday night? That's more dangerous than that street we crossed."

He smiled a little. "That was a close one. That was terrible."

"I'm sorry about that napkin."

"It's okay."

"No. It isn't. I'm going to call that guy Epstein in London and get you a signed photo."

"You don't have to."

But something had jumped in his eyes.

And eventually I did get him the photo, personally signed to him, and another to me for the A-1 office wall.

Right now, though, more pressing matters were on my mind.

Specifically, that swarthy face that blurred by in that Bonneville; but not so blurry that I didn't recognize him.

I was damn sure—well, pretty sure—that he was a Cuban who'd been arrested in November of last year by the Secret Service. I'd been working with them at the request of a friend of mine who was so famous that if I'd told my son, he would have accused me of bullshitting again.

Three weeks prior to the shooting of the President in Dallas, a similar scheme had been hatched, and thwarted, in Chicago. I had hauled in two Cuban suspects and delivered them to the Secret Service, who had let them go after JFK's motorcade through the Loop was canceled. I'd never seen either of the Cubans again.

Until tonight, anyway, when one of them tried to run me down outside the Stock Yard Inn.

CHAPTER 2

Late Summer 1962

From Moisant International Airport to New Orleans stretched a dreary ten miles of billboards, filling stations, strip joints, cheap bars, parking lots, neon signs, and sleazy motels. Of the latter, the one at 1225 Airline Highway appeared perhaps the most benign, an innocuous-looking low-slung yellow-brick building with its aqua awnings and towering three-tiered '50s-modern sign—

Town and
Country
MOTEL

—particularly if you were unaware it was owned and operated by Carlos Marcello, mob boss of Louisiana.

The motel's restaurant/lounge was horizontal to the highway. Behind it were two facing wings of guest rooms separated by an outdoor swimming pool edged at its far end by tall skinny pine trees. The trees helped conceal the bunker-like brick-and-cinder-block one-story building behind the motel.

That modest structure housed Marcello's office, out of which he ran such legitimate interests as a beer and liquor distributorship, shrimp-boat fleets, taxi and bus firms, and the tomato canning company that allowed him to claim he was principally "a tomato salesman." Some in law enforcement might point to a panoply of rackets including (but not limited to) narcotics, prostitution, extortion, and gambling ranging from casinos to the Town and Country's own B-girl-serviced lounge with its side room of slots.

We had just come from the airport, my client Paul Fudala and I. We weren't here to check in, although any time Carlos Marcello was your host, checking out was a possibility. A longtime veteran of the oil business, Paul was a client out of the A-1's newest branch, Las Vegas; he had hired me to have my people investigate a couple of potential investors in a new business venture, an oil additive he'd developed. Carlos Marcello was one of those prospective moneymen, but I hadn't been hired to investigate him. You didn't have to work very hard to know what Marcello's background was.

Paul had grown up in New Orleans and had been a childhood friend of Marcello's. For some reason, Paul had let slip to his old pal that I was doing his investigative work, and "Uncle Carlos" had enthusiastically said he wanted to meet me, "de famous private eye to da stars." The mob boss, as I am attempting to convey, had a mush-mouth drawl that mingled, or rather mangled, Louisiana and Sicily into a unique mess.

Paul was in his late fifties, a big white-haired cheerful guy with a nice tan and a Brooks Brothers suit not designed for this sticky, muggy heat. I was in a gray lightweight Botany 500, but it wasn't faring much better against the humidity.

Thankfully, the interior of the unadorned brick building behind the motel was air-conditioned. If anything, it was meat-locker cold. Just inside the building were two facing offices. On our right a closed door was labeled PHILLIP SMITH—a lawyer on staff, Paul said—while on our left an unlabeled door stood open, revealing a nice-looking middle-aged brunette in a short-sleeve pale yellow silk blouse with a jeweled brooch. Eyes friendly behind jeweled cat's-eye glasses, she greeted Paul warmly by name.

"Frances," Paul said, smiling at her and taking the hot-pink-nailed hand she offered across a desk piled with paperwork, "it's been too long. We're half an hour early—should we go back and kill time in the Lounge, or is the Little Man in?"

The Little Man was Louisiana's big man, of course.

She slapped at the air. Her drawl was an easily understandable second soprano. "Oh, you boys just go on down and see Mr. Marcello. He said send you all in whenever you got here."

I followed Paul down the hallway of unadorned cream-colored brick.

"She was pleasant," I said.

"She's married to Carlos's top man—guy who runs the Town and Country. Nofio Pecora? You'd never guess butter-wouldn't-melt Frances runs a call-girl ring spanning four states. Texas, Mississippi, Alabama."

"You said four states."

"Well, Louisiana, too, naturally."

Naturally.

At the end of the hall, the office labeled CARLOS MARCELLO stood open, revealing the Little Man himself, hunkered behind a big uncluttered mahogany desk in a spacious, dark-paneled, handsomely appointed, plushly carpeted office that might have belonged to a bank president. The walls were all but covered with huge framed aerial photographs of a sampling of what Paul later informed me were Marcello's Louisiana properties.

Busy on the phone, our host smiled at us both, nodding, waving us into two tufted leather chairs opposite him while he continued his business.

He was a squat, bullnecked, broad-shouldered man. His crisp-looking short-sleeve white shirt with silver-gray silk necktie revealed muscular if short arms. His head was a broad, oversize oval, dark hair graying and receding, eyes dark and wide-set, nose beaky, mouth oddly sensual, cleft chin resting on a fleshy second chin. To me he looked like the oldest, meanest elf on St. Nick's staff, the guy who kept the other little fuckers in line.

"No . . . no . . . yeah . . . . *What*? *Dat* dog don't fuckin' hunt . . . .

Yeah, dat's right, dat's right . . . . *No*! You tell dat muthafucka he kin go *fuck* hisself! And ah don't mean dat in no *fun* way . . . ."

This went on for a while. Glancing around, I noticed an area over a brown-leather couch where the aerial photographs gave way to family photos and a few celebrity ones. Marcello with his arm around Sinatra, for example, taken maybe around 1950 when the mob was underwriting Frankie's comeback. One photo had been taken at an outdoor rally and showed a teenaged Marcello grinning and shaking hands with the Kingfish himself, Governor Huey Long.

I'd done a job for the Kingfish, back in '35, and helped out his widow in '37; but since then I had rarely returned to the Pelican State. Maybe that was because, once upon a time in Louisiana, I'd almost become a generous serving of Yankee Gumbo. Oh, you'd like the recipe? Well, you jes' take one tub o' lye and add y'seff one Yankee. Stir. Then pour the ol' tub in the nearest swamp.

When I'd been facing getting served up that way, a young, illiterate, bullnecked hood had been one of the flunkies I'd encountered. That teenaged hoodlum was just a hired hand, and we hadn't really tangled. He had just helped set me down in a wooden chair in the back room of a ramshackle bayou restaurant called the Willswood Tavern and gone back out front to serve his customers, leaving me to the whims of a political stooge named McCracken and an imbecile called Bucky Boy. I wasn't even sure the hood knew my name, back then. I knew his, all right.

I'd first encountered Marcello on that job for Huey, in '35, in the French Quarter, when Carlos was just a kid loading Chief slot machines in back of a truck. I'd have never guessed that by 1947, at age thirty-eight, he would assume leadership of the Louisiana Mafia. Like Kennedy patriarch Joe, Carlos had gone partners with New York's Frank Costello—Kennedy in booze, Marcello in gambling.

Anti-organized crime crusader Robert Kennedy having been the kid of a fellow Costello accomplice was an irony Carlos never forgot—although I'd be shocked if he knew what the word irony meant.

Not that he was a dummy. Far from it. Carlos Marcello was perhaps the most autonomous mob boss in these United States. The Mafia had, after all, put down its roots in Louisiana long before Chicago, New York, and New England. The loose structure here, so intertwined with Pelican politics, provided mob boss Marcello uncommon independence and power. He did not answer to the national commission of Cosa Nostra bosses, who considered Louisiana a foreign country, and rightly so.

Marcello had learned early on to insulate himself from accomplices, or if not, silence them. For a junior-high-school dropout, he was uncommonly shrewd, and generous—his six brothers all held responsible positions in his enterprises. As one would expect of a Louisiana kingfish, he also had a knack for exploiting greedy, cowardly public officials.

"Dat's all ah got to say about dat," Marcello said into the phone, keeping the elves in line. "Tony, don't you call me back with no bad news now, you hear? . . . Give my love to Lucy and da twins."

And he hung up. He rose to shake hands with us. He was barely five feet tall, yet he still managed to give an impression of size.

"Well, fuck me sideways," Marcello said, "how long it been, Paulo?"

"Maybe two years," Paul said, finishing up a handshake. "I don't get home much as I should. . . . Carlos, this is Nate Heller."

Marcello grinned at me. There was something charming about it. Also something chilling. He had dark, inverted-V eyebrows that gave his otherwise pleasant face a devil's-mask quality.

"So dis is da famous private eye," he said, shaking my hand. If my fingers were toothpaste tubes, he'd have made a hell of a mess. "Like on the tee-vee, huh?"

"Something like that," I said, smiling.

We all sat down.

"Now, Nate . . . or ya prefer Nathan?"

"Nate is fine."

"Now, me, ah don't stand on no damn ceremony. Ya can call me Carlos, or Uncle Carlos. We gonna be great frien's."

"I hope so, Carlos."

"You pals wid da Silver Fox, ah hear."

He meant Johnny Rosselli, a Chicago Outfit guy who traveled in the highest of low circles.

"John and I go back a long way," I admitted.

Marcello sat forward, leaned on two elbows, cocked the big head, arched one upside-down V. "You go back all de way to Frank Nitti days, dat right?"

"I knew Frank. I was just a kid then. We did each other favors."

"And now you a regular Jimmy Bond, ain't ya, son?"

I just smiled.

Was this mere friendly banter? Or was there menace in there? Certainly condescension, since most men my own age don't call me "son."

The Little Man leaned back, rocked easily in his high-backed leather swivel chair. "You boys want some refreshments? Ah don't drink dis time of day, but don't let dat stop you. Me, ah wouldn't mind a Coke-Cola."

"Coke would be fine," Paul said, as I nodded. My client had a nervous smile. You would, too, if you were about to talk business with Carlos Marcello.

Carlos punched a button on his phone and got Frances on the speaker, and the madam of a four-state call-girl ring said, most pleasantly, that she'd run over and get us some Coke-Colas.

The meeting began and I quickly became a third wheel. Paul explained to Uncle Carlos that he already had the financing for production of the new oil additive, the merits of which he spent two or three minutes on, then emphasized he hoped Marcello could fund distribution of the product. Our host seemed interested and agreeable, and asked many smart questions in that stupid-sounding Cajun drawl.

About halfway through this discussion, Frances arrived with little cold-sweating bottles of Coke. She wore an orange skirt to go with her yellow blouse and had a figure nice enough to work for her own prostie ring.

As the business talk grew more serious, an edge came into Carlos's voice. "Now, Paulo, you come to me 'cause there ain't nobody in Louisiana dat could distribute dat oil thing a yours better dan Uncle Carlos. We both know dat. Didn't ah get slots in every corner of dis state?"

"Yes," Paul said, nodding. "Louisiana would be a fine place to take the product out for a trial run."

"But ah wanna have a gar-on-tee dat ah in for de long haul and a nice slice, when dis thing gits rolled out."

"Well, of course, Uncle Carlos," Paul said, a quaver in his voice. "I wouldn't have it any other way."

Marcello was giving his old friend that classic Mafia stare. I'd seen that same no-nonsense boogey-man whammy delivered by mob bosses from Nitti to Ricca, Accardo to Giancana, and was convinced these guys practiced that glaring glower in the mirror. I almost laughed. Almost.

"You know dat loyalty's da most impotent thing under da sun to Uncle Carlos. Ah don't take kin'ly to muthafuckers dat screw my ass over."

Despite the meat-locker air-conditioning, Paul had beads of sweat on his forehead.

"Uncle Carlos," he said, and the "uncle" seemed goddamn silly, considering they too were about the same age, "we been friends since we were kids. Surely you can't doubt—"

Marcello cut the air with the edge of a thick hand. "Frien's and bidness, dey don't always go t'gether so good. You and me, Paulo, we ain't never done no bidness together. So ah don't mean to sound like no hard-ass muthafucker . . ."

Like hell he didn't.

". . . but it like when ya crawl in bed wid some broad, and you think, should ah slip on de rubber or not? We ain't usin' no rubber here, my frien'. We is bareback all de way. You *still* wanna do bidness with Uncle Carlos?"

"Very much."

The stare melted into a big smile, mitigated only by the devilish eyebrows. "Well, dat's fine den." He turned his now-friendly gaze on me. "Nate, you min' if ah steal you away for a spell? You boys stayin' at the Roosevelt, right?"

Both of these questions struck me as non sequiturs, but Paul said, "Yes, I can drive our rental to the Roosevelt and meet up with Nate later, if you'd like some time with him."

"Well, ah surely would," Carlos said. "Ah wanna ask him about dem investors of yours he been lookin' into—always like to know who ah'm gettin' in bed wid."

Rubbers again.

"'Sides which, we got mutual frien's, Nate and me. We might wanna discuss about dis-and-dat, Paulo, dat might not be somethin' a fella like you need to hear."

Paul considered me mobbed up, so he understood that. I didn't consider myself mobbed up, despite all the gangsters I'd known and even consorted with over the years, but I always let clients like Paul think I was. Good for business. But occasionally it put me in an awkward position. Like now.

Paul took off, and then it was just me and Carlos in the bank-president office. That wasn't scary. I could handle that. I did wish I'd brought the nine millimeter, though, even if I wasn't licensed to carry it in Louisiana.

"Listen, son," Carlos said, leaning forward, "dis is no place for you and me to shoot da shit."

"It isn't?"

"Naw, and anyway, ah wanna take ya out to Churchill Farms. On da West Bank. Got sixty-four hunnerd acres out dere, man. Like to show you around de property, some. Ah got plans out dere, an' we can talk real good, over dere."

I had heard of Churchill Farms. It was said to be a remote farmhouse on the bayou where Carlos often took business associates and guests for private talks. Some of those business associates and guests didn't come back. Yankee Gumbo, anyone?

"I'm fine talking here," I said with a shrug.

"Naw, naw," Marcello said. He was reaching for the phone

again. "We get us some privacy, Nate." Into the phone, he said, "Jack, bring de car aroun'."

When he hung up, he said, "Dat's Jack. He my personal barber and driver like. You gonna love Jack."

Jack was a big guy, six two easy, the Frankenstein monster in a suit and tie, with a nice slicked-back haircut. He was waiting at the end of the hall for us, and opened the door onto bright sunshine. That sunshine did not keep me from seeing the message posted on the inside of the door, for all of Uncle Carlos's guests to read on their way out:

THREE CAN KEEP
A SECRET
IF TWO ARE DEAD.

We rode in back of a bronze Caddy with hulking, well-groomed Jack—clearly as much bodyguard as barber or driver—up front at the wheel. Carlos and I actually did talk about the investigations that I—or anyway, my agents—had done into the various investors Paul Fudala had assembled to back his new product.

"Dese is good folk?" Marcello asked, frowning earnestly. "Good bidness-type people? Rely-upon-type people? No crooks in de woodpile?"

"No, they're upstanding citizens. Solid investors." Hilarious, wasn't it, that the boss of the mob in Louisiana was so careful about who he got in "bidness" with?

Moving off the main highway onto Marcello's property, the Caddy navigated a narrow strip of bumpy dirt road that seemed to go on and on. This wasn't a private drive—we passed a shrimp-packing plant that Marcello said was his—but if we had met another car, passage for both would have made a tricky dance.

As we rumbled along the rutted dirt road, a white egret here or a blue heron there would swoop skyward from the bordering marshes. If this represented Marcello's six-thousand-some acres, what he owned was a swamp, a vast one with mud-brown ponds, Spanish-moss-hung gray cypress, and emerald-green palmettos.

Our conversation trailed off and, after a few minutes of silence, Marcello noticed me watching out the window as the eerie landscape glided by.

"Dere's where we get rid of de bodies," Marcello said, pointing past me out the window, then laughed, hee-hee-hee.

Big joke. Once, a long time ago, I had run into that swamp, away from underlings of the teenaged Marcello's boss.

"Hey, Heller, you a Jew?"

"I'm half a Jew."

"How da hell kin a man be half a goddamn Hebe?"

"My mother was Catholic. My pop was an apostate Jew."

"A pos what? What dat?"

"It's a Jew who doesn't believe in the faith."

"You one?"

"I'm nothing."

"You don't believe in nuttin'?"

"I believe in money."

"We got dat much in common. Anyway, good thing ya ain't a full-on Hebe, 'cause ya know what we do with dem, in dese parts, don't ya, Nate?"

"No, what's that, Carlos?"

"Why, we jes' roll 'em outta de car into de ol' swamp. Dey plenty a snakes in dere."

Alligators, too.

He gave me a playful shrug. "Aw, hell, son, I'm just funnin' ya. Think ah'd kill me a Jew jes' for shits and grins?"

I didn't reply. My eyes caught the driver's in the rearview mirror, and he gave me a little eyebrow shrug. I guess Jack wasn't so sure. Not that it mattered to him—he was pure Italian.

"What de hell, Nate, snakes ain't no never mind to no mongoose."

Was he referring to what I *thought* he was referring to? Was *that* what this visit was about?

A clearing emerged from the marshy landscape and two rustic buildings appeared before us: a small, remodeled barn, painted white, with the kind of narrow first-floor windows a pioneer shot at Indians out of, and a shed around which milled goats and chickens. Dive-bombing swallows and green-bottle flies were swimming out there through the humidity.

Jack pulled around on the gravel apron near the former barn's front door, and we got out of the Caddy. But apparently we weren't going in right away—Marcello was wandering toward where the swamp edged the clearing. I followed him. Jack stayed behind, sitting on a small cement front stoop, smoking a cigarette, looking bored.

I stood beside Marcello. Shit, he was short—I felt like Wilt Chamberlain. He had his suit coat folded neatly over an arm as he gestured toward the swamp. The afternoon was starting to die and sunlight lanced through the ghostly trees, making a blur of a panorama that he seemed to be repainting with a thick, gesturing hand.

"First thing ah gonna do, ah gonna put one of dem marina deals in dere. For boats and shit. Ah already got a hunting camp down over dere, dat direction—duck blinds and dat. But dat jus' the start of it."

He walked to another position and I followed him. The view was the same, blinding with sun, but he began painting with his hand again.

"We gon' drain out mos' a dis shit. We gon' have shoppin' centers and a big-ass airport and a sports stadium and housing, you know, dem condom minimums."

Fucking rubbers again.

"Ah gon' turn some of dis dicey shit o' mine over to my brothers, give dem a shot. Me? 'Fore ya know it, ah'm gon' be strict legit. Ah done what it took ta ride out the damn Depression, an' never let it stand in my way, da kinda shit dey give guys like us, Nate, wops and micks."

I had apparently been promoted to a full-fledged mick.

"I'm sure you'll be a very rich man," I said, squinting into the sun.

"Ah'm already a very rich man. But dis way dey can't fuck wid me so much. Ah'll be fuckin' respectable, son. So why does some people wanna give me shit, is what ah wanna know!"

What the hell was he talking about?

Finally our tour moved indoors. The barn-turned-farmhouse was straightforward and plain . . . although the upstairs was a handsomely furnished meeting room with a long conference table, lush carpeting, and wood-paneled walls, again adorned with framed aerial photographs of his properties. Downstairs was simple, the furnishings straight from the Montgomery Ward showroom—a small bedroom with one dresser, a dining room, a modern if spartan kitchen.

That was where we wound up, seated at the kitchen table. Jack the barber remained outside with the darting swallows and greenbottle flies. There were no countertop appliances, unless you counted the little hi-fi, like a teenage kid would have in his room. Immediately my host put on an LP—*Connie Francis Sings Italian Favorites.* Then he went to the refrigerator and took out a platter of sliced cheese and salami, which he brought over to the gray-topped Formica table and set down.

"Scotch all right?" he asked.

Rum was my preference, but I said, "Scotch is fine."

He got a bottle out of the cupboard, poured several inches each into a couple glasses, and left the bottle on the table as he sat back down.

He nibbled some provolone. I nibbled some salami.

He said, "So, how often you see dat rat bastard Bobby dese days?"

I didn't think he meant Darin or Rydell or Vee, even though they were all Italian. Connie was no help—she was busy singing "Arrivederci Roma."

"Not in a long time," I said.

Which was a lie, but not one Marcello was likely to see through.

Gingerly filling the silence, I ventured, "That was a shame what he put you through last year. I read about it in the papers."

Bobby Kennedy had been attorney general only three months when he made perhaps his most audacious move against organized crime. He arranged for Marcello, reporting in for a routine quarterly meeting at the New Orleans immigration office, to be grabbed by INS agents, handcuffed, and hauled off for immediate deportation. Marcello was actually born in Tunisia, but Kennedy pretended that a forged birth certificate, once used by Marcello to obtain a Guatemalan passport, was real.

"Livarsi 'na pietra di la scarpa!" Marcello blurted, his dark eyes bulging and bloodshot, his hand gripping the glass of Scotch so tight I thought it might crack. "Dat's an old Sicilian saying, man."

"Is it?"

"Ya wanna know what it mean, man?"

"Naw, that's okay."

"It mean, 'Take the stone out of my shoe!' Don't you worry about that little Bobby son of a bitch. He gon' be took care of."

"You don't want to do that, Carlos," I said gently. "That could get you in one hell of a lot of trouble."

But he wasn't listening. His eyes weren't bulging now, they were looking inward, and his mushy mouth let the words out softly.

"Dey jus' snatch me, man, dem damn feds, dey grab my ass and don' let me call home or nuttin', don't lemme get my fuckin' toothbrush, man. Dat fuckin' Bobby, he jus' dump my ass in Guatemala City wid no money, no clothes, no nuttin'."

We sat and drank. I took it easy, but he was putting it away. The more he drank, the more mush-mouthed his speech became, not surprisingly. The farmhouse was cool, window air conditioners going, but his forehead was sweat-beaded. When he got up to turn the Connie Francis record over, he seemed a little unsteady.

He sat back down hard and talked a little bit about Paul Fudala and the fun they'd had in the French Quarter as kids, getting laid young and often.

"All de boobies back den was big, and all de pussies was tight."

Dose were da days.

He talked about legit business deals and repeated his plans for draining Churchill Farms and creating housing and commerce where snakes and alligators now thrived. Then he got up and put on *Connie Francis—More Italian Favorites.* She was singing "That's Amore" when he brought up Bobby Kennedy again.

"You still got dat Bobby bastard fooled, Nate?"

"Not sure I follow, Carlos."

"Back in dem racket committee days, when you was workin' for Bobby? Little bastard never knew you was *really* workin' for Jimmy, did he?"

That was Jimmy as in Jimmy Hoffa, the Teamsters president the McClellan Committee had been investigating; but actually Hoffa was the bastard I still had fooled. I'd been Robert Kennedy's double agent—an old secret that could still get me newly killed.

Marcello leaned forward, gestured with his glass of Scotch, amber liquid sloshing around. The redness of his eyes was like Christopher Lee in a Dracula picture.

"Lemme tell ya somethin', Nate. Dis Bobby done me and my family wrong. We went through two months of hell, me and Jackie."

Like JFK, Carlos Marcello had a long-suffering wife named Jacqueline.

"Ah got my ass bounced aroun' Guatemala like a fuckin' rubber ball, man, stuck in dis jail, stuck in dat hotel. Den dey say dey is sendin' me home, and dey drive me to da Honduras border and what da fuck, dey dump my ass *again.* Dis time ah got my lawyer wid me. Fuck lotta good he done, middle of de goddamn jungle wid mountains and shit all aroun'. We walk seventeen miles, Nate, we walk eight hours in de wilderness like some fucker in da Bible. An' here ah is in a bidness suit and tie, hikin' like a fuckin' Boy Scout under de tropical sun. Ah pass out three times in de dirt, and one time ah look up and tell Mike, my lawyer, ah tell him, if ah don't make it, you tell my brothers what dat goddamn rich-kid Bobby Kennedy done to me. Tell 'em to do what they got to do."

I sipped Scotch.

Connie sang, "Return to Me."

Quietly I said, "You can't hit the attorney general of the United States, Carlos. You're not in the jungle now."

"Ah know dat," he said, shrugged, and finished his latest glass. He poured some more. "Wouldn't do no good, nohow. His brother Jack, dat bastard gonna hit us wid everything he got."

"Right."

"But ya know what dey say in Sicily, man."

"I don't know."

"You wanna kill de dog, don't cut off de tail, man, cut off de head."

"What's that mean, Carlos?" Though I thought I knew.

He frowned. "It mean de dog, he keep bitin' you, you only cut off his tail. But you cut de damn dog's *head* off, de whole damn dog gonna die . . . tail and all."

He nibbled at some salami. Threatening to kill the President gave him an appetite.

"Carlos, Bobby would come after you so hard that—"

"Ha! You don't know much for a Chicago boy, Nate. Who will da new president be? Lyndon Baines Johnson, dat's who. And he hate Bobby like poison. He fire that li'l bastard faster den shit."

We finished our Scotches. I hoped he didn't see me shaking. We walked out the back way into the muggy night and Carlos reached a hand up to settle on my shoulder. *Why had he told me all that? Jesus, why me? Had he got drunk and let his mouth run to where later he'd sober up and want me dead?*

Standing at the edge of the swamp, where darkness had settled and the moon was touching black unknowable ripples with silver, he said, "Dat Bobby, he still tryin' to deport my ass, man. And Momo, too. And da shit he give Hoffa, who a good, hardworkin' man helpin' hardworkin' men! Gotta stop, Nate. Gotta damn stop."

"This is out of my league, Carlos."

His smile was a horrible thing, the kind of smile one of those alligators out there would give you before taking a limb away for lunch.

"Don't play humble, man. Ah mean, hell, you part of dat mongoose deal, right?"

There it was again—*mongoose*. Only with a capital M, as in Operation Mongoose: the unholy marriage between the CIA and the Mafia. Their joint attempts to assassinate Cuba's Fidel Castro may have failed, but it had been a marriage nonetheless.

"I'm just a little tiny cog in that wheel," I said.

"Come on, now! You only set up de whole damn deal."

Yes, I had officiated at the marriage. Marcello had not been part of the original Miami meeting in '60, but he and Florida boss Santo Trafficante were thick as, well, thieves. So it was no surprise he was in the know.

I had been approached by a CIA spook I had history with who asked me to serve as a go-between mutually agreeable to both sides—I had that reputation of being mobbed up, remember.

Marcello squeezed my shoulder. "Tell me how dat little prick thinks he can get in bed wid us, and then fuck us over. You tell me dat, son."

It was something I had never understood myself. Bobby and his brother Jack were both well aware of Operation Mongoose. And yet Bobby had still pursued his dream of being the man who took down the Mafia.

"You want me to encourage Bobby to back off," I said, thinking I was finally getting it.

He didn't say anything. Just squeezed my shoulder.

But as he was walking me back toward the bronze Caddy, he said, "We come a long way, Nate, from de back room of de Willswood, ain't we?"

So he'd known me all the while.

He called out to his driver, who was still sitting on the cement stoop, smoking. "Hey, Jack! Take Mr. Heller here on back to de Town and Country, and send a couple boys back. Ah'm gonna camp out here tonight."

I said, "I'm stayin' at the Roosevelt, remember?"

Marcello gave me the alligator grin again. "Yeah, yeah, ah know.

But Jack here is a hell of a barber. He got his own barber chair back at the motel and everything."

Jack joined us and Carlos dug some bills out of his pocket and pressed them into his driver's hand. "You take Nate here on back, and give him a nice close shave. He look like he could *use* one."

The Little Man was waving from the porch as we drove off.

We hadn't gone very far when I sat forward from the back and said, "No offense, Jack, but I'm gonna skip the shave. You thank Carlos for me anyway. Just take me to the Roosevelt."

Jack nodded. "Sure thing."

Since I was carrying a message for Marcello, I figured Jack probably wouldn't have pulled anything, once he got me in that barber chair. Not unless Uncle Carlos had figured to make *me* the message.

And on the ride back, Jack didn't try anything, just dropped me off with a friendly nod out front of the Roosevelt Hotel on Baronne near the French Quarter, home of big boobs and tight pussy.

I'm sure Uncle Carlos's personal barber would have done a nice job for me. I just figured I'd had a close enough shave today already.

CHAPTER 3

September 1964

The well-dressed queue down Walton Street, laughing, chatting couples and little groups of affluent-looking men, extended half a block. Not unusual outside the Playboy Club at nine P.M., and had this been a Friday or Saturday, not Tuesday, they'd have been standing four abreast. Their goal was the colorful entryway that engulfed the sidewalk, a horizontal box of modern art–inspired yellow, blue, and green panels, and larger off-white ones with the familiar bunny-head-on-black symbol. The cool, slightly breezy evening was pleasant enough to wait out in, and the heady charge of being part of the In Crowd was palpable, as cigarette smoke trailed skyward like lazy, unimpressed ghosts.

I edged on by—I didn't have to wait. As they say, I knew Hefner "when." The A-1 had been on retainer with Playboy since 1955, investigating threats, scams, and lawsuits, and I'd long been part of Hef's inner circle. So I had a free membership and a permanent reservation anywhere in the club.

The lobby at once established a subdued atmosphere of low-key lighting, dark paneling, and modern furnishings, like a bachelor pad got out of hand. Circulating, greeting club members and their guests, was a small battalion of Bunnies, as the waitresses in their skimpy, satiny costumes were called.

Bunny Teddi took my Burberry—no hat: this private eye swore off snap-brims when Jack Kennedy took office—and deposited it at the coat check counter. At the sign-in desk, I requested that Bunny Cheryl not add my name placard to the wall display of key holders in attendance. The name of the man I was meeting was absent, as well.

It would be.

From the lobby, abuzz with well-dressed patrons and helpful underdressed Bunnies, walk-ins were shuffled one flight down to the Playmate Bar. This pleasant purgatory, with its endless bar, countless black high-backed stools, and walls of backlit nude pinup photos, was overseen by half a dozen bartenders and as many Bunnies. Some of the latter worked 26 tables, the same dice game that B-girls in Chicago bars had played with suckers since the Fire.

Those who called ahead were sent one flight up to the Living Room, a dining room with piano bar, legendary for its remarkable buck-and-a-half buffet. For a more secluded atmosphere and dining that wasn't a buck-fifty, the VIP Room was up another flight. Showrooms featuring the likes of Ella and Sammy took up the top two floors, but my stop was the VIP Room, where After Six apparently had the clothing concession, not counting those skimpy Bunny costumes. My dark-blue Hanover Hall herringbone would just have to do.

The VIP Room was the only place in the Playboy Club where you could find some privacy—a dimly lit, soundproofed space with flickery candles in orange glasses that made the LeRoy Neiman paintings on the walls seem even more expressionistic. A Negro jazz trio managed never to drown out the tinkle of ice cubes and the laughter-spiked conversation.

My friend Edward "Shep" Shepherd—if a high-level spook could be considered anybody's friend—had managed somehow to put an empty booth on his either side, despite the crowd waiting down on Walton Street, not to mention those damned souls suffering the attention of Bunnies in the Playmate Bar.

Of course, most of those below weren't VIPs, while Shep certainly looked the part in his navy Brooks Brothers with his silk tie of wide black stripes and narrow red ones. What did CIA security chiefs make a year, anyway? Or was that Top Secret?

Shep was studying the menu like it was a U-2 photograph of a Soviet missile installation. He reminded me of a middle-aged version of Robert Morse from *How to Succeed in Business Without Really Trying,* sporting a similar sly, gap-toothed grin and twinkle in those dark-blue eyes. Those eyes were getting pouchy now, the blond of his hair getting lost in the gray. He was, as usual, drinking a Gibson, the pickled onion gone, always an immediate casualty with Shep.

Shep had done me a favor, a dozen years back, when I first butted heads with what they were now calling the Company. Two years ago he had done me no favors by enlisting my help in initiating Operation Mongoose, calling upon my patriotism. Whenever somebody tries to appeal to your patriotism, put one hand over your wallet and the other hand over your family jewels.

"Nate, what a singular pleasure," he said, a fluid trace of the South in his lilting drawl. He gestured to the empty side of the booth. "I'm so very pleased about this coincidence."

I slid in opposite him just as the jazz combo was starting up a swingy "Charade." The coincidence he mentioned was that I had called him on Sunday hoping to come out to D.C. and see him. But he had said that "coincidentally" he was going to be in Chicago "the Tuesday after Labor Day." We could get together then, if I pleased.

I pleased.

Like most detectives, I have an extremely low opinion of coincidences. I might have felt better about this one if I could have inquired about what non-Heller business brought him to town. But unless he were to offer up the information, a CIA agent like Shep is not someone you ask that kind of question. Nor could I ask him, *Am* I *the reason you are in Chicago*?

His eyes were sleepy as his smile split his face. "How the hell is that boy of yours? Sam? Is he a senior this year? My God, the time flies."

"Actually he's a junior. He spent most of August with me. Put him on a plane home on Sunday. He was back in school today."

"Such a fine young man."

I didn't remember Shep ever meeting Sam, but I didn't mention that.

"And *your* son?" I asked. "Your daughter? Still in college?"

"Bradley has another year, Susan graduated. She's working at a Manhattan bank. She's engaged to a fine boy in pre-law. Won't hurt her to have a little real-world experience before providin' me with some grandchildren."

Bunny Vicki, as part of her real-world experience, took my order for a gimlet. Those damn satiny costumes were just ridiculous, bunny ears, bunny tail; and I knew from several Bunnies I'd dated that even the best endowed of them had to stuff their bras to create that cleavage. The effect of long legs was phony, too, just the high-on-the-hip cut of the skimpy garment. What a crock. Magnificent.

"Fitting we should talk about our kids," I said.

Shep's eyebrows raised as he sipped his current Gibson. "How is that, Nate?"

I told him about the hit-and-run incident after the Beatles concert, and that my glimpse of the driver convinced me I'd recognized him. This I did to a backdrop of the jazz combo noodling on "Call Me Irresponsible."

Shep, who'd listened intently behind a furrowed-brow expression, asked, "Did you report this?"

"I'm reporting it to you."

"So the police know nothing of it."

"No."

"What about Martineau, at the Secret Service?"

"No."

"It *was* one of the Cubans, though."

"I'm not absolutely sure. I was busy at the time, getting my ass sideswiped. Pretty damn sure, though."

"*Which* Cuban?"

"Ramon Rodriguez. According to the ID he had on him last

year, anyway. I was in on the interrogation. He and his pal Victor Gonzales said they were Cuban exiles from Florida up to look at investing in real estate here in Chicago. According to them, their landlady must have been crazy, saying they had high-power rifles in their room, with the President's motorcade route marked on maps and in a newspaper."

Shep had stopped sipping his Gibson; he didn't take things much more seriously than that. His hands were folded before him like a minister listening patiently to a parishioner's problems.

"I understand the Secret Service elected not to hold them," Shep said.

"And isn't *that* odd?"

"Why, were any rifles found? Or that map and the newspaper?"

"No. But once the President canceled his trip to Chicago, the two suspects were released. Just flat-out fucking sprung."

He fluttered his eyelashes like a modest Southern miss. "I don't see what that has to do with me, and, uh . . . my resources."

I leaned forward. Spoke very softly. "Shep, don't shit a shitter. Consider who it is you're talking to."

I didn't have to say it. The Company and Cuban exile factions had been in league long before the Bay of Pigs fiasco and well after. The exiles, like the Mob, were part of Operation Mongoose and the plot to assassinate Castro.

As was I, goddamnit.

"I helped you people out," I said. My tone was casual, conversational, befitting the setting; but he could hear the edge. "I wish to hell I hadn't, but I did. Now I am one of the handful outside of your rarefied circles who knows for a certainty that a conspiracy took down the President."

"Jesus, Nate," he whispered.

Bunny Vicki arrived with my gimlet and another Gibson for Shep. She did the classic Bunny dip as she served them; she was a lovely blonde of maybe twenty-three and for a night with her, you would gladly kick your grandmother's teeth out. And yet right now I couldn't have cared less.

When she was gone, I said, "But I haven't done anything about it. I didn't survive all these years in Chicago not knowing when to back off. If Uncle Sam wants the world to think a lone nut pulled off that hit, I can look the other way. Just don't tell me it's patriotism."

Very quietly he said, "I'm sorry, Nate, but it *is* patriotism. Suppose this thing were traced back to Castro? You and I both know the Beard had a perfectly good motive for this terrible thing."

Yes he did. Hadn't the Kennedy administration tried repeatedly to kill him?

"And how," Shep continued softly, "do you suppose the public would have reacted to their beloved President bein' killed by a Commie dictator just ninety miles from our shore?"

I said nothing.

"President Johnson, he wasn't about to risk nuclear war, nuclear annihilation. Director Hoover submitted evidence indicating this Oswald character was a pinko nut from way back, and from everything I understand, the Warren Commission will be reaching that same conclusion."

Rubber-stamping it was more like it.

I sipped the gimlet. "Say, isn't your old boss Allen Dulles on that 'blue-ribbon' commission? Who was fired by Jack Kennedy after the Bay of Pigs screwup? Where was *he* on November 22, 1963?"

"Careful, Nate. . . ."

"I'm trying to be. I did my best to save Jack Kennedy's life last November, and a hell of a lot of good it did him or me. I'm on to more important matters."

"Such as?"

"Such as, are you people trying to kill *me,* Shep?"

"No!" He glanced around at the other diners, knowing his voice had jumped up over the jazz and the chatter. Much softer but with equal force, he said, "Hell no."

"Why should I believe you?"

He frowned, and actually looked hurt. "Why *ask* me, if you're not prepared to believe me? You think you've become a loose end, is that it? Well, I can assure you the Company doesn't view you that way. We view you as an asset, and a valuable one."

"Is this where I say, 'Gee whiz, thanks'?"

"No. But I understand your . . . bitterness. Your boy might well have been killed by that car."

"I won't have my son put in harm's way, Shep. I will not fucking have it. I can take care of myself, but he's just a boy. Do I have to tell you? You're a father. How far would you go if a child of yours was threatened or . . . worse?"

He drew in a breath, let it out slowly. "No, you don't have to tell me. But I would ask you a favor." He sat forward. "Should another attempt be made, don't assume the worst about me and the Company. Report it to me. I will try to help."

"Is that right?"

"I will, Nate. I swear to you. What more can I say?"

"Plenty."

He took a quick sip of the Gibson, then his drawl disappeared into a more rushed, if hushed, cadence. "It's possible rogue elements were involved in this awful thing. Don't blame the Company itself, man. Christ, I would like to root those elements out myself."

"My God, but I would like to believe you."

He sighed. Actually fucking sighed. "The nature of the world, Nate, is that you can't be sure. The business of spycraft is lying, and I could be lying to you right now."

"Your brand of reassurance lands on the soft-sell side, I'd say."

"Nate, I'm just asking you not to assume it's us, if this should happen again. And if it *should* happen again, let me know. I *will* try to help. And frankly . . . and it pains me to say it . . ."

"Say it."

He shrugged just a little. "If the Company wants you dead, Nate, you're going to be dead. Hell, if they want me dead, so am I. So you might as well trust me, Nate. There really is no other option."

The jazz combo was playing variations on "Once in a Lifetime."

"Fine," I said. "I get that. I'm a big boy. But, Shep?"

"Yes?"

"If I see that Cuban again, I'm going to kill him."

Another little shrug. "Fair enough. . . . Shall I wave that little cottontail over and order us dinner? I'm going to have red meat tonight, and screw my doctor and his damn cholesterol."

What the hell. I let Uncle Sam buy me a decent meal.

That, and the words he'd given me, was the best I could hope for out of Shep tonight. For what it was worth, I believed him. He was as close to a decent man as I knew in that foul line of work.

And, anyway, the CIA wasn't the only group that might have sent someone to tie off a loose end named Nathan Heller.

Chasen's on a Saturday night could be tough to get into. But Johnny Rosselli wouldn't have had any trouble getting a reservation at the venerable West Hollywood eatery.

Tonight he sat in a curved, tufted-leather-upholstered booth entertaining a beautiful blonde starlet in what was apparently a one-sided conversation. She didn't have to talk, not in a black low-cut gown like that, with natural cleavage those Bunnies back home might envy.

The booth they shared was big enough for four or maybe six, but Rosselli rated the real estate—he had long been a mob conduit for Hollywood. Around sixty but fit, the Silver Fox was handsome enough to be an actor with that flashing smile, immaculately cut and combed silver-gray hair, and blue-gray eyes set off by the kind of tan you could get shuttling between Vegas and Hollywood. Patrons not in the know might even have taken him for a motion-picture industry bigwig, a producer maybe, with his sleek gray suit with black lapels (Pierre Cardin?) and darker gray tie with matching silk breast-pocket hanky.

Rosselli hadn't noticed me yet. Like him, I usually didn't have any trouble getting into Chasen's, but my partner Fred Rubinski of the A-1 LA branch had made a call just in case. This was after

Fred called around to the mobster's half dozen favorite restaurants to see which one he was taking his latest starlet to on Saturday night.

My son, my ex-wife, and I rarely dined together as a family, if that's what we were, but I had insisted. Both were intrigued that I'd flown out to their corner of the USA at such short notice, particularly since Sam had just spent a month in mine.

We were ensconced in our own lushly padded leather booth, just like such regulars as Alfred Hitchcock and Gregory Peck, neither of whom were here tonight, though we didn't rate a name plaque like they did. A few celebrities could be spotted—Sinatra's pal Don Rickles at the bar, and Dean Martin and Jerry Lewis in separate booths with their individual wives, neither party acknowledging the other. Otherwise, star-gazers seemed out of luck, though you could bet this crowd included talent scouts, publicity agents, and studio execs, and you never knew who would enter next under the famous canopy out front.

The Hollywood A-list restaurant, at the corner of Doheny Drive and Beverly Boulevard, had a slightly cluttered, men's-club feel—a model TWA plane courtesy of onetime regular Howard Hughes flew over the bar, and autographed celebrity photos rode the knotty-pine walls. Waiters in tuxes played chummy with the patrons, famous or not, and would grill the famous "Hobo" steak table-side—three salt-encrusted slices of New York strip on buttered toast. Drinks were notably strong and the atmosphere borderline raucous. This was, after all, where midgets had once jumped out of a big cake for Jimmy Stewart's birthday.

The noise level was a plus for my purposes.

"All right," my ex-wife said. "I'll bite. What's the occasion?"

My ex-wife in her mid-forties looked fantastic. She was small, almost petite, and had dark-brown hair and violet eyes. She'd retained her figure over the years, and she'd once been a model for calendar artists, so it was a nice figure. As Margaret Hogan, she had been in a few movies, and even in a town where women over forty were considered ancient, she could still turn heads.

Sam was between us in the curve of the booth. He was in the Maxwell Street knockoff Beatle suit, while his mother wore a white wool suit threaded with black and a black silk cowl-necked blouse, not a knockoff. Givenchy, probably, knowing her expensive tastes. I was in a green worsted by Cricketeer, pretty hot stuff in Chicago, nothing special out here.

"Peggy," I said, "why don't we order first? Anything you like."

"Please don't call me that. You know it irritates me."

I insisted on calling her Peggy because that was the name I'd known her by. Out here everybody called her Maggie, including her husband, who was out of town on a shoot, not that I'd have invited him.

"Order," I instructed her. "Pretend you're trying to get an extra child support check out of me, which on this menu won't be hard."

She gave me a dirty look—she didn't like me saying things like that in front of Sam, who was oblivious to them. Right now he was sneaking a look at Jerry Lewis.

We ordered. My ex and I both got the Maude's salad and Hitchcock sole—she hated that we still liked the same foods—and Sam ordered the famous chili. How famous? Not so long ago, that other violet-eyed beauty, Liz Taylor, had servings sent to the set of *Cleopatra.* In Rome.

"I'm going to ask you to excuse me," I said, sliding out of the booth. "I'll be back before the food gets here."

"Nathan," Peggy snapped. "What is going on?"

"If I told you," I said cheerfully, "it would spoil your meal."

"Goddamnit, Nathan!"

But I was already halfway to Rosselli's booth, which was when he recognized me. A moment of surprise—*what, that I was still breathing?*—was replaced by a big smile. It seemed genuine, but this was Hollywood, remember.

"Nate Heller!" he said, extending his hands with palms up, as if to prove neither held a weapon. He turned to his date. "Sweetie, this is Nate Heller, an old Chicago pal of mine."

The little blonde smiled weakly and nodded. He did not introduce her by name. If, in years to come, she ever graduated from starlet to movie star, I didn't recognize her.

"Hope I'm not intruding, Johnny," I said. "I'm here with my family."

I gestured over to the booth, where Peggy was frowning a little and Sam was rubbernecking. Dean Martin's direction, this time.

"Aren't you divorced?" he asked, rather delicately for a hood. "If I'm not speaking out of school."

"Yes, that's my ex-wife, but we're still friendly. You know, just because you divorce a woman, it doesn't mean she isn't still the mother of your kid."

Rosselli nodded several times at this sage observation, while the blonde was frowning, trying to work it out.

I leaned in, resting a hand on the linen cloth of the booth's table. "Could I impose on you, John, for just a few minutes? Just a few words?"

His eyebrows went up. "Certainly, Nate. Be a pleasure to catch up."

"I'm not really here just to socialize, John."

Now the eyebrows came down, frowning just a little, in thought, nothing sinister, really. "Is it business? Is it personal?"

"Both." I smiled at the blonde. "Miss, would you mind powdering your nose for five minutes?"

She was thinking about that when Johnny nudged her, saying, "Go on, sweetie. Boy talk."

So the blonde slid out, swayed off, and I slipped into the booth. They hadn't been served anything but rolls yet, plus Rosselli was working on a glass of what was almost certainly Smirnoff on the rocks. I never knew him to drink anything else.

There was also what I would bet a hundred bucks was a Shirley Temple that the blonde had been drinking. What the hell—Chasen's was where they invented it.

"Nate, I admit you have my attention. And I'm a little concerned. What is it, man?"

Without any preamble at all, I told him what had happened

after that Beatles concert, including that the hit-and-run driver had been one of the two Cubans I'd picked up for the Secret Service when that first assassination attempt on JFK had been squelched.

"What do you make of that?" Rosselli asked cagily.

"When somebody swings out of one lane to run me down in the other, I figure he has a grudge. Or anyway a goal."

"One would think," Rosselli allowed.

I leaned toward him and he leaned toward me.

I said softly, "The Warren Commission will be hanging the JFK hit on that Oswald character, any day now. Somebody doesn't want me to spoil things. Somebody thinks I might talk."

"About what, Nate?"

"About Operation Mongoose, John. About Cubans and spooks and Outfit guys thinking the Kennedy boys ought to be taken down a big goddamn peg. About the attempted Chicago hit three weeks before Dallas that the Secret Service has kept mum about."

He backed away a little, frowning again, and now something sinister had found its way in. "Are these really things that should be discussed in a public place?"

"I might get killed in a private place, John."

The frown melted into a sad smile, the blue eyes in the tan face hooded. "Nate, Nate, what you are you saying? You know you're a friend."

He meant not just to him, but to the Outfit, and the other crime families around the country with which they were aligned.

"I'm a friend to your friends," I said, my voice even, "and the CIA considers me an asset. My guess, though, is that the Cubans feel otherwise."

He drew in air and sighed it out. His expression was sympathetic. "Can I help?"

"You can level with me, John. You can answer the big question."

"Ask it."

Across the way, an ancient waiter was serving Chasen's signature desert, the Coupe Snowball—a scoop of vanilla ice cream, sprinkled with shredded coconut and drizzled with chocolate sauce—to an attractive young couple who were about to share it.

I asked, "Have all my good friends decided that the world would be a safer, better place without Nate Heller in it?"

He waved that off with a diamond-ring-laden hand. "Oh, that's an outlandish suggestion! How can you even say that, Nate?"

"Yeah, it's crazy. Friends don't kill friends. But Johnny, as a friend, I'm going to ask you to pass along to any of *your* friends who might be interested that I am nobody to be worried about. I keep things to myself. I have a long reputation of keeping things to myself that goes back to Frank Nitti. More recently, two years ago? Carlos Marcello told me who he was planning to kill, and I kept quiet about it."

In this instance, not true: I had conveyed Marcello's message to Bobby, and he had pooh-poohed it. It was all Mafia braggadocio, Bobby said. It was all that Scotch talking.

The jovial gangster's expression was solemn now.

"That's right, Nate," Rosselli said, nodding just a little. "You're absolutely right. Your reputation for discretion is widely known."

My smile was amiable. "On the other hand, it's also widely known that I *am* somebody to worry about if fucked with. I brought my family along tonight to make a point, Johnny. My son might have been hit by that car. And my ex-wife, don't tell her, but there's still a part of me that loves her. Call me a romantic."

The jeweled hand held up a traffic-cop palm. "Nate. This ain't necessary. . . ."

"Tell your friends that if my boy or my ex is touched, I will become extremely unfriendly. That if they try to kill me, that's one thing. I can handle myself, and even take what's coming to me, if necessary."

"Nate . . . Nathan . . ."

"But if your friends try to get to me through my family, they won't like what happens next."

He was shaking his head now, firmly, though his voice was subdued. "Nate . . . threats . . . please. That's no way to talk."

"I don't threaten. I do warn. John, I'm too tangled up in this to go public. It's that simple. Tell anyone you think might benefit from a warning that I am not a loose end that needs tying off. But I *can* be a loose cannon if crossed."

He was nodding. Smiling, too, though it was on the forced side. "I understand. I see your point. And I respect you for this. I really do."

I slid out of the booth. "Good. Enjoy your meal, John. Attractive girl."

She was on her way back, navigating the waiters in the aisle with grace, getting looks from men in various booths. Five minutes almost on the dot. I wondered if she'd really powdered her nose all that time.

Teeth blossomed in the brown face. "I'm gonna get her a screen test, Nate."

"I bet you are."

I went back to our booth.

"Who is that?" Peggy asked. "Somebody important?"

"Very," I said.

Our food came and we didn't talk much. I was busy thinking.

Thinking about how I was going to break it to Peg that our son and for that matter her lovely self were going to be guarded day and night by A-1 operatives until further notice.

CHAPTER 4

Feeling half asleep, I got to the Monadnock Building just after nine A.M. on Monday, a sunny fall day that was doing my bloodshot eyes no favors. I'd spent yesterday in Hollywood with my son, taking in *Topkapi* at Grauman's Chinese, dining at Musso & Frank, and goofing off poolside at the Beverly Hills Hotel. Then after Sam's mom picked him up, I caught the red-eye back to Chicago. Hence my red eyes.

In its day the largest office building in the world, the Monadnock was a towered-over, sixteen-story, gray-brick relic now. But as the home base of a nationally prominent private detective agency, the Monadnock couldn't be beat for class or mood or history. Going in the main entrance on West Jackson, I passed the rear display windows of stores facing Dearborn and Federal, moved past the open winding stairwells, and caught the elevator to seven.

We maintained the corner suite of this floor. The frosted glass-and-wood exterior hadn't changed since we moved in, although I now did give billing to a partner:

A-1 Detective Agency
Criminal and Civil Investigations
Nathan S. Heller
President

and smaller,

Louis K. Sapperstein
Vice President

My Hollywood partner, Fred Rubinski, got similar billing out there, only with the same size lettering as me—always a tough town to negotiate billing in.

In the reception area, with its blond Heywood-Wakefield furnishings and framed Century of Progress posters, sat a slim woman in her early thirties, reading *Redbook.* She looked prim and crisp in a tailored gingham plaid dress, her blonde hair flipping up at the chin, a style maybe a little young for her, but she had pretty enough features to overcome it. She glanced up at me with big blue eyes and a tiny, hopeful smile touched with pale red lipstick.

I gave her a nod and a smile and moved on.

More likely a girl looking for a job than a prospective client. Well, we could use another swimmer in the secretarial pool. Not much chance she was after investigative work—she just didn't have the seasoned look of the ex-policewomen we hired.

I paused briefly to acknowledge our receptionist, who wanted to be called Millie now—she felt this was an improvement over Mildred, and maybe it was.

Millie, a dark-haired doll in her late twenties, had a pleasant manner and was sharp as hell. She had shifted from her Jackie Kennedy fixation in favor of Mary Tyler Moore from *The Dick Van Dyke Show.* It was working okay, though she and office manager Gladys Sapperstein had recently gotten into it over the issue of wearing slacks to work. Today Millie wore a navy blue dress with a V neck and no sleeves.

"Good morning, Mr. Heller," she said, chipper. She was on her feet, taking my Burberry to hang it up for me. "How was Hollywood?"

"Great," I said. "I got you Morey Amsterdam's autograph."

"Really?"

"No."

Sharp but gullible.

She crinkled her chin and warbled, "Mr. *Hel*-ler . . ."

She said that like Laura Petrie said "Rob" on *Van Dyke,* and I hadn't decided yet whether it was cute or annoying.

We had a regular Monday morning staff meeting at eleven, so the bullpen with its modern metal desks—I don't like cubicles—was well-populated, only a handful of agents out on assignment. Age and sex and color varied—we had three Negroes now—and all our agents had police or military police backgrounds. A wall of windows looked out onto Jackson Street while another wall was home to a lineup of metal four-drawer files.

Office manager Gladys Sapperstein was my partner Lou's wife. They had no children, unless you counted me. Her office was between Lou's and mine, and right now she was poised outside of it, her hands filled with paperwork.

Her eyes narrowed as she saw me ambling in her direction. She met me halfway, still an attractive woman after all these years (I'd hired her in 1939)—a busty, pleasingly plump brunette about sixty. She looked like the kind of teacher whose lap a fifth-grade boy wanted to sit in, but didn't know why.

Right now her lap and much of the rest of her was in a green and yellow floral dress and, like Carlos Marcello's secretary, she wore jeweled cat's-eye glasses, though I'm fairly sure she didn't run a four-state call-girl ring.

"Can I bring you coffee?" she asked.

"No thanks, Gladys. I had plenty at home, trying to get my engine started."

"Car trouble?"

"No. *My* engine."

"You noticed the girl in our reception area." This was delivered in an I'm-stating-the-obvious fashion.

"Why, because she's a looker? Is that how you think my mind works?"

"Yes," she said. It was two questions that deserved only one answer. "She's a prospective client. She has an appointment."

"When?"

"Nine-thirty. She's a little early."

"Well, there *is* a staff meeting. . . ."

"Really, and you were going to attend that, were you?"

"Gladys, you know I never miss a staff meeting when I'm in town."

An eyebrow arched. "Never?"

"Seldom." I checked my watch. "Well, I guess I do have time, at that."

"Almost an hour."

"Give me fifteen minutes, then send her in. Good morning, by the way."

This rather typical conversation should have been over, but she was still blocking my path. "Actually, Lou would like to talk to you about the client first. That young woman is a family friend of his. Could I send him in?"

"You're asking my permission?"

"You're in charge around here, aren't you?"

"Could I have that in writing?"

She just looked at me.

"In triplicate," I added.

And now she granted me a smile. She said, "Oh you," and slapped my arm and walked away, putting some wiggle in her fanny. She did both of those things, in that order, about once a day, if I was lucky.

Soon I was behind the old scarred desk in my inner sanctum, the desk (like me) a dinosaur dating back to a one-room office over the Dill Pickle in Barney Ross's building on Van Buren. Throughout the early years of the A-1, I had lived in that office, which had a Murphy bed and bathroom. Deluxe stuff.

I'd come a distance. This inner office was as big as its whole Van Buren Street predecessor. No Murphy bed, but a comfy leather couch, padded leather client chairs, a row of wooden filing cabinets, and walls where faces from my past stared at me—celebrity clients, celebrity friends, in a few cases celebrity lovers, from Sally Rand to Marilyn Monroe.

I did get around, like Sam's other favorite group, the Beach Boys, said.

Sam's framed picture was not on the wall—it was on the desk, twice: a nice solo studio portrait, and a snapshot with his mother, which was maybe an excuse to be able to look at that lovely face of hers. How many times had I said, or at least thought, *I could* kill *that bitch!* Yet now, with the threat of . . . of *what*? . . . hanging over me and Sam and maybe Peggy, I could only wonder if everything I'd accomplished and all the money added up to a big nothing. That every shady deal I'd made, every evil I'd witnessed, every body I'd buried, was finally going to catch up with me.

A shave-and-a-haircut knock told me it was Lou. He had picked that up from Paul Drake on *Perry Mason,* I figured.

"Come in," I called.

Bald, bulbous-nosed, bespectacled, he came over and sat, no hello, no preamble, resting his sturdy, muscular frame in the chair opposite, sitting forward as I leaned back. He wore a pale blue shirt and darker blue clip-on tie, shirtsleeves rolled up to the elbow. He was past seventy, but only the wire-frame bifocals tipped it at all.

"How did she react?" he said.

He meant Peg.

"She surprised me," I said.

"Yeah?"

"No recriminations or any such shit. She appreciated my concern. Approved the precautions. Remember, Peg was Jim Ragen's niece. She lived through all of that."

Ragen had run a racing wire service here in Chicago for bookies nationwide. It had got him killed when he refused to sell out to the Outfit. Peg had been around "underworld figures" all her life. Hell, she even dated a Capone bodyguard before she met me.

"Yeah," Lou said, as if reading my mind. "She dated Bugsy Siegel for a while, too."

"Thanks for reminding me. But he preferred 'Ben.' "

Lou sat back, grinned. "Maybe so, but he's not going to do anything about it now, is he? . . . You know, two men, twenty-four hours—even for the president of the agency, that's going to run into money."

"I got money."

"Not a bottomless pit of it, you don't. How long do you figure you can keep it up, round-the-clock surveillance?"

"I don't know. Long as I have to."

He was playing it casual but the eyes behind the bifocals were studying me. "Are you going to do anything else about almost getting killed by a runaway Cuban?"

"I could always go to Miami and see if I can find any Cubans named Gonzales and Rodriguez." I shrugged. "I talked to my CIA contact, I talked to my Outfit guy. What else can I do?"

Lou and I had no secrets, or anyway not many. He even knew about my visit with Carlos Marcello; and he was in on most of what had gone down with Operation Mongoose.

"You sometimes take steps," he said.

"I've taken them. What, do you expect me to crack the JFK killing? I already know who did it. I knew who did it before it was done."

"Question is . . . are you a loose end?"

"All I can do is wait, Lou."

"Wait, and keep your powder dry."

Now I sat forward. "If they get in my face, I'll defend myself, and I'll do it in a messy way. Anybody who wants me dead won't want the kind of noise I will make along the way."

"What kind of noise?"

"Shooting back. Shooting my mouth off. All kinds of noise."

He folded his arms like Big Chief Rain-in-the-Puss. "Your pal Bobby isn't in a position to help you out anymore."

Robert Kennedy had stepped down from the attorney general's chair to run for United States senator in New York.

"He will be someday," I said.

"Oh yes, someday he'll be president like his brother, who they shot, if memory serves. In the meantime, you look over your shoulder. And keep your kid and ex-wife under armed guard."

"I detect a critical tone. You have a suggestion?"

"You could go public with what you know."

I laughed. "What, go to the feds? J. Edgar was probably sitting in the window next to Oswald, on a box of schoolbooks, handing him rounds. The papers? I'll be dead before the ink dries—before anything I reveal could turn into hearings and trials. Maybe I could give Hef one of those interviews he sticks in the magazine between nudie shots, to keep him straight with the postal authorities."

Lou said nothing. He was frowning. He knew I was right.

"I wish I could help," he said finally, uncrossing his arms. Then he shrugged. "Only suggestion I have is to go on about your business. Get your mind off this mess with some work."

"So go ahead and tell me," I said.

He blinked behind the bifocals. "Tell you what?"

"About the girl in reception. The family friend."

He took a moment, clenched and unclenched his hands, then said, "She's kind of a family friend of yours, too, Nate. Her father was Jack Halloran."

Halloran had been a veteran copper on the Pickpocket Detail with us in the early thirties. He quit to take a job as a deputy sheriff in Geneva, where I heard he'd done well for himself, making it to sheriff and holding the office for decades, finally running for mayor and winning when he was in his sixties. But he was no one I'd stayed in touch with.

"You said 'was,' Lou—he's deceased?"

"Heart attack two years ago. But that's nothing to do with this, other than just the general bullshit and hardship that kid out there has been put through."

"She's a kid in her thirties, though, right?"

"I suppose. I don't know her exact age. I just know her problem. And it's tricky as hell. There's a political aspect to it."

"Local?"

"Local if you live in Texas. Also national."

"Texas? I thought she was from Geneva, Illinois."

He ignored the question. "You've read in the papers about this character Billie Sol Estes?"

"Yeah, but I don't know chapter and verse. He's some kind of con man, scamming the government. Pyramid scheme crapola. Pal of LBJ's, right?"

"Right. He's currently in stir. He bribed government officials, took advantage of federal loan programs for farmers, and made millions peddling mortgages for nonexistent fertilizer tanks."

I laughed. "A genuine bullshit artist selling fake bullshit. Beautiful."

He gestured offhandedly. "Well, you may want to chat about this with a couple of your old pals. Good ol' boy Billie Sol was shaping up to be a major embarrassment for the Kennedy administration, before the assassination. No connection to them, but Johnson may have been an accomplice in those scams."

"That's crazy."

"Not really. Johnson has a reputation for that kind of thing, and Bobby Baker and Billie Sol were scandals that quieted down all of sudden when he became prez. Never forget that Lyndon B. won his first election by having a ballot box stuffed. And I've heard he blackmailed his way onto the ticket when Jack ran."

I shrugged. "That's nothing I ever discussed with Bobby. You said 'a couple' of old pals?"

"Yeah, your old boss McClellan's one of the guys who exposed Billie Sol."

Senator John McClellan had been head of the rackets committee, a father figure to Bobby Kennedy and officially my boss, when I was on that payroll. I knew him fairly well. I could probably get him on the phone if need be.

I asked, "What does this have to do with that young woman out there?"

"Maybe plenty. Possibly nothing." He sat forward again. "Estes is in jail, yes. But he's kept his mouth shut. Refused to testify on his own behalf. Is apparently protecting whoever else is in this . . . maybe including the President himself."

"Then why doesn't the President just give him a pardon?"

"Maybe he will, right before he leaves the White House and heads back deep-in-the-heart-of. But I don't think so. This is very dirty stuff, Nate. A pardon for Billie Sol would be an admission of guilt."

"So what? Sleazy underhanded practices netted some shady politicians some greenbacks. That sounds like Texas, and it sounds like Chicago, and it sounds like Everywhere USA."

But Lou was already shaking his head. "No, no, Nate, we're talking murder here."

I frowned. "Whose?"

"Well, we can start with a guy named Henry Marshall. He's the Texas farm official who first blew the whistle on Estes. In June 1961, before he could testify about any of what he dug up, Marshall conveniently committed suicide."

"People do that sometimes, under stress."

He looked at me over his glasses. "Marshall must have been really stressed to shoot himself five times in the stomach with a rifle."

"Oh. That kind of suicide."

"There have been four more. In April of '62, right after Estes was charged with fraud, his accountant committed suicide. Carbon monoxide, hose attached to his pickup's tailpipe. But the guy also had a bad bruise on his head."

"That's one. What's two?"

"A building contractor partner of Estes who died in a suspicious plane crash in early '63."

"And three?"

"Early this year, a major business partner of Estes, recently convicted as an accomplice, facing a prison term. He was 'accidentally' killed working on the exhaust pipe of his car. The tools scattered around him in the garage, around and under the car. Only they didn't have a thing to do with the repair he was supposedly making."

"Dead of carbon monoxide poisoning, too?"

"Yup. And bruised on the head."

"That leaves one more."

Lou nodded. "But I need to back up. This one's not in chronological order, because it needs some context."

"By all means. Context away."

His hard dark eyes narrowed behind the wire-rims. "Seems the Marshall 'suicide' just didn't sit well with a certain Texas Ranger name of Clint Peoples."

"You made that up."

"No," Lou said, grinning, shaking his head, "this badge-wearing, horse-riding Texas Ranger did a shitload of investigation, and managed to get a DA on his side, and together they got a judge to authorize an exhumation. This was in March of '62."

"They dug Marshall up."

"They dug him up. And the county coroner's autopsy showed that, despite the five gunshots in the abdomen, the cause of death was actually carbon monoxide poisoning . . . administered *after* an incapacitating blow to the head."

"Jesus. Somebody sure wanted to make sure this son of a bitch was deceased."

Lou was nodding. "So it would appear. And now we come to the fourth murder . . . the fifth, counting Marshall himself. Which happens to bring us home, Nate. Sweet Home Chicago."

"How so?"

"Seems Billie Sol wormed his way into owning a big piece of a company called Commercial Solvents. He bought huge quantities of liquid fertilizer from the firm, through the Chicago office. The office manager, a Joseph Plett, committed suicide in Evanston . . . the day after Marshall's body was exhumed."

"Carbon monoxide poisoning again?"

Lou nodded.

I held up four fingers. "Okay, four murders, maybe five." I added a thumb. "One in Chicago. So what does this have to do with Jack Halloran's daughter sitting out in our reception area?"

"She isn't just Jack Halloran's daughter, Nate. She's also Mrs. Joseph Plett."

. . .

She was the girl you fell in love with in high school, ten or fifteen years later, holding up just fine—blue-eyed, pretty smile—but if you looked close, you saw tragedy there. In the crow's feet, in her slightly sunken cheeks and the gentle lines in her forehead that time would turn to grooves, possibly prematurely. She sat next to Lou across the desk from me, perched on the edge of the chair, hands folded in her lap, like a wallflower hoping for the next dance.

"I hope you don't think I'm terrible," she said, "being so concerned about money and everything. First and foremost, I want Joe's name, his memory, cleared. We're good Catholics, Mr. Heller, and I couldn't even bury my husband in consecrated ground."

Her voice was firm, her eyes clear. There would be no tears today. The death of her husband was over two years ago. This was about dealing with the aftermath.

"You have a right to worry about your own welfare," I said, "and your children's. That insurance policy would have brought double indemnity, making it . . ."

"Five hundred thousand dollars," she said. It was a number she'd become familiar with. "As it was, we got nothing."

I said, "No payout in the case of suicide is standard."

"But it wasn't suicide."

"From what little I know so far, I'd be inclined to agree. But I'd like to hear more about why that's *your* opinion."

"Certainly." She cleared her throat. "First of all, we have three children, Mr. Heller. Our son Alec is ten, Judy is six, and Beth is two and a half."

"Beth was born shortly before Mr. Plett's death?"

"That's right. Joe was giddy over that little girl, loved her to pieces. He loved all his kids, and he loved me. We were happy. He was making good money, and we were very compatible, in . . . well, in every way."

"How old was your husband, Mrs. Plett?"

"Please call me Marjorie, Mr. Heller."

"Marjorie," I said, and smiled. "That's a very pretty name. One of my favorites." I'd known a girl called Marjorie once. "And call me Nate, please."

She showed me the smile again, briefly. "Yes, Nate. Well, Joe was thirty-one. A healthy, happy thirty-one, with everything to live for."

"Husbands and wives can have secrets from each other, Marjorie."

"The only secrets he had, if he had any, would have been related to business. It's obvious this Billie Sol Estes individual was a bad sort."

"He's a con man. But he's not a murderer."

That puzzled her. "How can you say that, Mr. Heller?"

"Nate. Well, he wasn't brought in by the cops on the Marshall killing, at least as far as we know, and he was already behind bars when the other suspicious deaths occurred. Including your husband's. Had Joe ever suffered from bouts of melancholy?"

She shook her head. "Nothing unusual. Who doesn't get blue from time, Mr. Heller? Nate."

"No, you're right. We all have our dark days. But did you ever see him get really low? Did he ever drink to excess?"

"No," she said, with no hesitation, "and that's one of the suspicious things that the police, damn them . . . I'm sorry . . . but they just *ignored* it."

"What is?"

She raised a hand as if it held something invisible. "There was a half-empty bottle of whiskey on the front seat next to Joe, in the car. But the coroner said there was no alcohol in his body."

I glanced at Lou, who just nodded a little. He'd obviously already heard the basics from her.

"I understand there was a note," I said.

"Yes, Nate. Would you like to see it?"

"Please," I said, but she was already digging in her purse.

She handed me a well-worn, folded-in-four photostat of the

note. It said: BELLS EVEN TOLL WHEN A RAT DIES. THE BURDEN OF GUILT IS ON MY SHOULDERS. NO ONE ELSE IS TO BLAME. ALL OF YOU LIVE AND BE HAPPY WITH A CLEAR CONSCIENCE.

"Typewritten," I said softly. "Unsigned."

Lou was just shaking his head.

She said, "Joe was a letter writer, Mr. Heller. Handwritten letters. He wrote his parents and his sister at least once a month. He never used a typewriter except at work. And hardly ever there, because he had a secretary. If he were going to do something crazy like this, he'd write it out. He'd sign it. But he never *would*!"

I'd been wrong. Tears did come. She got some tissues from her purse and Lou edged his chair over to slip an arm around her. I waited. Didn't take her long to settle down.

"I found him in the morning," she said. Swallowing. "In our garage. When I went to bed, he was working in his little home office, in the den. He said he was expecting some phone calls from the federal agents who he'd been talking to about this Estes criminal. Did I mention that? That federal agents had contacted him?"

"No. FBI?"

She nodded vigorously. "Yes. Anyway, he was still up when the kids and I went to bed. The garage is on the other side of the house, and the front door, too, so if he let somebody in, or if somebody broke in and did this, you know, quietly? We'd never know."

"Were there any signs of a break-in?"

"No. But if someone came around and it had to do with business, Joe would let them in. I'm sure he would. He would never have guessed that . . . well, that's just not how he was."

"He was talking to FBI agents. He must have known there might be danger."

"But that Estes louse was in Texas. And Commercial Solvents is headquartered in New York."

I wasn't sure I followed that logic, but I nodded. "Marjorie, what's your situation now?"

"I sold the house, but we didn't have much in it. Still, it paid off the mortgage and gave us enough to go on for a while. We're living with my mother now. Dad's gone, as I think you know. You were friends, weren't you?"

"Yes."

"I work odd shifts as a waitress not far from where we live. Back in Geneva now, so Mom can babysit. I'd like better work, but all I have is a high-school education. If we had the life-insurance money, possibilities would open up. Maybe I could go back to school. Or just live on it till the kids are grown."

I raised a hand. "We'll look into this, Marjorie."

She sat forward so far she almost fell off. "I understand this will be expensive. Is it possible I could pay you on a time schedule? I know a retainer is standard, but—"

"Marjorie, we'll take this on, on a contingency basis. Reasonable expenses and ten percent of what we get out of the insurance company."

Her eyes grew very large. "You would *do* that?"

"Yes. But there's no guarantee we'll get anything out of them. So you'd be on the hook for the expenses."

"That's fine. That's fine. Do you think there's a possibility that . . . ?"

"I do. These other suspicious deaths, two with carbon monoxide poisoning as the murder method, make proving foul play a real possibility."

She smiled. For the first time I couldn't see the scream behind the smile. "Thank you, Mr. Heller. Nate. Thank you. This is the first glimmer of light my family has seen in a very long time."

"Family's important," I said, Sam smiling at me from his picture on my desk. Even the ex had a smile for me.

I came around and walked her to the door, then let Lou take her to do the paperwork in Gladys's office. We worked through a lawyer's office when client cases had sensitive issues that might benefit from confidentiality.

A few minutes later, Lou was shut back inside my inner office and seated across from me again.

"A *third* of that insurance money on a contingency case is standard," he reminded me, grinning. "If it gets around that Nate Heller has a heart, we'll be out of business."

"Fuck you," I said. "What did you think of that suicide note?"

"You first."

"Everything in it seemed aimed at silencing other potential witnesses—'bells even toll when a rat dies'? If you talk and get killed, it says, 'the burden of guilt' is on your own shoulders, 'no one else is to blame.' "

Both his eyebrows went up. "Yeah, and those left behind can have 'a clear conscience,' because you caused your own murder."

"And the text of the note got in the papers?"

"Oh yeah." His eyes narrowed. "Carbon monoxide MO sure makes it sound like one guy is doing this."

"It does. One guy among several in a dirty business, elected to cleanup duty."

He nodded, then asked, "So what now?"

"You'll need to handle this on the Chicago end. That garage is a very old crime scene, but give it a gander. Talk to neighbors and see if anybody saw anybody around that night who didn't belong, or anything suspicious. And get the police files on this thing, look at the photos if there are any, talk to the dicks who worked it, see if you can locate the coroner who called it suicide."

"What I would do without these work tips? What about you, Nate?"

"Well, I'm taking the advice I've been given so often by so many."

"What advice is that?"

"I'm going to hell," I said cheerfully. "And Texas."

CHAPTER 5

The boy in me had been expecting a rambling mission-style structure with a hitching post for horses, while the grown-up me figured on an anonymous modern building with an American flag and parking lot of patrol cars. What the Waco branch of the Texas Rangers turned out to be was a pair of crowded, cluttered rooms among half a dozen others at the rear of the first floor of a defunct department store in a section of the downtown that looked like a war zone.

What lived up to expectations was Captain Clint Peoples himself, a rangy hombre in his fifties with dark graying hair in a military-short cut and a ready smile that didn't keep me from noticing that those steady blue eyes didn't blink much. One of the two rooms was his, half as big as the bullpen shared by nine two-man desks, counting his secretary's just outside his office door. About eleven Rangers in plainclothes were making phone calls, typing reports. This might have been the bustling bullpen of a precinct house in Manhattan, except for the drawls.

Right now we were shut inside the captain's office, the door muffling but not defeating the bullpen clamor. With his back to a scarred old rolltop desk shoved against the wall, Peoples sat facing me in a visitor's chair. There wasn't much else to the room except a quartet of metal filing cabinets and a bulletin board of WANTED posters. No framed photos or citations on the cracked-plaster walls, despite this man being a celebrated lawman, veteran of countless arrests leading to convictions, and shoot-outs leading to dead perps.

A window air conditioner chugged in this room, as did one in the outer room. It was ninety degrees outside, and humid, and if this was fall in Waco, I wasn't anxious to summer here. The heat hadn't taken a toll on me, though, as I'd moved rapidly from an air-conditioned car into the cooled building. I was casual in a yellow Ban-Lon and a lightweight brown H.I.S. suit, the coat of which my host had already invited me to hang on the coat tree in the corner, where his own jacket and a multi-gallon Stetson worthy of a Texas Ranger already resided.

Like his Rangers, he wore street clothes—a short-sleeve white shirt with dark-brown tie, cowboy boots glimpsed under tan chino trousers; but a small gold CAPTAIN badge was pinned just above his breast pocket. A .45 automatic with fancy ironwood grips rode high on his right hip, and he was smoking a cigar, a big one. The air conditioner cut the smokiness in the air, and anyway it was a good cigar, so I wasn't bothered.

We had already gone through with the handshaking ritual, and his secretary, Ruth, delivered us both cold bottles of Dr Pepper ("The native drink," Peoples said). It was just after two o'clock in the afternoon, after I'd driven down in my rental Galaxie from Dallas, where American Airlines had deposited me around eleven. I'd checked into the Statler Hilton, freshened up, and made the ninety-minute drive to Waco on Highway 77. The ride had been surprisingly rolling and green, Waco itself a modern city dropped into a big bowl formed by low hills. An ancient suspension bridge bisected the town, taking me over the muddy Brazos at South First Street and Austin Avenue.

"I appreciate you seeing me at such short notice, Captain," I said.

"That was some high-powered advance scout you sent lookin' for me," he said, blowing out a little smoke signal of cigar smoke, his eyes amused.

"It was nice of Senator McClellan to make that call," I said.

"Impressive, you workin' for him and Bobby Kennedy on that rackets committee."

"More impressive if we'd sent Hoffa to jail."

He nodded, smile fading. "Now and then a big one gets away," he said, as much to himself as to me. Then his smile returned. "But the senator is one of the good ones. He tried damn near as hard as we did to put a certain party away."

"What party is that?"

His smile turned sly and he rolled the big cigar around in it as he rocked. "We'll get to that. We'll get to that. Mr. Heller, what do you know about the Texas Rangers?"

"Pretty much what I've seen in the movies and on TV. Which I figure is about as accurate as what you've seen about private detectives."

He let out a laugh. "We're not a Wild West show anymore, Mr. Heller. We're with the Department of Public Safety—us and the Highway Patrol and licensing bureaus and so on. We're essentially the state's detective division—we help out sheriffs and police departments, if investigatin' a major crime is beyond their means. And of course we handle fugitive apprehension, since a fleein' felon doesn't confine himself to county and city boundaries. Roadblocks, aerial reconnaissance, all your standard modern police methods."

"What, no horses?"

"Oh, we still have horses, Mr. Heller. There are lots of places left in Texas where it takes a horse to get there." He shifted in the chair. "I do apologize for these cramped quarters. When I spoke of 'modern police methods,' I was definitely *not* referrin' to these sloppy surroundings."

"Are they temporary?" It had that feel.

"They are now." He shrugged and puffed cigar smoke. "When Company F got relocated to Waco, a few years back, all we got was these couple of rented rooms, some cast-off office furniture, and a cleaning crew that comes in once a month, if the mood strikes 'em."

I jerked a thumb toward the street. "You know, this looks like a nice place to live, college town, trees along the river—lots of industry, I understand. Must be close to a hundred-thousand population."

"Not quite yet. Gettin' there."

"So why does your downtown look like East Berlin? This building included."

He half-turned to tamp cigar ash into a glass tray on his desktop. "That's a sad one, Mr. Heller. Terrible tornado blew through here in '53, right down the middle of town. Killed well over a hundred. Chewed up hundreds of buildings and spit 'em out. This downtown was one of the main casualties."

"Well, they obviously rebuilt it."

"Some of it. Some they never got around to. And in the meantime a new shopping center went in. *That* killed the downtown deader than the tornado."

"That's happening places where there hasn't been a tornado. But Waco's disaster was ten years ago—what makes these quarters 'temporary' now?"

He grinned. Those blue eyes even granted me a blink. "Remember how you got here, Mr. Heller? How you made your way back to us through the driver's license testing area, and those offices with pretty young girls and callow young men in them?"

"I believe my memory goes back that far."

"Well, we took to walkin' various suspects through there for questioning back here in No Man's Land. On a fairly regular basis, we rounded up some fairly unsavory types, on prostitution and vagrancy and drug dealing and such like."

"Ah," I said.

"I'd already been hounding the Powers That Be about the need for a separate facility for Company F's Rangers. And I have a few influential friends in the community, including a former mayor or two and assorted Chamber of Commerce folk."

"So when do they break ground?"

He grinned around the cigar again and his eyebrows flicked up. "Next May, Mr. Heller. Next May. Now, you didn't come all this way to hear about *my* problems—at least not my problems with these cramped quarters."

"No." I sipped Dr Pepper. Not bad for a regional drink. "I'm told, by Senator McClellan among others, that you're the man to talk to about the Henry Marshall 'suicide.' "

"It's an interesting story, Mr. Heller." He wasn't rocking. "And I would be glad to tell it. But there's another story—at least as interesting as that one—that you really should hear first."

"By all means," I said.

Let me tell you about another Texas boy, Mr. Heller. Born in Mount Pleasant, Texas, back in 1921. Name of Malcolm Wallace, "Mac" to most. His daddy was a hardworking man, a farmer who later signed onto road crews, and he must have been proud of his boy, making good grades and keeping out of trouble.

By high school, Mac stood a broad-shouldered six foot, and kept right on pulling down high marks, and was popular enough to get elected vice president of his senior class. Something of a football star, too, till he hurt his back and had to quit. After he graduated high school, the boy joined the Marines, this was before the war, around '39 . . . oh, you were in the Marines, too, Mr. Heller? I was a bit too old to serve myself, I'm afraid.

Anyway, Mac Wallace served on the USS Lexington, *an aircraft carrier, but he took a tumble off a ladder in 1940 and, wouldn't you know it, injured his damn back again. Got himself a medical discharge, and . . . you, too? No kidding, Mr. Heller. Section Eight, huh? Guadalcanal? That'd do it. Still, I bet you jumped right smack in the swing of things, back on the home front.*

So did Mac Wallace. He enrolled at the University of Texas, over in Austin, and was active in student groups, some of a type that a less charitable man than myself might term pinko. But he wasn't no oddball or nothin', no. He was elected student body president, and kept pullin' down top marks. When the university's president was fired because of his socialist ways, Mac headed up a student protest, led eight thousand kids in a march. The movement failed, but it got in all the papers. He was for sure a young man worth watching.

Here's a picture of him—you can have that, Mr. Heller, I had that made for you. That's him about 1945—handsome devil, look at that curly dark hair, those moody dark eyes, regular Tyrone Power type, but kind of studious-looking too, don't you think, in those wire-rim glasses. Later on he preferred black-rimmed jobs. I got an older picture of him, which you can also have. But I'm gettin' ahead of myself.

Brainy as he was, it still took him something like seven years to get his degree, partly 'cause he switched majors a bunch of times, finally settling on economics. Plus, he was working his way through, taking various jobs, at least till the G.I. Bill kicked in, in '44. I should mention he was chosen to belong to the Friar Society, sort of the Texas version of Yale's Skull and Bones, if you've heard of that. Figured you had. Anyway, that put this fast-rising young man on a path to the highest reaches of business and government in the Lone Star State.

The Friars' is probably how he met up with Edward Clark, LBJ's man, his top legal counsel and financial adviser. Later on, Clark would introduce Mac to Lyndon, but I'm gettin' ahead of myself again.

Where was I? Oh, after graduation Mac married a good-lookin' gal named Mary Andre DuBose Barton. Her daddy was a Methodist preacher, but they had some powerful relatives up and down the family tree. Unfortunately for Mac, his young wife was a wild one. You know how preacher's daughters can be. In divorce proceedings against her, years later, Mac said she was a sexual pervert. He told me himself that she was a whore and a homosexual. And frankly there's evidence to back him up.

What kind of evidence? Well, Mary Andre Wallace was picked up on several occasions by police at notorious make-out spots, public parks primarily, with other women. Stripped down to their undergarments. Apparently Mary Andre liked both boys and girls, and Mac didn't like that at all. I won't bore you with all the ins and outs . . . that didn't come out right, did it? . . . but he up and hauled the little woman off to New York, where he did a couple of semesters at Columbia, going for a doctorate. Top marks again. He was doing some teaching, too. They had a kid, and then the gal got pregnant again, and she would get real wild during the pregnancies, boy howdy. Her own mama called the police on her for having sex with both men and women in Zilker Park.

Anyway, Mary Andre claimed Mac got violent with her, hitting and raping her and so on, and she filed a divorce petition, and Mac didn't bother fighting it. But he must have carried the torch, 'cause he remarried her some time later. My apologies for this mixed-up chronology, but Mac Wallace led a pretty mixed-up life after college. Not that he wasn't doing respectable work. Taught at two or three colleges, winding up back in Austin, where his wife took their young son.

Finally Mac got tired of Mary Andre's catting around, and took a big step toward respectability and the kind of career he had seemed headed for, before his ill-fated marital union. His connections with President Johnson, of course he was Senator Johnson then, led to a job in Washington, D.C., with the Department of Agriculture. Once again, seemed like Mac was going places.

There's another interesting LBJ tie-in, by the way—while he was separated from his wife, Mac dated Lyndon's sister, Josefa. This may indicate that Mac was his own worst enemy, since Josefa was herself a wild child who caused LBJ considerable embarrassment—divorced twice, a heavy drinker who liked to dally with both men and women, even worked in a brothel for a time.

This is where a feller named Doug Kinser comes into the story. We're going to set Mac Wallace aside, just temporarily, and take a look at Doug, an Austin boy who grew up loving the game of golf. He realized a dream when his brother went in with him to open up a little pitch-and-putt nine-hole golf course by the downtown lake in Austin.

Now, golf wasn't Doug's only enthusiasm. He also loved theater. He even went to New York to give acting a whirl, which is where he met up with Mac and his wife Mary Andre. All three were involved in some amateur theater there, when Mac was studyin' at Columbia. But by 1950, Mac was in D.C. working for the Department of Agriculture, while back home in Austin, Mary Andre was gettin' involved in local productions with Doug. Josefa Johnson was part of that thespian group, also. Kind of funny how some people get those two words confused—thespian and lesbian?

Well, those words got confused a lot when Doug was pursuing his other enthusiasm—having sexual affairs with willing ladies. He particularly liked what the French call ménage a twat. That means a threesome, but I can tell by your silly grin that you knew that already.

So now if you been keeping score, we got Mac Wallace havin' an affair with LBJ's wild-gal sister, Josefa—well, Mr. Heller, I call it "an affair" because Mac was still married to Mary Andre at the time. She dropped her divorce petition, though they weren't living together, at least not steady. Hell, any way you look at it, it was a mess. Particularly considering that Mary Andre and Josefa were both having affairs with our friend Doug, sometimes two at a time, sometimes all at once.

Now here's an item that may or may not be significant. As a law-enforcement officer, I will caution you that it is not even close to evidence. But it sure as hell is suggestive.

Some time during or in between pillow talk with Josefa, Doug asked her to try to get her brother Lyndon to loan him some money to pay off some outstanding debts that were threatening his new pitch-and-putt enterprise. Apparently she went to Lyndon, got turned down, and went back again a couple times, after Doug pressed the issue. It's possible Lyndon might have viewed this as attempted blackmail. Possible.

Now, Mac was living in D.C. at the time, or anyway in Arlington, and late October 1951, he drove down in his shiny new blue station wagon to Dallas, where he borrowed a little .25 from an old college roommate of his, who happened to be in the FBI. That always makes me smile. He spent a couple of days talking to Mary Andre, and asking her to be a better wife, a more normal wife, and just what the hell had she been up to lately? Who'd been doing what to whom, he wanted to know, and that kind of thing. By all reports, he was calm and cool and collected. No talk of him slapping her around this trip. Anyway, he wound up in Austin a few days later, and drove to Butler Park, where the pitch-and-putt golf course was.

It was a lazy afternoon, sunny, kind of breezy, grass turnin' yellow with winter on the way. Golfers were fooling around nearby on a putting green, but that didn't faze ol' Mac. He walked right in the pro shop and confronted Doug, who was at the cash register, and a few words were exchanged. Then Mac shot Doug point-blank five times and killed him very damn dead. Well, yeah, Mr. Heller, I guess that does sound like "overkill," but remember, it was a little gun, so Mac was probably just makin' sure.

Anyway, when he come out with his shirt covered in blood, Mac waved the gun at the golfers nearby, told 'em to stay back, and then he drove off in that blue station wagon, a Pontiac. The witnesses saw the license plate was Virginia, not something you see every day in Austin, and they got the number and wrote it down. Mac got picked up right away, and there was some jurisdictional nonsense between the Austin police and the county sheriff, so the Rangers got brought in. It became my case, which is why I can tell you all this in an insider kind of way.

Mac was charged with murder, and right off the bat, he resigned his government job. Shortly after that, he got released on thirty-grand bail, thanks to a couple of LBJ's financial backers, and an attorney of Lyndon's, John Cofer, out of Ed Clark's office, showed up to defend Mac. Cofer's the same guy who defended Johnson for ballot-box stuffing in 1948.

Mac did not testify in his own defense. Hell, Cofer acknowledged his client's guilt—after all, we had the car, the bloody shirt, and a damn .22-caliber cartridge in the suspect's possession. What had me shakin' my head, though, was when the district attorney stated he could find no motive for the murder.

That's right, Mr. Heller. Nothing about the sex stuff came out at the trial, and certainly not that Josefa Johnson had been in a sex triangle with the murdered man and Mac's wife. Or I guess it's sex quadrangle, if you count Mac.

No evidence at all was introduced from either side about cause or extenuating circumstances. After a trial that lasted less than two hours, the jury found Mac guilty of "murder with malice aforethought."

Guess what he got for killing a man in cold blood? A five-year sentence—that is, a five-year suspended *sentence. Not exactly the "Texas justice" you hear so much about, like the kind all those colored boys on Death Row are waitin' on. First suspended first-degree murder sentence in Texas history. Maybe the only one.*

I hadn't been a Ranger very long, but I'd been a deputy sheriff and a highway patrolman, and could recognize the whiff of politics. The stench of it. Do I think LBJ directed Mac to kill a blackmailer? Hard to say. But any way you slice it, Mac sure did Senator Johnson a favor by shootin' a par five at the pitch-and-putt.

Peoples took a deep puff of his cigar, which had largely been forgotten in his ashtray while he spun his yarn.

He expelled some smoke, then said, "Hell's bells, that's rude of me. Would you like a cigar, Nate? I got a box of Senators right here. Made over San Antonio way."

Somehow a Texas Senator seemed fitting, but I said, "Thanks. Smells fine. But I'm not a smoker."

"Clean-cut fella, huh?"

"Not exactly. But I haven't smoked since I was in the Pacific, and then just cigarettes." I only got the urge when I was in a situation that recalled combat.

"Then can I have Ruth fetch you another Dr Pepper, Mr. Heller?"

"No thanks. But maybe you should call me 'Nate.' I'm starting to feel like we know each other."

Peoples grinned; even those blue eyes seemed to have warmed up. "Only if you call me 'Clint.' "

"Okay—but I thought the only Westerners called Clint were on TV."

That made him smile. "Nate, I ain't never been mistaken for Cheyenne *or* Rowdy Yates."

"I'll take your word for it, Clint."

He blew a smoke ring, just showing off, and rocked some more. "So let's talk about the late Henry Marshall, Nate. You know the basics, I believe."

"The very basics."

"The facts are easily laid out. Marshall was well-regarded, both as a man and a public servant. He worked for the Agricultural Stabilization and Conservation Committee."

"That's a mouthful."

"It is. He traveled a lot, and he worked hard—lived over in Bryan, nice family, who incidentally don't buy his suicide, neither. Had a ranch in Robertson County, which was a mostly a hobby of his. Place to get his mind off work, mending fences, seeing to crops, feeding cattle."

Peoples gave me a quick refresher on the case. After discovering that LBJ's pal Billie Sol Estes had been raking in over twenty million a year for "growing" and "storing" nonexistent crops of cotton, Marshall made his report to Washington, recommending a full-scale investigation and more stringent regulation.

"Suddenly Marshall gets offered a higher-up position in another department," Peoples said, "including a hefty pay raise, that would not so coincidentally make the Billie Sol matter none of his concern."

Marshall rejected the new position and instead spent the next several months meeting with various county officials in Texas as well as the farmers who'd been drawn unwittingly into the scam, and just generally spreading the bad word about Billie Boy.

Shortly after, Henry Marshall turned up dead in a pasture on his ranch alongside his Chevy Fleetside pickup truck.

"No suicide note, by the way," Peoples said.

I asked, "How can anybody buy a suicide shooting himself five times?"

"It was a .22 rifle," Peoples said with a shrug, relighting his cigar, puffing it back to life. "What the sheriff and coroner didn't think of—or if they did, conveniently forgot about—was that Marshall's rifle was bolt-action. He'd have had to hold the damn thing at arm's length to work the bolt to reload after every shot, getting wounded every time—two of 'em 'rapidly incapacitating' wounds, our staff coroner said. And here's the kicker—ol' Henry had a bum right arm, from an old farm injury. Couldn't hold the damn thing out straight if his life depended on it."

Or his death.

I said, "Sounds like the exhumation brought all the evidence out. So is it murder on the books now?"

Peoples shook his head glumly. "No. There was a ringer on the grand jury, a relative of the sheriff's, who wouldn't budge. Either the sheriff was bought or just didn't want to look stupid. Also, an FBI agent came in, looked at the evidence, and called it suicide, too."

"And those guys are generally pretty good," I said. "That's a hard one to figure."

"Your Senator McClellan couldn't get anywhere, either, even after he stood up at his committee hearing with the rifle and showed how hard it would be to work the bolt action at arm's length *without* a bum wing."

"So it's a closed case."

"Not from where I'm sitting." His frustration dissolved into a sly grin. "You wondering yet, Nate, why I started by telling you the sorry tale of Mac Wallace?"

"You know I am."

"Here's that later photo of Mac I promised you." He handed it over. "That's still over ten years old—he's camera-shy, our man Mac."

Wallace no longer looked like a college kid—the glasses were black-rimmed, the eyes cold, hair still dark, the strong jaw resting on fleshy support, eyebrows dark and heavy, but still a broodingly handsome man.

"Latest photos available come from the Doug Kinser murder trial in '52," Peoples said. "But take a look at this sketch."

Though crude, it resembled Wallace, all right—black-rimmed glasses, similar hair.

"Where does this come from?"

"A sketch artist of ours drew it from a description provided by a gas station attendant who gave directions to a man looking for the 'Marshall place' the afternoon of the killing."

I sat shuffling through the two photos and the police sketch, feeling the hair on my arms prickle and it wasn't the work of that window air conditioner.

I said, "You're saying Mac Wallace killed Henry Marshall."

"I have not a single solitary doubt. Would you like to hear how I see it? My reconstruction, as the big city lawmen say?"

"Clint, you know I would."

. . .

It's a beautiful Saturday, with birds twittering and flittering, in a part of Texas that looks green and lush in late spring. Marshall—who earlier drove around stopping to talk to some farmer friends, who found him in fine fettle—is puttering around the ranch.

Mid-afternoon, after stopping at a gas station for directions, Mac shows up unannounced at Marshall's little spread. It's possible he tries to reason with Marshall, maybe offers him another, bigger bribe. Might be he threatens him and his family. Maybe it turns into an argument—Mac's a volatile fella, real bad temper. My guess is, he pistol-whips Marshall, dropping him to the ground with his head cut along one side and his eye bruised up real bad.

Mac rigs a plastic liner to the exhaust of Marshall's pickup, and starts the truck. And now I'm just guessing, but I think something spooks our man—maybe traffic on the country road nearby.

Marshall's .22 bolt-action rifle is in the back of the pickup, stowed there for getting rid of varmints. Impatient with or unsure of his murder method, Mac uses the rifle to shoot Marshall five times in the side of the lower torso.

Here's the best part, Nate—the next morning, Mac goes back to that filling station, and tells the attendant that he changed his mind yesterday, and never did go out to the Marshall place.

Enough to make you wonder how he got those high marks in college.

"That gas station attendant is lucky to be alive," I said, shaking my head. "And Wallace has never been brought in for it?"

"For what? A suicide? But I can tell you this, Nate. Mac Wallace has no alibi for the Marshall murder, and those other 'suicides'—that accountant in El Paso, the building contractor flying out of Pecos, the indicted business partner in Amarillo—he has none for those, either. I believe he got a lot better at staging suicides. And he was in Texas at the time each of those kills occurred."

"You think Wallace is, what? A kind of hit man for the Johnson crowd?"

"My guess is LBJ is way above the fray. But he has had some big bad nasty folks backing him from day one—oilmen, industrial folk, powerful lawyers. Or it could be Billie Sol reaching out from behind bars. He's appealing his sentence, you know. Dead witnesses have a certain eloquence, but they don't get called to testify."

"I have another for you," I said, and I gave him the information about Joseph Plett's suicide.

He wrote it all down on a spiral pad.

When I was finished, he frowned at his own notes. "This Plett fella—the date of his death, why that's just one day after we exhumed Henry Marshall."

"Yes it is."

He sighed wearily. "Well, this one's out of state. I won't be able to check on Wallace's whereabouts on this 'un. Maybe you have people who could do that."

"Why, doesn't Wallace live in Texas?"

"He works for a Texas firm, Ling Electronics, in Dallas, but they transferred him in 1961. Oh, he comes back a lot, for reasons that probably don't *always* have to do with helping somebody kill their self. One possible item of interest, he was in Dallas on November twenty-two of last year."

"Clint, you can't be suggesting—"

"An individual known to be a hatchet man of LBJ's was in town, is all I'm saying. On the other hand, ol' Lyndon benefitted much as anybody from that particular hit."

I was starting to think maybe Captain Clint Peoples needed to be fitted for a tinfoil Stetson.

"Since movin' out of state," Peoples was saying, "Mac Wallace has spent a hell of a lot of time back home in Texas . . . visits that correspond to some nasty, suspicious deaths."

And deaths didn't come any nastier or more suspicious than JFK's, I had to admit.

I said, "Where did that electronics company move Wallace to?"

"Mac's workin' for the Ling branch on the West Coast."

Now the hair on my neck was prickling. "Where on the West Coast?"

"Southern California," Peoples said. "You know, Disneyland and movie stars—the Los Angeles area."

CHAPTER 6

As the Galaxie made its way up Highway 77, through a rural landscape that might have been Illinois were it not for the occasional cotton field, the sun began to set in a vivid expressionist blaze, throwing long blue shadows across my path. Like a futuristic mirage, a skyline rose from the flat terrain, modern monuments to insurance and banking, cold stone and steel but with touches of color, the blue Southland Life towers, the red horse riding the Mercantile Bank.

I'd had much to think about on the drive back to Dallas, and a conducive atmosphere to do it in—traffic had been light, and the landscape soothingly monotonous. The panic I'd felt at hearing that murderer Mac Wallace was within easy reach of my son and ex-wife had faded—Peoples having told me that Wallace was currently in Dallas, doing a project at the Ling Company's home base, and staying at the Adolphus Hotel.

"We kind of keep an eye on what ol' Mac's up to," Peoples told me, "when he's back in these parts."

That was apparently a fairly new policy for the Rangers, else some "suicides" might not have occurred.

Or maybe they would have. It had only taken driving a few miles out of Waco into wide-open spaces under an endless sky to acquire enough distance to decide that Captain Clint Peoples had become a kind of rustic Ahab with a white whale called Mac Wallace. No question Wallace had killed that pitch-and-putt fucker, that was a matter of public record; but all Peoples had on Mac for the Henry Marshall murder was a crude police sketch, a lack of alibi, and a hunch.

I had asked him, "Did you bring Wallace in for a line up for your gas station attendant to make an ID?"

"Didn't have enough to haul Mac in," Peoples admitted. "I showed our witness Wallace's picture, that same one from '52 I gave you, Nate, and he said he was pretty sure that was the fella."

"'Pretty sure' doesn't cut it."

"No, and the pump jockey isn't cooperating anymore. Not since he got a couple of very threatening anonymous phone calls."

That, too, indicated Peoples might have been right about Wallace in the Marshall murder, but it was still goddamn thin. Nonetheless, I would call Lou Sapperstein tonight and have him check on Wallace's whereabouts when Joseph Plett was killed in Chicago, and do a background check on him in California. We would put the convicted killer under surveillance when he returned to Anaheim, until I was convinced he was no threat.

Of course, if he *was* a threat, I'd do something about it myself, since I also had a streak of Ahab in me.

But right now I was in Dallas, and Wallace was in Dallas, too, so maybe I could get a jump on this particular lead.

I didn't bother going back to the Statler, instead pulling into the parking garage next to the Colony Club, the town's most celebrated strip joint. In the parking garage, I got my nine-millimeter Browning in its shoulder sling from the trunk where I'd snugged it behind the spare tire. I wasn't licensed to carry in the state of Texas, but if I was going out seeking a guy who got suspended sentences on murder one convictions, I figured better safe than sorry.

When I exited the ramp, the sidewalk was splashed with the club's neon. Looming over me was a sign worthy of the Vegas strip, white neon on undulating orange:

COLONY
CLUB

DANCING

FLOOR
SHOWS

and below that a marquee, black letters on white:

GIRL SHOW

JADA

CHRIS COLT
WITH HER 45'S

PEGGY STEELE

3 OTHER EXOTICS

Welcome to downtown Dallas, where nobody lived except conventioneers, businessmen on the road, and other lonely, horny men. When the Dallas working day was done, the rush was on to bedroom communities—executives heading north to the Park Cities, lesser white-collar types to far north Dallas and select neighborhoods in Oak Cliff and Lakewood, while the labor force took buses south. No stadiums for sports to bring them back, either, and only a few movie theaters, the Capri, the Palace, the Majestic.

That meant the primary entertainment options were the girlie clubs—Abe Weinstein's Colony and his brother Barney's Theater Lounge. Jack Ruby's Carousel, I noticed, on the other side of that parking ramp, was shuttered, a casualty of history.

Might seem funny that one of the classiest, most famous hotels in Dallas was right across the street from its biggest strip joint, but the twenty-two-story, Beaux Arts–style Adolphus depended on conventioneers, too. I crossed Commerce Street, dodging only light one-way traffic, figuring to eat in the Century Room.

I would eventually join the other out-of-town males at the Colony Club, if for no other reason than I had spent a couple of memorable nights with the exotic dancer named Jada (actually Janet Adams) when she played Chicago last year. But I had learned long ago not to eat at strip clubs, since food was never the attraction and when you got a hair in your soup, it had unfortunate resonance. Add to that the possibility that Mac Wallace might be dining at the restaurant in his hotel, and the Century Room it was.

Once upon a time the Century Room had been the "Hawaiian" Century, with bamboo and native bark on the walls, palm trees with coconuts, and an animated mural of volcanoes, mountains, and breaking surf tied in with a tropical rainstorm effect. Now it was space-age modern, brown and gold, looking like a high-class Denny's. Too bad. At least the Planked Gulf Trout Adolphus hadn't changed with the times, except for the price—a buck twenty-five after the war, two-fifty now.

What the Century Room didn't serve me up was Mac Wallace, even though I lingered through my meal and went through two vodka gimlets. The weeknight diners at the Century Room consisted of married couples celebrating a birthday or an anniversary, couples who might have been married but probably not to each other, and lonely men-about-town. None of the latter were the pitch-and-putt slayer.

Traffic hadn't picked up any when I crossed Commerce again into the neon fog of the sidewalk under the Colony Club's looming sign. For all that sleazy grandeur, the address was 1322½, meaning the nitery was one floor up, the glass-brick entry a modest recession between a liquor store and the parking ramp. Under a rounded canopy, glassed-in showcases at right and left presented racy posters and photos of Colony girls past and present, with an emphasis on Candy Barr, who'd got her start (and her name) here. Through the door with its porthole window, I went up thickly red-carpeted stairs to a small landing where an overly made-up attractive blonde in a low-cut red gown sat behind a semicircular black-leather-upholstered counter trimmed in silver. She wanted two dollars and I gave it to her.

There was a time when two dollars got you more from a blonde like that.

The club room was impressively large, dominated by a performance stage with an Art Moderne look that had really been something in the '40s. In those days, you would see the likes of Louis Armstrong and George Gobel here, and Bob Hope would hop up on the stage when he was in town, to do a free bit. The strippers were just part of the show.

Now they *were* the show. When I'd been here maybe ten years ago, the featured musical group was the popular George Shearing Quintet. The combo onstage tonight was Bill Peck and His Peckers. Somehow I didn't think Johnny Carson would be booking them on *The Tonight Show.*

Still, the place had remnants of class—the formidable stage, maybe twenty-five by thirty, was elevated, with a shiny black metal rail to keep horny patrons from getting too friendly with the exotics, as strippers liked to call themselves these days. Black-leather-upholstered booths and chairs, linen tablecloths, plush carpeting, and flickering candlelight added up to a dreamy ambiance.

I'd already had those two gimlets across the street, so from my ringside seat I just ordered a Coke from a smiling, busty black-haired waitress in a tuxedo jacket and black mesh hose. The waitresses pushed champagne, which was how you got them to sit with you. You shared a bottle with them, but they didn't drink much if any, utilizing a trick of pouring the champagne from their glasses into the ice bucket. My perky dark-haired doll tried hard, but I didn't want her company or the champagne.

That and wine and beer were the extent of alcoholic beverages that could be legally sold in a nightclub in Dallas. That was why there was a liquor store downstairs, and a cover charge outside. You brought a bottle in a brown bag and ordered setups.

Getting desperate, the waitress pointed out a doorway in the back corner. "I give private dances in the VIP room upstairs. You'd love it, there's these dark-blue mirrors and velvet couches. Real intimate and sexy. If I'm not your type, sweetie, some of the dancers are available. Just let me know. . . ."

The lights came down, and I sat rather glumly through the MC, a guy named Breck Wall who used to be Jack Ruby's man, doing a painful comedy routine with a guy in old-lady drag, a bad version of Jonathan Winters's Maude Frickert ("My living bra just died"). The first stripper was a pretty, stacked brunette called Peggy Steele, who according to MC Wall was "The I-Don't-Care Girl," and she didn't. As the Peckers played "Blue Skies," she moved listlessly around in a dark-blue strapless gown with a glittering bodice and gradually peeled to pasties and a small rhinestone-studded bikini bottom. Then a corny comic in a red derby accompanied his tired song parodies ("How dry I am, how wet I'll be, if I don't find the bathroom key") with a banjo and I decided Bob Hope probably wasn't going to show up tonight.

Blonde Chris Colt was next, with her "forty-fives," a description that did not refer to the toy six-guns on her hips. To "I'm an Old Cowhand," she pranced in a rhinestone-studded Western pants outfit that zipped off until she was wearing just two sheriff's-badge pasties, a skimpy G-string that exposed a little tumbleweed, and white boots. This cowgirl was usually the headliner, but not with Jack Ruby's headline stripper, Jada, on the bill—suddenly famous in the wake of the assassination.

And Miss .45's applause had not died down when Jada came strutting out to the Peckers singing, a capella, *"Ja-da, Ja-da, Ja-da Ja-da jing jing jing."*

She was an amazing-looking woman—though she was only five-foot-five or -six, her tower of flaming red hair, which somehow also reached her shoulders, conspired with high heels to make her seem larger than life. Flesh that had been creamy white in Chicago was now a dark-berry tan, her lipstick bright red, her full lips constantly flashing a wide, white Marilyn-esque smile; her wide-set blue eyes with the long fake lashes and curving eyebrows gave her the overemphasized glamour of a female impersonator, only she was definitely female.

Her spangly, feathery white evening gown with long white gloves didn't last long before she was down to red pasties and a half corset that showed off her full, shapely bottom. Her hourglass figure made the pert breasts seem larger than they were, and the lushness of her curvy figure was matched by a charismatic command of the stage, a laughing mastery she held over all the men in the audience.

Those blue eyes flared with surprise and even delight, seeing me seated ringside, and she blew me a kiss. I grinned at her, and she laughed, bump-and-grinding her way over to the leopard-skin rug on which she was about to perform the explicit routine that had made Jack Ruby mad at her. So afraid he'd go to jail over it, he'd sometimes turn the lights off on the stage.

Tonight the lights stayed on, though her pasties and G-string didn't, and this was merely the end of the first act. She got the kind of sitting-down standing ovation only the sexiest strippers could get, and pranced off laughing. The MC came out and announced the show's second half would begin in thirty minutes, the band taking a break as Twist music got pumped in.

Not five minutes passed before Jada flounced out from a door beside the stage, wearing a green robe with a green feathered collar, to sit with me at my little ringside table. The lights were up and her star presence got a lot of wide eyes and whispers going around us, but nobody came over and bothered us. An autograph is not what a guy wants from a stripper.

She grabbed my nearest hand with both of hers and leaned in and kissed the air a few fractions of an inch from my mouth—she couldn't risk smearing that elaborate lipstick job.

"Nathan Heller," she said, in a rich alto thick with a Latin accent, "you are a bad boy not telling Jada you were coming to town."

"Hi Janet. What's with the accent? Gonna go on the road and play Lola in *Damn Yankees*?"

She gave me half a grin. She was even sexier when she wasn't trying. Dropping the accent, she said, "These Texas chumps think I'm from Brazil," though there was now a hint of the South. "Doesn't hurt an exotic to be a little *more* exotic, and I also don't have to explain the tan."

"You look good any color. You're going on again?"

"Better believe it, buddy—I close the show. I'm the headliner, and doesn't *that* give Miss Big Titties from Big D heartburn. Ha! Me with my two tiny handfuls."

"You don't hear me complaining. When did they close down the Carousel?"

"Around when Ruby's trial started. It was a drag there. A club like that lives and dies on big spenders, buying champagne to impress girls they'll never get. After November twenty-two, all we got were beer-drinkin' reporters and curiosity-seeking tourists, with dumb questions about Ruby and Oswald."

"Like did Ruby know Oswald, and did Oswald frequent the club."

"Right. Stupid shit like that."

"Did Ruby know Oswald? Did he frequent the Carousel?"

"Sure. But, like, I'm gonna tell *that* to some hick from Iowa?"

"I'm from Illinois."

"But you ain't no hick," she said, grinning at me. My God, that smile was as wide and glittering as a Cadillac's front grill. "So, Nate, how long are you in town for?"

"Not sure. Tonight at least. You busy after? When do you get off?"

She touched my nose. "When I get off, Nate, is kind of up to you, isn't it? As for when I get out of *here,* last show's over at midnight. You want to take me over to your hotel, or come to my place? It's nice. It's in Turtle Creek."

"You headlining strippers must make good bread."

"Exotics."

"I stand corrected."

Her eyebrows, already high, went higher. "You working a case? I thought you were too big a shot to work cases anymore."

"Please. We call them jobs."

That made her laugh. She was easy to make laugh. You might assume she was easy in other ways, and admittedly, like a lot of girls in Texas, she'd been to the rodeo before. But I like to think she was picky. She picked me, didn't she?

"So, Janet, are you, uh, tied down to anybody right now?"

"You mean am I between marriages? Yes. Am I shacked up with anybody? No. I gave up men for Lent."

"Lent is over."

"That makes this your lucky night. So—is it an interesting job? You *do* know this town is a real drag these days, right? At least in the club we get out-of-towners, though not near enough."

"Why a drag?"

"Ah, hell, Nate, ever since Kennedy got killed, this burg is under a cloud. Everybody feelin' guilty, feelin' sorry for themselves. Talk about a bad rep. Tourism is *way* the hell down. Who wants to come to a town with a police department like ours?"

"Oh I don't know," I said. "Look how fast they caught Ruby."

It would have taken a beat for most strippers to get that joke, but Janet was sharp and she exploded with laughter. When she laughed like that she made a very unladylike, unsexy honk that made me like her all the more.

I glanced around, now that the lights were up, to see if Mac Wallace had strolled over from the Adolphus for a little entertainment. Despite his protestations of morality, he was a guy who had been, after all, attracted to a very wild bisexual wife and for that matter the President's scarily out-of-control sister.

Josefa Johnson, by the way, was deceased. Died under vaguely suspicious circumstances, according to Captain Peoples—a cerebral hemorrhage, Christmas day, 1961. Contrary to state law, there was no autopsy, no inquest, the death certificate signed by a doctor who hadn't examined the body; she was promptly embalmed and buried. Peoples saw the hand of the LBJ's hit man in this—and it was even thinner than his Henry Marshall theory.

Still.

"Lights up there are pretty bright," I said. "You probably can't see the audience very well."

"Not that bright. I can make eye contact. I saw *you* sitting here, didn't I? Why?"

"You come out and sit out front like this, sometimes?"

"You think you're the only man in my life? But I'm not reduced to pushing the champagne, I'll have you know."

"Just wondered if you've seen this man," I said, and I showed her the 1952 photo of Mac Wallace.

"Well, sure I have," she said, as if speaking to the village idiot. "He's been in here three or four times a week all month. He's here right now."

"Yeah?"

She nodded toward the back, where I had to swing all the way around in my seat to see.

And I saw, all right, saw him in one of the pink booths lining the rear wall—the dark hair, the black-rimmed glasses, five o'clock shadow on a handsome oval face. He wore a dark suit and a dark tie, very undertaker-looking, and he was pouring from a bottle of booze into a glass of ice.

"I didn't see him come in," I said.

"He was here before the show went on. I think maybe he was upstairs with one of the girls. One of the strippers who doesn't get billing, and could use a little cash."

"They like to be called exotics," I said, which was as witty as I could manage feeling this poleaxed.

She got up and leaned over and gave me another almost kiss. "Honey, I got to get ready for my next set. You be good. And if you can't be good . . ."

"Be careful," I said, "yeah I know."

I was facing the stage again. Checking my watch, I could see the show's second half would start in about ten minutes. Wallace didn't seem to be going anywhere, but I wasn't taking any chances. I tipped a waitress a buck to show me to a table toward the back, putting his booth just behind me to my left. When the lights came down, I would be able to adjust my chair to keep track of him without being obvious.

I did just that.

The second act was strictly strippers, the three girls who didn't receive name billing, then the cowgirl and finally Jada again, doing an even wilder routine. My attention was on Wallace, however, who was sitting sullenly working on his bottle, a pint of Jack Daniel's. He put it away slowly, but he put it away.

When the lights came up at midnight, there was no last call, because public imbibing, even the BYOB variety, was illegal past the witching hour. The Colony did serve sandwiches and coffee, and about a quarter of the audience stayed for that. But Wallace just sat there sipping bourbon on ice (he'd gone through several setups), and I overheard two waitresses arguing over who would tell him to stop.

"Not me," my tuxedoed dark-haired doll from earlier whispered. "He's got a bad temper, particularly when he's tight."

The other waitress, a blonde, whispered, "He doesn't look tight."

"He's one of those gentleman drunks. You know, he says excuse me after he belts you one?"

I had spent the second half of the show trying to figure out what my move was with Wallace. If he hadn't been drunk, or anyway tight, I might have just approached him, introduced myself, and said I wanted to talk to him. Like I would with any witness or potential suspect. But I decided to try a less direct approach.

I got up, and was walking past his booth in the direction of the men's room when I stopped and pointed at him in friendly way, smiling tentatively, and with a little slur in my voice said, "I *know* you, don't I?"

He was tipsy, so I was tipsy.

"I don't think so," he said in a mellow baritone touched with a tinge of Texas, his eyes half-lidded, dark and cold behind the lenses of the dark-rimmed glasses. His face was smudgy with beard—five o'clock shadow turned midnight blue. There was a slight plumpness to his cheeks and under his dimpled chin, adding a touch of babyface to his slightly dissipated leading-man looks.

I didn't overplay. No need for a full-on drunk act. The Colony Club already had enough corny comics.

"Maybe I don't," I admitted, then pretended to think. "Or did I see you in the paper? While back. Is that it?"

A small smile appeared under a Roman nose—just a curl at either corner of his rather full, sensual mouth, showing a slice of white teeth, startlingly so against the dark need-to-shave.

"I know *you,* though," he said.

"Yeah? So where do we know each other from?"

The teeth disappeared but the slight smile otherwise remained. He nodded next to him in the booth, motioning me to join him.

What the hell—I slid in. Plenty of room.

He said, with an even slighter slur than the one I'd already abandoned, "You're Nate Heller."

Shit.

"So *where* do we know each other from?" I repeated, somewhat lamely.

"I know you from magazines," he said. "*Life. Look.* I even read about you when I was in college—true detective magazines."

He was in his early forties and I was in my late fifties, so that was possible.

"That's who I am all right," I said pleasantly, as if we were still just a couple of guys striking up a conversation in a bar.

" 'Private Eye to the Stars,' " he said. "Isn't that something? And you worked on Lindbergh, too. And the Harry Oakes case in Nassau."

He really had read those true detective magazines. That slur had gone from his voice, but his talkativeness bore the fluidity and slight over-enunciation of somebody inebriated trying not to show it.

I snapped my fingers. "And that's where I know *you* from! I read an article in one of those magazines, too—on that murder you committed. Five-year suspended sentence for first-degree murder. You must *know* people, Mr. Wallace."

The smile disappeared. He didn't frown, though—he had a soft-lipped, blank look that was much worse than a frown.

"Call me Mac," he said, and offered his hand.

I shook it, and his grasp was rather limp, and clammy, like shaking hands with a corpse.

"And I'm Nate. A couple of guys who made it into the true detective mags, having a little impromptu reunion. Too bad they don't serve liquor after midnight in this town."

He shrugged. His tie was snugged up, giving him a formal look. What kind of guy sat drinking brown-bag bourbon all night and never loosened his damn tie?

"There's a little joint down the street," he said, "called the University Club that has a deal with the police. We could go down there."

"Well, okay. I'm buyin'."

"All right."

On the way out, I asked the black-haired tuxedoed waitress to let Janet, that is, Jada, know that I had run into an old pal, and that I would catch up with her tomorrow night. I let Wallace lead the way out, since I was not anxious to get pushed down a flight stairs, maybe in a sudden fit of despondency.

On the street he paused to light up a cigarette in front of the closed liquor store. He asked me if I wanted one and I said no, that smoking was one bad habit I didn't have. A group of four businessmen emerged from the Colony, sloshed, and staggered over to the Adolphus.

Then Wallace said, "I'm not stupid, Heller. Just be straight with me. Who knows? Maybe I'll answer your questions."

"Why not start with, where were you on May 22, 1962?"

He gave me a dead-eyed baby-face stare. "I should know that, should I? That's just fixed in my memory, is it?"

"Here's a hint—it's the day after they dug up Henry Marshall."

He turned toward the street, as if gazing at the fancy hotel across the way. His eyes had narrowed slightly. "So that's what this is about? That Plett suicide?"

Jesus! Was he admitting it?

He saw my surprise and said, "I read about that in the papers . . . to continue a theme."

"You remember reading about a killing in Chicago that happened over two years ago?"

He nodded, his expression smug. "I do. Got a lot of press here. It was part of the Billie Sol Estes scandal. That got lots of play in Texas, Nate. . . . Shall we walk?"

We headed down the street, at an easy pace. Traffic was almost nonexistent and the sidewalks couldn't have been more barren if the bomb had dropped.

"Let me guess," he said, and the slight smile was back. "Captain Clint Peoples. He told you all about how I'm President Johnson's assassin of choice. *That's* what you meant by that crack—I must 'know people.' "

Walking, side by side.

"You were a golden boy," I said, "who Senator Johnson helped out. I mean, he did keep you out of the death house, right? Since you helped him with his sister."

He stopped and I stopped. The night was cool, almost cold. The sky was a deep rich blue with pinpoint stars, like the fake ceiling of a strip joint. We faced each other.

His eyebrows, heavy and dark, tensed. "How exactly did I help him with his sister?"

"Well, probably one of two ways. Through intermediaries, like the Outfit guys back home do it, Johnson suggested you remove a mutual problem, namely that golf-course putz who was banging your wife and your girlfriend and his sister. That sounds like three people, doesn't it, but it's only two."

His small smile turned sideways. "You take liberties, Nate, with new friends. I mean, we just met."

"The *other* way would have been that you really did decide all on your lonesome that Doug Kinser needed killing . . . and LBJ and his crowd offered to help you stay out of jail, if you agreed not to testify and spread embarrassing sex stuff about his sister."

"I choose none of the above." His eyes managed to be cold and hard while seeming uninterested.

"In either case, Johnson and his cronies now knew they had a man who could kill in cold blood, and that might come in handy. For example, in the case of that Billie Sol Estes scandal you mentioned? A killer like that might be willing to stage a few suicides."

He was shaking his head, just a little. "Do you know what kind of people you're accusing?"

"Rich people? Powerful people? Corrupt people? That kind?"

"There's no truth to any of this, Mr. Heller."

"What happened to Nate?"

"If you harass me, I'll get a court order. If you go public, I'll sue you for slander or libel. Or maybe the people you're accusing will do something else."

"I'll get depressed, you mean? Suck on a tailpipe?"

"What do you want from me?"

"Here's an idea. Now, please don't consider this blackmail, although that's what it is. I don't care to go toe-to-toe with you Texas boys. I might wind up with a branding iron up my ass or become a rare white lynching victim. But that Joseph Plett you mentioned, his wife and kids got screwed out of a $500,000 insurance settlement because the insurance company doesn't pay out on suicide."

"Do I look like I have half a million dollars in my pocket?"

"No, but Lyndon's oil and arms buddies spill that kind of bread, not to mention that guy Edward Clark's law firm. Pass that along as a compassionate request for the welfare of a family who became casualties in that situation comedy starring Billie Sol Estes. Why is he still alive, by the way?"

And now a barely perceptible sneer. "You think you're very smart, don't you, Mr. Heller?"

"Smart enough, generally."

"Maybe not this time," he said, and he punched me in the belly.

Fucking sucker punches, anyway.

I was doubled over, which made it convenient for me to jam my head in his gut, though because of his blow I didn't have much power, just enough to make him stumble back a step. He swung and missed with his right and I swung my right and clipped him on the nose, just a glancing blow. His left came around and caught me under the right eye, though not with the power his other hand might have brought. But his back was to a building and I gripped him by the sport jacket and slammed him into the stone.

It jarred him, but he managed to shove back at me, and I lost my footing and went down on my ass. He came over and kicked me in the side, but when he tried to take a second helping, I caught him by the foot and shoved him backward, his arms windmilling.

He managed not to fall, but by the time he had regained his balance, I was facing him with the nine millimeter in my hand and about two feet between us.

The bad thing, the really nasty thing, is that he didn't seem to give a shit. He smiled, really smiled big for the first time, seeing the gun. He flicked the fingers of both hands in his own direction.

"Go ahead, Heller. Shoot me. You'll hate yourself in the morning if you don't."

Shoot him with a gun that wasn't licensed in the state of Texas. Shoot him on a public street where several cars had already gone by and not slowed down to get involved. Shoot him and let thousands of answers die with him. Shoot him and maybe go to jail, and how had that worked out for Ruby? Or Oswald, for that matter?

He was laughing as he walked off somewhat unsteadily—from the booze or the fight or both—in the direction of that after-hours club.

I put my gun away and hobbled back to the Colony Club, my side hurting like hell, a rib busted maybe, and somehow got up the stairs and into the nightclub, where Jada, in a plaid cloth coat and very little makeup and looking like the Janet she really was, was coming from backstage.

She put her hands on her hips and said, "Well, look who's here! I thought you were standing me up!"

"I changed my mind," I said, and passed out.

CHAPTER 7

Someone once said that there was no excuse for Dallas even existing—that it sat in the midst of nothing and nowhere, the land around it dry and black and providing would-be farmers with no more than a crop of headaches and heartbreak. Calling the Trinity—alternately a trickle or a flood—a river was typical Texas bluster. No oil derricks towered in or near Dallas, nor was there gas or sulphur. Back in the 1870s, the railroad came only because some shady businessmen tricked and/or bribed the Houston and Texas Central Railway to build there.

Nothing here happened by accident, nature, or happenstance. Men made Dallas. Men made their city a leader of banking and insurance and manufacturing, and the Southwest's center of fashion and culture, too. In 1964 it was home to half a million people, most of whom would gladly tell you that Big D did everything bigger and better—bigger steaks, fancier parties, more air-conditioning, taller buildings, better-dressed women, better-looking girls. Or anyway that was their attitude before Jack Kennedy made their town his last stop and their improbable city became a national disgrace.

I was staying with Janet Adams, aka Jada, stripper or (if you will) exotic dancer, in a high-rise luxury apartment house in an area once dominated by grand old homes as lovely as the trees lining the banks of Turtle Creek. Some of those lavishly landscaped residences were still there, but many had been pushed out by apartment complexes, filled with stewardesses, stenographers, salesgirls, models, and receptionists.

It was Thursday, early afternoon. In a lounge-style deck chair, I was stretched out wearing a bathing suit but also a short terrycloth robe, to cover up my bandaged ribs and some nasty bruising. On the cement beside me, on a towel, Janet lay on her tummy, her red hair pinned up like a crazy turban, her bikini top unsnapped, so she could soak up sun and get even darker. Periodically I rubbed some suntan lotion on her. Otherwise, I was just living behind my Ray-Bans, watching girls in their twenties swim and sun—a relative handful at half a dozen, mostly stewardesses I would venture, since the other single girls living here were probably at work. They were ridiculously beautiful. How I wished rubbing suntan lotion on Janet and ogling bikini-clad young women paid a living wage.

Though this was my second day as Janet's guest, it was my first time down by the pool. Tuesday night, Janet and two other dancers at the Colony Club had gotten me down to her car, a white Caddy convertible, parked in the same next-door ramp as my rental Galaxie. I barely remember this, but I do know that I have never had less fun in the company of eager-to-please strippers.

I also barely remember the trip to the emergency room at Parkland Hospital. I was X-rayed, found to have two cracked (but not broken) ribs, got taped up, shot up (with Demerol), and given a five-day supply of drugs (Demerol again).

I woke up in Janet's bed late the next morning. She was there, a nurse in green halter top and short shorts, to walk me to the john, feed me some more Demerol, and put me back to bed. That evening, I got up, was able to get myself to the john and then avail myself of a tan cotton robe (no shortage of abandoned men's clothing at Janet's), and joined her in the living room of a very nice but very underfurnished apartment. In fact, the furnishings were right out of a thrift shop, what little there were.

We sat at yellow-Formica-topped table that June Cleaver would have tossed out around 1956, eating TV dinners and sipping cans of Schlitz in her modern kitchen. Swanson frozen fare was all she cooked for herself, she informed me. What the hell—it was better than I'd got in the service. She was still in the dark-green shorts outfit—it went really well with her red hair—and was having the meat loaf. I had Salisbury steak.

"What's the story on this place?" I asked. "It's got to run you one-fifty a month, easy."

"Two bills," she said, chewing meat loaf.

"Meaning no offense to a gracious hostess, but the interior decoration is strictly Early Goodwill."

She grinned at me. "Don't you get it? I'm part of the suitcase set."

"What's the suitcase set?"

"We're kind of high-class nomads. You move into an apartment in one of these high-rises, then move out again in two or three months. These places offer the first month free, you know."

Sounded more like low-class moochers to me, but I kept it to myself.

"I didn't know," I said.

"Sure," she said, digging into her aluminum pocket of peas. "Anyway, I don't need a year-round residence in Dallas. I spend as much time in New Orleans."

Working Carlos Marcello's clubs.

"And sometimes," she was saying, "Austin and Fort Worth, too. It's a little circuit. I'm just winding up a two-month stint at the Colony, then a few weeks in New Orleans at the Sho-Bar, and back to Big D at the Theater Lounge, Abe's brother's joint."

"I thought they were famous for their amateur nights."

"Yeah, and boy did that use to drive Jack batty. Or battier, anyway."

She meant her Carousel boss, Jack Ruby.

"You know," she was saying, "he was stuck paying exotics guild minimum. And the amateur girls down the street got bupkus."

The guild was the American Guild of Variety Artists. My old pal Barney Ross, the onetime triple-division boxing champ, did PR for the AGVA in New York. I had grown up on the West Side of Chicago with Barney. So had Ruby.

"Anyway," Janet was saying, eating her mashed potatoes without enthusiasm, "the Theater Lounge books a headliner in, to shore up these amateur-night cunts."

Okay, so Janet wasn't always elegant. Like the thrift-shop furniture, she didn't really belong here. But she had rescued me last night and was feeding me today, so she could be as vulgar a little cunt as she pleased.

While she was getting ready for work—she did her makeup at home, because the Colony's dressing room was shared by all the dancers—I used the kitchen phone.

I got Lou Sapperstein at home, and he was cross with me: "Where the hell have you been? I pressed the desk clerk at the Statler till he admitted you weren't in your room last night."

"I stayed overnight with a stripper friend."

"Well, that doesn't mean you shouldn't check in! I was about ready to start calling the hospitals, or the Dallas city morgue."

I explained that I'd taken a beating from a suspect in the Plett murder.

"Get something to write with," I advised him.

"Okay, but first, the whole Plett job, this whole Texas trip of yours . . . something really crazy happened. Something good, maybe even great, but crazy as hell."

"What?"

"This afternoon Mrs. Plett gets a call from that insurance company and is told she's getting the full half a million. They told her they were doing a reappraisal of certain cases, and that the circumstances of her husband's death were questionable enough that her double-indemnity claim would be honored. Two years after the fact! You ever hear of such a thing?"

"No. She called and told you all this?"

"Yes. She wanted to know if we were responsible for her good fortune"

"What did you say?"

"I said I believed we were. *Were* we, Nate?"

"Probably."

I gave him a brief rundown on Mac Wallace, per Captain Peoples and my own experience—minus the suspicions about LBJ and JFK—and how I'd told Wallace our investigation would cease if our client got her money.

"I'm a little surprised," I said, "that it came from the insurance company. I didn't know how the payoff would happen, but never figured on that way."

"Well, it's a Dallas-based company, if that tells you anything."

I also told Lou that even though the insurance company had come belatedly through, I wanted Wallace's whereabouts at the time of Joseph Plett's "suicide" looked into. And that when Wallace returned to California, he was to be kept under surveillance until further notice.

"That could be expensive, Nate."

"We'll be getting fifty grand from Mrs. Plett."

"True. This guy Wallace is very likely a contract killer."

"More like an in-house assassin."

"And we're going to let him walk?"

"Our job is to get our client satisfaction, and if that insurance payout does the trick, then we walk away."

He gave me a long-distance sigh. "Agreed."

"Was the client happy?"

"Very. Nothing about clearing up her husband's suicide was even mentioned. For that kind of dough, who needs consecrated ground?"

"Then it's over."

I told Lou I'd likely be heading home tomorrow, and we said our good-byes.

In her living room, Janet positioned me in a threadbare armchair before a little black-and-white portable TV on a wheeled stand before she left for work that evening. I had taken some Demerol with my Schlitz and I fell asleep in the chair before *The Beverly Hillbillies* turned into *The Dick Van Dyke Show.* I dreamed a weird episode of the latter staring the A-1's receptionist, Millie.

When Janet nudged me awake, the TV was hissing with snow on the screen.

"You shouldn't have slept in that chair," she scolded. Her blue eyes narrowed under a high bare forehead—she wore no makeup and her painted-on stripper eyebrows were gone, leaving only the faint shadow of shaved-off real ones. She should have looked grotesque, but her pretty eyes and cute nose and full sensual mouth made up for any shortcomings.

"Tell it to the Demerol," I groaned. "That stuff put me out like Cassius Clay."

She helped me out of the chair. She'd already hung up her cloth coat, and was in a red-and-brown plaid lumberjack shirt and jeans and sandals. Her flaming mane was pulled back in a ponytail with enough hair for a real pony's tail. Even minus stripper wardrobe, she was a cartoon of a woman. But in a good, Al Capp–drawn kind of way.

Once I got up, I realized I was feeling better. But I didn't argue when she led me into the bedroom and deposited me there, tucking me under a cool sheet.

"Get to sleep," she said, turned off the light, and walked briskly into the adjacent bathroom, closing the door, leaving only a slash of bright light under it. Shortly the sound of the shower began. I could hear her singing in the echoing booth. Took me a minute, muffled as it was, but then I made it out: "Everybody Loves Somebody Sometime."

That made me smile. Dino, hitting the charts, knocking the Beatles off their perch. Sorry, Sam.

Then she started singing "Love Me Do," and maybe my son had the last laugh at that.

I propped myself up in bed with two pillows, working to find a position that didn't strain my aching ribs. Well, they didn't ache that much after the Demerol, anyway. There wasn't much bruising showing, either, as mummy-like bands of adhesive tape covered the majority of my purple badges of honor.

The door opened and let steam out and she was poised there in the fog of it. She pulled a shower cap off and lots of red hair escaped, wild and undisciplined, and she began toweling off her curvy body. No pasties, no G-string. Just a woman with a classic hourglass figure, no skinny *Vogue* model this, more an escapee from *Cabaret* magazine. Her breasts rode her rib cage as if she was serving them up, like cupcakes on trays, and her pubic triangle was trimmed way back, the better to stay within the confines of her G-string onstage. That nether hair matched her head's improbable flame color. If only her hairdresser knew for sure (as the TV ads speculated), he or she was doing double duty.

"Are you up?" she asked, still framed in the doorway. Light poured out, providing moody illumination in the otherwise dark bedroom.

"Are you kidding?"

She smiled, and padded over like a little girl, jiggling in all the big-girl places. She was giggling, too, which was cute as hell coming from such an experienced broad. She stood next to me where the sheet tent-poled and she batted playfully at it, making it wave hello at her, as she grinned and licked her lips.

"You *are* feeling better," she said. Then her expression grew serious. "Listen. I know you're hurting. We don't have to do anything. I'm pretty tired myself. But if you do feel like it . . ."

I reached my hand out, like the Frankenstein monster about to learn that fire is hot.

She batted that away, too, and gave me as impish a smile as she had in her. "Wait. I want to get your opinion on something. Just wait there."

I nodded, my bruised body throbbing, but at least some of the throbbing was pleasant.

She went over to a dresser that looked like it had been salvaged from a shipwreck, and bent over, showing me the heart-shaped behind that had made her infamous, and which suddenly made me understand the meaning of cupid's arrow imagery. She grabbed some things out, and almost ran back into the bathroom, where the steam had dissipated, and closed the door.

It didn't take her long to come back out, leaving the door open to provide some backlighting. She was wearing a little nurse's cap and a very short-skirted white nurse's uniform.

"What do you think?" she asked, arms spread, palms up turned, in *ta-da* fashion. "It's for the act."

I said nothing. My mouth had dropped open and didn't seem to be able to function for anything but sucking in air.

"It's a little different," she said thoughtfully, and she strutted a few steps, then shook her head, dissatisfied, saying, "Without music, without heels, it's not the same."

I curled my finger and she came over dutifully. I threw the sheet off. She placed a hand gently around me and stroked. "Are you sure you're up for it? Well, I mean that's *obvious*. . . . I could use my hand like this . . . or my mouth like . . ."

As she leaned over the bed, her hair flopped over and hid her as her head descended upon my lap and she suckled me, gently, tentatively, then began a slow up-and-down motion that was hypnotic as she went gradually, so gradually, deeper and deeper, until she had all but engulfed me. At the perilous moment, I gently entwined my fingers in that red mane and eased her off.

"I don't mind," she said, with a smile both loving and nasty, tongue flicking, invisible eyebrows raising.

"Get on. Ride me. Ride me, cowgirl."

"Can't you see I'm a nurse?"

"I have a good imagination. Just . . . take it a little easy."

"I'll be gentle. I'll be ever so gentle. . . ."

I swallowed, gestured to the nightstand. "I have something in my wallet . . ."

She shook her head and the hair was a red shimmery smear around her lovely face. "It's a safe time. Don't worry."

This was a notorious stripper who got around. Some might call her a slut. She could have twelve kinds of diseases. Using a rubber was an absolute must. It would be insanity otherwise. She tugged the white skirt up over the red triangle and I let her climb on. A bareback cowgirl nurse, sucking me up into the wet tight warmth that the men she danced for could only dream of.

Her intentions of being gentle were reflected in her easy, loving cadence. Which lasted almost thirty seconds before the bump-and-grind she was so famous for began, that frantic, jungle-beat gyration accompanied by long hair hanging over me and whipping me, whipping me, whipping me, as she ground into me with a hunger that expressed itself in crazy swivels, working herself into my lap like she wanted to tear me off and take me with her. She was jungle-beast noisy, too, squeals and screams, seemingly lost in the throes of orgasm throughout, and when she finally did come, the noise fell off into a whimpering.

Meanwhile my ribs were screaming—all the Demerol in the world could not have stopped it—and I was in such exquisite pain when I came that if I had died at that moment, I wouldn't have minded.

"Next time," she whispered, and gave me a peck of a kiss, "we'll let it all hang out."

She climbed off like a little girl getting off a carousel pony and padded into the bathroom, the twin globes of her fabulous behind jiggling like Grandma's Jell-O salad under the pulled-up short white skirt. I lay back, wilted and worn, but the hurt seemed to have subsided, the hurt of my ribs that is. Because she rode me raw.

That night I woke up once, to use the john and take some more Demerol, and when I climbed in bed next to her, I was out like a switch had been thrown.

Now it was Thursday and I was feeling much better, sitting by the pool and being a letch behind my Ray-Bans. I was temporarily shacking it with a female who could make any heterosexual male's wildest, dirtiest dreams come true, and yet I was still watching young stewardesses swim and frolic. Being a man is such a humiliating task.

Janet turned over and sat up and had me close the snap on the back of her bikini top. "You look chipper," she said. "Is that a gun under your towel, or are you glad to see me?"

"It's a gun. Also, I'm glad to see you."

"Little ol' me? I should feel honored, with all this prime cooze on the looze. So—you want to stay with me, till the end of my Dallas run? We could have a good time, Nate."

"I know we could. Not sure I could survive it, but I do know." I stretched. Actually stretched. "I think I'd like to go to the club with you tonight."

She smirked. "In the mood for some more quality entertainment—like those shitty comics of ours?"

"Well," I said, and my hand around the nine millimeter grip tightened, "I *am* in the mood for entertainment. Has Mac Wallace been back around?"

"He was in his favorite booth last night. Why?"

She didn't know it was Wallace who cracked my ribs. I'd told her I was mugged. She had thought that was funny, since I was a guy with a gun and yet some asshole had gotten the best of me. I thought it was a riot myself.

"Just wondering," I said.

The bill hadn't changed—same bad comics, same stacked strippers, from lackadaisical Peggy Steele to busty Chris Colt to gyrating Jada. The difference was that tonight I watched from the wings. This new position gave me some refreshing angles on the peelers, but also a more inconspicuous sideways view on the audience.

As promised, Wallace was in that same back booth, again pouring brown-bagged bourbon into glasses of ice, getting quietly if not noticeably sloshed. During the show's second half, he rose and went off toward the men's room.

I took the backstage steps to come out a door to one side of the elevated platform and cut along the side of the club. The mostly male audience—the house was about two-thirds full—saw nothing from their wide eyes but the near-naked girl onstage, a short, curvy number with a taffy-colored bouffant. Her gimmick was that pieces of her fringed outfit seemed to drop off of their own free will as she did the Twist to Bill Peck and his Peckers playing "Irresistible You."

When I reached the men's-room door, I taped on a hand-lettered sign (which I'd fashioned at Janet's apartment) that said CLOSED FOR CLEANING. This was necessary because there was no lock on the door of the good-sized restroom, with its half a dozen urinals and four stalls.

Within the dreary but fairly clean yellow-walled john, one guy was washing up, another was just coming out of a stall, and Wallace was pissing at a urinal. I washed my hands, watching Wallace in the mirror while the first guy left and the guy who'd exited a shitter came over and washed his hands beside me. Both were gone when Wallace did the little dance men do to coax out those last few droplets, and he didn't recognize me until he was washing up. I was standing nearby using a paper towel.

"Something I can do for you?" Wallace asked blandly. As before, his handsome oblong face with its baby-face plumpness was smudgy with beard, the eyes cold and dark behind the black-rimmed glasses. He was again in a black suit, though his necktie was red tonight.

"I think you already did," I said pleasantly. "I hear Mrs. Plett's insurance company decided to pay out her claim. Only took them two years."

"Typical bureaucracy." He was washing his hands, faucet running hard. He looked at me in the mirror and his smile was small and smug, his dimpled chin jutting. "Not that I'd know what you were talking about."

"You know what I don't get?"

"Why don't you tell me."

I watched him closely, figuring he might throw soapy water in my face.

"I don't get," I said, "how a pinko student protestor grows up to be the willing arm of a bunch of right-wing Texas fascists?"

Looking at me in the mirror wasn't enough. He shut off the faucet and turned his head toward me, frowningly. "The President is a great man."

I chuckled. "So that's it. The ol' strange bedfellows routine. Your pitch-and-putt benefactor Lyndon feathers the nests of his oil buddies, so he's free to do good in the world."

Tightly, Wallace said, "He's done a *lot* of good."

"I'd agree. Took a Southern conservative to push civil rights through. And there's the war on poverty. We'll forgive him Vietnam, 'cause he's got to throw the military-industrial boys *some* kind of bone. It's the old ends-justifies-the-means gambit. I get it."

"You may," he said.

"What?"

"Get it."

And he flicked the soapy water on his hands toward my eyes, but I was ready, and ducked it, and slammed a fist into his belly. When he doubled over, I grabbed the back of his head and kneed him in the face. He didn't go down, but he wobbled. I took out the nine millimeter and slapped him alongside the left temple, and *then* he went down.

He looked up at me, drunk with pain, his face smeared with red from his nose and his mouth, his eyes seeking focus, and I took him by the lapels of his undertaker's suit coat—a little tricky with a gun in my right hand but I did it—and I hauled him over and into the first stall.

"Your face is a mess, Mac," I said. "Let me help."

I shoved him face-first into the toilet bowl and flushed it several times. My son called this a swirly. I called it plain old-fashioned fun.

Wallace was coughing and sputtering and spitting water when I turned him around and sat him down hard on the can and shoved the snout of the nine millimeter in his neck. My eyes bore in on his dark ones, blinking now, no longer half-lidded.

"Listen, Mac, I don't care whether you killed Henry Marshall, President McKinley, or Cock Robin—none of that is my business or my concern. You saw to it that my client got her payout from the insurance company, so we're square."

"What . . . what . . . what . . ."

I had no idea what he was asking, but I answered anyway: "This isn't my way of thanking you for that, it's my way of settling the score for the other night. Nothing more, nothing less. Now, I understand you live in California."

He frowned, beads of water running down his face like tears that started at his scalp. His hair, which wasn't very long, nonetheless looked stringy as seaweed.

"My ex-wife and my son live out there," I said. "Why would I tell you that? Because it's only fair, since I will kill you or have you killed if you are ever seen anywhere near them or where they live. You may think you are one deadly motherfucker, and you might think you could find me and kill me. And probably you could. But I employ just under one hundred hard-ass ex-cops, any one of whom would just love to teach you how to *really* rig a fake suicide. Do I make my point?"

He just looked at me, gulping air, face running with water droplets.

I slapped him—just with my hand, not the gun.

"Do I make my point?" I asked again.

He swallowed and nodded.

"Good," I said.

And left him there.

This time I followed Janet home, my rental Galaxie tagging after her convertible Caddy like an eager puppy. I was feeling pretty damn good. I was feeling no pain on Demerol, and a man in his late fifties had just kicked the ass of a hard case maybe fifteen years younger. Mac Wallace was an evil fuck, but I had put the fear of God in him. Or the fear of Heller, anyway.

And in bed, I took the lead, bending my redheaded benefactor over the edge of her bed, entering her that way, and the bump-and-grind was under me now and slower this time, with a yearning that made both of us very happy and maybe a little sad, because I'd already told her I was leaving tomorrow.

She was leaning back in bed, sheet at her middle, perky pointed titties bared, and she was smoking. Apparently she didn't know it was a cliché. I didn't crave a smoke, though earlier I had felt the urge, right before I cornered Wallace. But I hadn't succumbed. One must maintain control, after all.

"You wrapped up your job, huh?" she said.

"I did."

"Somebody said Mac Wallace limped out of the club, looking like he got his clock cleaned."

"Do tell."

"You did that, didn't you?"

"I sure did."

"You be careful, Nate. Don't get cocky."

"I thought you liked me cocky."

"That Mac Wallace character has important friends."

"Does he, now?"

"I hear he works for Big Oil."

"No, he's with an electronics company."

She shrugged. "One of the girls who dated him says he works for that nut with the window."

"What nut with what window?"

"Some Big Oil guy who owns the Texas School Book Depository. You know, where Oswald shot his rifle out the window? If you believe that shit. Anyway, this Big Oil guy removed the window and made some kind of display out of it, in his home. Like it was a damn . . ." She shuddered. ". . . *trophy* or something."

She had my attention.

I said, "Who told you this?"

"One of the girls I know from the old Carousel days. Rose Cheramie. She said they tried to kill her, too."

"*Who* tried to kill her?"

"Some of the shooters who got Kennedy. Look, you gotta consider the source. Rose is a junkie."

"She's at the club now? I don't remember a Rose dancing."

"No, she's working a club in Waco this week, I think." She drew in smoke and then let it out her nose in twin trails. "Shit, what is it with that goddamn Kennedy thing? Why can't everybody forget about it and get on with their goddamn fucking life?"

"You mean, like those tourists at the Carousel?"

"Yeah, them, and these damn reporters. I've had this one, this really famous one actually, hounding the hell out of me."

"Who?"

She shrugged, irritated a little. "You know that showbiz columnist, the one that's on that dumb game show Sunday nights?"

I sat up sharply. "You don't mean *Flo Kilgore,* do you?"

Flo had written an article exposing the chicanery surrounding the death of Marilyn Monroe; based largely on my investigative work, the piece might have won the Pulitzer, if her editor hadn't spiked it, giving in to pressure from the Kennedy White House.

"Yeah, that chinless dame," Janet said. "I'm surprised you didn't run into her at the Statler, 'cause that's where she's staying. What's that show she's on? *I've Got a Secret?*"

"*What's My Line?,*" I said numbly.

"Well, *I've* got a secret . . . I got a bunch of 'em." She pointed at one pert bare breast. "And I intend to keep 'em to myself. I'll live longer that way."

Looked like I wasn't leaving Dallas just yet.

CHAPTER 8

The soaring Statler Hilton had a Space Age look that screamed 1960s but was already almost ten years old. Its twenty stories were home to 1001 rooms and as many hotel employees, its innovations including conference rooms on lower floors, a mammoth ballroom with no pillars, and a heliport "taxi" service for the rich, though most guests were more impressed by the 21-inch custom TVs by Westinghouse in every room. The front of the hotel was the fork of its Y-shape, a concave facade that looked as cool as a cocktail but had the unintended by-product of creating an eddy that scooped up any trash blowing down the street to circulate by the front entrance like soiled confetti.

On a more positive note, that concave front also allowed for a Vegas-like drive off Commerce Street, and I pulled my rental Galaxie in and got myself out. It was mid-morning, a sunny, pleasant day, not as humid as other trips of mine to Dallas. I had a room here that I hadn't slept in for the last two nights.

That meant I was in the brown H.I.S. suit I'd worn interviewing Captain Peoples in Waco, not to mention during my dustups with Mac Wallace. So my clothing was a little ripe, even if I had showered occasionally over the past several days, though I hadn't bothered shaving yet this morning. The doorman must have been used to eccentric Texan millionaires—they said H. L. Hunt went around in near rags—and gave me no attitude as I handed him my keys for the valet parking.

After wandering through an impressive lobby with atomic-design carpet and floating staircases, I selected an elevator in facing banks under a futuristic metal lighting grid, all very Buck Rogers, but on the rear wall was a map of Texas that seemed somehow a relic. The ride up was accompanied by Mantovani's strings butchering "I Believe in You"—another of this hotel's innovations, but not a welcome one: elevator music.

My room, 714, at first seemed to have no bed, just modern furnishings in rust, yellow, and brown (with matching abstract-shape drapes) dominated by a couch, which Detective Heller deduced was actually a twin bed with one side flush to the wall, along which propped-up cushions provided seating for two, facing the TV opposite.

I took a long, hot shower, letting the jetting water drill me like a friendly machine gun. First thing this morning, at my request, Janet had removed the adhesive strips that had mummied around me, supporting my ribs. The ER doc at Parkland had been good enough to have a sweet-looking young brunette nurse shave away the body hair before he'd applied the bandages. I'd been in so much pain, I barely noticed her.

So the strips had come off, and I was sore, but I was still on Demerol tablets, cutting the dose in half to keep me alert. And to make the pills last longer.

I finally shaved, splashed on some Prince Matchabelli aftershave (Black Watch), slipped into some dark-gray Jaymar Sansabelt slacks, a gray-striped Van Heusen shirt with a dark-gray narrow knit tie, and a Madisonaire sport coat from Lytton's in Chicago.

I looked goddamn good and nowhere near my age, even if I did feel far older, the ribs aching, the bruising mercifully covered up. But I should pass muster with a certain very famous lady.

Not that I had a date lined up with her or anything. I just knew she was one of the other guests in another of the thousand rooms in the Statler. But this female was no stranger to me, and I knew she would just be getting around to breakfast about now—a quarter to eleven. And her breakfast would be a martini.

I can't always be right—she was having a Bloody Mary.

In my defense, she had skipped breakfast and gone straight to lunch, a shrimp salad with Thousand Island dressing. She sat alone at a table for four, tucked in a corner of the vast and currently underpopulated Empire Room, the restaurant that converted to a showroom with name entertainment after dark. The furnishings were modern here, though the tables wore linen cloths, and the room was on the bright side, the partition walls bearing Mondrian-style plastic squares of color—red, aqua-green, black, white, yellow—like the Playboy Club's sidewalk-spanning entryway.

I hadn't seen her in two years but she looked just fine, if every year of her age—mid-forties—her brown hair in a forehead-baring bouffant, her nice slender shape in a piebald shift; she wore starry earrings and a single strand of pearls that was vivid against her alabaster complexion. No Texas sunning for her.

This was Flo Kilgore, *New York Herald Tribune* show-business columnist, nationally syndicated and a genuine household name, primarily due to her spot on the panel of *What's My Line?*, the hit Sunday night game show.

Flo glanced up at me with blank disinterest on her heart-shaped face, apparently assuming I was a waiter, then her big blue eyes widened and brightened, her cheeks dimpling, her smile pretty and dazzling white, if thin-lipped, over her only bad feature, the weak chin that Frank Sinatra and Johnny Carson made such cruel fun of.

"Nate! You've been on my mind!" She scooched her chair back and got to her feet, holding out arms with white-gloved hands. "Have I conjured you?"

I gave her a kiss on the cheek and a hug, and took the chair next to her that she gestured to as she settled back in.

"No magic involved," I said. "I'm just wrapping up a job. Figured on heading back to Chicago this afternoon."

She reached out and held my right hand with both of her gloved ones. "I wish you'd stay! There's something you could help me with."

"Really?"

Though there were no other patrons within a dozen tables of us, she leaned forward and whispered confidentially, "It's the biggest story of my career. Scoop of the century."

"What, are Liz and Dick splitting up?"

"Don't be mean. Anyway, I'm off the Hollywood beat and back on Broadway where I belong."

"Dallas isn't Broadway."

"No, but it's home to the story that's going to net this little Indiana girl a Pulitzer. I already have a book contract from Bennett."

She meant Bennett Cerf, publisher of Random House, her fellow game-show panelist.

I said, "Why were you thinking about me, of all people?"

"Two reasons, really. One is for a favor, which is to ask you to contact a friend of yours."

"Who?"

She raised a gloved hand, like a prim lady traffic cop. "Not yet. You need background first. But the other is to see if I can hire you."

"For what?"

"For a bodyguard."

"One of the things I'm known for," I said, arching an eyebrow, "is famous clients of mine who've been killed, despite my best efforts. Amelia Earhart, Sir Harry Oakes, Mayor Cermak, Huey Long. . . ."

"Judging by those last two," she said coyly, "you must be something of a expert in the realm of political assassination."

She had no idea that I was way ahead of her on that mysterious scoop she was dangling.

I asked, "Why would you need a bodyguard?"

Now both white-gloved hands patted the air, like Jolson milking the audience for an encore. *You ain't heard nothin' yet.* "We'll get to that, we'll get to that. . . . Why don't you have some lunch, and afterward, we'll talk business."

A waiter came over and I ordered a steak sandwich, rare, cottage cheese, and a Coke, which arrived quickly, and Flo and I made small talk throughout lunch. She had a teenaged son and daughter, and of course I had Sam, so that carried us a while. Despite her upbeat mood, she revealed she'd been through some rough times of late.

Two of her various marriages had been to a former actor and sometime Broadway producer named Frank Felton. Two years ago she had married him a third time. Over the years, depending on whether they were hitched or not, they had a sporadic radio show, *Breakfast with Flo and Frank* (the martinis and Bloody Marys going unmentioned) on WOR in New York. They'd also had one of the first open marriages I ever heard of, but that hadn't kept them from getting divorced twice. Her other marriages had been to younger men, both pop singers, one famous, one not.

"I've been burning the candle at both ends," she admitted. "Booze and pills . . . like poor Marilyn."

"Not exactly like poor Marilyn, I hope."

"No. I wouldn't say I'm that far gone. But since I saw you last, I've checked in three times at Leroy Hospital to wean myself off the goodies."

"So that's just tomato juice, then?"

"No. I didn't say I stopped drinking, just stopped drinking so much. Anyway, that's how Frank and I got back together. He was taking the cure at the same time as me, and one thing led to another. I'd been doing the radio show alone, and, well, we'd always had such great success at WOR as a twosome."

"I'm glad that's going well for you."

"Actually, it isn't. Frank fell off the wagon badly. Nate, I can't bring myself to divorce him again, but I should. You know how he would fill in for me when I was off on a story, doing the breakfast show alone?"

I didn't, but I said, "Sure," because celebrities hate it when you don't know things about them.

"Well, sweetie, he went on the air drunk, oh, a bunch of times, and we got canceled. Can you imagine? *Canceled.* An almost twenty-year run, and in an eye blink, *phffft.* And that was a lucrative gig, too."

"I'm sorry."

Her eyebrows flicked up and down. "You know, the newspaper business isn't what it used to be. I'm in about half as many papers now, although very soon that will change. That . . . will . . . *change.*"

We ate in silence briefly. She was searching diligently, ace reporter that she was, for one last shrimp in that salad.

I said, "So you're back in Frank's town house in Manhattan?"

"Yes. Had to sell the Beverly Hills house, the one on Roxbury where you and I worked on the Marilyn case, remember?"

"Like Chevalier says, I remember it well. The money that brought in should have helped."

"No. We barely covered the mortgage. Oh, I don't mean to poor-mouth. *What's My Line?* is just a damn juggernaut. Can't kill it with a stick. And . . . listen, there's something else I need to tell you about. Right now. At the outset."

At the outset of what? I wondered.

She leaned forward and this time used just one gloved hand to hold mine—well, I didn't have a white glove on. But she held it.

"Nate, there's a new man in my life."

"You mean Frank."

"I most certainly do not mean Frank. At my age, I may not need to divorce him over it—he has his chippies, he always has had. But I'm in *love,* really, truly in love, so there won't be any funny business between us, this go-round, Mr. Nathan Heller. No hanky-panky."

"Not even just hanky?"

She giggled. She was an easy mark for me in the laughter department. Squeezing my hand, then withdrawing hers, she said, "No hanky, no panky."

The waiter cleared our dishes. Flo turned down an offer of coffee (as did I) and said, "We really need to go somewhere private to talk."

It was getting more crowded now, as the lunch hour approached, and people would be recognizing her, coming over for autographs.

Frowning, she said, "We can't go to my room. You'll think I'm wacky, some paranoid fruitcake, but . . . I really think the CIA may be watching me."

I didn't tell her that they might be watching me, too.

"Why don't we go outside," I suggested. "There's a garden patio overlooking St. Paul Street."

"Oh, yes, with the sculpture. They can't bug the great out-of-doors, can they?"

"The great out-of-doors is full of bugs, silly."

She laughed at that. I told you.

The Empire Room emptied into a brick patio housing a lush garden, in a vaguely Japanese fashion, above street level on the west side of the hotel, with squared-off areas for various flora including a pair of fifteen-foot magnolias. Center stage, at the lower of two tiers, was a rotating abstract stainless steel and gold-plated sculpture called *A Wishing Star*, twelve feet high, fifteen feet in diameter, reaching for the sky like a massive benign claw. We took a backless stone bench near a small reflecting pool.

"You remember how I began in this business," she said. "That I was the youngest woman ever to work the crime beat in Manhattan?"

"Oh yes," I said, though I needed no reminding. She still interrupted her columnist duties to cover famous murder trials, like Sam Sheppard and the recent Finch-Tregoff barn burner.

"But this, Nate, this is the *big* one. You'll never guess what."

"Kennedy."

That seemed to startle her. "How did you know?"

"Well, first, this is Dallas. It's kind of *the* case around here, y'know? And second, I didn't just run into you, Flo. I heard from a friend that you were in town, and that you were poking into the assassination. And came looking."

"What friend?"

"Janet Adams."

"Jada! I haven't gotten *anywhere* with her." She sat forward, half turning toward me, with that shark-eyed look great journalists get when they smell a lead. "Can you help me on that front? There are a *flock* of Ruby strippers I haven't been able to get to. My God, that would be *fantastic* . . ."

"Slow down," I said, holding up a palm. "I *might* be able to help. First, fill me in. I want to know what you've been up to."

Her smile was smug but cute. "Keep an eye on the papers next week. That'll show you what I've 'been up to.' "

"Which is?"

She gave me a pixie look, like she'd gotten away with a cookie or two from that jar on top of the refrigerator. And with those gloves, no fingerprints.

She said, "I'm running a story that showcases Jack Ruby's Warren Commission testimony."

I frowned at her. "The Warren Commission report isn't coming out till the end of the month. And it's considered Top Secret. And you have an inside source?"

"I do. And you know not to ask."

"I know not to ask. So what does Ruby say that's so newsworthy? I'm not somebody who buys that screwball feeling sorry for Jackie Kennedy and just blowing his stack . . . even if Ruby *is* a guy known for blowing his stack. It just never included killing people in a police station basement before."

She sat up straight on the bench, folding her white-gloved hands in her lap, like a little girl at a very proper function. "Last June, Ruby was interviewed in his jail cell by Earl Warren himself, and Gerald Ford, a congressman from Michigan, a crony of the President's. Ruby has a kind of ostentatious way of speaking, convoluted . . . like Jerry Lewis trying to sound smart in an interview."

"I know," I said, nodding. "I know Jack."

Her eyes flashed sharply, then narrowed shrewdly. "I *know* you know him, Nate . . . and we'll get back to that. But the thing is, Ruby kept dodging questions, and saying his life was in danger, and that he wanted to be taken to Washington, D.C., where it would be safer for him to talk freely."

"His jail cell here in Dallas is bugged, obviously."

"Obviously. But the chief justice told him that a D.C. transfer was impossible, because the Commission didn't have police powers, couldn't protect him properly."

"That's bullshit. Just bring in the FBI!"

"Right," she said, with a dismissive shrug, then her manner grew intense. "Ruby also kept mentioning LBJ, saying what a wonderful, great man our President was, and that he just *knew* LBJ could set things straight about him."

"Hmmm. What do you make of that?"

Her smile was tiny and merciless. "I believe Ruby knows things that he believes he can use to trade his way off Death Row."

"But not in Dallas."

"Not in Dallas. Ironic, isn't it? He was like an unofficial member of the PD here, the best friend a Dallas copper ever had, comping them at the Carousel, fixing them up with his girls. Probably the local mob's bagman, which explains why he was around the station so often, and had such easy access."

I was nodding. "He certainly didn't have any trouble waltzing into that police station the morning they moved Oswald."

"No." She made an openhanded gesture. "But now he sits in a Dallas jail cell, where every dirty cop in town can get to him. If he talks, and not just his usual gibberish, he can wind up as dead as Oswald. As dead as Jack Kennedy."

"What do you want from me, Flo? Besides the bodyguard gig."

She placed a hand on my shoulder. Her eyes were intense in a different way now. This was a personal gaze, from one friend to another. From one lover to another.

"Nate, you grew up on the West Side of Chicago. Your best friend was Barney Ross, and Barney was, and is, a good friend of Jack Ruby's. I finagled a very short interview with Ruby at his trial. Nate, Ruby likes me. He's a fan of *What's My Line?*"

"He'd make a great 'mystery guest.' "

For once she didn't laugh at a dumb gag of mine. "I want to talk to him again. In depth. Away from his jail cell. But he's been politely declining through his attorney."

Melvin Belli, one of the top defense men in the nation.

I shrugged. "I'm not that tight with Jack. We aren't really friends. I did a job for him, a long time ago, but . . ."

"But *Barney Ross* is still a good friend of Ruby's. If Barney put the word through that Jack should talk to me, and that you will be along as Barney's surrogate, maybe . . . just *maybe* . . . I can get the interview that will crack this case."

She had a hell of a reporter's mind, this kid from Indiana, this game-show celebrity, this gossip columnist.

Shaking her head, she was saying, "I know it sounds unbelievable, Nate, but I am convinced there was a conspiracy behind Jack Kennedy's murder."

Should I tell her that she was preaching to the choir? That last year I had helped the Secret Service shut down an attempt on JFK's life that had been mounted in early November, just twenty days before Dallas? That the players had been the same—the Mob, rogue CIA, exiled Cubans, right-wing crazies?

She was saying, "My source inside the Warren Commission says the results are going to be laughable. They are all too anxious to show that Lee Harvey Oswald was a lone, unaffiliated assassin, and Ruby a psychopath who, by the way, has no real connection to the Mafia."

I shook my head. "I know the government's been selling the lone-nut theory on Oswald, but how can they deny Ruby's connection to the Mob? He's a *mobster,* for Christ's sake."

"The whole thing smells fishy to this girl reporter. Nate, it's too convenient and simpleminded that some nut kills the President of the United States, then escapes from that little trifling matter to kill a policeman, only to be apprehended in a movie theater under circumstances that defy every tenet of police procedure, then to be murdered himself under extraordinary circumstances."

"Well, yeah."

"I've been digging, Nate, and I've come up with incredible stuff, starting with the police log that chronicles their minute-by-minute activities. Police Chief Curry was in the first car of the motorcade, and when he heard the shots, his first command was to get a man to the top of the overpass and see what happened there."

"I've never heard this."

"Of course not. Because the next day, Chief Curry told the press that the shots had come from the Texas School Book Depository, and that his first order had been to surround and search *that* building."

I frowned in thought. "But in reality his first real concern was the overpass and that grassy slope the President's car was moving toward when the fatal shots were fired."

She was nodding, nodding, nodding. "At about eight miles per hour, yes. Here's something else for you to chew on. The police radio description of Oswald came from an eyewitness, a Howard Brennan, a steam fitter sitting on a concrete wall more than a hundred feet from the sixth-floor corner window that Oswald supposedly shot from."

Then Flo told me a darkly amusing story about how she and her husband Frank had reenacted the assassination from a window of their swanky five-story town house in Manhattan.

"Frank used a broomstick for a rifle," she said, "and I went down and outside to East Sixty-eighth Street. I stood approximately where the steam fitter had, hoping none of the neighbors were watching, and let me tell you, Nate, describing a suspect seen from that distance proved impossible."

"This was in broad daylight?"

"Yes, and the steam fitter claimed he saw Oswald walking around inside the depository, with no change in height when he came over to fire his shots. Well, it's been definitely proven that the assassin had to *kneel* to fire."

"Interesting."

"Oh, Nate, and there's so much more! I've got evidence indicating the rifle used wasn't a Carcano but a Mauser—there was a fucking switch! And do you really think it's credible that Jack Ruby killed Oswald out of *love* for Kennedy?"

"All mobsters hate the Kennedys."

"Right! Or that Ruby, the biggest police buff in Dallas and probably the Mob's payoff man, never even *met* Officer J. D. Tippit?"

I shifted on the hard stone of the bench. "Honey, you do understand this is a risky road you're heading down?"

She snorted a laugh. "Do you really think they'd kill a celebrity?"

"Ask Jack Kennedy."

The rotating sculpture was making a slight squeak above the gentle lap of the reflecting pool.

"Listen," she said, softly, "I understand the danger, better than you know. Hell, I have eighteen phones in my town house, and I'm convinced every one is tapped! Or do you think I'm paranoid, like some people do?"

"I don't. I think this is chancy as hell, and if the kind of people are involved that *seem* to be involved . . . you might want to walk away."

She shook her head. "This story isn't going to die as long as there's one real reporter alive." She sighed. "Nate, I know the perils."

"Perils? This isn't a Saturday matinee serial, Flo."

"You think I don't know that? Why do you think I was so happy to see you walk back into my life?"

"My charm? My smile?"

That did make her laugh, a musical ripple that went well with the reflecting pool. "Well, of course, darling . . . but mostly I want a big strong man to be my bodyguard, though I do need you to do a better job than you did for Mayor Cermak."

"That doesn't set a very high standard. But have you had death threats? Or damnit—has someone tried—"

"No! No. But there's a disturbing pattern emerging just the same, as I dig deeper into this morass."

I frowned again. "What kind of pattern?"

"A pattern of death. Probable murders, and outright ones. Faked suicides."

I felt the back of my neck prickle, as it had in Captain Peoples's office.

"Some of the witnesses I wanted to interview, Nate, aren't available—they are conveniently deceased. Would you like a rundown? Probably just a partial one, because I don't know of *everyone* involved, not yet anyway."

"Please."

The day after the assassination, Jack Zangretti—an Oklahoma mobster who ran a lavish illegal casino and motel—informed friends, "A man named Jack Ruby will kill Oswald tomorrow, and in a few days, a member of the Frank Sinatra family will be kidnapped just to take some attention away from the assassination." Frank Sinatra Jr., was kidnapped for ransom on December 8, 1963, making national headlines. No such headlines were made when simultaneously Zangretti was found floating in a lake with bullet holes in his chest.

Bill Chesher, thought to have inside information linking Ruby to Oswald, died of a heart attack three months after the assassination.

Hank Killam, a painting contractor who lived at Oswald's boardinghouse, claimed that he had seen Ruby and Oswald together. His throat was cut when he was tossed through a department-store window, four months after the assassination.

Four men met in Jack Ruby's apartment after visiting Ruby in jail just a few hours after the killing of Oswald: Bill Hunter, a reporter from California; attorney Tom Howard; Dallas reporter Jim Koethe; and Ruby's roommate, George Senator. The latter had disappeared, and the other three were dead. Hunter was "accidentally" shot by a police officer. Howard, forty-eight, died of a heart attack.

"Jim Koethe was killed last week," Flo said, "stepping out of his shower in his apartment here in Dallas. A karate chop to the neck.

Place ransacked, but the only thing missing were the notes on the book he was working on—guess what the subject was?"

"Places to see in Dallas?" I asked.

She cocked her head, smug and serious. "What does all this sound like to you, Nate?"

It sounded all too familiar. And the odor was reminiscent, too—the same smell as the convenient deaths in the Billie Sol Estes scandal.

"A cleanup crew," I said. "Removing witnesses, tying off loose ends."

"Acquila Clemmons would probably agree with you. From her front porch, she witnessed the killing of Officer Tippit. Saw two men—the gunman was short, kind of heavy, the other tall and thin in khaki trousers and a white shirt. Didn't want to talk to me, because a Dallas PD officer warned her she might get killed on the way to work."

"Good advice."

"I've saved the best for last," she said. "The strange tale of Warren Reynolds."

The Reynolds story began with Officer J. D. Tippit, shortly after two P.M. on November 22, reportedly cruising for suspects matching Lee Harvey Oswald's description (as provided by the steam fitter, remember?). Officer Tippit pulled to the curb on Tenth Street, supposedly seeing a suspect matching the description. For some reason, Tippit got out of his squad car and came around to talk to the suspect but was shot and killed instead, falling near the front right fender. Two witnesses saw a man running from the scene. Neither identified Oswald as the runner.

The first such witness, Warren Reynolds—who owned and operated Reynolds Motor Company on Jefferson Boulevard, just west of the murder scene—pursued the man, heading south on Patton Avenue, but lost him a block later.

Two months after the assassination, after news reports identified him as a Tippit witness, Reynolds was questioned by the FBI.

He said that Oswald was definitely *not* the man he saw fleeing, gun in hand, from the Tippit killing.

Two days later, at nine P.M., Reynolds went into the office of his car dealership. The lights were out, the fuse apparently blown. Someone waiting in the darkness shot Reynolds in the head, point-blank.

Miraculously, Reynolds stumbled to the telephone and summoned help, and survived the shooting. A petty local criminal, Darrell Wayne Garner, was arrested, but was freed after a young woman named Betty Mooney gave him an alibi.

"Betty Mooney," Flo said, "was one of Jack Ruby's strippers."

Shortly after, Reynolds's ten-year-old daughter was nearly abducted. Threats and further intimidation followed.

"Earlier this year," Flo said, "Reynolds changed his story. He decided the man he saw fleeing was, in fact, Lee Harvey Oswald."

Domingo Benavides, seeing Tippit's body in the street, had stopped behind the squad car and rushed up to help, calling in the shooting on the dead officer's own radio. He found two spent cartridges, .38 autos, which he initialed for Dallas officer J. M. Poe. The casings were apparently replaced with .38 Super cartridges, which would work in a .38 revolver—the .38 autos would not. Domingo's initials were absent from the Super cartridges, as well.

More problematic was the description of the shooter that Domingo provided, that of a suspect with dark, curly hair and clothing and physical attributes that didn't match up with Oswald's.

"Domingo was the closest witness on the scene, by the way," Flo said.

Domingo began receiving death threats, but it was his look-alike brother, Eddy, who was killed—shot in the head in February '64.

"I got all of this last instance secondhand," Flo admitted. "Domingo isn't giving interviews. By the way, Betty Mooney? The Carousel Club stripper who alibied the possible shooter in the Reynolds attempted murder? She was arrested by the Dallas police this February for disturbing the peace, and hanged herself in her jail cell. Using her toreador pants."

"That's quite a list."

"Oh, it's longer. There are more in New Orleans, where Oswald lived right before moving to Dallas, and where Ruby often went to troll for new strippers. That's my next stop."

I held up both hands. "Whoa, Nellie. Let's stick with Dallas for now."

Her eyes flashed and her smile winked sunlight. "Then you'll help me?"

"What exactly do you have in mind?"

"I have several witnesses to interview. And if you could get Jada, or Janet Adams, to talk to me, and maybe line me up with a few others among Jack Ruby's girls, that would be fantastic. I'm not as flush as I once was, but I can offer a thousand a week. A week here, then a week or maybe two in New Orleans. What do you say?"

"I say I need to think about it," I said. "I've been away from the office and have to check in, and see what's on my desk."

"Is whatever-it-is-on-your-desk bigger than the Kennedy assassination?"

"No, but it's safer. Whatever-it-is."

She tried to pull off a pout. "You'd just leave me here, to my own devices?"

"Just a poor little defenseless girl reporter? Give me the weekend. Don't you have to fly back to New York and do your show Sunday night?"

"Yes," she admitted with a nod, "I'm booked out tomorrow morning. But I'll be back at the Statler by this time Monday." She sat forward, her gloved hands girlishly in her lap. "Oh, Nate, please consider it. You're the *perfect* man for this job."

"I'll call you in New York late Sunday night. After the broadcast."

She kissed me on the mouth.

Then she gave me an impish look that should have seemed silly from a woman her age but wasn't at all. "Now, don't get any ideas, Nathan Heller."

But I had a lot of ideas, none of them, for once, having to do with getting laid.

And most of them had to do with the VIP whose blessing, even permission, I would need before saying yes to the girl reporter.

CHAPTER 9

"You'd think I was the fucking Beatles," Bobby Kennedy said, holding back a sheer curtain, looking out the hotel-room window at the mass of people on the street ten stories below, their murmur like an insistent surf on a reluctant shore. The jacket of his black suit was off, waiting neatly laid out on the bed, and he wore a black tie on a white shirt whose shirtsleeves were rolled up, in a perhaps misguided rich-kid attempt to connect with workingmen.

"And that's a bad thing?" I was seated in a comfortable chair nearby, sipping the Coke I'd been provided by a staffer. "They love you, Bob. Yeah yeah yeah."

He smiled humorlessly, shaking his head, the familiar tousle of dark-brown hair bouncing. "Don't kid yourself, Nate. They're here for him. They're here for him."

He let the curtain take the window, brightness still filtering into a gloomy bedroom with no lights on. He seemed to prefer the shadows.

In half an hour, the Democratic candidate for senator of New York would be addressing this crowd, supposedly getting them stirred up, but right now that was hard to imagine, as he dropped dejectedly into the chair opposite me, slumping there.

Days ago I had heard about the funk Bobby was in from Bill Queen, the ex-NYPD cop and current Manhattan branch A-1 agent who was Kennedy's personal bodyguard. Senatorial candidates didn't get Secret Service protection, even when the candidate's brother was an assassinated president.

Bill was also how I was able to get in to see Bobby without any red tape, a phone call getting me right to Steve Smith, Bobby's campaign manager (and brother-in-law). And now I was sitting in the bedroom of a suite at the Statler—the venerable and very non-Space Age Statler in Buffalo, New York, that is. Not Dallas, out of which I'd flown yesterday afternoon.

About fifteen minutes ago, after working my way up from the lobby showing my ID to half a dozen interested parties, I'd entered the suite, where a bustling bunch of aides were in the outer area, some sitting, some pacing, almost all smoking. Included in this group was my man Bill, but also Steve Smith, the only guy in the room with his suit coat on, though his narrow red-and-blue striped tie was loosened.

Smith was a dark-haired, athletic-looking guy in his thirties, a former hockey goalie with a wry sense of humor and an unflappable nature. Like the others in this mostly male clubhouse (a few "Kennedy Girls," secretarial types, all young and pretty, were tagging along with clipboards and pencils here and there), he was in shirtsleeves and looked frazzled for a guy normally cool.

The air was blue from cigarettes, so I said by way of greeting, "This must be that smoke-filled room I've heard so much about."

"Nate," Smith said, grinning. "Welcome to the monkey house."

He looked a little bit like the young Joseph Cotten, though with a wider face. He offered a hand and I shook it, then he curled a finger for me to join him in as quiet a corner as the campaign hubbub would allow.

"Maybe *you* can get Bob out of his funk," he said. "He *likes* you."

"Doesn't he like you anymore, Steve?"

"Right now he doesn't like anybody much, including himself. This campaign has hardly started and we're already getting kicked in the ass."

My forehead frowned and my mouth smiled. "I can't believe that. I mean, that guy Keating is well-liked enough, I guess, but he's basically the smiling uncle you dodge at Christmas."

Smith was shaking his head. "Don't count Keating out. He's a Republican but he's a liberal one, and that makes him credible in this state. Good voting record."

I nodded toward the street. "There's a mob scene going on out there. They're crazy about our blushing boy. Took me half an hour to push my way through."

And it had—out on Delaware Avenue at Niagara Square, old and young, men and women, blacks and whites, strained against the police lines.

"Don't be fooled," Smith said. "A good share just want to see a Kennedy in the flesh—that's no guarantee they'll vote for him."

"It's a start."

"Yeah," he said with a humorless smirk, "but they haven't heard him talk yet." He spoke in a barely audible whisper. "Nate, the little fella's been stinking on ice. He's flat, and when he isn't flat, he's screechy. He's nervous and he mumbles. Oh, he's loud enough when he's snapping at reporters, and you can sure hear that he's got nothing bad to say about his opponent."

"Doesn't he want to win?"

The campaign manager shrugged in exasperation. "I don't know at this point, Nate. I really don't know. Maybe *you* can reason with him. *I* just know he's blowing it."

"So why bust your ass for the guy, Steve?"

"Because Jean wants me to," he said, referring to his wife, who was also Bobby's sister, of course. "Anyway, it's like I always say—ask not what the Kennedys can do for you, ask what you can do for the Kennedys. . . . You can go on in, if you can get past your own man. Bobby knows you're stopping by."

Bill Queen was indeed sitting in a chair near the bedroom door, a bald mustached paunchy guy in his fifties in a brown suit and brown-and-yellow tie who was Central Casting's idea of a cop, and Central Casting was right. He was reading *Playboy* magazine, or anyway looking at the busty blonde in the centerfold.

"Nice work if you can get it," I said.

Unashamed, he refolded the Playmate and got to his feet. "I have a boss who can appreciate the finer things."

I pointed to the magazine in his hand. "Those girls in there are young enough to be your daughter."

"I don't have a daughter, Nate." He nodded toward the door and did Groucho with his eyebrows. "*He's* in a mood. Hell, he's always in a mood. You shoulda warned me about the guy."

"What mood would you be in, doing rallies on streets with high windows all around, if you were him?"

"Oh, that doesn't faze Mr. Kennedy. Hell, he sits up on the backseat of a convertible like a beauty queen, waving and giving the crowd that sad-puppy smile. Sometimes he stands on the roof of a parked car to see 'em better. It's like he's askin' for it."

That sounded like Bobby. "So are Hoover's boys cooperating?"

The ex-cop nodded. "I call them every morning, like you arranged, and they give me the latest death threats. Steady stream of 'em, Nate. Or do you think Hoover's just trying to look vigilant for his old boss?"

"I don't think J. Edgar gives two shits about what his 'old boss' thinks."

Bill jerked a thumb at the closed door nearby. "Well, you tell your friend, in future, to listen to me about security measures, would ya? Then maybe I'd have better things to do with my time on this assignment than pound my pud in the john to Miss October."

Bobby heard me come in and met me at the door, shaking my hand and giving me his shy, almost bucktoothed smile, which with his rather high-pitched voice suggested an Ivy League Bugs Bunny. "It's been too long, Nate. Too long. Can I, uh, get you something to drink?"

I asked for a Coke and he yelled out to a Kennedy Girl to get us both one. She swiftly returned with a warm smile and two chilled bottles. Then she was gone and we were shut inside the hotel bedroom, which was smoke-free—Bobby was not a smoker, actually was adamantly against it, though he clearly didn't forbid his staff. He wasn't much of a drinker, either, as the sodas indicated, though he was by no means a teetotaler.

We exchanged a few pleasantries as I tried to get used to how skinny he looked. I hadn't seen him since late October '63, though I'd talked to him on the phone a few times, post-assassination, and he'd seemed himself. But in the flesh, he appeared to have shrunk, all but swimming in the white shirt and black trousers. Almost a year later, and he was still wearing black. His face seemed sunken, gaunt.

"Tell me, Nate, do you really have something to talk over with me, or, uh, did Steve Smith just want you to come and give me a pep talk—get me off my duff and into this thing?"

"I really do have something to talk about. And I don't think it's going to boost your spirits any. Just don't jump out that window, when you hear. Anyway, some college girls down there would just catch you and drag you off to have their way with you."

That made him smile, although his eyes lacked their usual spark. "Doesn't, uh, sound half-bad."

I gestured toward the muffled roar. "If you're not up for this race, why the hell did you get in it?"

Everything had happened so recently—he hadn't even announced his candidacy until August 22, and only resigned as attorney general at the beginning of the month.

His face tried to remember how to summon a big smile. "Remember what Steve McQueen said in *The Magnificent Seven,* Nate?"

"Don't believe I do."

"About the man who jumped into the cactus? 'It, uh, seemed like a good idea at the time.' "

That gave me a chuckle. "And now you find you have no taste for jumping into cactuses."

"Or caucuses." He sighed, gave up a tiny shrug, then sipped at his bottle of Coke. "They say I'm a carpetbagger, and, uh, well, they have a point—I did move out of New York in the sixth grade.

The party bosses in New York hate my guts, and the Jews think I'm anti-Semitic, like my old man."

I raised a finger. "Don't forget the far left. They think you're a ruthless McCarthyite."

He nodded glumly. "That's why I don't want to go after that nice old man, Keating, and have the press hang that 'ruthless' sign around my neck again."

"Hell, they'll do that anyway." Outside, the murmur seemed to be building, a low dull throbbing with occasional accents of shouts or laughter. "Maybe you owe it to that crowd out there to give it the ol' college try. Tell 'em Keating is a Commie or a dog-fucker or something."

He'd been sipping the Coke and almost choked on that as he laughed. He set the bottle on the little table next to him, on an issue of *Newsweek* with his sullen picture on the cover. "You're still a pisser, Nate."

I was loosening him up. Good.

I shrugged. "So who cares, if they're here for Jack? *You're* the one who's here, man. Don't disappoint 'em."

He was studying me carefully, his smile still there, but having melted some. "Okay, uh, so that's your pep talk, Coach Rockne. But that's not why you're here, is it?"

"No." I met his eyes, those bluer-than-Jack's blue-green eyes. "You know the subject we haven't discussed, the few times we've talked lately."

". . . I do."

"You also know that I'm probably one of the few people who's not in government, the Mob, the John Birch Society, or some Cuban exile group who knows that a conspiracy took your brother's life."

He said nothing. He wasn't looking at me now. He was staring past me, into the past maybe or God knew where.

I kept my voice even, and didn't push. I let the words do that. "What went down last year in Chicago, Bob, just twenty days before your brother was killed, involved the same sorry cast as Dallas. I even met Oswald, briefly."

His eyes flashed to life. "What?"

I nodded. "And guess who introduced him to me? Jack Ruby."

Now the eyes tightened. "The hell you say. Where?"

"Where else? A strip club. Not in Dallas or New Orleans, but on South Wabash, in Chicago, a little less than a month before the tragedy."

"What was discussed?"

"It had to do with that Hoffa matter I told you about, which isn't pertinent. What *is* pertinent is that Ruby, and Oswald, who were chummy as hell by the way, knew who I was, in the greater scheme of things."

"Don't be coy, Nate."

"This room is secure?"

"Your man says it is."

"Then it's secure." I sipped Coca-Cola. Rolled its sweetness around in my mouth, swallowed, and said, "Ruby knew I was instrumental in putting Operation Mongoose in motion. Bragged me up to Oswald, who'd been rabble-rousing at the University of Illinois, Urbana, pretending to be a Commie."

Bobby's hands had been on the arms of the chair like a king at his throne. But now those hands tightened into bony, veiny things. The darkness of the room dropped shadows into the hollows of his face and the skull beneath the skin was apparent. Seconds ticked by as he sat there brooding as the words *Operation Mongoose* hung in the air between us.

"In large measure, Nate," Bobby finally said, "that's why I haven't come forward. Why I have in my own, uh, measured way gone along with this Warren Commission travesty."

That made me sit up. "Don't tell me you knew who Oswald was, *before* the assassination?"

His silence spoke volumes.

"Jesus! You . . . you *knew* that Oswald was part of Mongoose?"

A man in his thirties should not have been capable of so world-weary a sigh. "Well, I knew that Oswald was one of ours. A CIA asset, an FBI asset. You don't just defect and trot off to Mother Russia like Oswald did, then a year or so later traipse back into the country and get a warm welcome from the State Department."

"Why would *you* know about a small fry like Oswald?"

"One of our Cuban assets brought me a photo of Oswald passing out pro-Castro leaflets in New Orleans. I'd asked this Cuban individual to keep me informed on any, uh, alarming exile activity."

"What was so alarming about passing out leaflets?"

"Well, Oswald was also tight with Carlos Bringuier, an anti-Castro exile who had a strong grudge against Jack and me. We'd cracked down on Cuba raids, post–Bay of Pigs, you know. I did a little checking, learned that Oswald was a FBI asset."

"What a surprise."

"I assume he was also CIA or his Russian adventure wouldn't have been possible. At any rate, in New Orleans he was obviously playing both sides—one day pro-Castro, the next day against. So I told my Cuban asset to, uh, steer this Oswald character a wide path—they wanted to *kill* him, just to see who would take his place! These Cubans are crazy, Nate."

"No shit," I said, working to make my brain not explode.

From day one, Bobby had known Oswald was no lone nut!

"Damnit, Bob, you were still AG! Why didn't you unleash the Justice Department on your brother's murder, while you were still in a position to control things? And don't tell me you were depressed, I'm sure you were, but I'm only *half* Irish and, Jesus, I would have stormed the gates of hell for revenge, in your place."

That was a little purple, but it made the point.

Bobby had to take a few breaths not to rage back at me; but that funk of his was keeping the legendary temper in check.

"Nate, the minute Jack was killed, my official power began to evaporate. Lyndon ignored me, wouldn't take my goddamn calls, and Hoover? He invented new ways to fuck me over, daily."

"That's not hard to believe," I said.

Bobby was gesturing to the murmuring window, saying, "Why do you think I'm putting up with this horseshit dog-and-pony show? First I have to get into the White House, and then I can really get this goddamn crime solved. And this Senate seat is the stepping-stone, even if it, uh, does make a goddamn carpetbagger out of me."

"No other reasons for waiting, Bob?"

He frowned in irritation. "Well, of course there are. You and I both suspect that this conspiracy involves government elements. If that became common knowledge, at this juncture, it would *tear* the country apart! And then . . . well, uh, you know the rest."

I did know. Jack and Bobby had sanctioned Operation Mongoose, marrying the CIA to the Mob to fight a secret war against Castro, largely depending on assassinating the man code-named "The Beard." Were that known to the public, the Kennedy legacy would not just be tarnished, but destroyed.

And since Bobby was far more accountable for Mongoose than Jack, who had rubber-stamped it on his brother's say-so, that made RFK—in a convoluted but inevitable manner—responsible for JFK's assassination.

Bobby Kennedy had been paralyzed with grief, yes . . . but also with guilt.

"Anyway, on a, uh, very basic level," he said almost casually, "I didn't trust the FBI to investigate Dallas."

"I don't blame you. But somebody should."

"Somebody is. In a very low-key fashion, I've put some of my own best people, from the Get Hoffa squad, on the case. Walter Sheridan, for one."

"Good choice," I said, nodding.

His smile came out a little forced. "And I've thought about, uh, hiring *you*, too, Nate . . . but I would assume you aren't doing much fieldwork now."

"That's a job I might consider," I admitted, then sat forward. "But let me ask you something first, Bob. This Warren Commission farce is wrapping up soon—have you testified? Or, are you planning to?"

He shook his head. "Well, you're right, it is a farce. My political enemies control it, I mean Dulles is an obvious CIA spy on the thing—did you know until recently Lyndon lived across the street from Hoover, and that, uh, Ladybird, Lyndon, Hoover, and Clyde Tolson would have regular Sunday dinner together?"

"Cozy. I can just picture them holding hands and saying grace. Norman Rockwell should paint it. Or *Mad* magazine."

He smiled briefly but his expression immediately darkened and he shook his head slowly several times. "You would not believe what that fucking commission put Kenny O'Donnell through."

O'Donnell was one of Bobby's best friends and advisers.

His eyes unblinking and empty, Bobby was saying, in a voice so hushed I could hardly make out his words, "Kenny heard at least two shots fired from that grassy hillock . . . in front of the motorcade? So did Dave Powers—they were in the Secret Service backup car, right behind Jack. They saw and heard the whole horror, Nate. When Kenny reported what he'd witnessed to the FBI, he was informed that he was *mistaken* about the direction of the gunfire. He was told that the shots came from the book depository and that he should testify to that fact. They were both told that if they did not change their story, the results could be . . . damaging."

"To whom?"

A little fatalistic shrug. "The country, I would suppose. Or possibly themselves. Still, Dave wouldn't budge from his story, and, uh, was not then asked to testify. Kenny went along with them, though, and I asked him why he'd done that, why had he lied, and he told me he just didn't want to stir up any more pain and trouble for my family."

"Did you tell him to come forward?"

"Nate, he was under oath. He'd committed perjury. I wouldn't ask him to do that, not when he'd been trying to do the right thing by the Kennedys. Anyway. Now is not the time for these . . . revelations."

My laugh was hollow. "What, you want to wait till your friend can correct the record, and receive a presidential pardon, huh?"

He held up a hand like the cops outside, keeping back the crowd. "Suffice to say I have refused to testify. To avoid that, I agreed to give Warren a signed letter stating I didn't believe there was a conspiracy behind Jack's murder."

Of course, unlike Powers, he hadn't been under oath.

I said, "You've made similar statements in public."

"It's what is needed at this point. I mean, there would be blood in the streets, if right now the American people found out what really happened in Dallas. Oswald the lone killer, Ruby the sorrowful nut, it's a myth that keeps the public reassured . . . while in the meantime, I authorize a sub-rosa investigation."

"You want to know who to go after," I said, "the day you hit the Oval Office."

"Correct. Which is why Steve and everyone around me is right—I need to get my head in this game." He had a tortured expression now, as he glanced at that window. "But, Nate, they look at me and they see Jack . . . and I *know* what a joke that is."

"Cut that crap. Quit sniveling. And I'm not convinced you should wait till you're President. That's a little like me giving up sex till I can get next to Kim Novak."

I'd made him smile again—not that easy a task under the best of conditions.

He said, "You, uh, *are* the Private Eye to the Stars, aren't you, Nate? I would think, uh, a meeting with Miss Novak could be arranged."

Sooner or later, when you were hanging out with the Kennedy boys, bedding beautiful movie stars came up in conversation.

I sat forward again. "Bob, a lot of the American people already aren't buying the lone gunman theory. Maybe when the Warren Commission puts its report out that'll change . . . but I don't think so. People have questions."

"Do they?"

"Sure! Like how can there be a lone gunman when the Parkland docs say one of the bullets entered the throat? Or how can a guy using a shitty twelve-buck mail-order bolt-action rifle squeeze off three expert shots in under six seconds?"

"You've seen the same tasteless articles I have," Bobby said, with a derisive tone and a sneer to go with it. "These so-called assassination buffs, they're creeps and kooks, even if they *have* asked some of the right questions."

"Well, here's one they missed—if Oswald was a pro-Castro pinko, why would he shoot a president who was trying to improve relations with Cuba? Of course, you and I know that Oswald was a CIA asset. So maybe his motive was the Bay of Pigs fiasco."

Irritation was showing in his face again. "Nate, stop it."

"This isn't going away, Bob."

"I know it isn't. And when I'm in the White House, it's going to be exposed."

He meant it would be exposed when he had the power to manipulate the facts to whitewash himself and his brother in Operation Mongoose. And as the guy who had set up the first meeting between the players in that sad game, I was just fine with that.

"Then," I said, sitting back comfortably, "I need to tell you what I've been doing in Dallas the last week or so."

And he sat forward. Not slumping now.

I gave it all to him, including the Billie Sol Estes cleanup effort, though I wasn't convinced it had anything to do with the dead witnesses in Dallas, similar though the approach might be.

"I don't know," he said, and shuddered. "Flo Kilgore? A gossipmonger? A silly game-show celebrity? That's not my idea of a credible investigation."

That rated a laugh. "You aren't conducting a credible investigation, Bob. You are, in your own words, mounting a very timid, subrosa one. Why not let Flo be your stalking horse? She's going to do it anyway."

"And if you accept her job offer," he said, thinking it through, "then you'll know what she's found, and you can control the situation."

"To some degree," I said, nodding. "And I can report back to you. Plus keep my eye on preserving the Kennedy legacy. But I didn't want to take her money without you giving the okay."

His expression remained thoughtful. "I appreciate that. But it's not like I could stop you, Nate."

"If you said walk away, Bob, I'd walk away."

His smile was barely there, but it meant a lot. "Thank you, Nate."

"And I may walk away, anyway."

"Oh?"

I told him how this had begun, with what appeared to be an attempt on my life disguised as a hit-and-run accident. And I told him how, afterward, I'd approached both my CIA handler and my primary Mob contact, and had been assured they were not responsible.

"Thing is," I said, "I promised them I'd stay out of any inquiry into the assassination, or anyway implied as much. I presented myself as a loose end not worth tying off."

"But now you find yourself in Texas," Bobby said, "in the midst of what looks like a concerted effort to, uh, tie off various loose ends."

"Yes. A cleanup crew. Getting rid of pesky witnesses and annoying snoops. And you may have noticed that I fall into both categories."

He was frowning in thought, his fingertips tented. "Who do you suspect in this?"

"Not CIA. As my handler said, if the CIA wanted me dead, I'd be dead by now. The Billie Sol aspect, if it ties in, might indicate Texas oil. But Ruby, and whether anybody can connect him to Oswald, pre-assassination, seems to be the focus."

"Which means mob."

I nodded. "Which means mob."

He cocked his head. "And this began with a Cuban trying to run you down."

"Yup."

"And you're someone else who saw Ruby and Oswald together."

"Right." I shrugged. "Who knows? Maybe everybody's trying to kill me."

"Nate," Bob said, some spark back in his blue eyes, "considering how long you've been around? Everybody's got a reason."

"Glad I finally cheered you up," I said.

The sound from the window seemed to be intensifying. "You didn't really know Jack well, did you, Nate?"

"No."

"Half the days he spent on earth he was in intense physical pain—scarlet fever, terrible back pain, and just about every conceivable other ailment in between."

Including VD, I thought.

"We used to joke that a mosquito took a hell of a risk biting him." He was smiling with the memory. "On a trip around the world about ten, twelve years ago, he, uh, got so sick I thought we'd lose him. *His* Senate campaign? He spent it on crutches."

"No kidding. Did *he* bitch?"

"Not once. I never heard him say anything resembling God had dealt him a bum hand. If you were close to him, you knew when he was having trouble, because his face got a little whiter, the lines around his eyes a little deeper . . . maybe his, uh, words a little sharper. Those who didn't know him so well didn't pick up on anything."

"If you want to honor his memory, Bob, then do me a favor and let my guy Bill Queen tighten up your security."

But he wasn't hearing me. He was saying, "When that Jap destroyer sank his PT boat, Jack swam and swam, rescuing six of his crew, leading them to this small island, towing his badly burned engineer all the way. Then he went for help—he swam for two or three hours in the black cold of that water and that night, and then tread water and finally just drifted till dawn, his mind a hallucinating jumble, his only clear thought that he was going to die and then when he didn't, it changed him. He told me so many times, 'You've got to live every day like it's your last day on earth.' "

That had been the nobility of Jack Kennedy, all right. Also his weakness—it had put him in bed with Marilyn Monroe and Judith Exner and so many other willing women.

But who was I to talk?

We spent another five minutes with family chitchat, shook hands, and then I left him there, with his brother and the waiting throng.

CHAPTER 10

This was the same kind of warm sunny fall day that had greeted John F. Kennedy last year when he and his wife Jacqueline and their entourage emerged from Air Force One at Love Field late on the morning of November 22. That had been a Friday. This was a Monday, just after two P.M. Traffic was medium, the tourists minimal, the citizens of Dallas at work or otherwise occupied. Meanwhile, a New Yorker named Flo Kilgore was giving a Chicagoan named Nathan Heller a tour of the most famous crime scene of the twentieth century.

On the edge of downtown Dallas, west of Houston Street, was the landscaped triangular city park called Dealey Plaza; there Elm, Main, and Commerce Streets converged at a triple underpass, Elm turning into Stemmons Freeway, while at the south, east, and north, like battlement walls, tall buildings loomed over this grassy oasis in a modern city. Where Main Street entered the Plaza, and at the outer edges of Commerce and Elm, decorative colonnades with fountains and basins stood on either side, dispassionate observers from another age. The grassy slope within the Plaza that had been above and to the President's right was bounded by a seven-story turn-of-the-century rust-brick building—the Texas School Book Depository—on the corner of Elm and Houston. A sidewalk to the south, a parking lot to the north and east, and a railroad bridge over the triple bypass completed the crime-scene picture.

The President's motorcade eased down Main, turning right at the Criminal Courts Building, going one block west past the Dallas County Records Building, just south of the Dal-Tex Building, finally turning left on Elm, heading toward the underpass on the way to Trade Mart, where Jack Kennedy's next event awaited. Of course another event had intervened.

The President's car had been second in line, making it only a third of the way to the underpass before the first shot came, one of at least three. Officially, all the gunfire had emanated from the east corner window of the sixth floor of the book depository, supposedly the work of a malcontent with a blurry grudge against society.

I parked my rental Galaxie in the lot behind what the press had dubbed the Grassy Knoll. Flush with the parking lot was a wooden picket fence; at our right, past the parking lot, were train tracks, and behind us the lot was bordered by the train-switching station, while at our left rose a scuffed-looking white WPA-era monument to the memory of newspaper publisher G. B. Dealey.

From the corner of the fence where its left side met its front, the view was blocked at far right by a tree, but otherwise provided a clear shot, so to speak, across the three lanes of Elm Street. At left two flights of cement steps rose from the sidewalk to that memorial that had provided citizens perches from which to watch the motorcade, and a path for police and brave bystanders to run up to try to spot and even stop the shooter they thought they'd heard, and seen by way of white puffs of smoke from his gun.

Flo stood at that picket-fence corner and pointed a pretend rifle toward Elm Street. "A sniper shot from here."

"You sound sure of that."

My girl reporter looked touristy and not immediately recognizable as the famous regular on *What's My Line?*, dark wispy bangs hiding some of that high forehead, a ponytail utilizing the hair that usually made up a bouffant, her sunglasses large with white frames. She was in a light-pink blouse and dark-pink slacks with red shoes, like Dorothy in *The Wizard of Oz,* only not glittery.

And there was no doubt we weren't in Kansas anymore. Wonderland, maybe.

Me, I was a tourist type myself, in Ray-Bans and a black-banded straw Stetson (this Texas sun had me back in hats again), a white-and-shades-of-gray vertical-striped seersucker sport shirt, charcoal Leesure slacks, and Italian loafers. Stetson yes, cowboy boots never.

"I *am* sure," Flo said, leaning an arm between pickets. "This is where any number of witnesses say they heard the shot coming from. One of those witnesses was an army man home from basic training, taking pictures of the President to show his buddies back at the base."

"Is this somebody you talked to you, or was it your pal Lane and his bunch?"

She had been working, off and on, with a lawyer from New York, Mark Lane, who had associates investigating the assassination. He was writing a book, which made me skeptical. Of course, Flo was writing one, too. But she was paying me.

"I talked to the soldier," she said. "His name is Gordon Arnold. He was standing right over there."

She indicated the grassy incline, maybe three feet from where we stood.

She was saying, "Said he felt a bullet whiz past his ear, heard the crack of a rifle, and that it was like standing under the muzzle. He hit the dirt and another shot flew over him."

"Okay. So where's his film?"

"A Dallas uniformed police officer, or somebody dressed as one, came around from behind the fence and grabbed his camera and ripped out his film. Then the officer headed back here to the parking lot and was gone."

"Well, it's no surprise the Dallas police had a man posted in this lot."

"Actually, it is, because they didn't, according to their log. Nate, no uniformed man was assigned to this spot."

"So you're saying there was a fake cop back here? That maybe a shooter was dressed as a cop?"

"I can't think of a benign reason for it," she said. "There were fake Secret Service agents up here, too."

"According to Arnold?"

"And four others, one of them a Dallas police officer. But Arnold won't go on the record because of the witness deaths."

Couldn't blame him.

I asked, "How did he know they were *fake* Secret Service agents?"

"He didn't," Flo said. "I found that out myself—the Secret Service didn't have anybody posted up here. They didn't have anybody posted anywhere except in the motorcade."

Sounded like Jack Kennedy could have used Bill Queen's security advice, too.

She aimed her pretend rifle at Elm Street through the space between pickets. "Pow. That's the shot that knocked Kennedy's head back. Just like in the Zapruder film."

Amateur photographer Abraham Zapruder had stood on a pillar of the retaining wall of the nearby Dealey monument and filmed the President's motorcade with his little Bell & Howell Zoomatic as the limo rolled by into carnage and history. *Life* magazine had published grisly frames from the home movie, making Zapruder rich and the public sick. But they hadn't seen the worst of it: Flo's Warren Commission source told her the complete film graphically depicted Kennedy's head being thrown back, indicating a shot from the front, not from behind the President, where Oswald would have been, in a book depository window.

She pointed to her red shoes and my Italian loafers. "Just here, by the fence, were footprints, and cigarette butts, like one or two people had been standing a long time."

"This is according to the cops?"

"According to railroad workers on the overpass, who heard shots and saw puffs of smoke, and came running. Nate, the smell of cordite was in the air—Senator Yarborough said so, and any number of bystanders. People thought somebody was shooting at Kennedy from those bushes."

"Then how did the book depository get the attention?"

"It didn't at first. Cops right away focused on this parking lot. Dozens of police and bystanders rushed up here."

We walked around the fence at left and past the monument, and started down the two flights of steps that led to the wide sidewalk along Elm. Pausing at the cement landing between flights, Flo pointed to the center lane where an X quite literally marked the spot, like the ones superimposed on crime scene photos in the old true detective magazines.

"That's the head shot," she said.

"That's a hell of distance from the book depository," I said.

"Something like eighty-five yards," she said. She pointed down the street, toward the depository, to another X. "That's the first shot, the neck shot. But it may have come from the Grassy Knoll, right where we were standing."

I gestured farther down. "Why didn't Oswald shoot when the limo made that slow turn at the intersection?"

"There are workers at the depository who say Oswald was downstairs in the second floor break room, so maybe he didn't shoot at all."

"Well, I presume the cops gave him a paraffin test." That was the process by which gunshot residue on skin and clothing was determined.

She nodded. "They did, and it came out positive on his hands, and negative on his cheek."

"Indicating he fired a handgun recently, but not a rifle. That suggests guilt in the Tippit shooting but not the assassination."

"So it would seem, but I'm told the FBI considers the paraffin test unreliable."

Then why had they been using it for decades?

I cast my eyes around. Tall buildings, fences, and sewers—carte blanche for snipers. "If you're right about the Grassy Knoll shooter, that means there were multiple shooters . . . and this is a perfect spot for triangular fire. What's that building there?"

"The Dal-Tex."

"That rooftop would be ideal."

"Prisoners in the jail, overlooking the Dal-Tex, saw a man on that roof . . . but I'm told they weren't interviewed by the Commission."

I pointed here and there and around. "We're looking at a kill zone where multiple shooters could fire from all sides. And the *least* likely source of a fatal shot is that book depository."

"Oswald claimed he was a patsy," she said, smiling. "Maybe he was."

She'd obviously already made up her mind about that, but I now knew that whatever Oswald had been, he was just a cog in the complex wheel of a military-style operation.

I said, "You're sure you can get us in the book depository?"

"This will be my third trip. The office manager loves me, Nate. It's all about serious journalistic credibility. . . . That, and identifying the occasional 'mystery guest' on *What's My Line?*" As she said that last bit, she was laughing.

Someone was sobbing.

We glanced toward the sound coming from the monument behind us and saw a young couple in their early twenties, the boy's expression grave as he hugged the weeping girl to his chest. They were dressed like tourists, too. I hoped they would have more fun at the next attraction they took in.

"Am I terrible, Nate?" Flo whispered, grabbing my arm. "Making light of this?"

"You aren't making light of this," I said, patting her hand where it gripped me, "and I'm not, either. We're just a pair of old pros at a crime scene. Anyway, there's no ghosts here. It's too goddamn sunny."

That seemed the only haunting aspect of the place—that it was just a small, rather spare-looking sun-washed park with a handful of cold-looking monuments and a patch of green cut through by traffic lanes, a humdrum city scene that in no way said Texas, much less tragedy.

The Texas School Book Depository entrance on Elm was up six or seven steps to glass doors and a sign that said:

NO ADMITTANCE
EXCEPT ON
OFFICIAL BUSINESS

Those doors were unlocked, however, and took us into a very nondescript, wood-paneled reception area. We put our sunglasses away, and Flo checked in with the receptionist. Soon we were met by a manager—about forty, in horn-rimmed glasses and an off-the-rack brown suit—who was pleased and impressed to see his "friend" from TV stop by again. Flo introduced me, by name, as her assistant.

Chatting with Flo about last night's show (Henry Fonda was the "mystery guest"), he walked us cheerfully through typical drop-ceiling office space where young women and a few young men sat at metal desks, making phone calls or pounding typewriters, the din not unlike that of a newsroom. The manager walked us up several flights of stairs at the rear of the building, past the lunchroom where Oswald had been controversially spotted immediately after the shooting.

On the ride up the service-type elevator, I asked the manager, "Is it true the original window in the sniper's nest was taken out, as a sort of souvenir, by the building's owner?"

"Yes, sir, it is. Colonel Byrd displays it in his home."

"To what purpose?"

He shrugged, and no trace of opinion could be discerned from his tone. "As a conversation piece, I assume."

With a grin, I asked, "This Colonel Byrd is one of your Texas oil tycoons?"

"You could say that. He's a co-owner of Ling Electronics, among other things. Admiral Byrd's nephew, you know."

The elevator shuddered. We had reached the sixth floor, just as it was occurring to me that if this building had been controlled by a conspirator, that would provide an assassin (or assassins) easy access.

To America this floor was history, but to the book depository, just warehouse space still in use (though no one was around right now but us) with boxes of books piled high and making corridors among the open rafters and beams and brick walls. Arched windows let in plenty of dust-mote-streaming light to reveal that the place was a fairly disorganized-looking, messy affair, the building a dingy nonentity, particularly considering its celebrity status among other American edifices.

"Old building," I said to the manager, as he led us toward the Elm Street side. "I assume the School Book Depository's been here a good long while."

"Oh, no, Mr. Heller. We only moved in last year. A few months before the tragedy, actually."

Wasn't that interesting?

The area near the window from which Oswald was said to have shot—the "sniper's nest"—was literally roped off, with metal folding chairs as occasional hitching posts. Flo had told the manager we just wanted a brief look and he stood by patiently, a respectful distance away, while we stepped over the rope like gate-crashers.

There wasn't much to the nest—just a wall of books blocking any view of someone standing, or crouching, at the window, plus a two-box stack by a box propped on the sill, an apparent arrangement for a sniper to steady a rifle against them. Nearby was another book box that could have been used as a seat by Oswald, as he waited for his target to roll by.

Flo was watching me; she'd seen all this before. "What do you think, Nate?"

"I think it's a farce. The idea of trying to shoot out that window with those boxes in the way, plus that water pipe by the window? Nuts." I jerked a thumb to the left. "Can we check out the next window over?"

"Of course."

It was just as I'd thought. This window was a view onto Houston meeting Elm, where the President's limo had slowed almost to a stop. I pointed my finger where the car would have made its slow curving turn, thirty-five yards below.

Bang.

Oswald wouldn't have needed a second shot from this perch.

Or at least, I wouldn't have. I wouldn't have needed a rifle with a scope, either—I could have used my goddamn nine-millimeter Browning automatic. If it hadn't been tucked away in the trunk of the Galaxie, I might have used it for a little dramatic show-and-tell for Flo's benefit, although the depository office manager might not have dug it.

"You may be right," I told her, "about Oswald being a patsy. He sure as hell didn't shoot Kennedy from that supposed nest—or if he *did* shoot, he sure as hell didn't hit him."

She frowned at me in thought. "So that sniper's nest—it's all theatrics? To cover what the real murderers were up to in the . . . kill zone, you called it?"

I nodded. "Oswald may have been a conspirator, and he may have been a nut, too, for all I know. But he was not a lone nut."

She was nodding slowly.

Still at the window, I pointed down. "Anyone positioned in this building, intent on killing Kennedy, would have shot him when that limo made its left turn, with the target facing the shooter. You don't wait till a target is going away from you, and nearly out of sight, before shooting."

"*Somebody* was seen shooting from the other window, by a number of witnesses. One or two identified Oswald."

"Well, I'm not saying Oswald or somebody didn't shoot from that window. It only makes sense, though, one way."

"Which is?"

"Multiple shooters. Your Grassy Knoll, for sure. Dal-Tex maybe, or some other tall-building rooftop. . . . Let's let your nice friend over there get back to work."

We headed toward him, smiling. He smiled back.

Quietly, Flo asked, "What do you suggest we do next, Nate?"

I gave the sniper's nest a dirty look as we passed it. "Something more worthwhile."

"Such as?"

"Talk to some strippers."

. . .

"Janet Mole Adams Bonney Cuffari Smallwood Conforto," Janet said with a shrug, in response to Flo's request for her full name. "What can I say? I been married a few times."

She tapped her cigarette into a tray and released twin dragon fumes of smoke from her nostrils. The redhead, who—like her questioner—had her pile of hair pulled back in a ponytail, was sitting in a booth in the Colony Club, well before opening . . . just two closer to the restrooms than Mac Wallace's booth had been.

Janet had agreed to talk to Flo and me, as well as to arrange for several other Carousel Club veterans to do the same, one of whom was due here later.

I was on the other side of the booth sitting next to Flo, across from the lovely if slightly ill at ease Janet, and between us on the tabletop was a silver-and-black Sanyo micro-pack portable tape recorder, with reel-loaded cassettes that recorded twenty minutes, then flipped over for another twenty. It was like something out of James Bond.

Janet was in a pale green blouse and darker green shorts, wearing minimal makeup. She looked good that way, but like the club around us, wasn't done any favors by the lights being up. She was twenty-seven or -eight, and looked ten years older. She was smoking Salems.

Flo asked, "How long have you known Jack Ruby?"

"I never met Ruby before June of last year," she said. "He came and caught my act at the Sho-Bar in New Orleans, and offered me a gig on the spot. Said he'd never seen a sexier act. Said he'd pay big money for me to headline for him, twice what he paid any other dancer."

I asked, "Doesn't Carlos Marcello own the Sho-Bar?"

"I don't know who owns it," she said, shrugging again. "But his brother Pete hired me, so maybe that tells you something. As for Ruby, he was a loon from word go, but headlining in a Dallas club appealed to me. My ex and me had a club go bust in the French Quarter not long before, and I was on my own again, so it was a chance for a new start."

Flo asked, "How did it work out?"

"Well, the Carousel never did draw like the Colony. But me, personally, I did great with the audiences. Ask Nate—men go crazy over me. But that Ruby could be a horse's ass. He hires me because I'm . . . *uninhibited* onstage, right? 'The sexiest thing I ever saw,' he says. Then I go to work for him and he shuts the lights off on me and docks my pay for being 'raunchy,' when all I did was flash a little gash . . . uh, what I mean to say, Miss Kilgore, is . . . give the occasional customer a little peek under the G."

"He docked you for being too wild onstage?"

"Yeah, and I said if he didn't pay up, I was gonna sue him and then he *threatened* me."

I said, "With violence?"

"Oh yeah. I took him to court on a peace bond over it. He was a hothead, ask anybody. One of those guys with a 'little man' complex. If some a-hole was causing trouble in the club, he wouldn't let his bouncer take care of it, no, he had to toss the bum down the stairs himself."

"Did he ever hit you?"

"No, but I thought he might. And he carried guns around all the time, waved 'em around, and I mean, he was obviously a little unstable."

Flo asked, "Unstable enough, hotheaded enough, to kill Lee Harvey Oswald out of love for Kennedy?"

"Oh, he didn't love Kennedy," she said with a snort of a laugh, a fresh cigarette in her mouth as she lit herself up with a little silver Zippo. "He hated the Kennedys, Bobby particularly. I don't know where they get that garbage about how he was trying to prevent Jackie from . . ." She played it melodramatic. ". . . *the heartache of a trial*!"

"Did Oswald ever come into the Carousel? Did Ruby know him?"

Janet thought about that, the vaguely oriental eyes unblinking. Drew on the cigarette, held in the smoke, let it out in a big blue cloud. Then she gestured with a red-nailed finger. "Turn that gizmo off."

Flo clicked it off.

"That's a dangerous subject," Janet said, sitting forward, with a smile devoid of humor. "Dying is getting contagious in this town, if you discuss that subject."

Flo held up her hands, palms out. "Off the record, then."

She sighed smoke. "They knew each other, okay? Oswald came in, half a dozen times, but I don't think he cared about the girls. He might've been a homo. Never looked at the stage, anyway. I figure, if a guy would rather talk to Jack Ruby than watch me strut my stuff? *That's* a homo."

"He and Ruby were friendly?"

"They'd sit at a table and talk. That cop joined 'em once or twice. You know, just about every cop in town came in the Carousel, for free beer and food and girls."

"*What* cop?"

"The one Oswald wound up shooting. Tippit. He was a pal of Ruby's. Ruby's best friend was that cop's landlord."

I saw Flo's eyes tighten, and I had that familiar prickly sensation along the back of my neck myself.

"And don't ask me what they were discussing," Janet said, shaking an open palm at us, "because I don't know. I noticed 'em from the stage—I never circulate in a club much. Listen, it's a little-known fact, but Ruby swings both ways."

Flo touched the switch on the recorder. "May I turn this back on?"

Janet nodded, exhaling smoke out her mouth.

Flo said, "Swung both ways. Go ahead."

"He was with women sometimes, but it was more like he was proving a point. And he had this funny habit of, if he got one of his dancers to put out for him? She was on borrowed time. He lost respect for her. 'Little cunt has no class,' he would say. And she'd be gone."

I asked, "Did he come on to you?"

She grinned. "That's the one that takes the goddamn fuckin' cake. He asked me to move *in* with him."

"What?"

"Yeah. I know! He knew I didn't like him, and he didn't like me, really. But he liked what I stood for."

Flo asked, "What do you stand for?'

Her smile was enormously self-satisfied. She seemed to sense that Flo and I had the kind of rapport that might suggest sexual intimacy, and that was giving her just a little attitude mixed in with the apprehension.

"For being the kind of spectacular piece of ass," she said, "that any red-blooded man would kill the Pope in the front window of Neiman's to spend one night with."

I said, "But what you're known for is not what he wanted out of you?"

She shook her head, and the red ponytail swung. "No, he said I'd have my own bedroom and it would be strictly platonic. He just wanted to show me off to the neighbors, the *world*. To make people think he was the kind of man's man who could rate, well . . ."

"A spectacular piece of ass," Flo said pleasantly.

Now Janet liked her better. "Right. Listen, there's, uh . . . one other thing." She gestured for Flo to switch off the tape machine again.

When it had clicked off, Janet said, "The morning of the twenty-second of November, last year . . . you know what day that was, right?"

"Right," Flo and I said.

"Well, that morning, I stopped by the club. He was there early, a lot, doing business-type things, and, anyway, he'd hired me clear through the start of this year, but stopped paying me even though I was still working. This was maybe a week before the assassination I mean, that I quit. Well, I went around to collect my costumes, which are very expensive, I'm known for my fancy costumes, and also to get what back pay he owed me. I was outside his little office and I heard him on the phone. He was talking to somebody and don't ask me who it was. I might have an idea, but do not fucking ask, okay? Anyway, he was upset. He said he didn't want to be part of 'this thing.' "

Flo, sitting forward, asked, "What thing?"

"That wasn't clear. You need to understand, that was *not* clear. But I gathered he was going to be involved in some kind of . . . something really bad, something really big. And also he said, 'I never been party to killing anybody in my life,' okay?"

I said, "But he couldn't have been talking about Oswald—this was before Kennedy even hit town."

"I don't know, Nate," Janet said, and her nerves were showing, her hands trembling, her eyes moist. "Maybe killing that rabbity little homo was already on the program, how should I know? Or maybe Ruby didn't want to be part of killing Jack Kennedy. If you really want a dumb goddamn stripper's opinion."

I reached over and took one of her hands and smiled at her. "That's 'exotic dancer,' okay?"

She nodded and smiled a little-girl smile; she'd been one a million years ago.

"Anyway," she continued, "I was leaving, trying to just sneak out without being seen, and suddenly he's back in the doorway of his rathole and saying, 'Hey, Jada! You want something?' And I said, oh, I could see you were busy and, you know, didn't wanna bother. And he says, 'I know I owe you some money, doll. Next week be okay?' And I say sure. And he says, 'Why don't we bury the hatchet? Come back and work for your Uncle Jack.' And I say, maybe, and he says, 'But not tonight. We're gonna be closed tonight.' And I say fine, but I'm thinking, something big sure as hell *is* going down—closing the club on a Friday night? Was he kidding?"

Flo said, "And this was *before* there was news of the assassination?"

"It was before the goddamn *assassination*! Anyway, I went over to the Alamo Court, on Fort Worth Avenue, where I was staying, and threw everything I owned in a couple of suitcases and I jumped in my Caddy and I booked it. Jesus, people were already lined up on the street to see the President, happy as clams to be in Dallas. Me, I just wanted out. Oh-you-tee, out. I knew I could always get work in New Orleans, and then, *fuck,* I *hit* this guy."

I said, "What?"

"I struck a goddamn pedestrian, okay? I was hauling ass, but luckily he wasn't hurt bad, just kinda clipped him, the guy, Charles Something, and I tried to give him some money but he was real pissed and yelling, so I took him over to a clinic where he got examined and stuff, X-rayed and that, and I was trying to say, I'll pay for everything, just let me give you my name and you got my license number, but I gotta get the hell out of Dallas, okay? And they finally did."

"What did you do then?"

"What do you think? I got the hell out of Dallas. I was maybe half an hour out of town when the news came over the radio." She looked past us. "Oh. Rose is here. You should talk to her, now."

CHAPTER 11

You could see the pretty girl she once had been inside the puffy visage, before droopiness touched the big brown eyes that had witnessed too much. She had a pale indoor look rare in Texas but common to B-girls, her hair dishwater blonde with hints of gold, rising in a permanent wave over a heart-shaped face around which more blonde hair cascaded to the shoulders of a yellow blouse whose cheerfulness was offset by a frayed collar. All her features were nice, though the nose may have been missing some cartilage—men had knocked this female around; she carried abuse on her slightly hunched shoulders like the heavy load it was.

She may never have been a headliner, but even now she had a nice figure, making it easy to buy her as a credible act on a strip club bill, drenched in the forgiveness of red and blue stage lighting. Easier still to imagine her working the dingy mini-trailer-park bordellos behind bars and gas stations along scrubby strips of highway, and providing a lonely man a shabby fantasy that led to temporary relief.

I'd have been surprised if she were past thirty, even if she did look near forty. Her slightly hooded eyes and her languid manner confirmed *drug addict,* but she wasn't high at the moment, sitting across from Flo Kilgore and me.

The tape recorder was fine with our guest. She chain-smoked Parliaments as we talked. Maybe she thought filter-tip cigarettes were healthier. Well, she was right in a sense—they were healthier than shooting heroin, which is what Rose Cheramie ("That's my stage name, I like it better than Melba Marcades") had been on, last year, on the evening of November 20.

"I don't mind talking," she said in a husky, even ravaged, alto, "and I'm not afraid, hell, I talked to all sorts of cops about this and nobody seems to give a shit. So what's the harm?"

"We appreciate your willingness to be interviewed," Flo said, but the stripper didn't need much interviewing. She launched right in, in a Texas drawl that managed to sound lazy and rapid-fire at once.

"I'm not as young as I used to be, and I never was no frisky firecracker like Jada. So stripping is just one way to make money for me. Sometimes, when gigs're slow, I turn a trick or two. Guess I trick more than strip these days, and also, not often, when things get tough, y'know, I run dope sometimes. This particular time I was doing it for Jack Ruby, before he got himself famous. Years ago, I used to strip at his old club, the Pink Door. It's closed now."

Sitting forward, Flo asked, "You ran illegal drugs for *Jack Ruby*?"

Rose laughed; it was like sandpaper rubbing against itself. "That makes it sound like he was the boss. He was no big shot. Just another goddamn go-between. They got layers, these bent-nose boys, like a cake. Anyway, Pinky—that was his nickname back in the Pink Door days, I never did call him Sparky like some do—he does what he's told, like any small fish. The run I was making was from Miami to Houston, but we was stopping off in Dallas. To pick up the money . . ." She raised her black, mostly painted-on eyebrows. ". . . among *other* things, to say the least."

I asked, "You had the dope with you, Rose?"

She shook her head, exhaling smoke. "No, we're picking up the stuff, and I was only along so a girl could make the trade, money for smack. It's less . . . conspicuous. I mean, the guys with me, these two were hard-core badasses and looked it. I figured them for Italians at first, but turned out they was Cuban. Shouldn'ta surprised me. Y'know, you can't shake a stick in Miami without hitting one of them Cuban spics."

"So I hear," I said, watching her light up a fresh Parliament off a book of matches labeled GAEITY CLUB.

Waving out the flame, she said, "The plan was, pick up the money to pay for the stuff in Dallas, then go to Houston and check in to the Rice Hotel, meet up in a bar with this sailor comin' into Galveston, give sailor boy the cash for the ten kilos, and then hightail it back to Dallas and trade the dope for my kid."

I frowned at her and Flo was wincing in confusion.

"Trade for your kid, Rose?" I asked. "What do you mean?"

She shrugged. "I was kinda bein' forced into this thing. They was blackmailing me to do it. One of 'em was holding on to my baby boy for, you know, collateral. On the plus side, I was gettin' eight grand."

Gently, Flo said, "Rose, it's the assassination we're investigating. You do understand that?"

"You mean, what does running dope have to do with shit?" Nobody smiled at the unintentional pun. "Thing is, these Cuban pricks got to talkin' loose in front of me. It was a long trip and we got friendly, had a couple three-ways at motels. Felt like a vacation to me, though they was making sure we was making good enough time to get to Dallas when they was expected. These guys, they seemed . . . really keyed up, ya ask me. They was laughin' way too much."

I asked, "Drunk?"

"Not *that* drunk. And not hopped up, neither. They just kept makin' these weird, in-jokey comments—'Things to do,' one of 'em says, like he's reading off a list. 'Go to Dallas. Pick up money. Kill the President. Go to Houston. Pick up dope.' "

Flo and I exchanged glances.

Rose blew out smoke. "When I was in the backseat, sleeping—they *thought*—they got *really* loose-lip about it. 'We're gonna kill that lying son of a bitch.' 'That bastard is gonna pay.' And do you know who they was talkin' about? John Kennedy is who! This was . . . the Wednesday night before it happened."

I asked, "What did you think about that, Rose?"

"I thought it was fucked up. I thought maybe I should bug out, maybe find a cop or something and try to stop it. They had a fucking rifle with a scope in the trunk, you know. So when we stopped for an overnight, after the three-way and they got drunk and fell asleep, I kinda . . . well, I didn't call the cops. See, everybody thought I was clean, I was straight, but really I was still using. I thought a taste might help make this Kennedy thing go away. I had two cardboard boxes of my crap in the trunk, next to that rifle? Clothes of mine and baby clothes and also down in there, hidden away, was my works."

"Works?" Flo asked.

"Needle and so on," I said quietly.

Flo mouthed, "Oh," and nodded.

"So the next morning," Rose went on, "they saw my works in the john and the geniuses figure out I wasn't clean and had junk along, and yelled at me and slapped me around and I just kind of took it. I figured they needed me, so they'd get over it. I was the contact for the sailor, you know? We keep driving, and driving, and then we stop in this little shit bump, Eunice—we're in Louisiana now—and it's like maybe five thou pop, but they like to party in that little town, and we stopped at the Silver Slipper Lounge, a bar that Ruby had a piece of. Maybe the Cubans were contacting somebody, maybe they were just thirsty, I dunno. I knew the place a little, I tricked there before, they had little trailers out back. Manny was a nice man, Manny Manuel I mean, the manager?"

"Rose," I said, "can we stay on the subject please?"

She gave me a flirtatious look. "I *am* on the subject, Handsome. I'm all *over* the subject." Then her expression grew serious. She flicked ash into a tray.

"See, I'd been thinking about what they was saying about the President, just kind of getting in a real funk about it. I tried to make myself think they was kidding or something, but they were for real, man. They were part of . . . part of something *bigger* than they were, and it excited their asses. This sounds crazy, but it's almost like they were doing the dope run so that if they got picked up, *that* would be what it was for."

As opposed to killing the President.

"So we're drinking and talking, and I say something like, 'What do you wanna kill John Kennedy for? What did he ever do to you? He's got a wife and kids, you know.' And one of them Cubans says, 'The Bay of Pigs is what,' but the other one is already swinging on me. Right there in the damn nightclub. He cold-cocks me and I'm off the chair and on the floor, and when I wake up, Manny is pushing the Cubans through the door and outside, tellin' 'em he doesn't run that kind of joint. Manny helps me up and I thank him and I go back outside and they're waiting, they grab me and they toss me in the backseat and one Cuban crawls in back after me and the other gets behind the wheel and peels out. They're going maybe fifty and we're out of town now with nobody around when the Cuban with me in the backseat opens his door and I get kicked out and go rolling. The car screeches to a stop, and then I see them both get out, and one opens the trunk. I try to get to my feet 'cause I think they're going for that rifle, but they was just after my boxes of stuff, and they tossed them on the roadside and just took off."

This must have been what Janet meant when she told me Rose said the "shooters who got Kennedy" had tried to kill the woman.

Flo said, "How badly were you hurt?"

She shrugged, spoke through exhaled smoke. "Not serious, bumps and bruises and scrapes, but back at the club, somebody saw those guys grab me and told Manny, and he got concerned, bless him, and drove out looking for me. He found me, all bloody and hitchhiking, and took me to the hospital there in Eunice, to the emergency room. They cleaned me up but said they couldn't admit me because all I had was bruises and scrapes, and then I told them I was having drug withdrawal and could they help me, and they called the cops. A nice officer I met before . . .'cause I worked at the Slipper from time to time and the cops knew all the girls there . . . anyway, this nice trooper named Fruge—it's an easy name to remember, 'cause of the dance?"

She did a sad little pumping of both fisted arms, indicating the Frug.

"Trooper Fruge," she went on, "took me to the little Eunice jail. I said I had something important to tell him but he said I could tell him in the morning, because he had to go to the policeman's ball that night."

"You're kidding," I said.

"No, unless maybe *he* was, but I wasn't really on top of things, because I was coming down and I was coming down fast . . . I hadn't fixed since last night . . . and they put me in a jail cell and I got awful hot and took off all my clothes and I was really climbing the walls. I don't mean that as an expression. I was climbing them, trying to, anyway. So they called Fruge, at the dance I guess, do you think maybe he was doing the Frug? Ha. And anyway, he came back with a doctor, the coroner I think, who gave me a sedative and that helped. The next morning Trooper Fruge drove me over to this nuthouse in Jackson, not 'cause I was nuts or anything but they did drug withdrawal there, and on the way I told him about killing Kennedy."

Flo said, "This was Thursday, the twenty-first."

"Yeah, I guess it would've been. So I told Trooper Fruge, I said, 'These fucking Cubans are *crazy*, they're going to Dallas to kill Kennedy when he comes to town.' I told him everything, just like I done to you—the drugs, my baby, everything. I wanted help getting my kid back, y'know? Also, I didn't want to see Kennedy killed. Fruge had this other trooper come and hear my story and I told it again. But that was it. The two troopers just went away, and I told the doctors about Kennedy, and the nurses, and everybody just kind of nodded, 'cause they had committed me for drug withdrawal and thought I was delirious or some shit."

I asked, "No one else came to talk to you?"

"Not till after the assassination. Jesus, I mean, I was in the hospital rec room, watching TV on Friday, and I see this news thing with people lining the streets in Dallas, and I start screaming, like a crazy person, which there was no shortage of in there, 'Somebody's gotta do something! They're gonna kill the President!' Nobody paid any attention to me. Then the cars came on the screen, the, uh, what's it, motorcade, rolling by, and I yell to the nurses and other patients, '*Watch,* you assholes! It's gonna happen! It's gonna happen!' You couldn't see it on-screen, but there was these pops, and then this commotion, and I said, '*See!* See! I am *not* nuts!' "

"And *then* Fruge came back?"

"Not till Monday. Not till after Pinky had shot his girlfriend."

"Pinky?" I said. "You mean Ruby?"

Flo asked, "What do you mean, 'girlfriend'?"

"Oh, Pinky and that Oswald character," Rose said, "they was shacked up off and on for years. I saw those queer sons of bitches sitting together at the Pink Door and later the Carousel, plenty of times."

I asked, "You told this to Fruge?"

"Yeah, him and a bunch of other troopers. I played to smaller audiences in my time. Fruge said he was going to report what I said to the Dallas cops and the FBI, too, but neither of those ever questioned me. I run into Fruge a couple months later, and he said he called the FBI but they wasn't interested in the Cubans 'cause they already had their man."

Meaning (the late) Oswald.

"And," Rose continued, "Fruge said he called some cop named Fritz on the Dallas PD, and told him the story, too, and this Fritz guy said he wasn't interested, neither."

"That would be Captain Will Fritz," Flo said, with a glance in my direction. "He was in charge of the assassination investigation."

"Well, whoever or whatever he was," Rose said pleasantly, smiling as she lit up another Parliament, "he didn't bother talking to me. Sometimes it pays to be an unreliable junkie . . . oh, but I'm straight now. Don't get the wrong idea."

"We won't, Rose," I said.

She shrugged, sighing smoke. "That's all I know about the Kennedy thing. If there's nothin' else, I could use the bread we agreed on. . . . Bus trip from Waco ain't free, you know."

This was directed at Flo, who had arranged to pay Rose two hundred for her expenses. This wasn't strictly journalistically kosher, but I thought Flo got off cheap, even if the Waco bus trip had cost maybe fifteen bucks.

"One other thing," I said to Rose, who was about to slide out of the booth. "You used to go out with a guy named Mac Wallace, right?"

"Yeah. Few times. Maybe . . . two years ago. When I was dancing at the Carousel. I cut that shit off fast."

"What kind of guy was he?"

"Well, he's a big good-looking guy, but kind of a creep. Very smart, but broody, like Brando. I'll tell you one thing, he's a bully when he's drunk. Likes to knock a girl around. Likes to kind of . . . well, rape you, when it isn't even necessary. Who needs that crap? Why? What does he have to do with the Kennedy assassination?"

"Nothing," I said. "Probably unrelated."

Probably.

"I'm a regular here at the Colony Club," the fresh-looking young blonde said, then raised a cautionary finger. "Not a stripper. I'm a singer. Strictly a singer."

"Really, Bev?" Janet said with a smile. Aka Jada had, at our final guest's invitation, joined us in the booth for the interview, sitting next to the petite brown-eyed blonde, whose pixie-cut ratted platinum hairdo emphasized her vague resemblance to Connie Stevens. She was wearing a red-and-green plaid bandana-ish blouse, gray shorts, and minimal makeup. Almost pretty, definitely cute.

"Well," Beverly Oliver said to her friend, giggling (she seemed barely out of her teens), "I guess you caught me, honey. I used to come up on the bus from Garland, it's about a forty-minute ride, and enter the amateur night at the Theater Club—Abe's brother Barney runs that. And then later here, at the Colony. But I only went down to a bikini."

"You'd have made a mint stripping, doll," Janet said, making her red ponytail swing with a shake of her head, grinning at her little protégée.

"Nope. I'm a singer, Sunday, Monday, and always. And an old-fashioned one. You didn't see me here last week, Mr. Heller, 'cause I sometimes do a week at the Embers in Houston."

I said, "Bill Peck and His Peckers back you up here?"

"No! Joe Garcia's little orchestra. Don't look for any Beatles or Herman's Hermits from this girl—maybe some Pet Clark. But I'm a Joni James, Kay Starr kinda thrush. You want to hear 'Blues in the Night' or 'Bill Bailey,' you've come to the right chile."

In any case, she was a natural performer, and the tape recorder didn't faze her—she liked talking in front of it.

"'Bill Bailey,' huh?" I said. "Billy Daniels or Bobby Darin style?"

"Okay, *you* caught me, too, Mr. Heller. I'm enough of a teenager to like Bobby better. I'm only eighteen."

Flo, surprised, asked, "How old were you when you stripped at those amateur nights?"

"Fourteen," she said with a shrug. "Fifteen."

I said, "Janet gave me the impression you worked at the Carousel."

"Well, yes and no," Bev said. "I never sang there and certainly didn't strip, though Jack had amateur nights himself, just trying to compete."

"Jack Ruby," Flo said.

"Yes, we were friends. He was never really my boss. I worked for him, but in a limited way. Like, I hosted some of his after-hours parties—I'd mix drinks, sit around and visit, that kind of thing."

Janet said, "Jack said Bev had more class than his regular waitresses, and any dancers at those parties were busy rubbing against the guests, if you know what I mean."

Bev said, "I spent a lot of time in the Carousel. Jack liked me.

Liked to be seen with me. I thought he had a crush on me or something, but he never made a play. I took a couple trips with him where I sat by the pool in a bikini, and it was more like he was showing me off than really had any interest."

I asked, "And you didn't have any interest him in?"

"Heck no! I mean he was nice, but not nice-looking, everybody knows that by now. But a big heart, good to his girls, always loaning them money. He would bring down-and-outers in and give them food and so on. That side of him, nobody knows."

The side everybody knew was the kill-Lee-Harvey-Oswald-in-the-basement-of-the-Dallas-police-station one.

Janet prompted, "Tell them about Oswald."

"Well, honey, you were there," she said to her pal. For the first time a topic seemed to give her pause. "*You* go ahead and tell them."

Janet, seeming like the mother to this little girl, ordered her: "No. I already talked to these nice people. It's your turn."

Bev shrugged and her well-sprayed pile of platinum hair bounced like the single object it was. "There wasn't much to it. I saw Oswald in the Carousel only twice. The first time, he and Jack were really friendly. Janet was sitting with them, and Jack called me over, and he said, 'Beverly, this is my friend Lee Oswald. He's with the CIA.' I said hello, but I guess it was clear I wasn't impressed. This friend of Jack's was just sitting there kind of sullen, not friendly at all. Kind of giving Jack a dirty look. Jack said, 'Do you know what the CIA is?' And I said no, and almost added, 'And I don't care.' And Jack says, 'He's a spy like James Bond.' I think Jack was a little tipsy, but he always liked to boast, so maybe not."

I said, "What was the other time?"

"Well, that was strange. Oswald was in the audience and he started heckling the comic, Wally Weston, who I think was doing some kind of political skit. Oswald yelled out that Wally was a filthy Commie, and Wally—he was a World War Two veteran—boy, was he PO'ed! He jumped into the audience and smacked

Oswald in the puss. Then Jack came over and dragged his 'friend' out and tossed him down the stairs. Which was something he did a lot to unruly types. Amazing he didn't kill anybody."

Well, he did actually, but not by throwing Oswald down the stairs.

Flo asked, "Were there ever prominent people in the club. Politicians? How about policemen?"

"Oh, yeah," the little blonde said, nodding. "Policemen particularly. They were sort of touted to come into the club with free coffee and Cokes and pizza and so on. They provided free security—Jack never had to hire more than one bouncer. There were politicians, too, and some very rich people. Oilmen. Surprising when you think about it, because really, the Carousel was rather sleazy."

Janet said, "That's why I was one of the few headline performers Ruby ever managed to book into that shithole. Agents said his club didn't meet the high standards that dancers like me expect."

Bev said, "But Jack was always trying. He wanted to bring Candy Barr back, for instance, when she got out of prison."

Janet smirked. "That tells you something, Nate—Candy Barr is Ruby's idea of class."

"Jack's always been a guy in search of class," Bev said reflectively. "He thinks that *things* bring you class and that the people you *know* give you class. He's never figured out that class isn't something you can buy."

I asked, "Did you ever see Cubans in the club?"

"Funny you should say that," Bev said, with an odd expression, as if I'd just guessed her weight. 105. "My boyfriend, Larry, got into a conversation about Cuba once with this weird guy named Ferrie." She thought for a while. "His first was David, I think. I probably only remember it because . . . this is terrible, but he *was* a fairy. He liked boys, I mean."

"Okay," I said. "But 'David Ferrie' isn't a Cuban name."

"No, no, but I'm getting to that. Well, Larry and this Ferrie character start talking about Cuba, how dangerously close to America that Communism is all of a sudden, and how we ought to take it over again, and start the gambling back up, and that somebody ought to do something about Castro."

"All right," I said, interested.

"Larry and Ferrie . . . ha. I'm a poet and don't know it." She gave me a little-girl grin, then got serious again. "Larry and Ferrie were agreeing about this subject. But Ferrie starts getting agitated, raving and ranting and all."

She shook her head and the platinum hair damn near moved.

"That Ferrie was strange," she said, and shivered. Might have been the air-conditioning but I didn't think so. "By strange, I don't mean dumb or stupid, no—he was very, very intelligent but . . . an odd duck."

Janet said, "Ferrie was in the Carousel a bunch of times. He's from New Orleans. You see him sometimes over there in the Sho-Bar. A first-class oddball."

Flo asked, "In appearance or behavior?"

"Both," the two women said, and then Bev giggled and so did Janet, the younger girl turning the hardened stripper into a momentary teenager.

Bev said, "He's a good-sized guy, around six feet, maybe a hundred ninety pounds. He had some kind of disease where he lost all of his hair. So he wears this crazy reddish fright wig and he paints on black eyebrows."

"Like a stripper," Janet said, pointing to her own similarly painted-on eyebrows. I felt sure they looked better on her. "He's got this kind of *anteater* look."

"Anyway," Bev said, "getting back to Larry and the Cuba conversation. Out of the blue, maybe kidding, maybe not, Ferrie says to Larry, 'How would you like fifty grand to go to Cuba and kill that bastard?' Excuse my language, but that's what he said, or anyway Larry said that's what he said. So Larry says no thanks and just gets up and drifts away."

I asked, "Was this Ferrie guy drunk?"

"No," Bev said. "He's just a nut. There was an after-hours party I was working, the week of the assassination. The Monday night before. There were some Cubans there, and Ferrie, too."

"How about Oswald?" I asked.

"No. But Ferrie got into a shouting match with one of the Cubans, and took out a gun and was waving it around! Jack went over and wrestled it away from Ferrie and called him an SOB, said someday somebody would shove that little gun up where the sun don't shine. Funny thing, though—Jack didn't toss Ferrie out, like he did with most people making a ruckus. Things quieted down, then I went over to Jack and said, 'I don't like this at all, I'm sorry, but I'm out of here. Things are getting too hot for this little blonde.' Jack said he understood and I left."

Janet said, looking from me to Flo, "There's another reason I asked Bev to talk to you. Something that doesn't have to do with the Carousel Club. She was *there*."

I said, "Where?"

"At Dealey Plaza. She saw the assassination, Nate. Right there on Elm Street. Ringside seat."

Bev was nodding, and Flo's eyes were so wide, I thought they'd fall out of their sockets.

"Tell us, please," I said.

"It happened right in front of me," Bev said quietly. Her eyes were looking into the memory. "I had a brand-new movie camera that my boyfriend gave me—Larry worked for Eastman Kodak—and I wanted to make sure I could get some really good pictures of the President. I'd been to a party the night before and took a cab over there that morning. My car was already in the parking garage next door, here."

She gestured with a thumb.

"Anyway, I start walking up Commerce, looking down the side streets to see if I could get a place close to the curb. It was just absolutely packed. There's no way to even get up close enough to see him, let alone take film of him. I keep walking and walking, oh at least ten blocks to Dealey Plaza, across from what they're calling the Grassy Knoll now."

She shifted in the booth, sighed, and Janet gave her a supportive little nod. The girl was trembling but her voice was strong, clear.

"I got lucky and found this area where almost nobody was standing—by a father and his little boy—and I thought, 'This is gonna be a great place to get pictures!' And I start filming as soon as the motorcade turns onto Elm Street."

Flo asked, "When you heard the first shot, did you react? Did the camera shake?"

"No, I never even knew that Mr. Kennedy had been shot until the . . . the *fatal* shot. That was definitely a different sound. There was a bang, bang, bang and then a buh-*boom*. The bang, bang, bang sounded like those little firecrackers people throw on the sidewalk. Then I saw the whole back of his head come off, and the blood flying everywhere." She swallowed. "I guess I went into a state of shock, then. Everybody else is on the ground, and I'm still standing there, frozen, with my camera in my hand, like a doofus."

I asked, "Did you think the shots had come from the book depository?"

"No," she said firmly. "But there was smoke drifting over the picket fence. At the time, frankly, it never occurred to me it was gun smoke. I figured there was a car in that lot that started up. But people went running up the hill. You mentioned the book depository, and even people from there, they were running down to that Grassy Knoll."

The girl paused, as if shock was settling in yet again.

Flo asked, "What did you do next?"

"I . . . I walked across the street to the little slope, where everybody was gathering. I saw some people who kind of looked official, taking people and talking to them. I thought, 'They're gonna want to talk to me in a minute,' and I hung around a while, but nobody approached me. I made eye contact with a Dallas cop I knew from the Carousel. I could tell he recognized me and figured, if they needed me, he'd know where to find me. So I left, without anybody questioning me, and went to my car. I didn't hear that the President had died until I got out on North Central Expressway."

Janet said, "Tell them about the two men who came to see you at the club the next day."

"Actually," Bev said, "it wasn't the next day. I didn't go to work Friday night—I don't think the Colony was even open, but I didn't go. I didn't come here to work Saturday night, either, and of course I didn't go to work Sunday night, after what Jack did to Oswald."

She sipped at a glass of water we'd provided.

Then she picked up: "Monday night, I got here at my normal time, a quarter till eight, and there were two men waiting at the landing halfway up the stairs. I wasn't concerned because a lot of times people going to the Colony would wait there for the rest of their party to catch up. As I got to the landing, the taller of the two men stepped forward. He showed me FBI identification. Said, 'Young lady, we understand you were taking pictures when the President was killed.' I said, 'Yes sir, I was.' Said, 'Have you had the film developed yet?' I said, 'No sir, I haven't.' Said, 'Where's the film?' I said, 'Still in my camera.' Said, 'Where is your camera?' I said, 'In my makeup kit, right here in my hand.' It was a train case, and I held it up. He said, 'Well, we want to take that film and develop it and look at it for evidence, and we'll get it back to you in a few days.' That was November 25, of last year, and that's the last I heard of it."

Employees of the Colony Club were drifting in—waitresses, bartenders, musicians, a few dancers. The clink of glasses accompanied the lights coming down, transforming the dreary-looking club into the kind of classy venue that Jack Ruby would so dearly love to run.

"That's an incredible story," Flo said.

"Really," Bev said, with a shrug, "it's simple—I was down there that day standing between twenty and thirty feet from the President when he was shot. I was taking a movie that three days later was confiscated by a man who identified himself as an FBI agent. All there is to it."

I said, "And you've never told anyone before?"

"No," Bev said. "Mr. Heller, Janet said I could trust you. That you are a good man. And of course I know Miss Kilgore from TV."

"You could've cashed in on the free publicity," I said.

She gave me a look wiser than her years. "Mr. Heller, if they can kill the President of the United States, they could kill a two-bit songbird like me and it wouldn't even make the back page of the newspaper."

CHAPTER 12

Over the next several days, Flo Kilgore and I interviewed a dozen witnesses. I had no part in lining any of them up, nor did she reveal to me how she had done so. I gathered it had been accomplished with the help of her friend Mark Lane and his people, but I didn't ask. I wasn't the lead investigator. In fact, I was just a glorified bodyguard.

Toward that end, and properly sobered by the interviews with Janet, Rose, and Beverly of the infamous Carousel Club, I was carrying the nine millimeter again, despite my lack of a concealed weapons permit. This meant, in rather warm Texas weather—did this state know it was goddamn fucking November?—I had to wear a suit, a lightweight tan number courtesy of a Maxwell Street tailor who knew how to allow for a clunky handgun in a shoulder holster under the left arm.

A number of the witnesses went over the same ground, chiefly people present that day in Dealey Plaza who had seen puffs of smoke and other suspicious activities around the picket fence on the grassy knoll.

Like Lee Bowers, a railroad towerman for the Union Terminal Company, who the morning of the murder saw three unauthorized cars enter the parking lot, drive around, and leave. One driver was using a walkie-talkie. Bowers also saw two strangers—one middle-aged and heavyset, in a white shirt and dark trousers, the other in his mid-twenties in a plaid shirt, standing ten or fifteen feet from each other—both near the picket fence around the time of the shooting. He also reported seeing "a flash of light or smoke or something" that caused him to feel that "something out of the ordinary happened by that fence."

Like building engineer J. C. Price, who was standing on the roof of the Terminal Annex building at the south end of the plaza, opposite the Grassy Knoll, who saw a man running, fast, away from the fence toward the railroad yard, carrying something that looked like a rifle.

Like railroad supervisor S. M. Holland, who saw rising from the knoll "a puff of smoke about six or eight feet above the ground right from under the trees."

Like *Dallas Morning News* reporter Mary Woodward, who was standing in front and to the left of the fence and heard a "horrible, ear-shattering noise coming from behind us and a little to the right."

Two of the interviewees were of particular interest, and import. The first was Deputy Sheriff Roger Craig, who met us at the Statler, where we sat midday at a corner table in the currently underpopulated Coffee House and Grill, an offshoot of the Empire Room.

The off-duty deputy arrived in a light-blue short-sleeve sport shirt and dark-blue slacks. He was tall, slender, dark-haired, probably about thirty. He could easily have played a cop on television, though his Texas near-drawl might have typecast him as the deputy he was. He was fine with being recorded.

Flo ordered a coffee and I had a Coke on ice, but our guest said water would be fine. He had that odd combination of assurance and shyness that you sometimes find in his profession.

"Here I come all the way to Dallas," Flo said, mildly flirtatious (he was a handsome man), "and the first deputy I meet isn't in uniform."

"Well, Miss Kilgore, I'm off-duty for one, and for another, I'm a plainclothes man. A detective, like Mr. Heller here."

Any civil-service detective who was like me should be watched carefully, but never mind.

"You know how this works, Deputy Craig," I said. "Just tell us your story."

He did.

"The morning of November twenty-second," he said, his voice a warm baritone, "Sheriff Bill Decker called in all his plainclothes men, myself included, and informed us President Kennedy's motorcade would be coming down Main Street. He wanted us to stand out in front of the courthouse, at 505 Main, to sort of represent the sheriff's office."

I said, "Not to aid in security for the President?"

"No. We were told the security had been arranged by the Secret Service and the boys in blue, the Dallas police. We were to take no part in it whatsoever."

Flo said, "So you were all just standing in front of the courthouse when the assassination took place?"

"That's right. A bunch of flat feet standing flat-footed." He frowned and I read embarrassment in it. "There was a lot of stupid animosity toward the President among the sheriff's men—hell, I may have been the only one who voted for him. I remember around quarter after twelve, just standing there stoked to think I'd be like four feet from the President of the United States, I said to Deputy Sheriff Jim Ramsey that the motorcade was late. And Ramsey said, 'Maybe somebody shot the son of a bitch.' That really brought home how all the other men around me resented being there, felt they'd been forced to acknowledge the presence of someone they hated."

I asked, "Did you sense anything wrong, before the first shot?"

His eyes narrowed. "Well, something *was* bothering me—like any trained cop, I was just looking around, checking for anything that seemed out of place. That's when it occurred to me—there weren't any officers guarding the intersections, or controlling the crowd, either. Not that there was anything I could do about it."

"This is before the motorcade approached."

"Right, but then suddenly cheers started and there President Kennedy was, him and his beautiful wife, smiling and waving, and his smile was infectious. Right then, I wasn't a deputy sheriff, I was just an American citizen getting caught up in the moment. Then the limo made its turn onto Elm Street, and it was only seconds before the first rifle shot."

For several seconds, nobody said anything.

He swallowed and took a deep breath and let it out. "You know, I'll take a Coke myself."

I called the waitress over, ordered it, and when she was gone, said to him, "Once you heard the shot, what did you do?"

His eyebrows flicked up and down. "Well, I ran like hell toward Houston—I was maybe fifteen feet from the corner, but before I got there two *more* shots rang out. I couldn't believe it, it couldn't be happening, but of course it was, and I kept running, ran across Houston and beside that little pool, on the west side, that reflecting pool, and I knocked a guy out of my way and he splashed in. I ran across the grass between Main and Elm, people scattered on the ground like they were gunshot victims, too—I even stopped and checked a mother and child to see if they were okay. The President was long gone by now . . . in every sense I guess."

His Coke arrived and he had a sip.

Flo said, "We're told the immediate reaction of many was to head for the so-called Grassy Knoll."

He nodded. "I saw a Dallas Police officer run up the there and go behind the picket fence near the railroad yards. I followed his lead, and, man, behind that fence, that was complete confusion, utter hysteria."

"So," I said, "people were behind the fence at this point, and in the parking lot?"

"Oh yeah. I began questioning witnesses, and pitched in to help the Dallas uniformed guys restore order. When things got calmed down some, I started in questioning people who were standing around at the top of the incline, asking if anyone had seen anything strange or unusual before or during the shooting."

"Had they?"

"Well, a number of people thought the shots came from the area of the Grassy Knoll or from behind the picket fence. But the most interesting, and I think reliable, witness was a Mr. Arnold Rowland. He and his wife were standing toward the top of the knoll on the north side of Elm. Something had caught Mr. Rowland's attention waiting for the President to arrive. Approximately fifteen minutes before the motorcade got to Dealey Plaza, something caught his eye—a white man standing by the sixth-floor window of the Texas School Book Depository building in the southeast corner, holding a rifle equipped with a telescopic sight."

"Did Mr. Rowland alert anyone?"

"No. He thought they were Secret Service agents—a natural enough assumption for a citizen."

" 'They'?"

"He also saw a darker-complected male—colored, or Latin maybe—pacing back and forth, in the southwest corner window. I passed Mr. and Mrs. Rowland along to another deputy, and I understand the Warren Commission has talked to them, although the wife didn't see anything."

He sipped his Coke again, and I sipped mine, letting him take a moment to further gather his thoughts. I could sense Flo's excitement, which I shared—this felt closer to being there than had our tour on foot the other day.

"Well," he said, allowing himself a sigh, "traffic was heavy by this point—the patrolman assigned to Elm and Houston had left his post, probably dealing the crowd and the chaos. I made my way over to the south side of Elm, to look for any signs of bullets striking the curb or the street or anything. By now it had been established that the President had been shot . . . this must have been around twelve-forty . . . and that's when I heard a shrill whistle."

"What kind of whistle?"

He held two fingers near his mouth. "Like a kid whistling, to get your attention. Coming from across the street. I turned and saw a white male in his twenties running down the grass from the direction of the book depository. A light-green Rambler station wagon was coming slowly west on Elm. The driver was a husky-looking Latin, with dark wavy hair, wearing a tan Windbreaker.

Driver was looking up and leaning over at the guy running down toward him. The station wagon pulled over and picked him up—guy was wearing a long-sleeve work shirt and faded blue trousers."

He leaned forward and his eyes moved from Flo to me.

He said, "I didn't know it at the time, but it was Oswald, or somebody who looked a hell of a lot like him. I tried to cross Elm Street to stop them—the two of 'em were obviously in a hurry, and were the only people not running *to* the scene. That's human nature when there's a shooting or an accident, you know, go check out the scene. But they were heading away, so I immediately tried to cross the street, to take the two into custody. Only traffic was too heavy by now, and I couldn't get to them before they drove off, going west on Elm."

"You reported this?"

"You bet. Right away I brought it to the attention of the authorities at the command post at Elm and Houston, in front of the book depository. I told a Secret Service agent, or at least that's how he identified himself, what I'd seen. He didn't seem too interested. Sheriff Decker himself heard this exchange, and yanked me to one side and told me the suspect had already left the scene. That's when I got pulled in on what was the first real search of the depository."

"Decker led that?"

"No. He left that to me and a couple of other deputies. We went up to the sixth floor, which was very dark and dusty. The south side of the building seemed the logical place to start. Immediately we found three spent rifle shells that struck me as arranged, deliberately placed there, in plain sight on the floor by the window. A small brown paper lunch bag with some chicken bones in it was on the floor, too. I called across the room for Dallas Police ID man, Lieutenant Day, to bring his camera over, which he did. Then we started searching the rest of the floor."

"The rifle hadn't been found yet?"

He shook his head. "No. We did find it, but that's a . . . story in itself."

"Oh?"

He was nodding as he sipped Coke again, and for the first time he smiled, a small odd smile that didn't last. "We neared the northwest corner of the floor when a deputy called out, 'Here it is.' I went over. Two rows of boxes were stacked close, but when you looked down between them, there it was, on the floor—a rifle on a strap with a telescopic sight, with the bolt facing upward. Lieutenant Day came over and so did Captain Fritz of Homicide. Day retrieved the rifle, activated the bolt, ejected one live round of ammunition. Day inspected the rifle briefly, then handed it to Fritz, who held it up by the strap and asked if anybody knew what kind of rifle it was. Deputy Weitzman, who knew a lot about weapons, used to run a sporting goods store, gave it a close look and said it was a 7.65 German Mauser."

"What?" I said, sitting up. "Not Oswald's famous piece-of-shit Mannlicher-Carcano?"

He shook his head. "No. A Mauser."

"You're saying at some point a switch was made?"

"I'm saying a deputy who knew his stuff said it was a Mauser, and a bunch of other law-enforcement officers agreed with him. Right about then, word of Officer Tippit's shooting came in, and it was chaos again."

He sighed and the waitress came over and asked if he'd like a refill. He looked up at her, nodded and smiled, his second of the afternoon; she smiled back—yes, he was handsome, all right.

I said, "That's a hell of a story, Deputy Craig."

"Oh, there's more. As the afternoon went on, and information came in, and Oswald was arrested at the Texas Theatre, I became convinced that I had seen the assassin and his driver making their getaway from the scene in that Rambler. They would only have to drive six blocks west on Elm and they'd have been on Beckley Avenue, with a straight shot to Oswald's rooming house. That *might* have given Oswald time to kill Tippit, which the official story really doesn't—him taking a bus, getting stuck in traffic, getting off, catching a cab, and so on."

"Did you ID Oswald as the guy picked up by the station wagon?"

He nodded and another smile emerged, briefly. "I did. Later that afternoon, I called Captain Fritz at the PD and gave him the description of the guy I saw, who Fritz said sounded like their suspect. He asked me to come take a look at him. I got to Fritz's office a little after 4:30, was given a peek through the door at Oswald, sitting there by Fritz's desk."

Flo was watching and listening with the rapt attention you might give a Hitchcock thriller.

Craig continued: "I made the ID, and Fritz and I went in together. He told Oswald, 'This officer saw you leave the crime scene,' and Oswald, real defensive and sullen, said that he'd already told them that. Fritz then said, 'He saw a Latin fella pick you up in a station wagon,' and Oswald replied, leaning forward on Fritz's desk, forceful as hell, 'That station wagon belongs to Mrs. Paine' . . . who was apparently a friend of his wife's, and he didn't want to see her 'dragged into this.' Oswald seemed disgusted, like he'd been let down or even betrayed, and Fritz was sort of playing 'good cop,' because he almost seemed like he was consoling Oswald, who said, real depressed, 'Now everybody will know who I am.' "

That sounded to me like an undercover agent whose cover had been blown.

"Miss Kilgore," he said, sitting forward, firm but pleasant, "I will be glad to cooperate with you any way I can. This has smelled like a cover-up to me since the day it happened, and because I have refused to be part of it, my career has hit a dead end. I expect any day to be fired over one trumped-up thing or another. Just four years ago, I was named Officer of the Year. I nailed an international jewel thief. Do you know that? Officer of the Year."

His voice was steady, but his eyes were moist.

Beyond the Dealey Plaza underpass—through which an assassinated president had been whisked away into history books that would one day be boxed and stacked in the nearby depository—

stretched the city-within-the-city known as Oak Cliff. The boarding-house where Lee Harvey Oswald had roomed, and the street where he possibly shot J. D. Tippit, and the movie theater where he was arrested, were all in Oak Cliff.

Two hundred seventy-five thousand of Dallas's citizens also lived there, in the small, older homes close to downtown, and newer houses and apartments farther out. Chiefly a blue-collar community, with considerable natural beauty—in particular the woods and hills of Kessler Park—Oak Cliff was convenient for those working downtown. Young men on their way up would have a home in Oak Cliff only temporarily, relocating their families to more status-friendly North Dallas when raises allowed.

On a quiet side street in Oak Cliff's newer section lived a young woman who was not on her way up, having already realized her dreams. Most likely she owned the modern six-room bungalow. Unlike much of Texas, the oak tree in her modest front yard realized this was autumn and was spilling leaves. A knock at an antique oval front door quickly summoned the lady of the house, petite, curvy, in her thirties, with a pixie-ish reddish-brown hairdo. Her prettiness was on the pixie side, too, heart-shaped face, wide-set brown eyes, pert nose, and dimpling smile.

"Well, look who's on my doorstep," our hostess said, in a lazy, Scarlett O'Hara–ish way. She looked primly festive in a brown-and-orange flower-print cotton dress with flounce sleeves and a full skirt. "Why, when I heard Flo Kilgore wanted to chat with me, I was simply flabbergasted. Come in, come in."

We did, into a living room arrayed with Early American antiques. Only a few framed family photos on one wall—our hostess with two young boys at various ages—were indicative of this century. She had apparently cleaned the room to perfection, knowing a TV star was coming by.

Flo, looking chic in a royal-blue crepe dress with A-line skirt, gestured toward me with a white-gloved hand. "Mrs. West, this is my investigator, Nathan Heller, from Chicago."

Mrs. West nodded with a smile that had turned forced as she

said, "Mr. Heller, welcome to my home," and I wondered if I'd somehow already managed to get off on the wrong foot with her. Probably she hadn't expected Flo to bring anyone along.

"Miss Kilgore," she said, her hands fig-leafed before her, "I would much prefer you call me Madeleine, or if you favor the formality, make it Mrs. Brown—my name by my late, first husband. I do not live with my present husband."

"Certainly, Madeleine," Flo said. "And call me Flo, please."

"And I'm Nate," I said with a smile that she returned without anything forced about it this time.

"I generally don't indulge in alcohol in the afternoon," she said, "but I can get you something, if you like. Or iced tea, perhaps?"

Flo said iced tea would be fine and I agreed.

"Shall we sit on the patio?" Madeleine asked, and led us through a modern kitchen to a sun-dappled cement slab on a backyard given over to flowers, vines, shrubs, and small trees. Flo and I were directed to black wrought-iron chairs with all-weather floral cushions at a matching round table under an umbrella. We sat as Madeleine returned to the kitchen to fetch glasses of iced tea.

When all three of us were settled, Flo removed the recording gizmo from her purse and Madeleine shook her finger in a gently scolding fashion. "I'm sorry, Miss Kilgore . . . Flo . . . but I won't be recorded. You will, I'm afraid, have to take notes."

"Well, that will be fine," Flo said, and her smile was as forced as Madeleine's earlier one had been.

As Flo dug in her purse, Madeleine said, businesslike, "Now, perhaps Mr. Lane didn't make it clear, but I cannot at this time be quoted. Perhaps in the future. But *not* at this time."

Flo, settling in with her spiral pad and ballpoint, said, "I understand. For the present, you'll be an unnamed source, close to President Johnson."

"That will be fine," she said, and sipped at a straw as long as her tall narrow glass. "That will be fine."

Since 1948, Madeleine West, or Brown, had been the mistress of Lyndon Baines Johnson. They had a son together, one who closely resembled his father (that had been clear in my glance at those family portraits). Senator Johnson had bought her this house in 1950, and seemed to support her well if not quite lavishly. Apparently she had married a man named Brown for cover purposes. Flo knew all of this going in, and knew as well that Mrs. Brown was irritated with her lover/provider, for spending so little time with her since assuming the presidency. Whether Mrs. Brown knew of another LBJ relationship with a White House secretary—which had also resulted in a child—was unknown.

I had already cautioned Flo that Mrs. Brown's current irritation with her longtime benefactor might color what she shared with us this afternoon. Or—and this was more likely—that her sharing it with us was at once a blackmail threat and a life-insurance policy.

Flo asked, "When did you meet Lyndon Johnson?"

"Right after the Box 13 scandal, in the election of '48—perhaps you'll recall the ballot-box stuffing accusations that dogged Lyndon?"

"So they were just accusations, then?"

"Oh, my no, Lyndon and his people did that, all right. Well, they were celebrating, and I must say that night is engraved in my memory. When that tall Texan walked into that ballroom, so charismatic and handsome . . . why, everyone there gravitated towards him, including this little girl. I was seduced by the very sight of him."

I sipped my iced tea and managed not to make a face, either at the sugared Southern style of the drink or at Madeleine Brown's *True Romance* magazine twaddle.

"At the time," she was saying, "a girl just starting out, I was working for the Glenn Advertising agency, only a few steps away from the Adolphus Hotel, where the party was held . . . in the Crystal Ballroom?"

Was she asking me? I wasn't there.

"He was just a typical Texan—both feet on the ground, smiling, warm, just terribly sexy. We were introduced by someone who did business with the agency, and I danced with the man of the hour, and it was so overwhelming, just to be in his arms."

Looked like it was going to be a long afternoon.

"Lyndon invited me to another party that night. This was next week at the Driskill Hotel in Austin. I said yes, and he had someone fly me there and I waited for him in his suite, but the only party was the two of us. I became his second wife that night."

Confused, I asked, "You were married?"

"No, my dear. But 'mistress' is a word with such unpleasant connotations. And when Steven was born, we became Lyndon's *other* family, though I never had the privilege of being called First Lady."

My hunch was that Johnson had his first lady when he was about thirteen.

Flo said, "Having a relationship with a married man must have been difficult for you."

"Oh, yes, I'm a good Catholic girl, you know. My parents raised me that way, and after every time I was with Lyndon, in those first years, I would go to church and confess. But then I would just turn right around and sin again. Anyway, our relationship was hidden to the outside world. No one but Lyndon's insiders ever knew."

"And God," I pointed out.

Flo shot me a flash of irritation.

But Madeleine merely nodded, saying, "And God, yes. A client at the agency was our cover-up man—he would alert me of Lyndon's arrival in town, or arrange travel to Austin or elsewhere, and the hotel room where I was to be, and tell my boss I was needed on business." She leaned toward Flo, woman-to-woman. "These are precious moments to me, fleeting moments to share with the man I loved."

Flo asked, "You knew he would never be yours?"

"That's right. There was plenty of romance—perfume, flowers, and material things, like this house and a new car every year. But there was also . . . do you embarrass easily, Mr. Heller?"

"I blush at card tricks," I said.

Flo gave me another quick look.

"Well, then hold on to your hat," she said (I was wearing the Panama by Stetson again), "because I intend to be frank, sir. While we certainly talked and enjoyed each other's company, these stolen moments were primarily sexual. We both enjoyed each other that way. He was a *wonderful* lover. A stallion between the sheets."

The thought of this cute dish in bed with LBJ was cringe-inducing.

Flo asked, "And when he found out you were expecting?"

"He was furious at first . . . then worried for us both. He was so terribly ambitious and already had his eye on the presidency. He feared the Mafia or somebody would find out about us and use it against him."

Kind of like she was doing now.

Madeleine gestured with an open hand, as if introducing a debutante. "You see, Lyndon was created by two millionaires from here, H. L. Hunt and Sid Richardson. I know them both well. You look skeptical, Mr. Heller. Well, Dallas is a small city, and it was smaller still in the '50s. Keep in mind, I was an account executive at the most important ad agency in town. I would figure and analyze budgets, direct client marketing, purchase media time, and travel to radio and TV stations all around the state. I rubbed shoulders with the high and the mighty. Take Hunt, for instance. I saw him every weekday morning—we parked our cars side by side in the same lot."

I asked, "Why was Hunt backing Johnson? LBJ's a liberal in many ways, and even a guy from Chicago knows that H. L. Hunt is just slightly to the right of Attila the Hun."

Her smile was wide and those dimples were something. "Oh, yes, Hunt's a John Birch Society boy. He's the one that backed that 'treason' ad in the paper the day Kennedy came to town, and passed out circulars calling the President a traitor. But H.L. *believed* in Lyndon, and in the power of money. Funny thing is, he dressed like some poor old man. Richest man in America, in near rags."

Flo asked, "What did Hunt think of John Kennedy?"

"Oh, hated him like poison, of course. But H.L. was practical, and patient."

I asked, "Patient how?"

"Well, when Lyndon was going to lose the nomination for President, back at the '60 convention? Hunt got together with old Joe Kennedy and worked out a deal for Lyndon to get on the ticket. That's how he became VP, even though JFK couldn't stand him. And Hunt said to me, 'We may have lost a battle, honey, but we'll win the war.' "

"Meaning?"

"I'll let you draw your own conclusions, Mr. Heller. Nate. I *will* say that after the assassination, H.L. told me, 'Well, we won the war!' "

"You're saying Hunt was behind the assassination."

"I'd call him the . . . linchpin of the oilmen around here. Some say Lyndon was behind it, and I asked him, point-blank, right next to me in bed, and he said that was bullshit, that it was Texas oil and those . . . pardon my French . . . 'fucking renegade intelligence bastards.' "

"For what reason?"

"Kennedy was calling for big cuts in the oil depletion allowance. He was stopping mergers under antitrust. The market dropped, steel fell. And he was gonna close a bushel of military bases here and overseas, and was gonna pull out of Vietnam. *And* he was talking about dismantling the CIA. I mean, he did fire that Allen Dulles *and* his second in command, our mayor's brother. Mayor Cabell changed the motorcade route that day, you know. . . . More iced tea, Nate?"

"No. No, I'm fine."

She smiled impishly. "Here's something nobody outside of Dallas knows. H. L. Hunt and Jack Ruby are pals. Jack used to set up these great poker games for Hunt—old boy's an avid poker player."

"You know Jack Ruby?"

"Everybody around here does. You *do* know the Carousel was right across from the Adolphus? If you passed Jack on the street, and you didn't know him, he would stop you and give you his Carousel Club card. Jack was everywhere in those days. He knew everybody in the Dallas Police Department. *He* hated Kennedy, too."

I gave her half a smile. "Madeleine, you don't seem like the type to hang out at a strip joint."

"Oh, I'm not. I don't know if I was *ever* there during regular hours. They opened at seven-thirty P.M., I believe. No, Jack liked to be around important people—said they were 'classy.' He'd open up in the afternoon, or any time, really, for fellas like Hunt or anybody in politics or business to duck in for a little privacy or fun. Fix 'em up with gambling or girls. I heard Jack Ruby could have somebody beat up for fifteen bucks and killed for a hundred. No, Jack was a buddy."

She seemed awfully cavalier about murder, for a nice Catholic girl serving up too-sweet tea on a patio surrounded by flowers.

Flo asked, "What was your reaction when Ruby killed Oswald?"

Madeleine paused. For once, the free-flowing words stopped and she chose them carefully. "I thought he was at the police station because somebody asked him to do that, and he had no other choice than to do it."

Flo leaned forward. "I understand you saw Lyndon the night before the assassination."

The dark eyes flashed and so did a smile. "Yes, he surprised me that night. I didn't know he would be there. I was asked to attend a party at Clint Murchinson's residence—he's another of those oilmen behind Lyndon. His son John was living there at the time, because Clint had a stroke—like old Joe Kennedy—and was moved to more accommodating quarters . . . although he was there that night, all right."

I asked, "What was the occasion of the party?"

"It was in honor of Edgar Hoover. He was a big pal of Clint's and of Lyndon's. Then, of course you know, Edgar was a lifelong bachelor, and had his friend Clyde Tolson with him to . . . you know, several of those oilmen were life-long bachelors, too. They all loved horse-racing and gambling, and they would go off on these holidays together, and, well that's neither here nor there. Where was I?"

"The party," Flo said.

"The party! Well, the guest list couldn't have been more impressive. For example, Richard Nixon was there . . ."

I said, "*Nixon* was in Dallas during the assassination? Does he have an alibi?"

That last had been kidding on the square.

Flo said to me, "Nixon was in town for Pepsi Cola. They were a client of his legal firm." She nodded to our hostess. "Please continue."

"Well, Hunt was there, Sid Richardson, George Brown . . . George brought Hoover in on his private plane. All the oilmen, who I call the Great White Fathers. Bankers like John McCloy, who's on the Warren Commission. And all kinds of society people from Dallas. But Lyndon didn't get there till the party was breaking up, at eleven or even midnight. And he and Hunt and a few others, including Nixon and Hoover, went into the library and locked themselves in for, oh, maybe ten minutes."

She paused to sip her iced tea.

"When Lyndon came out of there, he saw me and came up and he was red in the face. Like he'd got himself an instant sunburn in there. He had this just . . . dreadful look. I asked what was wrong, and he whispered, in this terrible grating voice, 'After tomorrow, those damn Kennedys will never stand in my way again. That's not a threat, it's a promise.' I'll never forget that. How could I?"

Flo said, "Do you realize what you're implying?"

"I do. But I don't know what happened in that room. I don't know what was discussed. Maybe somebody shared inside news that Lyndon was being dropped from the ticket, and he intended to tell Jack Kennedy off."

Or perhaps he'd been told of the imminent assassination and had worked himself up some righteous outrage over previous Kennedy humiliations to help rationalize his role in the crime, even if that role was simply foreknowledge.

Flo said, "Forgive me, Madeleine, but my tracking of the whereabouts of the major figures in the case puts Johnson at his hotel at the time. He was *seen*."

She waved that off. "Lyndon had a look-alike cousin who filled in for him, if he was slipping out. Somebody who could pass for him, if it wasn't up close or in conversation."

I guess his mistress would know.

"Now, not *everybody* still at the party went into that private conference," she was saying. "For example, Mac Wallace didn't."

I about fell out of the chair. Flo, who knew of Wallace through me, glanced my way, knowing I'd react.

I said, "You *know* Mac Wallace?"

"Sure do, bless his heart. He's Lyndon's number one hatchet man, and that's not exactly a figure of speech. Mac made seventeen, eighteen people disappear that I know of, or anyway strongly suspect. You know, he was a man with a future, smart as a whip, but then he got mixed up in that love triangle with Lyndon's no-good sister, and lost his head and shot that poor golfer. Lyndon bought his friend out of that jam, but you know, that was the end of any kind of normal life for Mac."

"You don't hold it against him, being a murderer?"

"Oh, I kind of feel sorry for him. He's certainly a terrible man now, but once he was so promising." Her eyes tightened as something occurred to her. "You know, we had this wonderful colored girl who all but raised my two boys when I went back to work at the ad agency. She was with us for many years. She traveled with us, and one time on a trip to San Antonio, I believe it was, she accidentally came in on Lyndon and me at a most inopportune moment. She scurried out, and Lyndon said, 'Say good-bye to her.' I thought he was joshing, but she disappeared the next day. No one has seen her since. I asked an attorney who's been my go-between with Lyndon if he knew what became of her. And he said, 'What do you think? Mac Wallace.' . . . Now, Mr. Heller, you look dry as a bone. I simply have to refresh your tea."

She took the glass from my hand and went off to do that while Flo and I looked at each other in blank amazement.

Then Madeleine was handing me back my tall glass and I said, "Doesn't it bother you, these killings?"

She sat. "Killings bother any Christian, Mr. Heller. Why, I would mourn the untimely demise of any person. But these were political decisions. They were deemed necessary. We're not talking about just any man. We're talking about a powerhouse of a man who became the President of the United States. A man I love very much. He did what he had to do, to do the very good things that he has done. For Negroes. For the poor."

I could think of one "poor" Negro he hadn't done anything good for—the nanny who raised her boys.

Madeleine's expression was grave now, her brown eyes boring in on me—no pixie in them at all. "Had the assassination not happened the day it did, Lyndon would probably have gone to prison—or at least the Kennedys would have shuffled him out of public life in some way. All because of his involvement with two good friends, two wonderful men, Billie Sol Estes and Bobby Baker. Funny how some of the people who were going to testify against Lyndon found themselves in the middle of homosexual scandals, or like that Marshall fella, who shot himself five times."

"Mac Wallace," I said.

"Yes, Nate," she said pleasantly. "Without a doubt. And Flo? Can you understand why it is that you can't use my name? Next time Mac Wallace is in town, I don't want him dropping by."

CHAPTER 13

The twenty-two story building at 3525 Turtle Creek Boulevard, of tinted, reinforced concrete and Mexican brick, was the most prestigious apartment house in Dallas.

Built in 1957, 3525 (as it was known) was home to such famous residents as Greer Garson, Jimmy Dean, Senator John Tower, Fabian, and assorted oilmen and wealthy widows. The restaurant off the spacious, modern lobby, the Turtle Room—with its continental cuisine and seventeen-foot, floor-to-ceiling windows on three sides, looking onto magnificent landscaping—was open to the public. The on-site nightspot, Club 3525, however, was for private members only, though of course Flo Kilgore was an honored guest, on the off chance she might mention the place in her nationally syndicated column.

3525 had made the papers before—a while back, a socialite's body had been found floating in the swimming pool; then department-store widow Minnie Marcus had been relieved of seventy grand in jewelry in a daring robbery; and, not long ago, the club had been raided by the city vice squad for after-hours drinking (the more elderly residents had complained about the noise).

Detective Nathan Heller of Chicago was investigating none of these crimes. Instead I was spending a quiet evening at 3525, first dining on French fare at the Turtle Room in a setting rich with teak and polished crystal, and then in the club, listening to the Bill

Black Combo play jazz with a saxy flare that wouldn't have been wrong for the Colony. Eat your heart out, Bill Peck and his Peckers.

The crowd here was young, at least for 3525—couples in their thirties and forties, Twisting and Frugging on a small dance floor by the modest stage, pretending they were in their twenties. The room was black booths and mirrored walls with red-and-blue stripper lighting on the stage and dance floor.

Needless to say, I didn't spot Greer Garson.

Flo had spoken to a number of fans, but signed few autographs, as this was too hip a room for that. She looked very mod in a yellow white-polka-dotted miniskirted dress, with a matching bow in her indestructible bouffant, as seen on TV. She was trying too hard to look young, but the lighting helped.

"Bill Black isn't in the combo anymore," she said when they went on break. "Ailing."

We were sitting close in a booth for four, a martini for her, a vodka gimlet for me.

"Used to be Elvis's backup band," I said, showing off.

"That's old news. Early this year, they opened for the Beatles—at the Beatles' request—on their first American tour."

"They're going to be here next week."

"Bill Black?"

"The Beatles."

She smiled a little. "Surely not at Club 3525."

"Only after hours. They're going to be at Memorial Auditorium a week from tonight."

This was Friday. Since Monday, we had interviewed fifteen witnesses, and Flo had plenty of material for an assassination exposé, perfect to appear right after the Warren Commission announced its results, at the end of the month.

But she remained disappointed that I hadn't been able to arrange an interview with Jack Ruby. That seemed out of the question, for this trip anyway, because we were both set to fly out tomorrow, her to New York and *What's My Line?*, and me to Chicago and the A-1 Detective Agency.

I had talked to Barney Ross on the phone several times, in his office at the Milton Blackstone ad agency in Manhattan. Though we had all grown up on the West Side, Barney was much closer to Ruby than I was.

"Belli's not going to be involved in the appeal," Barney said, meaning Ruby's famous defense lawyer. "His new defense team is led by a guy named Clinton. Sam Houston Clinton."

It would be.

"I got feelers out," Barney said, "to find somebody I know who knows this guy. If I can get the new man to pass my message along to Sparky, you'll get in."

Sparky was Ruby.

I said, "They may want you as a character witness again."

Barney, as a famous ex–boxing champ, had testified for Ruby at the Oswald murder trial. Ruby had been convicted in March. Justice moved fast in Texas. Or anyway something moved fast.

"Maybe not," Barney said, and sounded embarrassed. "Some people say my testimony worked against Jack. Because of my drug habit."

Barney, who'd been a Marine and served with me in the Pacific, had come back from Guadalcanal addicted to morphine, whereas I'd come back mildly nuts enough to rate a Section Eight. Checking himself into a VA hospital for help, Barney had famously kicked the monkey on his back.

But the prosecution had used Barney's addiction—and that as kids, he and Ruby ran errands for Al Capone—to suggest Barney was some kind of mobbed-up lowlife. In the scheme of things, his testimony hadn't mattered, but it had been an embarrassment for the ex-champ.

"You know," Barney was saying, "I helped raise money for the defense, on the first trial, and I'll offer to do the same on the next one."

"That should get a lawyer's attention."

"They say money talks."

"And whispers and screams. Just see what you can do."

I told him I'd be in Dallas through Saturday.

I'd also been on the phone with Captain Clint Peoples in Waco, calling him about checking on Rose Cheramie's seemingly absurd story. Just yesterday the Ranger had called me back, confirming it.

"Everything the Cheramie girl told you lines up with what the trooper, Frank Fruge, says," Peoples reported.

"So what?" I said. "It could still all just be a wild story she told Fruge."

"Well, keep in mind Fruge did find her along the roadside where she'd been dumped. And because of the Kennedy angle, he checked up on the details of her story."

"Yeah? Such as?"

"Seems the girl mentioned names in the drug scheme—of the boat, of the sailor, and the hotel in Houston where she had a reservation under an alias, which she also gave the trooper."

"And it all checked out?"

"To a tee. Fruge even took her to Houston to work with the Customs people, for her to help them take the drug ring down. But apparently word got to her accomplices and the thing fell apart."

"I didn't know about that. She didn't mention it."

"Well, Nate, the key thing is, the Customs folks say the names she gave 'em were all known for criminal narcotics activity. And that Rose's story remained consistent with no discrepancies."

"Thank you, Clint. I appreciate this."

"It might be a good lead into the Kennedy killing."

"Yeah, if anybody was investigating it."

"Aren't *you*, Nate?"

"Don't spread it around. Listen, Clint, you said the Rangers keep tabs on Mac Wallace."

"Well, this Ranger does."

"He's checked out of the Adolphus, you know."

"I *do* know. Early this week. What you may not know is he's back in California, at his day job for Ling in Anaheim. Home of Disneyland?"

I had a sudden flash of following Wallace into the "It's a Small World" boat ride and drowning him.

"Thanks," I said. "I'll have my A-1 people out there confirm that."

Right now the Bill Black Combo was playing their big hit, "White Silver Sands," inspiring Flo to drag me out on the little dance floor to Twist to it. The crowd was old enough that in the subdued club lighting I could get away with it. You might consider it just plain sad that a man zeroing in sixty would make a fool out of himself that way, but it made my spine pop and saved me a trip to the chiropractor.

We were on the dance floor when Janet AKA Jada came in—I'd asked her to join us after her last set at the Colony. She had left her stage makeup on and wore a lime-green fringed go-go dress that barely covered what Jack Ruby used to turn the lights down to conceal.

Seeing me doing the Twist made her laugh giddily, and who could blame her? She joined us on the dance floor (to "Don't Be Cruel") and we were a threesome, if not exactly like the one Rose Cheramie made with those two Cubans. Whether any of this crowd knew she was the famous/infamous Jada of the Carousel, I couldn't tell you.

But when she started to go to town, smiling big, eyes flashing, unleashing tendrils from the tower of red hair, the rippling fringe going a hundred miles an hour, the other dancers (including Flo and me) simply gave up and gathered around, clapping to the band's infectious beat and smiling just as big as Janet.

When the combo started in on "Harlem Nocturne," nice and easy and jazzy, Janet latched on to me for a slow dance, and Flo—with a funny little smile—graciously capitulated, heading back to the booth.

With her curvy body plastered to me, Janet buried her face in my neck. "Why don't you come home with me tonight?"

"It'd be rude."

"I can't believe you'd rather fuck that skinny bitch than me."

She ground herself into my groin. Soon she murmured into my ear, "*Hello* there. I remember *you*. . . ."

"First of all," I whispered, "she's not a bitch. She's a lovely woman, and she isn't skinny. She's got a nice figure."

"As nice as mine?"

"And second, I'm not fucking her. I'm working for her as an investigator. You know that."

"You've fucked her before, though, right?"

"This is a pretty swanky club for that kind of talk."

"I thought so."

We moved in a little circle on the crowded dance floor, smoke floating like fog, or was that steam?

"Anyway," I managed, "we aren't an item, you and me. You can't be jealous."

"I'm not jealous in general, Heller."

"Oh?"

"I'm just jealous tonight. . . ."

Adjusting my trousers as I came down off the slightly elevated dance floor, glad for the subdued lighting, I let Janet lead me by one hand to the booth, where I slid in beside Flo, and Janet slid in after me. In four decades as a private eye, I'd never been so pleasantly surrounded.

We chatted. The band was loud but not deafening, and we were toward the rear. Janet asked how the investigation was going, we said fine, Flo thanked her for her help lining up the other Carousel girls, that kind of thing. Janet reported a good house this evening for both shows at the Colony and that Beverly Oliver, back on the bill, got a nice reception.

But we were having to raise our voices somewhat to be heard, and I suggested we go outside and find a quiet place to talk.

The pool—where I was pleased to see no corpse floating—was a circular affair that fed a little waterfall that emptied into a smaller pool, the two levels nestling in an angle of the building adjacent to a natural ravine. The terraced area overlooked a city park; the night was warm with no humidity, the sky a Maxfield Parrish blue with a scattering of stars, as if Mrs. Marcus's stolen jewels had been cast there carelessly. The muffled sound of Bill Black playing their hit "Smokie" provided background music, and somewhere in the night a dog barked, but not keeping time. We found a trio of white deck-style chairs and had this little patch of Texas heaven to ourselves.

Flo seemed somewhat confused, having no idea why I'd want to talk to Janet about anything, while Janet just seemed pleased by the attention.

"Something occurred to me just the other day," I said to the exotic dancer, "that should have much sooner."

"Oh?"

"Mac Wallace's presence all those evenings at the Colony Club may not have been innocent."

Janet laughed once. "Nothing is innocent about Mac Wallace."

"That's good to keep in mind. When I arrived in Dallas, I was looking at Wallace in terms of suspicious deaths related to the Billie Sol Estes scandal."

Janet nodded. "Helping suicides along."

"Right. But as you know, Flo and I have been looking at the assassination, looking hard. And it's a crime littered with dead witnesses. Many of them have died the same kind of suspicious deaths as those tied to the Billie Sol Estes case."

Flo, getting it just a beat before Janet, said, "Wallace may be responsible."

"I doubt there's one person responsible. I believe it's a kind of a cleanup crew." I turned to Janet. "And it's possible that Wallace was at the Colony Club to watch you."

Her small sneer was big with self-confidence. "*All* the men who come to the Colony Club are there to watch me."

"Not that kind of watch. The keeping tabs kind. He may have been stalking you. Getting your patterns down."

The smile disappeared. "Am I in danger, Nate?"

"You may be. Wallace isn't in Dallas right now, but again . . . others on this cleanup crew may well be. Do you own a gun?"

She nodded. "A little .22. Should I carry it?"

"You should. Don't leave the club at night alone. Don't put yourself at risk. What's your upcoming schedule?"

"Tomorrow night I'm wrapping up the engagement at the Colony. I'm off to New Orleans for two weeks."

"The Sho-Bar?"

She nodded.

"That's a Marcello place," I said, more to myself than them.

"One of them," Janet said. "Carlos isn't there a lot, but I know him."

"Are you friendly?"

"As far as it goes."

"If you see him, make nice."

"How nice? Sex nice?"

"That's up to you and your conscience, but I would suggest you let him know, without saying anything directly, that you can be trusted. That you are discreet."

Janet's eyes flashed wide. "Discreet? What about talking to you and Miss Kilgore the other day?"

Flo, picking right up, said, "Your name won't be used. You'll be a reliable source close to the Dallas club scene. That's a very common journalistic practice."

"Okay," Janet said. She sighed. Nodded. "Okay. . . . Listen, Nate, suddenly I'm not in the mood for drinking and dancing. Walk me out to my car, would you? I'd feel safer."

"Sure," I said. I turned to Flo. "See if you can reclaim our booth, or find a new one."

Flo nodded and went back inside.

Janet took my hand and walked me around the building, skirting cabanas curved around one side of the pool, and across manicured grounds overlooking the wooded view of the nearby park. The parking lot was filled with luxury vehicles, including her white Caddy convertible, which awaited, its top up. I opened the driver-side door for her and she got behind the wheel.

"You really do care about me, don't you?" she said, looking up at me, the paleness of her pretty face emphasized by moon- and starlight. Her blue eyes, with their oriental cast, seemed to stroke my face.

"I do," I admitted.

She reached over and unzipped me and fished out the part of me that was most interested. I glanced around. The parking lot was empty but for a couple on the other side, drunkenly stumbling toward their car. I was still looking in that direction when her mouth slowly, moist and warm, slid down the shaft, about halfway, and then began an increasing tempo, as she went deeper and faster.

I was almost there when she grinned up at me and asked, "Would you like to get in back of the Caddy? Nice and roomy."

What did she think I was, some high-school kid?

She slipped off the shoulder straps of her fringed go-go dress and tugged the thing to her waist and her small, pert breasts, thrust toward me by her prominent rib cage, met the cool air with a sharpening of their points, which were almost as red as her lipsticked mouth.

"I wouldn't mind," I said.

I wasn't gone long enough to be suspicious—fifteen minutes maybe, and it wasn't like Flo and I were having a thing. It was strictly a working relationship, although admittedly with a certain intimacy suggestive of what we had once been to each other.

We didn't dance again and conversation slowed. I'd risked a third gimlet, and she was on maybe her fifth martini, when I suggested we head back to the Statler. The first half of the drive back was silent, until she stopped pouting about whatever she imagined had happened (even if it had) and apparently started thinking about her story again.

She said, "Could somebody have been impersonating Oswald, at some of these sightings?"

She was referring to a handful of stories we'd heard from witnesses, in which the supposed assassin appeared to be purposefully attracting attention prior to the killing.

Albert Bogard, car salesman at Downtown Lincoln-Mercury, said that on November 9, Oswald test-drove a vehicle, Bogard riding along, as was customary. Oswald zoomed around the freeway at seventy MPH in a new Mercury Comet, as if trying to make an impression. Back at the showroom, Oswald—he wrote "Lee Oswald" on the back of a business card of Bogard's—said he was interested but didn't have the money right now. But a job coming up soon would make him flush, and he'd be back. (On the other hand, Oswald's widow, Marina, had told the authorities that her late husband did not know how to drive.)

Wednesday morning, November 20, a heavyset young man and a young woman entered the office of American Aviation Company at Red Bird Air Field, on the Dallas outskirts; waiting in their car, in the passenger seat, was a man in his early twenties. They approached American Aviation's owner, Wayne January, wanting to rent a small plane for Friday afternoon. They would be flying to southeast Mexico, near Cuba, and asked detailed questions about the available Cessna—how far could it go without refueling, what was its speed, how did it perform in certain wind conditions? It sounded like a recipe more for hijacking than rental, and January refused their business. He watched the irritated couple join the man in the car, January's suspicions (perhaps purposefully) aroused. He took a good hard look at the sullen young man who hadn't come in. Later he recognized that man as Lee Harvey Oswald, or someone who closely resembled him.

Several employees and patrons of the Sports Drome Rifle Range reported seeing Oswald behaving (in the words of one) in a "loud and obnoxious" manner. In early October, Malcolm Price helped Oswald adjust the scope on an Italian Mauser rifle. On November 17, Garland Slack said Oswald was next to him on the range, and Oswald suddenly began shooting at Slack's target instead of his own, in a rapid-fire fashion. When Slack objected, Oswald gave him "a dirty look I'll never forget."

On the morning of November 21, a hitchhiker carrying a brown-paper-wrapped package (about four by four and a half, containing "curtain rods") was picked up by refrigeration repair man Ralph Yates. Conversationally, he asked if Yates had ever been to the Carousel Club, and later wondered aloud if the President on his upcoming visit could be assassinated by a sniper in a high window. The passenger got off at the corner of Elm and Houston. Yates discussed the disturbing incident with a co-worker before the assassination, after which he took his tale to the FBI.

"It's possible someone was trying to incriminate Oswald," I said, "before the fact."

"With a *double*? That's crazy."

"LBJ has a double, if Madeleine Brown is to be believed. Worked for Mussolini and Hitler, didn't it?"

"Nate, that's spy stuff. How would a nobody like Lee Harvey Oswald get caught up in something like that?"

"Who knows?" I said. "It's a conspiracy involving some high-level people. Anything is possible, I guess."

I couldn't tell her what Bobby Kennedy had confirmed: that Oswald was an asset of both the FBI and CIA, and that the latter agency was eminently capable of such a deception.

"Maybe," she said thoughtfully, very coherent for a woman who'd downed five martinis, "it explains how Deputy Craig could see Oswald getting picked up in a station wagon when other witnesses put him on a bus and then a taxi."

"And maybe," I said, wishing I could say more, "it explains how an assassin resembling Oswald could be at a window on the sixth floor of the book depository when the real Lee H. was sitting in the lunchroom, sipping a Coke."

"Did you have sex with her?"

"Huh?"

"That vulgar stripper! Don't deny it. I can smell her on you."

"Don't be silly," I said.

Guess I should have washed up before joining her back at the club.

I dropped Flo at the front of the Statler without a word, expecting her to have gone up to her room by the time I got back from the parking lot across the street, but she was waiting just inside.

"You walked her to her car," she said. Her big blue eyes were wide in a porcelain face as emotionless as a bisque baby's. "You were worried about *her.* Can't you at least show me to my room?"

"Sure."

We got on the elevator and she stepped away from me, putting some distance between us. We were alone in the car.

We'd passed a few floors when she said, "Take me to your room . . . not for sex! I *told* you there's a man in my life. I don't want you and I don't need you, understand? But . . . please?"

Wasn't this the goddamnedest argument I'd ever had?

"Sure," I said.

She came over and grabbed on to my arm with both of hers and pressed herself close. "I'm afraid. All this talk of . . . I'm *afraid.* You were afraid for her, weren't you? Don't you think that, that . . . *cleanup* crew of yours might want to do me harm?"

"Could," I admitted.

So we went to my room. She sat on the twin bed currently in its couch formation, with cushions propped against the wall. I turned on a table lamp, giving us not much more light than Club 3525.

"What do you have to drink?" she asked. She was sitting with her legs tucked up under her, heels kicked off, her polka-dot dress hiked, plenty of nice leg showing. But at my age, if she was here for sex, she'd better be prepared to wait a while.

I sat next to her and plucked the silly bow from her hair and tossed it somewhere. "Water from the faucet is what I have to drink."

"Very funny."

"There's a pop machine and ice down the hall. Glad to make the trip."

"Call room service. Get some gin and tonic."

"I don't like gin."

"I don't care what you like. Order something for yourself, too. *Herald Tribune* will pay for it."

"You've had enough to drink."

"That's your opinion. You work for me."

"Not right now. I'm off the clock."

She hit my chest with a little fist. "Gin and tonic. Right now! . . . Please?" She looked like she was going to cry. "I'm scared. You scared me tonight."

I didn't think so. I didn't think this little dame would scare unless maybe a goddamn bear was chasing her.

I asked, "What's this really about?"

Her chin crinkled. "My guy . . . my guy hasn't returned even *one* of my calls all week."

She wasn't talking about her husband.

"Sorry," I said.

"And then you . . . you haven't even had the decency of throwing me a pass. And tonight, you take that little slut out to her car, and what did you do? Fuck her in the backseat?"

She was a girl reporter, all right.

I said, "Don't be ridiculous. Janet was just scared, like you are."

"I *said* I could smell her on you! You think I would let you stick it in me after you stuck it in her? Christ knows what diseases she's carrying. Maybe she'll get pregnant! Think you'll live long enough to go to Junior's graduation?"

I took her by her spindly arms. "First, there already is a Nathan Heller, Jr. Second, it could be a girl. Third, no it couldn't, because I used a Trojan. I was in the Boy Scouts, you know."

Really I wasn't, but my words were like a splash of cold water in her face, and then she started to laugh and hugged me.

"Nathan Heller," she said, giggling, but it didn't sound happy exactly. "You are a scamp."

"Is that what I am?"

She pushed me away. "Now get me my gin and tonic."

"Okay," I said, and went over to the phone, but as I was reaching for it, it rang.

"Heller speaking," I said.

"Nate, it's Clint Peoples," the receiver said, as if that voice needed any identifying. "I'm goddamn sorry to call you so late like this, but I thought you should know."

"Know what, Clint?"

"The Cheramie girl is dead."

I grabbed a nearby chair and sat. "Christ."

"An auto-pedestrian accident near Big Sandy."

"What's Big Sandy?"

"A town in Texas, man, what do you think? Apparently Rose was just lyin' in the roadway with her suitcases scattered around and a driver came along and tried to swerve and miss her. He didn't. He struck her, just part of her, but . . . her skull was crushed."

"Jesus."

"That's all I know. I mean, this thing just happened. Came in over the wire. I will make calls tomorrow and have more for you later. Sorry to be the bearer."

"Thanks, Clint."

We both hung up.

Then I called down for the gin and tonic.

She stayed with me that night. She was afraid, as well she should be, and she drank herself to sleep. We did not have sex, if your prurient interest must be satisfied. She stayed in her dress, I was down to my underwear, my nine millimeter naked on the nightstand. We talked very little, before she drifted off, although the sense that we had caused that poor woman's death was there in the room with us, hogging the space.

Before the gin took her away, I said, "You'll go home. I'll go home. You'll write your story, and maybe win a Pulitzer. But that's all."

"What do you mean . . . that's all?"

"I mean the investigation ends here. You write your story, enjoy your accolades, and you can prime the pump for other investigators, whether cops or reporters, and let them follow your lead, and them take the heat. We don't get anybody else killed, understand? Not you. Not me."

She toasted her glass with mine. I'd sent down for some Captain Morgan.

"Okay, big boy," she said.

Her tiny, curvy body snuggled next to me in the twin bed, and with her in my arms, I remembered how much fun we'd had together in years gone by, which is what years do.

An insistent ringing turned out to be the phone again. My eyes somehow came open and I realized sunlight was streaming in. Our respective plane reservations weren't till the early afternoon, so we hadn't overslept, at least not dangerously. There was no reason to get up, or hadn't been till the phone started in.

She stirred, and I whispered, "Probably Captain Peoples again. Just go back to sleep."

She did, and I got the phone. I had a brief conversation, hung up, and came back and shook her gently awake. Her eyes were wide in a face that was pretty despite the smeared makeup and weak chin.

"That was Barney," I said.

"Who?"

"We got the Ruby interview."

CHAPTER 14

The Criminal Courts Building, overlooking Dealey Plaza, stood nine granite-trimmed brick-and-steel stories. The 1913-erected structure housed two Dallas county criminal courts, the offices of the sheriff and DA, and the county jail, which was a building within a building. Jailbreaks were impossible, it was said, until one occurred recently and embarrassed Dallas yet again.

Saturday morning, at ten o'clock, with Flo in the passenger seat, I pulled the rental Galaxie into the shallow basement of the Courts Building, eerily similar to the city jail basement where Ruby had shot Oswald. We got out and headed toward the elevator. We looked spiffy—I was in a gray Botany 500 (*not* tailored for a shoulder-holstered weapon, which was tucked in the car trunk) and Flo in a pink suit with leopard top and white heels and her usual white gloves. I felt we projected the class with which Ruby was so obsessed.

Joe Tonahill was waiting at the elevator, the only attorney from the murder trial who remained on the current Ruby team. The Stetson-wearing Tonahill (I was bareheaded today) was an aptly named mountain of a man, six four and three hundred pounds easy, with a narrow skull, out-of-control John L. Lewis eyebrows, and a shelf of a second chin that seemed to engulf the almost boyish face.

Tonahill smiled and nodded to Flo, saying, "Always a pleasure, Miss Kilgore. You're the only reporter Jack will talk to."

"Well, I'm honored," she said with a funny smile that added, *I guess.*

The small head on the huge body swiveled my way. "You'd be Nathan Heller," he said affably, and we shook hands. "I read about you in the *Enquirer.*"

"That puts the 'any PR is good PR' notion to the test," I said, as we exchanged smiles. "What's the drill?"

He gestured toward the elevator. "Jack, as you might expect, is kept separate from the general population. He doesn't even have a cell of his own."

"That doesn't *sound* like he's being kept separate."

"Sorry. I didn't phrase that as felicitously as I might. He's camped out in a corridor on the mezzanine level between the sixth and seventh floors. By the chief jailor's office. There *is* a little holding cell he can sleep in."

Tonahill reached suddenly inside his tan suit coat and for a moment I flashed on Lee Harvey getting surprised. But all he withdrew was a folded sheet of paper.

"I'm accompanying you up, but Jack has made it clear I'm not welcome to sit in on the interview. How would you feel about signing a document that has you working for me as an investigator, Mr. Heller? Providing you with the rights of confidentiality that Miss Kilgore enjoys as a member of the Fourth Estate?"

I looked at it. Simple and straightforward, it required my signature and for Tonahill to pay me "the sum of $1 and other good and valuable consideration." He handed me a pen and I leaned the page against the closed elevator door and signed it.

Handing the contract back to him, with one of my cards, I said, "I'll want a photostat of that for my files."

"Certainly," he said, and his smile was as tiny as he wasn't. He pressed the elevator button with a forefinger that made it disappear.

"You're forgetting something," I said.

His tufted eyebrows rose. "Oh?"

"Where's my dollar?"

He grinned and got out his wallet and I was slipping the buck in my pocket when the elevator doors dinged open. We got on board and Tonahill pressed 6-M.

Soon we were stepping into a vestibule and facing an office with E.L. HOLMAN, CHIEF JAILOR in black-edged gold on a light-brown door. We did not enter the office. Instead, a deputy at a barred gate at right recognized Tonahill, nodded, and allowed us into a narrow hallway. The deputy stayed at his post while Flo and I followed Tonahill, moving down the straight path to another gate and another deputy. Three more deputies were on the other side, the quartet of deputies the literal guards at Ruby's gate. Two of them sat at a little metal table in the white-walled windowless end-of-the-corridor space, which opened up into what might have served as a reception area, with another office door at left and a steel door at right. They were playing cards with their charge.

"Gin!" Jack Ruby said, and, hearing the metal grind and whine of the gate opening, threw his cards in and got to his feet with a smile. "Miss Kilgore. Nate Heller! What a pleasure to have such high-class company."

Ruby came over quickly, his thinning hair slicked back George Raft–style, his face freshly shaved. He looked a little like Uncle Fester, minus the lightbulb in his mouth, the black pajamas traded in for trim white short-sleeve jail coveralls, though his loafers and socks were *Addams Family* black.

He took Flo by the hand, in a gentlemanly way, as if about to ask her for the first dance. "This is such a rare, wonderful opportunity."

He didn't say whether that applied to him or her.

Then Ruby offered me a sweaty hand to shake, and I did, as he said to Flo, "You may not know this, but Nate and me go back to the West Side. We grew up together."

That was an exaggeration, of course, but not exactly a lie.

"How's Barney?" he asked, walking us over to the metal table, which the pair of deputies had vacated. They had left the cards behind. Tonahill was still standing near the gate, where all four deputies had now gathered, like flies around offal.

"Barney's doing fine," I said. "I'm grateful he arranged this."

Ruby waved that off. "Anything for Barney. He raised a hell of a lot of dough for my defense."

"He's going to do the same for your appeal, he says."

"What a stand-up guy. What a stand-up guy. Listen." He leaned in and whispered to me. He smelled of Old Spice. His eyes were like black buttons sewn onto his face, only buttons blinked more. "I can't let that lawyer sit in. I don't know if I trust him."

"You haven't fired him."

"Not yet. But this meet is strictly for you and Miss Kilgore. This is a one-of-a-kind interview, Nate. You are about to sit down with history. You want some water? I don't think I can talk them into coffee or anything, unless you're still here at lunch."

"No water, thanks," I said, and Flo said the same.

Tonahill hunkered in conference with one of the deputies, the oldest of the quartet. Then he came over and towered over us and said, "They've arranged for you to use room 7-M upstairs. It'll be more comfortable."

There was something accusatory in Ruby's pasty face as he said, "That's where Justice Warren interviewed me." He said this looking at Tonahill, then he turned to me and repeated it.

I said quietly, "I'm ahead of you, Jack. What do you see as our options?"

Ruby had already thought that over. "There's a visiting room on this floor, but I don't trust it any more than 7-M. That holding cell over there . . ."

He nodded toward a cubbyhole with its barred door swung open.

". . . is where I sleep and do my personal business."

He meant piss and shit.

He was shaking his bullet head. "Not appropriate for Miss Kilgore. Crowded and not what I would term pleasant—though I don't see how they would bug it."

I nodded. The only bugs in there would be cockroaches. But Jack was right, it wouldn't do.

Then I turned to Tonahill, who stood anxiously nearby like a guy waiting for an estimate from a shady auto mechanic. "Joe, see if you can get those deputies to stand down the hall a ways, on the other side of that gate. We're going to have our little talk with Jack right here."

Tonahill thought about that for maybe two seconds, nodded, said, "Okey dokey," and went over and ran it past the deputies. One went off to check with the chief jailor, but we went ahead and set up shop. I moved the little metal table flush against the far wall, and arranged Flo's chair so that her back would be to the deputies and Tonahill. I sat across from Ruby, who gathered the cards and set them to one side.

Tonahill got the okay, and he and the deputies positioned themselves on the other side of the gate, close enough to keep us in sight, far away enough to provide the privacy we needed.

Flo got the portable tape gizmo out and asked Ruby for permission to record him.

"Please," he said, nodding, so worked up he blinked once or twice. "Be my guest."

Then he folded his hands before him as if about to say grace and waited for the interview to begin.

Flo had a little notebook she was checking in, to make sure she hit every subject on her mind, and Ruby blurted, "Not everything pertaining to what's happened has come to the surface, you know."

"Is that right?" she said, flipping through pages, still getting ready.

"The world will never know the true facts of what occurred, my motives, unless you can get the story out. I trust you, Miss Kilgore. And Nate and me, like I say, we go way back—like me, he's had dealings with certain kinds of underworld types without ever selling his soul to them."

With a serious smile, I asked, "You never had to make that bargain, Jack? Isn't that what brought you here?"

His customary expression was that of a guy who just had water splashed in his face. "You got a point, Nate. I'm not sayin' you don't have a point. These people who have so much to gain and such an ulterior motive for . . . for putting me in the position I'm in, they'd do just about anything to keep the true facts from coming out to the world at large."

Flo finally jumped in. "Are these people in very high positions, Jack?"

"Yes." He unfolded his hands and, not hard, pounded a fist on the metal tabletop, making the deck of cards jump a little. "Yes! . . . You know, I *tried* to tell the truth to the Warren Commission."

She nodded. "Jack, I do know. I got an advance look at your testimony. But you told Justice Warren the same story you've *been* telling—about committing the crime for the sake of Jackie and Caroline Kennedy, to spare them the hardship of a trial."

A tiny smile flashed. "Don't you think I would make a good actor?" Now the high forehead clenched and he leaned in. "That was a story, Miss Kilgore, that my first attorney instructed me to tell. From the start, I wanted to tell the truth, but I couldn't, not here in Dallas. Not in this jail. I told Justice Warren, if they wanted to get the straight story out of me, they had to take me to Washington, D.C."

I said, "But they refused."

He gestured with open hands, eyes popping. "They refused! Why? *Why*? I said if they would take me back to Washington, that very night, and let me talk to the President, then I could prove I'm not guilty, and maybe something could still be salvaged."

Sitting forward, I said, "Jack, almost everybody in America was watching on that Sunday morning, and the rest have seen the instant replay—*you killed Oswald*. You can't be saying you're innocent of that."

"No, no, I'm not talking about that. Nate, you're a Jew—you know that there is no greater weapon you can use than to create this kind of falsehood about someone of the Jewish faith, especially of such a terrible heinous crime as the killing of President Kennedy."

Flo glanced at me and I at her, and she said to him, gently, "You feel you are being accused of killing the President?"

He nodded vigorously. "Of being part of a *conspiracy* to kill our beloved President."

I said, "Jack, you *hated* the Kennedys."

He shrugged. "I hate Bobby. I never had a problem with Jack. But if I am eliminated, there won't be *any* way of knowing what really happened. The Warren Commission, they muffed it, Nate, they eff you cee kayed it up, if you'll pardon the crudity, Miss Kilgore. I want to talk to LBJ, who I think has been told, I am *certain* has been told, I was part of a plot to assassinate the President."

"Why would Johnson have been told that?"

"Because . . . because he's been told. I know he's been told. By the people who plan to eliminate me."

Shaking her head, as if to clear cobwebs, Flo asked, "Who is going to try to eliminate you, Jack?

"They won't *try,* Miss Kilgore, they *will.* Maybe if you get out there with your story, I have a chance, but . . . you see, I have been used for a *purpose,* and there will be a tragic occurrence if you don't take my story to the people and somehow vindicate me, so Jews like me don't have to suffer because of what I have done."

I said, "That's what we're here for, Jack. To get your story, and get it out there."

"Good, because I may not be around for you to come and talk to again. You know, I told them I'd do a lie detector test, truth serum, anything. And then I could leave this world satisfied. I just don't want my people to be blamed for something that is untrue, for something that some wrongly claim has happened."

"Then your account of the Oswald shooting," I said, "was fabricated for you?"

"Yes. Yes. Yes."

"Then why do you keep repeating it?"

"Because the brave Jew killing the President's murderer is a good story. And because I have family. I don't want my brothers to die. I don't want my sister to die. I don't want my nieces and nephews to die. *I* do not want to die. But I am doomed just the same. And I am *not* insane. I was framed to kill Oswald."

I held up a calming hand and said, "Okay, okay. But let's back up. You hated Bobby, you said. You say you didn't hate the President, but Jack, nobody in mob circles loves *either* Kennedy."

He didn't deny it.

I pressed on: "So why are there so many reports that you were devastated by the President's death? That you were crying and weeping and wailing?"

"That's an exaggeration, but . . ." He gave me a knowing little grin. ". . . you were *always* smart, Nate. We've come a long way from that union hall in Lawndale, haven't we?"

Had we? That had involved a killing, too, of Leon Cooke, a former president of a junk-handler's union. Maybe Ruby had come a long way at that.

Now the stocky little man's focus was on me, perhaps because he knew I could follow him on the torturous journey ahead in a way that Flo Kilgore might not.

He said, "Maybe you don't know this, Nate, but back in the fifties, I was big in the Cuban realm, both before and after Castro took over. I made trips for people, I moved some guns, I helped Santo get out of there when they had him locked up. I was valuable, making things happen. But then when Castro threw all the casinos out, my influence, it was gone with the wind and, well, at least I had a life and a business back here in Dallas. I concentrated on that. That became my life and world. I was happy. I am competitive by nature. But you mentioned deals with the devil, Nate, right? And I admit, I like to be important, it's a weakness, but who doesn't savor the attention of powerful people?"

I said, "Can you be more specific, Jack?"

"Well, powerful people, they never talk to you direct, do they? So if I said Carlos Marcello, I would be trying to make myself sound more important than I am, and the humbling thing about what I've been through, Nate, is that I know I was not important. *Now* I am important, and that's the bittersweet taste, huh? Because now I wish I was not so important. I wish I was a small person again, a small successful person with his club and girls and his little dogs. I miss my little dogs, Nate."

"Jack, you say somebody contacted you on Marcello's behalf. Who? When?"

"A fella in New Orleans, smart guy, kind of on the weirdo side. We'll call him the Ferret. He's a pilot, in fact he and me, we go back a ways ourselves—we owned a plane together, in gunrunning days. I hadn't heard from him in a couple of years, not since the Bay of Pigs went south and all of the Cuba stuff went circling down the porcelain exit. Anyway, the Ferret—"

"David Ferrie," Flo said with a nod.

That startled Ruby, her knowing that name.

I asked, "What did Ferrie want?"

"He . . . he wanted some help with some projects the Cubans were working on."

"Cuban exiles."

"Yes. There's a big variety of different groups, but this is a pretty militant bunch, and well, sometimes I work both ends against the middle, and that can be dangerous, but it can also be profitable, and it covers a person's behind, you know."

She said, "You were an FBI snitch."

That startled him, too. And he seemed a little hurt.

"I guess you could state it like that, Miss Kilgore. That's a terminology that makes me uncomfortable, I would say 'informant' is a bit better, but yes. So I figured my FBI contact would not mind knowing what the Cubans were up to, and since casino interests like Mr. Marcello and Mr. Trafficante seemed to think Cuba might be returned to its former profitable glory so to speak, I lent my services, and my club after hours, for meetings and so on."

Flo asked, "You didn't hesitate getting involved again with these mobsters?"

"I was having money problems, tax trouble in particular, and anyway, I had business in Cuba with certain of these individuals that . . . Nate, can we *talk* about this in front of Miss Kilgore?"

"If you mean Operation Mongoose," I said, "yes."

That failed joint effort between the CIA and the Mob to kill Castro. That ridiculous French farce involving exploding cigars and poisoned food and tampered-with wet suits.

I said to him, "Miss Kilgore knows we were both part of that, each in his own small, respective way."

Dark eyebrows rose above eyes about as expressive as a shark's. "Does she know that . . . ?"

"That I ran into you in a bar in Chicago, in early November, last year? That you introduced me to your buddy 'Lee Osborne'? Yes."

Or, anyway, she did now.

This had taken some of the wind out of his sails, and I had to prompt him: "What mischief were the New Orleans mob and the Cubans up to? Or should I say, what did you *think* they were up to?"

". . . The idea was to embarrass the President," he said. His hands were folded again and he was looking at them. He seemed smaller suddenly. "Embarrass Kennedy with a phony pro-Castro demonstration when he came to Dallas. I think those oil-money Birchers who were in bed with Marcello and the Cubans were afraid that Kennedy was cozying up to the Beard. But that's just a small-time nightclub owner putting two and two together."

And he was getting four, all right: Bobby had told me that secret talks between a Kennedy administration rep and Castro himself were under way the day of the assassination.

Flo asked, "Where did Oswald fit in?"

"He was just a little foot soldier," Ruby said, "like me. He was an FBI informant, too, you know. And maybe more, maybe a spook—they sent him to Russia, huh? And some of those spooks were really pissed off at Kennedy, because of the Bay of Pigs betrayal, and, well, that should have told me something."

"A phony pro-Castro demonstration," I said. "Only it was a front for a presidential assassination."

Ruby nodded. "You're right, Nate, only I didn't know that at the time. The plan as presented was that a shooter would take a kind of potshot at the President, with Castroites catching the blame, which would then shut down any peace talk bull and maybe ignite the shooting war in Cuba that everybody wanted, the Birchers, the spooks, the hoods. Why else would Oswald, who was Marcello's guy—and maybe a spook or both, too—go around pretending to be a pinko?"

"Because he was being set up as a patsy," I said.

"*I* didn't know that. Believe me, I didn't try to put any pieces together, Nate, not up front. I just did what they asked, did whatever I was told."

"By Ferrie?"

"He was one of several. But the day before, that Thursday before, some nasty customers started showing up in town, Nate, from all over, specialized talent, I mean it was a goddamn torpedo convention . . . and it *did* start feeling like something else was up. Something big."

"Who showed up, for instance?"

"Well, for one, our old buddy Chuckie, from back home."

"Chuckie? You mean Nicoletti?"

Charles "Chuckie" Nicoletti was Sam Giancana's number one hit man.

Ruby nodded. "Rosselli, too. You know Johnny."

I knew Johnny.

"But," Ruby was saying, "he left before the big day, I think—maybe he was just putting things in motion, finishing touches."

"Who else?"

"Couple of Cuban hard-asses, don't ask for names, I could never keep track of 'em. Oh, and that creepy guy, Johnson's hatchet man, used to live here but is out on the West Coast now."

I exchanged glances with Flo.

I asked, "You mean Mac Wallace?"

Ruby nodded again, even more vigorously. "That freak would give Boris Karloff the heebie-jeebies. And there was this guy, maybe with some Cuban blood, who Oswald didn't know about but coulda been his brother."

Flo asked, "A double?"

"Not so close you'd call him an identical twin or anything, but easy enough to mistake for him. Also, some guy from Europe, a Corsican, I think. He was supposed to be a whiz with a rifle, and he was gonna be the one taking the potshot. Needed an expert for that, 'cause it wouldn't do to accidentally really whack the President, right? So we were told, anyway."

I asked, "You heard this at a meeting at the Carousel?"

He ignored that. "Why would they need three teams of shooters, Nate? That's what made it start to smell. If this was just a potshot, if they were just gonna miss the guy and put Castro on the spot . . . why a military action like that?"

"To guarantee a kill. Triangulation. Snipers from three sides."

As for the number of teams and the disparate players, that meant each faction within the conspiracy was providing a shooting team, two or three people each. To bind everybody together, to ensure silence by way of shared responsibility.

Or blame.

So you had Nicoletti and Rosselli for the Mob, who maybe also provided the Corsican specialist; the Cubans representing the exile group; Wallace as part of the Big Oil contingent; and other players as yet unnamed. Perhaps never to be named.

"I was in the military like you, Nate. I recognize that kind of thing when I see it. I would never be part of an atrocity such as this. Kill a *president*? I don't care if I didn't vote for the son of a bitch, I don't care if his brother *is* Bobby Kennedy and his father is a senile old bootlegger who betrayed us all, *kill a president*? I am *not* insane. Do I look insane?"

Was that a trick question?

I asked, "Oswald didn't know?"

Ruby shrugged. "He may have been putting things together like I did, as things came into play. Who can say?"

In Chicago, in late October, the first warning the Secret Service got of a possible assassination attempt set for JFK's November 2 visit came from an otherwise anonymous caller identifying himself only as "Lee."

Ruby sat forward. "But I think when that kid realized that Kennedy had been killed, he knew he was being set up. They'd sent him to work that day with a package of posters for the fake demonstration! That package was too small, but everybody uses it to say, Look! He brought a rifle to work! They told him to tell the guy who drove him there that they were curtain rods."

Curtain rods was what the hitchhiker told that truck driver was in his brown-paper package.

Ruby's upper lip curled back over his teeth. "Isn't it strange that Oswald, who hasn't worked a lick in most of his life, should be fortunate enough to get a job at the book depository two weeks before the President visits Dallas? Now where would a nebbish like Oswald get that information? Where could the people who put him in that building find out when and what the route would be? Only one person could get that information."

Flo said, "Who?"

He shifted in his metal chair, his expression coy. "Let's just say if Adlai Stevenson was vice president, there would never have been an assassination."

"Spell it out, Jack," I said.

"Well the answer is that that man is in office now."

"And that man is Lyndon Johnson?"

He was raving, yet keeping his voice soft enough not to be heard across the room. "And that man is Johnson! Who knew weeks in advance what was going to happen, because he is the one who was going to arrange the trip for the President—this had been planned long before the President himself knew about it. The one who gained the most by the shooting of the President was Johnson, and he was in a car in the rear and safe when the shooting took place. What would the Russians, Castro, or anyone else have to gain by eliminating the President? If Johnson was so heartbroken over Kennedy, why didn't he do something for Robert Kennedy? All he did was snub him."

I said, "Did you ever meet Madeleine Brown?"

That slammed his brakes on. He blinked. He shrugged. "Uh,

sure. Hot little number, in her day. Johnson has a good eye for talent, although that one was too smart for him. Got herself knocked up, milked him like a cow, money, cars, house. Why?"

"Just wondering," I said. "What did you mean, when you said Oswald was Marcello's man?"

"The summer before the assassination, he was a runner for a Marcello bookmaker. His uncle Dutz Murret's a longtime Marcello man. This is all well-known in New Orleans."

There it was: Oswald tied directly to the Marcello organization.

Flo said, "That still leaves the big question, Jack. Why did you shoot Oswald?"

He swallowed. "Because, Miss Kilgore, I had to. I got a call, and they told me I had to, and so I did, because I had to."

"A call from David Ferrie?"

"A call, Miss Kilgore, and I had to."

I said, "And *that's* what you were broken up about. Not Jackie and Caroline."

"I didn't want to shoot that kid! He was in so far over his head. He'd have already been dead if . . ."

"What?"

"Nothing."

Acquila Clemmons was sitting on her porch when she saw Officer Tippit killed. She said two men were involved—the gunman was a "short guy and kind of heavy," the other man taller and thin in khaki trousers and a white shirt. She had been reluctant to talk to Flo because a Dallas PD officer had warned her to stay quiet, saying she "might get killed on the way to work."

"*You* killed Tippit," I said.

Ruby shook his head. "I didn't say that."

"When Kennedy really *was* shot, you knew both you and Lee Oswald were dupes in this thing—you even went to Parkland Hospital to see if Kennedy would pull through, and when he didn't, you went looking for Oswald. Tippit died near your apartment, didn't he? You tried to *warn* Oswald."

"He was supposed to die that day," he said ambiguously.

"Who?" Flo asked.

I said, "Oswald. Jack here screwed this up for everybody. Tippit was supposed to kill Oswald—he was combing Oak Cliff, supposedly for a suspect based on the description over the police radio. He got out of the car to come around and take Oswald out, only Jack here rescued his pal. Didn't you, Jack?"

"I don't think . . . I don't think I should admit to a murder that maybe I didn't do."

I pressed: "Did Ferrie or Marcello suspect you? Is that why they sent you for the job? Or was it just a terrible coincidence? That you, the guy who could come and go as he pleased at the police station, were sent to do the deed."

"I went to that press conference Friday night," Ruby said hollowly. "I wanted him to see me. To understand he should keep quiet. But he kept saying over and over he was innocent, he was a 'patsy.' I *tried* to give him a pass."

"But it was the old, old problem."

"What?"

"He knew too much."

Ruby nodded. Sighed. "I guess . . . I guess that kid and I have that in common."

I heard footsteps. Tonahill was walking toward us. He paused halfway, looking massive and apologetic, and said, "That's all the time they'll give us."

It had been enough.

Ruby walked us to the gate. Our white-jumpsuited host stayed at Flo's side, as if he were walking her to the door after the prom and was hoping against hope for a kiss.

"I know you'll do right by me, Miss Kilgore," he said. "The sooner you get this out there, the better are my chances. They wouldn't fool with a famous person like you. Not a journalist."

That was a naive thing for him to say—not just because Kennedy's fame hadn't stopped anybody, but Ruby was an old Chicago boy. He surely remembered the *Tribune*'s man Jake Lingle getting it in that subway tunnel back in Capone days.

We bid Lee Harvey Oswald's killer good-bye. We did not discuss anything on our way back to the hotel. I guess we were both trying to absorb it all. The tape was in her purse, and that was what I referred to first: "Get copies of that made when you get back to New York."

I was dropping her at the Statler. She nodded and went in, while I went and parked.

Shortly thereafter, up in her room, perched side by side on her couch/bed, I said, "Ruby is right—don't sit on this. Get it written and out there. Once the genie's out of the bottle, we'll all be safer."

She was having a gin and tonic and I sipped at a bottle of Coke.

"I don't know, Nate," she said, frowning in thought, looking as cute as she was famous. "I owe Bennett a book. That's much bigger than a story."

"Doesn't it take a year or more for one to come out?"

"Not with a hot topic like this. They'll rush it—three months maybe, no more than five."

"That's a long time in Dallas. What about the Johnson stuff?"

"Think I should hold that back?"

"Probably. It's beyond the pale, Ruby's just speculating, and anyway that might get the whole project spiked. Remember what happened with the Marilyn story."

"I'll use my head." She took my hand and squeezed. "This isn't over, Nate."

"Sure it is. Go home. Write your story or your book, whichever suits you. And go back to covering Liz and Dick, and what does and doesn't flop on Broadway this season."

She touched my chest with a gloved finger. "We're going to New Orleans next."

"No we aren't."

She nodded firmly, and her big blue eyes locked onto me. "Yes we are. Unless you want to send me there by myself."

Fuck.

"Fuck," I said. "All right. When?"

"I want to get my thoughts down in chapter form. Or maybe

it'll be an article, but anyway written. I'll send you a copy, plus a dupe of the tape, and arrange for an interview with that Ferrie character. And maybe a few others in the ol' Big Easy. Make it . . . two weeks from next Monday. I'll book us a suite at the Roosevelt near the French Quarter. Okay?"

"Okay."

"I mean, we'll talk on the phone, before then, but . . . when's your plane?"

"Three hours."

"Mine's in two." She gave me her sexiest smile, which was fairly sexy. "Did you know that there's nothing more erotic to a girl reporter than a scoop?"

"I'll take two scoops," I said, and put my hands on her breasts.

CHAPTER 15

On Monday morning, back in Chicago, when I rolled into the A-1's suite of offices around ten A.M., everyone was happy to see me, or at least pretended to be—I was, after all, the boss. Millie asked me how Dallas was and I told her great, and that I'd gotten her John Wayne's autograph, but she merely informed me that John Wayne didn't live in Texas. She was learning. Gladys dug down deep and found a smile for me and said she was pleased to have me back, and I chose to believe her, though mostly she just wanted to remind me about the eleven A.M. staff meeting, as if we hadn't been doing that for decades.

I took my office manager up on her standard offer of coffee, and I was drinking it at my desk when Lou Sapperstein knocked shave-and-a-haircut, then leaned in without waiting for a response. His eyebrows were climbing his endless forehead, the dark eyes glittering behind the wire-frame bifocals.

I waved him in, and this big man in his seventies settled his still-brawny frame into the black leather client's chair, his own cup of coffee in hand. He wore a pink button-down shirt, red necktie with matching suspenders, and navy-blue slacks, proof that Pop Art was injecting way too much color into the world.

He asked, "How about filling me in on your summer vacation?"

"It's September, Lou."

"Your skills of observation remain keenly honed. What the hell happened down on the Panhandle?"

"Dallas isn't in the Panhandle."

"Too bad, because it's one of the few Texas terms I know. What gives?"

After our client, Mrs. Joseph Plett, had her double-indemnity claim belatedly honored, I'd been scheduled to come right back. All Lou knew was that I'd decided to extend my stay in Big D, having run into Flo Kilgore.

"I was just helping Flo out with a little investigative work," I said, probably too casually.

"In Dallas," he said, well aware Flo was an old flame of mine. "Covering a way-off-Broadway play, was she?"

"Not important."

His jaw tightened. "It's Kennedy, isn't it? You took a left turn into that, out of the Billie Sol Estes thing. Or is that a right-wing turn?"

His skills of observation remained keenly honed, too.

"You talked to Bill Queen in the Manhattan office," I said.

"I did. Also, over recent months, Miss Kilgore has received a lot of attention for her columns on the assassination. Thanks to her celebrity, she's the most credible of those conspiracy kooks."

"She's not a kook," I said, but didn't add that it *was* a conspiracy.

"Is getting into that area wise, you think, after what happened?"

"After what happened?"

He sat forward, on the verge of losing a usually kept cool. "After you and your son almost got run down! Tell me you weren't looking into other loose ends down there that got conveniently clipped off."

The image of a once-pretty dishwater blonde floated across my mind—Rose Cheramie.

"I don't keep much from you, Lou, but this time it might be better all around if—"

"Nate," he said, shifting in his chair, "we just landed a huge insurance paycheck for a client by sniffing at a suspicious suicide tied to a bunch of suspicious suicides in Texas. We still have your friend Mac Wallace under surveillance in Anaheim, and—"

"Keep him that way."

"How long?"

"Indefinitely. It's okay, Lou. I get a good rate. I have an in."

"Nate, it's just . . . what are you getting yourself into? What are you getting the *agency* into?"

I raised a hand in a gesture that was half *stop* and half *peace.* "Lou, I have been encouraging Flo to shut down her investigation. She has more than enough to write a hard-hitting piece of journalism that will get her the respect she craves, and maybe make some useful waves."

"That sounds dangerous."

"Potentially it is, but it's also potentially very high profile, and our role in it won't hurt business one little bit."

He sighed, nodded, leaned back. "You said you were encouraging her to shut it down, though?"

"Right. I'm meeting her in New Orleans two weeks from today for a few follow-up interviews, and then I promise you I will either convince her to write 'thirty' to this thing, or walk away."

He was shaking his head. "Nate, I'm just an old Pickpocket Detail dick."

"Right. You're an old dick. I get that."

"I feel like I should give you some fatherly advice right now, but you're a little old for that, and I'll be damned if I know what it is. What's in New Orleans, anyway?"

"Besides Carlos Marcello, you mean? Possibly some of the people who killed Kennedy, or who helped kill him."

"Jesus." He shook his head again. "Jesus H. Christ. You're going to get us all killed."

"No. Honestly, Lou. I'm on top of this. Really."

"Okay," he said. He reached over and collected my empty coffee cup, just helping out his wife. "Okay. . . . Uh, listen. It may not mean anything, but Mac Wallace isn't in California."

"What?"

"He flew out Saturday morning to Dallas. Does that matter? Your family is in LA, you're in Chicago, your friend Flo is in New York. Who does that leave in Dallas?"

Fourteen or fifteen witnesses we'd interviewed.

From the doorway, Lou said, "We don't have anybody in Dallas to watch the guy. There are agencies in those parts we could contact. What do you say?"

"No, I'll make a call myself. Have one of our LA men determine when Wallace is due back in California and pick him up then."

"You're the boss." He pointed at me and then at himself. "Now, if you get killed, then *I'm* the boss, right?"

"Right."

"Okay then," Lou said.

And he left me there with my apprehensions.

Coming into the office this morning, settling behind my desk in my inner sanctum, had given me a nice feeling of normalcy. As if everything that happened in Texas had been an episode, like a show on TV, and the show was over, the set clicked off.

But one of the witnesses, Rose Cheramie, was dead, just three days after we talked to her. Rose was a junkie and the kind of woman who could get herself killed lots of ways. But had we *gotten her killed? Had* I?

Clint Peoples wasn't in, but he called me back after lunch.

"Nate," the familiar mellow, folksy voice said, "I got some additional information for you, on the Cheramie woman's death, if you're interested."

"That's one reason I called."

"Driver in question, a Mr. Jerry Don Moore, from Tyler, was heading home. Comin' up level with a roadside parking area, he noticed three or four suitcases strewn on the highway, spillin' over the yellow line. He swerved right, to miss them, and then there in front of him was a woman lyin' prone on the shoulder, at ninety degrees to the road, head *on* the road, like the pavement's her pillow. He braked, says he doesn't know for sure if he hit her or not."

"How's that possible?"

"Moore says there was a sound, but it mighta been a shoe brake hitting on his old beater—it's got bald tires and a single headlight. The fella admits to speeding, and drinking, by the by. Some colored folks stopped and helped him, moving the suitcases, putting Rose in his backseat. Moore took her to a doctor he knew in Big Sandy, who got her to Gladewater Hospital, where she was DOA. Cause of death . . . let me give it to you exact . . . 'traumatic head wound with subdural and subarachnoid and petechial hemorrhage to the brain caused by being struck by an auto.' "

"Hardly a surprising diagnosis."

"Maybe so, but Nate—there was also a 'deep punctuate stellate wound above her right forehead.' Now, this type of injury—"

"I know what type of injury that is, Clint."

The result of a contact gunshot wound, the star-shaped wound from the bursting, tearing effect on skin of gasses trapped against flesh.

"Other odd thing is, Highway 155, where she was found? That's a farm-to-market road, runnin' parallel to US Highways 271 and 80. She'd have had a much better chance of hitchin' a ride on either of those."

"She was killed elsewhere and dumped."

"Not much doubt about that—for one thing, she had tire tread tracks on her damn head . . . and that junker's tires are bald, remember. Also, her estimated time of death was nine hours before she was admitted to Gladewater."

"What now?"

"Well, despite these anomalies, I'm afraid my sister organization, the Texas Highway Patrol, has already closed the case."

"Shit, that's a little fast, isn't it?"

"The officer in charge couldn't establish a connection between the driver and victim, and Rose's relatives do not wish to pursue the matter. If I may be blunt, Rose was a junkie prostitute, and those girls find imaginative ways to die each and every day. Wish I could say Mac Wallace doesn't have an alibi, but he's got one, all right—he flew from sunny Cal into Dallas on Saturday, and Rose died Friday."

"That was the other reason I called, Clint—to make sure you knew Wallace was back on your turf."

"As I mentioned the other day, we do keep track of the boy."

"I'm glad to hear that, because I don't have an A-1 office in them there parts to keep an eye on the bastard. I think I may have mentioned we've been maintaining surveillance on him in Anaheim."

"Well," he sighed, "can't promise the Rangers are watching him as close as all that, but I *have* made a sort of hobby out of Mr. Wallace. You have any particular concerns?"

"Miss Kilgore and I talked to a number of assassination witnesses, who seem to be a vanishing breed, to put it in Texas terms."

"You mean, more than a few folks are comin' down with a bad case of suicide?"

"Or a terminal dose of getting their skulls crushed by a car after getting shot in the head. Would you like a list of the people we talked to? Other than Rose Cheramie?"

He wrote the names down, then said apologetically, "There is no way or manner I can offer all these individuals protection . . . but if I see any incidents involving them, I will get right on it."

"And inform me, please. By the way, I'll be in New Orleans for a few days, starting two weeks from today. I'll be at the Roosevelt if you need me, or come up with anything."

"Got it. Take care now, in Louisiana. That's a foreign country, pardner."

"Pardner, huh? Havin' a little fun with me, Clint?"

"A mite."

When I'd hung up the phone, I sat there staring at it as if it might be able to give me the advice that Lou said he couldn't. Starting on the plane trip back, I'd been brooding over whether to fill RFK in on what I'd learned about his brother's murder. On some level, I'd been working for him in Dallas—on the investigating side, sure, but also keeping tabs on Flo and what she discovered.

But if I reported everything we'd learned to Bobby before Flo had a chance to get her story or book out there, Jack Kennedy's sibling might reach out with his considerable clout and squelch her efforts, even while plundering them for information. Still vivid in my memory was Flo's bitter disappointment—and mine—when the work we'd done uncovering the truth of Marilyn's murder had been spiked by her editor due to Kennedy family influence. It had created a rift between Bobby and me that had only recently sealed over.

I was still looking at the phone when it rang, which for just a second gave me a start, as if I had willed that to happen.

Millie was on the line: "Mr. Heller, I have a call here from New York, a gentleman who is not on our list. He sounds very upset, and is insistent on talking to you, but I can follow procedure and refer him to Mrs. Sapperstein if you prefer."

"Who is he?"

"Frank Felton."

I sat up. "Put him through."

Flo's husband. He'd been an actor once upon a time, and if Millie were ten years older, she might have recognized the name. Might.

"Nate, this Frank. Flo's Frank."

Though we'd only met a few times, his warm baritone, a trifle slurry, was immediately recognizable: he'd played Johnny Dollar on the radio for a while.

"Yes, Frank. Is everything all right? I watched the show last night, so I know Flo got back safely."

"She did, but I have . . . Nate, I have . . ." Damn, was he crying? "We lost her, Nate . . . she's gone."

"Gone?" My stomach tightened, as a sick feeling flowed through me. "She's . . . *dead,* Frank?"

"The damn booze mixed with pills. Damn booze and pills. How many times did I tell her . . . Listen, I can't really talk . . . I have a number of calls to make, but I know you were close. That you were just with her. She thought the world of you, Nate."

"Jesus. Frank, I'm sorry. So sorry. Hell. Was there any sign of foul play?"

"Foul play? No! Why would you . . . ?"

"Sorry to bring it up. You *do* know what story she and I were working on in Dallas, right?"

"Yes. Yes."

"Well, then I don't have to tell you she was exploring very dangerous territory. Very."

"No. You don't."

"When is the funeral?"

"Not till later in the week. To give her friends from around the country . . . around the world . . . a chance to get here, if they . . . they choose."

"Frank—was there anything disturbed? Anything missing, any signs of struggle or possibly anything indicating a search of her things?"

"No! Nate . . . she died in her sleep last night, just hours after *What's My Line*? She guessed two of the occupations, how . . . how about that? My little Florrie Mae." His pet name for her. He was crying again.

"I'm sorry," I said. "These are inappropriate questions right now. Forgive me."

"I . . . I understand. *She*'s an investigator, too. Her mind works like that."

She was still in the present tense for him. Me, too.

"Frank, would you approve my coming out there tomorrow? Talking to me, and giving me a chance to kind of look things over?"

"I don't know, Nate. . . . There are so many arrangements to make . . . people to talk to . . . and . . ."

"Just let me come out there and give me even half an hour."

"I . . . I suppose that would be all right."

"Tomorrow afternoon then?"

"Yes. All right. Fine."

"Frank, do you know what happened to the tapes she made on our trip? The interviews?"

"No, but I can check where she keeps such things."

"Do you have anywhere secure to keep whatever you find? A wall safe, locking file cabinet, something?"

"Well, yes, probably. Why?"

"Take whatever you can find from the Dallas trip, tapes, notes, and hide them away. Please. Do that *one* thing for me."

"All right, Nate. I'll . . . I'll see you tomorrow, then."

We said our good-byes. He had stopped crying.

My turn to start.

West Side Ford New and Used on West Cermak Road in Riverside was indistinguishable from scores of other such dealerships in the Greater Chicago area. Its best shot at standing out from the rest of the pack would have been advertising a certain probable off-the-books custom job.

Back in May of 1962, the cops checked out a parked '62 Ford sedan where two individuals were spotted ducked down on the floor of the backseat. The two individuals turned out to be notorious mob hit man Charles "Chuckie" Nicoletti and his frequent backup, Felix Alderisio. The officers discovered switches under the dash, one enabling the driver to disconnect the taillights (aiding in avoiding pursuit), the other opening a compartment in the center front-seat armrest fitted to hold shotguns and rifles. Reporters dubbed the vehicle the "hitmobile." Asked to explain why he and Alderisio were crouching in the backseat, Nicoletti said, "We were waiting for a friend."

Nicoletti grew up in poverty, his first killing (at twelve) that of his abusive father, then dropped out of school to join the slum delinquents known as the 42 Gang, whose members included "Mad Sam" DeStefano and Chuckie's current boss, Sam Giancana. In Outfit circles, Nicoletti was perhaps best known for cold-bloodedly eating his spaghetti while Anthony "the Ant" Spilotro squeezed Billy McCarthy's head in a vise till an eye popped out of its socket.

As to why I'd assume West Side Ford New and Used had done the hitmobile customizing: Chuckie Nicoletti was a co-owner and assistant manager there. This was essentially a cover story for the cops and FBI, of course, but Nicoletti was a charming guy for a psychopathic Mafia murderer, and got a kick out of selling cars.

And there he was on the lot, tall, affable, handsome for a hood, talking to a young couple in their early twenties about a shiny new red Mustang convertible. Several other salesmen in the brightly lighted lot—it was approaching closing time, eight o'clock—were similarly occupied. When I walked into the showroom, nobody was there but a busty brunette secretary on the phone at her desk, talking to her boyfriend. I walked past the various empty offices, found the central one labeled CHARLES NICOLETTI, ASSISTANT MANAGER, then went over to the brunette at her desk up front between showroom windows.

Smiling, I raised a finger, indicating I just wanted a brief word. She told her boyfriend to hold a second, covered the mouthpiece, and looked up at me with very big brown eyes, her lipstick a startling pink. She had a bouffant hairdo you could have bounced bullets off of, which considering who her boss was might come in handy.

"Sorry to interrupt," I whispered. "Just tell Mr. Nicoletti that a satisfied customer is waiting in his office to thank him."

She nodded, managed a smile, then went back to her important conversation, which seemed to be about selecting a discotheque.

Inside the glorified cubbyhole of Nicoletti's office, leaving the door slightly ajar, I checked the desk—there was no filing cabinet, just walls with a few sales awards and framed color photos of current model cars—and found a Browning .22 automatic among the paperclips in the center drawer. Despite the seemingly small caliber, a .22 was typical for a hard-core hit man, being a weapon that silenced effectively. I removed the clip, thumbed each shell into the wastebasket, replaced the now-empty clip, and returned the gun to its drawer.

Sitting in one of two customer chairs across from the desk, I unbuttoned the jacket of my suit coat to give me access to my shoulder-holstered nine-millimeter Browning—which did not silence well at all. I scooted the chair into a sideways position to see Nicoletti as he entered.

It was possible that he might be armed, but I doubted it. Similarly, he might be escorting that couple into his office to write up a deal, but I doubted that, too. Those kids were window-shopping or whatever the car lot equivalent was. This late in the evening, a deal would not likely go down.

I sat for maybe fifteen minutes, about ten minutes into which the lights dimmed in the showroom, followed by the sound of the secretary and various sales personnel gathering their things, saying good nights and going. If the secretary told Nicoletti about my presence, I didn't hear her do it.

He would return to this office, though, because a hat and raincoat were waiting on a metal tree in the corner. No weapon in any raincoat pocket, by the way.

When he came in, Nicoletti was already friendly and saying, "Susie said you were wanting to—"

And then Chuckie's smile froze and his words stopped.

Even pushing fifty, Chuckie Nicoletti cut an intimidating figure—broad-shouldered, six two, big hands with frying-pan palms and fingers like swollen sausages. His handsome features had a vaguely swollen look, too, and the white infiltrating his ridge of dark, carefully cut-and-combed hair stood out starkly against his Miami tan. His suit was charcoal black and tailored, his tie white and black and silk, wider than current fashion and with a knot like a fist.

"Hi Chuckie," I said as he stood in the doorway, the dark showroom behind him, neon signage giving him a halo of color. "Why don't you shut that?"

I wasn't holding a gun on him. Nothing so melodramatic. But my suit coat was open enough to make the butt of the nine millimeter apparent in its rig. So just melodramatic enough.

"Heller," he said with a smile that hid its uneasiness. "I thought you drove Jags. Decide to try a good old-fashioned American ride like Ford for a change?"

"Sit down, Chuck. I just need a couple of minutes. Not to talk cars, though."

He moved slowly behind the desk and eased down as if fearing I'd rigged the seat of his swivel chair to explode. "What subject?"

I moved my chair around to face him directly.

"I'm going to kind of build up to that." My words were calm but I couldn't keep the edge out of my voice. Since hearing about Flo earlier today, I had not been myself. Or maybe I was too much myself. "You were part of Mongoose, right?"

His dark eyes flared. He placed his hands on the edge of the metal desk, thick fingers on artificial-wood top, giving himself easy access to that .22.

"It's okay to say so," I said with a smile. "You can check with Rosselli about that. Didn't John ever mention my role? He can confirm I set up the first meet between him, Mooney, and Santo."

"Okay," he said, with the expression of a man adjusting his shower temperature. "I was part of that. Not that we never got nowhere with it. That prick Castro is still smoking Havanas."

"Yeah, and the poisoned ones never worked out, right? There was one plan I heard about, though, that might've come in handy—something about hitting Castro on his way to the airport from a high building. Using highly trained snipers. That's plural, because triangulation was involved."

Traffic on West Cermak was providing a discordant muffled soundtrack, an occasional horn honk stabbing the night.

His dark eyes were hooded now. "We're all CIA assets, Heller. You and me and John and . . . plenty of other people. If you're just trying to figure out who's on what side, that would put us on the same side. Same team."

"Okay." He didn't seem to be lying. On the other hand, he *was* a car salesman. "Chuckie, did John mention to you that earlier this month a Cuban tried to run me down? And that my son was almost a hit-and-run victim, too?"

"He did not mention that, no."

"I spoke to John, and he assured me that if somebody was out there tying off loose ends, he was not involved."

"I'm sure he isn't. He likes you, Nate."

Now I was Nate. Well, that was only fair. I was calling him Chuckie.

I said, "But the question is, are *you* involved?"

"In . . . tyin' off loose ends? Hell, no."

"You've tied off your share, Chuckie."

"I suppose I have."

"The estimate around town is twenty hits."

"That sounds about right."

"That's about half the Japs I killed in the Pacific, but not bad for local work."

Big white smiling teeth, caps or choppers, collided with his dark tan. "You done all right yourself, back in the States, ain't you, Nate?"

"I don't like to brag. Have we established that neither of us scares easy?"

He went for the gun and then I was just sitting there with him aiming its long snout at my chest. A head shot would have been messy here at the office. I waited to see if he'd fire or was just one-upping me.

"Why don't you tell me what this is about, Nate?"

"Does that feel a little light, Chuckie? It might."

He frowned.

"Because I removed all the bullets."

Then I got out the nine-millimeter and he clicked on an empty chamber, twice, then sighed. Set the gun down with a little clunk.

"Okay," he said. "So you're right. Neither of us assholes scares easy."

I kept the gun in my hand, but draped casually in my lap. As casually as a nine millimeter can be draped, anyway.

"I just got back from Dallas," I said conversationally. "A little bodyguard work for a reporter who was looking into the aftermath of the assassination."

"JFK."

"Not Lincoln. I could have said McKinley, but at a Ford dealership, Lincoln seems more politic."

"You are a fucking laugh riot, Heller."

"Coming from a guy as uneasily amused as you, Chuckie, I

take that as a compliment. So when Billy McCarthy's eyeball popped out, did you even miss a beat scarfing down that spaghetti?"

"That story you heard is inaccurate."

"Oh?"

"It was ziti."

We smiled at each other. We were both laugh riots who were not easily scared. And yet we were both good and goddamned scared, and I was fine with that.

I said, "The reporter was Flo Kilgore."

He frowned a little; it made white lines in his tan. "That skinny dame from TV? I heard on the radio she died. Accidental overdose, they said."

I ignored that. "We were interviewing witnesses to the assassination, plus some peripheral figures."

"What does that mean? Per what?"

"Fringe. Sidelines, but still in the game. They're dropping like flies, Chuckie. Accidental deaths like Flo. Sudden suicides. Car accidents. Some people are just getting threatened or maimed, but one way or the other, they're getting shut up."

"And this is a bad thing?"

I gave him half a smile. "I'm aware you were there, Chuckie. I know you were part of it. Maybe even a shooter."

His eyes narrowed. He was wondering if he could throw that .22 at me hard enough to buy him time to come around the desk and kill me with my own gun. Anyway, that's what I'd have been thinking.

I raised a "stop" hand and said, "That's between you and your maker. I'm not trying to solve the Kennedy assassination."

"No?"

"No. I already knew it was a conspiracy before it went down—I was in the middle of the Chicago plot early November last year, remember? And I know who the big boys are. Oh, not necessarily all of them by name, but it's oilmen and other right-wing wackos, and spook pals of ours from Mongoose and the Bay of Pigs, and their Cuban buddies, and of course, obviously, what we'll quaintly call the Mafia."

His eyes had disappeared into puffy slits. "If you know everything, Heller, what the fuck can *I* tell you?"

"Tell me this. Can I . . . can *you* . . . trust John Rosselli?"

"Huh?"

"When he says there is no Outfit cleanup crew dispatched to tie off loose ends, is he telling the truth?"

"On the grave of my kids," he said, holding up both big palms, "I don't know of any."

"I think you mean on the life of your kids, but their graves might be more apt at that, Chuckie. As I said, my boy Sam was almost run down, and that pisses me off."

He shrugged. "Sure. That's over the line."

"Good. It's nice to talk to a fucking professional for a change. I don't think it's the Company. I have a contact there who I trust, as far it goes. And I don't think those Cubans could organize a fart in the bathtub."

"You're tellin' me?"

"Then who *is* tying off the loose ends, Chuckie? And be careful how you answer, because I ask you as one loose end to another."

That got his attention.

"Only one possibility," he said, shaking his head as if saying no, which he wasn't. "That fucking Uncle Carlos. He's a law unto himself. We do business with him, we have a kind of . . . understanding with him. But he stands apart. He doesn't view this Thing of Ours as a club he's in."

"Most of the deaths are in Texas. Some that I haven't looked into yet are in Louisiana."

Chuckie nodded. "Marcello controls all of Texas and Louisiana, and he and Santo got Florida, too. So if I was to suggest something to you, Heller . . . as one pro to another . . . as one . . . *loose end* to another . . . if you want to shut this thing down, you already *know* where you have to go."

"New Orleans," I said.

"New Orleans," he said, nodding.

Where in two weeks Flo and I would have continued our investigation, before this latest convenient tragedy had come along. I'd be taking that Big Easy trip all right, but my next stop would be Manhattan.

I got to my feet and slipped the nine millimeter into its leather womb. "You'll find your slugs in that wastebasket, Chuck. If you reload your clip and come running after me, I'll know I misjudged you."

"You didn't, Nate."

He held out his big hand and I shook it.

Shook the hand of one of the likely assassins of John F. Kennedy.

CHAPTER 16

The brown-brick facade of the five-story town house on East Sixty-eighth Street, squeezed between similar nondescript buildings, concealed a glittering twenty-two-room world as imagined and executed by Flo Kilgore.

I had never set foot in the place before. Despite her fame and fashion, Flo had always struck me as a scrappy small-town kid who made it big. But this decadently elegant display—French doors, chandeliers, gilt-framed landscapes, rosewood furnishings—made sense only if Flo had seen *Gone With the Wind* at an impressionable age and grew up determined to replicate Tara in Manhattan. Hell, she even had black servants, although I didn't see any that looked like Aunt Jemima or Uncle Ben.

Of course, the blackest thing in this otherwise opulent town house was the unique room on the third floor, its four walls and ceiling black, as if painted overnight to mourn the town house's late hostess. It was filled with bizarre bric-a-brac—shelves of sculpted and wooden hands, toy banks, music boxes, and numerous variations on the American eagle. A big antique Revolutionary War–style snare drum had been converted to a coffee table with two red child-sized chairs. A gigantic oil painting of General Custer and his men chasing Indians (wishful thinking?) dominated the room, hanging over a low-slung sofa with black cushions and an intricately carved wooden frame painted an iridescent blue. Cigar-store Indians, positioned here and there, seemed to be viewing Custer with understandable skepticism.

Still, it was a lived-in space. Black throw pillows were on the dark-green carpet near a 21-inch TV (its cabinet painted black, of course) in one corner. Those kid-sized chairs by the drum table indicated this wasn't a living room so much as a family room, a rec room.

I'd worn a black Botany 500 suit with a black tie, out of respect, but I felt like I was disappearing into the stygian surroundings as I sat beside Frank Felton on the sofa. He was in a black suit, as well, with a black necktie, and we might have been two undertakers waiting to talk to the family, when of course he *was* the family.

"I'm afraid this room represents something of a practical joke," he said with forced cheer.

"Joke?" I said. I felt like I'd walked into a Charles Addams cartoon, in search of the punch line.

Felton was in his mid-fifties but looked ten years older. You could just barely see, in that reddish, puffy, vein-shot face, the handsome young comic actor he'd once been. His dark eyes had the seldom-blinking, slightly widened look of a man on a bridge admiring a sunrise as he contemplated jumping off. Only his voice retained its radio youth—*Yours Truly, Johnny Dollar. . . .*

"Well, Florrie Mae was so determined to make a gleaming showplace out of these digs," he said, "I suggested we have one fun room."

"Ah," I said, noticing on a nearby shelf a rustic wooden hand with candle-speared spikes rising out of the fingertips.

"Just a space where we could let our notions of the bizarre run wild." He grinned, displaying yellowed, questionable teeth. "A lot of times, we'd play 'Count the Eagles.' "

"Oh?"

He nodded. His eyes were staring past me into a memory. "We'd ask guests to close their eyes and test their powers of observation—

how many eagles had they noticed in the Black Room? That's what we call it, the Black Room."

"Catchy," I said.

"You wouldn't believe the parties this space has seen," Felton said. "I loved to plan the things, stage them like a film or Broadway production."

"Ah," I said.

"On one anniversary bash, we turned the Black Room into an inferno—simulated, of course—for a 'Saints and Sinners' costume party. So many beautiful people, frolicking among the faux fire and brimstone. We had gambling in another room, a small orchestra for dancing downstairs, an arcade with pinball machines, Moviolas playing silent movies. That ebony baby grand over there, top recording talent performed just for the privilege of being part of it all."

Probably not Sinatra—he and Flo had carried on a famous feud, her calling him a gangster, him calling her "the chinless wonder." I'd seen her cry over that.

Felton was saying, "Guests were challenged to come as their favorite sinners from mythology, literature, history. I left it up to Florrie Mae what sinners to choose for us. You will never guess what she picked."

"Scarlett O'Hara and Rhett Butler," I said.

He smiled in surprise and really looked at me for the first time. "Flo told you?"

"No," I said.

That stopped his incessant chatter, which was what I'd hoped it would do, whether I'd guessed right or wrong.

"Frank," I said, "I know this is difficult. But I want you to tell me what happened, in as much detail as you can manage. As much you can stand."

We sat in silence for perhaps thirty seconds.

"I didn't really see her the night before," he said finally, with a frustrated shrug. The dark unblinking eyes took on a desperate cast. "Can I get you something to drink?"

"No thanks."

Felton got up and, moving more side to side than straight ahead, went over to a liquor cabinet converted from an old wooden highboy icebox, painted black, of course. He was perhaps five nine, and looked more bloated than overweight. He poured himself several fingers of Johnnie Walker and returned, not sitting, though, standing before me, feet planted but weaving just slightly.

"You'll have to forgive me, Nate," he said. "I don't think I've stopped drinking since this happened."

I didn't think he'd stopped drinking since 1948, but at least right now he had a damn good excuse to drown himself in booze and sorrow.

"You were friends with Florrie Mae. You *know* about . . . us. Right? Right. You know how we didn't, well, stand in the way of each other's extracurricular activities. We just didn't . . . *flaunt* it at each other. Tried not to embarrass each other."

"They're calling it 'open marriage,' these days. You were one of the first couples I ever knew who so indulged."

His shrug was as overly elaborate as the house. "Well, we were grown-ups, Nate. We still loved each other, we were pals, and we . . . had our romantic moments, even after things cooled. I mean, we *must* have loved each other, right? We married each other often enough!"

"The night before she died, Frank. Tell me about that."

"The last time I saw her was with Julian Rusk, her hairdresser—he always comes here Sunday afternoon, to do her hair at home, before the show. Late afternoon. I said . . . break a leg, and she just . . . smiled and nodded. I rarely went to the broadcast with her and this was no exception. She and one of her producers went to P.J. Clarke's for a quick drink, after."

"Was that out of the ordinary?"

"No, no quite the opposite. From there she took her limousine—CBS provided that—to the piano bar at the Regency. Going there for cocktails was also customary—in fact, the show's staff always invited the contestants to join them and usually some of the stars, depending on who was available or anyway in the mood."

"What time did she get home?"

"I don't really know, Nate. I was in bed already. No one else was in the house—the servants don't sleep in, and our kids are in boarding school. Well, they're home now, but . . . anyway, she was here at 2:20, that much I can tell you."

"Did you check with the limo driver about what time he brought her back?"

"I did. She sent him home when he dropped her at the Regency."

Maybe she had a date.

"If you didn't see her, Frank, why are you so sure she was home at 2:20?"

"She called Western Union at that time and had a messenger come pick up her column. She probably had most of it written already, and made a few finishing touches, after getting back from the Regency bar. Her last column."

He sat back down next to me, leaned an elbow on a knee, and covered his face with a hand.

I gave him a few moments, then asked, "You said you'd already gone to bed. Did she join you, and in the morning, you . . . ?"

He shook his head. "No. At times we didn't sleep together. I'm afraid I snore, and Florrie Mae worked all hours. I have a bedroom on the fourth floor, Florrie Mae has a little bed in her office on the fifth. But she was found in the bedroom we share, the master bedroom. That's why I brought you to the Black Room, Nate—not out of any gallows sense of humor . . . though this is certainly a room where we had wonderful times." He pointed off to the right. "She was found in the bedroom just off of here. . . ."

From the Black Room we entered a blizzard of white—white walls, white furnishings with gold accents and antique brass hardware, though red relieved the white by way of a Florentine design on the spread of the king-sized bed, and a red tufted velvet headboard with matching slipper chair.

I stepped into the room, but Felton stayed in the doorway, as if the parquet floor was one big trapdoor waiting to be sprung on him.

He said quietly, "That's where she was found. Not by me. By Rusk, the hairdresser. He had an appointment to do her hair at nine A.M. She had a TV show to tape at eleven, guesting on *To Tell the Truth.* She was sitting up, a book in her lap—*Seven Days in May*—must have fallen asleep reading."

"And died in her sleep."

"Yes. There was no sign of any kind of disturbance, not even rumpled covers. So it must have been peaceful. She just slipped . . . slipped away. . . ."

"Do we know the cause of death?"

"It was the booze and pills, Nate. You know that."

"Too early for an opinion from the coroner?"

"Not officially, but Dr. Luke tells me it's 'the effects of a combination of alcohol and barbiturates.' "

Booze and pills.

I walked to the white nightstand. "Any pill bottles? Any kind of bottles?"

"Seconal, about half of her prescription still there. A glass of gin and tonic, about . . . a third of it left. She'd have to get up and go out into the other room for a refill."

"Will there be an inquest?"

"No, thank God. The doctor said Flo's death will be labeled 'circumstances undetermined.' "

"That's a common enough designation, but it leaves the door open for speculation."

"But she wasn't depressed, Nate!" He was assuming I meant suicide, and indeed there were rumors of that reported in the press.

"This talk of suicide," he said in a rush of words, "it pisses me off, really pisses me off royal. She was energized about her book for Bennett, that Kennedy thing, she was happy with her life, she . . ."

She had a new man in her life. He had to know that. But couldn't bring himself to say it.

"Show me her office, would you, Frank?"

On the way up the front stairs, I said, "How much do you know about the Kennedy book?"

"Just that she felt confident her reporting would make a real difference. She bragged, she was cocky—said she was going to 'blow the case wide open.' "

"You didn't talk specifics?"

"No. She talked with that young man from Indiana who's been assisting her. But otherwise she was protective, even . . . secretive. She said the more I knew, the more dangerous it was for me."

"She wasn't kidding. You *did* know what we were investigating in Dallas, Frank? The suspicious deaths of assassination witnesses?"

"That I did gather."

Her office on the fifth floor, with its single bed and desk in a corner with a typewriter, looked like the room of a teenaged girl, albeit a wealthy one—floral-brocade wallpaper, chartreuse carpet, embroidered organdy curtains tied back with taffeta bows. The only thing missing was the stuffed animals.

Frank stood beside me in the surprisingly small space. "This was her sanctuary," he said. "She called it the Ebb. As in ebb and flow? It's rare for me to set foot in here."

"Oh?"

"Rare for anyone but her to be in here."

The reddish face swung suddenly to me and he was close enough for it to be uncomfortable, his dark glazed eyes locking on me, like tics on a greyhound.

"Nate, on the phone, you asked about foul play. There were no signs of that downstairs, and nothing disturbed in here or anywhere in the house. But when you start talking about this Kennedy thing, you . . . well, you're *scaring* me, man."

I kept my voice calm, but did not duck the subject. "She's been publishing pieces on the assassination for over six months. Were there any repercussions? Any trouble of any kind?"

He frowned but the wide eyes didn't narrow. "Well, after she started publishing that Warren Commission material, about that Ruby character? We had FBI agents crawling all over the place."

"Really?"

He nodded. "They had a search warrant, but didn't find anything. They interrogated her down in the Black Room, like a suspect in a crime. They badgered her about the identity of her source and she told them . . ." His complexion paled to pink. ". . . told them she would rather 'die than betray a source.' "

I put a hand on his shoulder and squeezed. He swallowed. Closed his eyes.

I removed the hand and said, "Tell me about this young man assisting her. Would he have ever worked with her here in the Ebb?"

"Oh, yes. When I said no one was ever in here but Florrie Mae, I don't mean people assisting her. She had a number of protégés over the years. This one's name is Mark Revell. He's an entertainment writer for a paper in Indianapolis, Indiana, of all places. She met him on a movie junket of some kind and took him under her wing."

"Was it serious?"

"No." His smile was melancholy. "She was a romantic, Nate. Do I have to tell you that? That's the bad side of having an open relationship with a woman. A man can go from this one to that one, and it doesn't mean anything, it's just physical. *She* had to be in love . . . at least at the moment."

"Is Revell in Indianapolis now?"

"No, I believe he's staying over for the funeral. He's at the Regency."

So was I—the hotel was at Park Avenue and Sixty-first and an easy walk to Flo's town house off Park and Sixty-eighth.

"What about the hairdresser?"

"Julian Rusk? He lives in the Village. I'll get you his phone number."

"Thanks."

Now, finally, his frown was deep enough to make the eyes narrow. "Nate, you can't think Flo was a *murder* victim . . ."

"Circumstances undetermined, remember? The CIA has its own in-house Dr. Feelbad who can use drugs to simulate heart attacks or accidental deaths or you name it."

"You're saying someone came in, with me in the *house,* and did that, without my knowing?"

"It's five floors and a lot of rooms, Frank. You have that back entrance for the servants, with a stairwell giving access to everything. These spooks have pulled off much more complicated stuff."

"I can't believe it. No. That's far too Ian Fleming. That's as crazy as suicide!"

"You're not against me looking into it a little, are you, Frank?"

He flinched, as if I'd raised a hand to strike him. "No. Not in the least. Oh, those tapes and notes you mentioned?"

"Yes?"

"No sign of anything."

He showed me the top right-hand desk drawer that she kept locked—using a key from her center drawer to open it (not the greatest security)—and revealed it as empty. Had the Ruby tape been in there? If so, someone knew about the handy key, because the drawer showed no jimmy marks.

"Now," he said, "she might have hidden them away in one of her filing cabinets—there's a separate room for those, ten four-drawer files. It would take hours to go through them."

"Would you mind if I did that?"

"Could it wait till after the services?"

"No," I said. "I need this done as soon as possible. I'll make a call and have a man or two join me, from our Manhattan branch. In the meantime, if you'll show me to the file cabinets, I'd like to get started."

"Well, then, uh . . . I guess it'll be all right. There's family coming in, as you might imagine, and . . . but all right. Those tapes are Flo's legacy of sorts, and if you find them, that will be a good thing."

"If they *are* here," I said, "everyone in the house will be better off having them removed."

The puffy reddish face went blank with thought. Then he said, "Look—if you do find the tapes and notes, promise you won't give them to that kid Revell. He'd write his *own* book. When the time comes, maybe you can give that material to Flo's friend Bennett Cerf, and he can assign some *real* writer to it."

"That's fine," I said.

But the two A-1 agents and I did not find the Dallas tapes or notes. The cabinets were brimming with publicity releases and 8-by-10's, as well as clippings of Flo's columns carefully arranged by month and year, and coverage by other journalists of her own celebrity. It was not dull—"Hey, Mr. Heller . . . take a look at this Marilyn shot! Miss Cheesecake 1951!"—but it was also not fruitful.

One small piece of luck came my way when I got back to the Regency around eight P.M. The red-vested bartender in the hotel's chichi red-and-brown basement piano bar had been on duty Sunday night when Flo stopped in for that after-TV-show drink. She'd seemed cheery and "maybe a little high," he said, and had joined a nice-looking younger man in a dark-corner banquette (her regular spot), drinking gin and tonic, staying around till almost two A.M.

"Did you recognize this younger man?"

Bald, bulky, the bartender in his forty or so years had seen it all. "The gentleman had been in here before with Miss Kilgore, yes."

"Was he a hotel guest? Did he sign the tab to his room?"

"Miss Kilgore was paying, sir."

I made my way through the layers of subdued lighting and drifting cigarette smoke to a Negro piano player in a tux, noodling Cole Porter with a nice jazzy edge. He'd also been there Sunday night. Had Flo met a date at the club? *Of course, man! Real lady like Miss Kilgore wouldn't come listen to me play by herself.* Was Miss Kilgore's date a regular? *Couldn't say, man, couldn't say.*

Apparently all ofays looked alike.

Soon I was sitting in Flo's favorite booth with a nice-looking younger man of my own. He wore a collarless black suit with a gray button-down shirt, no tie—apparently he was in mourning, too—and his black hair was Afro-style, though this was apparently a perm, since he was white. Hell, he was pale. A slender five ten, he had the finely carved features of a male fashion model.

"I appreciate you coming up here to talk to me, Mr. Rusk," I said.

"Julian, *please,*" the hairdresser said, with an English accent that might have been real. "And do you prefer Nate or Nathan?"

"Either is fine," I said. "Something to drink?"

He liked that idea, and I waved a waitress over. He ordered a gin and tonic ("In honor of my late and very much lamented client"), and I had a vodka gimlet. On the phone, he'd known immediately who I was—familiar with my minor celebrity courtesy of magazines and tabloids, and aware that I was a good friend of Flo's.

Despite the possibly faked English accent, there was nothing effeminate about him—he was as masculine as Rock Hudson. But it was clear he was gay—something undeniably flirtatious flickered in his manner.

His eyes, which were a dark green, flashed and he smiled just a little. "Are you looking into her murder? I hope."

"Murder? My understanding is the coroner leans more toward accidental death."

"*He* didn't find the body, did he?" Rusk sipped his drink. "I could have told you my story on the phone, couldn't I? But you wanted to talk to me in person. Why? So you could look at me when I answered your questions. To what end? So you can size me up as a witness, or possibly a suspect."

I laughed just a little. "So far you're just answering your own questions."

"Touché. All right—do you want to grill me, or should I just tell my tale?"

"Go ahead and start. I'll jump in as need be."

He sighed grandly. "Well, I let myself in around eight forty-five that morning. Came up the same back staircase used by the servants."

"You had a key?"

"Yes. Not many did, but I fixed Flo's hair on a more-or-less daily basis. Not always so early, mind you—she had a television taping at eleven. Her dressing room is on the third floor, near that hideous Black Room, off the master bedroom—that's where she always had her hair done. I turned on my curling irons, and just idly walked into the bedroom, never thinking for a moment she would be there."

"Why? She shared it with her husband, didn't she?"

"Oh, she hadn't slept there for years, Nathan. They slept apart, Frank and Flo—don't let their breakfast broadcasts fool you." He shook his head. "I knew she was dead, right away."

"Just with a glance?"

"That's all it took. She was sitting up in bed, propped up with a pillow against the red headboard. The bed was spotless, as if she'd slipped under the covers and never moved an inch. She was dressed . . . very peculiarly."

"Be specific, Julian, please."

"All right. Well, normally she'd sleep in pajamas and old socks and her makeup would be off and her hair would be washed and just a mess, waiting for my rescue."

"I see."

"But she was dressed almost as if she were going out—hair in place, makeup on right down to her false eyelashes. She was in a blue matching peignoir and robe—nothing she would *ever* wear to bed."

"She was reading."

"Was she? That book, *Seven Days in May*? She read that months ago. She discussed it with me! And it was laid on her lap so perfectly, so you could read the title . . . only that was *upside down*—not in the right position for her to be reading it."

"Julian, that's a nice piece of deduction."

"Thank you, Nathan. You know, it was cold out that morning—we had a real cold snap. But the air-conditioning in the bedroom was on. Why?"

"If it was murder, perhaps to delay decomposition. Make the time of death harder to determine."

"Well, I guess you put *my* little deduction to shame, didn't you, Nathan? Let's see . . . is there anything else? The light was on, the overhead light, that is, not the nightstand. There was a water glass at her bedside, and a pill bottle, and her latest drink . . . but she was positioned in the very middle of that big bed and couldn't have reached either of them."

"Keep going. You're doing fine."

"I think that's about all. Oh, I would say rigor mortis had set in. Anyway, her hands were stiff. And there was lipstick on her sleeve. Why would that be there?"

"If she still had her makeup on, and someone changed her clothes after her death, her lipstick might have accidently made that transfer."

"My, you are a detective."

"Julian, you called it murder, right out of the gate. Do you have a suspect?"

"Just between us, Nathan?"

"Just between us, Julian."

"The best possibility would be the husband—isn't that always the case? Frank Felton's been unemployed for some time—his various ventures, from Broadway productions to that failed art gallery, exhausted all of his personal funds. And he was facing the possibility of yet *another* divorce from Flo—and this time there was a prenuptial agreement."

"But if she were to die before divorcing him, Frank would inherit the town house, I suppose."

"Oh, yes. And it's worth three hundred grand easily. Plus, there's bound to be a big life-insurance policy on a star like Flo—what, another hundred thou or two?"

"Probably. And retirement funds from the TV show." I mulled

that, then said, "But why the charade, putting her in the master bedroom? Can you see Felton dressing her in her bedclothes and carting her from one floor to another?"

"You've met the man, haven't you, Nathan? He was a producer. Those parties he mounted were like little Broadway shows, and were far more successful than those he actually tried to mount. Oh, he's *perfectly* capable of that kind of drawing-room farce by way of Hitchcock. And the master bedroom, why that's *perfect*—he would want the world to think he and Flo were still a couple, still enjoying connubial relations. The only problem is . . ."

"Yes?"

"It's a big one."

"Okay."

The hairdresser shrugged. "He lacks the balls."

"What about this Mark Revell?"

"He's a very pretty boy, Nathan. And he certainly has balls."

"Are you . . . implying something?"

"I am trying to avoid a vulgar term."

"What term would that be?"

"Fag hag. Vulgar and ugly, but I'm afraid it applies to my late client."

"How so?"

"Revell's in his twenties, he's very handsome, while Flo, lovely lady though she was, was what . . . fifty? He's an entertainment editor at a newspaper in Indianapolis, Indiana—do I have to draw you a picture? And somehow he manages to globe-trot with all kinds of famous larger-than-life females. Maureen O'Sullivan, Myrna Loy, Phyllis Diller, none spring chickens. Then there's Anna Maria Alberghetti, and Mia Farrow, and—"

"They're young."

"Yes, but certain women, for various reasons, like to be squired around by handsome, young, *non-threatening* males."

"Not Flo."

"No. Not Flo. You're correct, Nathan. She was a pistol. She liked her men and she liked them between the sheets and lively. She and

Revell went on movie junkets together to Rome, Florence, London, and shared lodgings. They met many times right here in this hotel—a suite on the nineteenth floor."

Revell was registered at the Regency right now.

Rusk was saying, "I'm sure she and Revell had a gay old time . . . in the old-fashioned sense, that is. *My* sense . . . if I may be frank? Is that Revell may be a switch-hitter."

"Do you have any reason to think he's bisexual?"

"Other than instinct? No. But strong show-business women like Flo are often attracted to the type. She dated Johnnie Ray, you know. *You* were good friends with her, I understand, Nathan. . . ."

"Yeah, and I've squired around some famous women, too."

"Marilyn Monroe, according to what I've read. Jayne Mansfield. And who's that old-time bubble dancer?"

"Sally Rand." I put my hand on his. "But, Julian? This time? You've made the wrong deduction."

And I patted him gently on the cheek.

He smiled and shrugged. "Can't blame a guy for trying," he said.

Was it my imagination, or was the English accent gone?

Half an hour later, Mark Revell was sitting across from me in the same booth. I'd called his room from the bar, and he'd immediately recognized my name. Like Rusk, Flo's protégé knew of both my reputation in the press and my friendship with Flo Kilgore. He was, as advertised, a handsome young man, under thirty, a sturdy six feet, in a muted glen-plaid suit with three-button jacket and matching vest—Cricketeer, I'd guess—with a gold tie with a single thin black stripe. His hair was brown, his look Ivy League, and he might have been a lost Kennedy brother.

"Yes, I'm an entertainment writer, Mr. Heller, for the *Indianapolis News*. On extended leave to work with Miss Kilgore . . . although I guess that's at an end now, isn't it?"

Revell sat with his hands folded and wearing an easy, friendly, rather wide smile. He had ordered a Coke and I'd followed his lead.

His eyes tightened as he thought back. "I met Flo earlier this year, in June I believe, on a press junket for reporters covering the film industry."

"Where was that exactly?"

His smile broadened and his eyes looked up into the pleasant memory. "We were in Salzburg on the set of *The Sound of Music.* I caught her arm when she stumbled, getting onto the press bus, and I said, 'Well, hello!' You know, in a way that said I recognized her as a celebrity. 'You know who *I* am,' she said. 'Who are *you*? Besides my savior.' We just hit it off like that, joking, giggling. We had drinks that night and the rest is history."

"History of what? A love affair?"

He frowned, shifted in the booth, almost but not quite offended by my bluntness. "Oh, you don't understand, Mr. Heller. It was definitely *not* a love affair, or anyway not a physical one. She was just this sweet funny lady, my bestest friend in the world. We talked on the phone every day."

Not in Dallas they hadn't. That was how I'd wound up in bed with her, one last time.

He was shaking his head slightly. "She was so soft, so romantic. Did you ever see her angry? I never did. I think the only conversations we had that were serious at all were about the Kennedy project."

"You knew about the Ruby trip?"

"Oh, yes. I didn't know she was planning to meet up with you, though."

I didn't bother explaining the accidental nature of that.

He was saying, "I know Mr. Felton thinks Flo and I were an item, but really we just *liked* each other, liked to be together, to ditch the pressures of this crazy old world and just *go*."

"Like to Rome and London."

He shifted in his seat, his smile one-sided now. "Mr. Heller, it was strictly platonic. There was a flirty aspect to it, sure, but there was no good-night kiss when I dropped her off. It just wasn't that kind of relationship. Not even close. I had other girls. She knew that."

Did he? I wondered.

I gestured skyward, to the heaven that was the Regency. "I understood that you and Flo sometimes met in your hotel suite."

"No. Maybe briefly for business, but not in the way you mean. After all, we were co-workers, Mr. Heller. I was involved in the Kennedy project, too."

"Did you see her the Sunday she died? Did she share any materials with you from the Dallas trip?"

"I called her in the afternoon. She *never* said much about the Kennedy investigation on the phone, for obvious reasons. No, I don't have any idea what happened in Dallas."

That last statement tried a little too hard for my taste.

"I only know bits and pieces," he said. "I was a sounding board for the Kennedy stories in her column, and also for what she was planning. I don't know if you know this, Mr. Heller, but she was going to write a book. If she did the story for her paper, she might win acclaim, but she was after more—a big score, big money."

"What do you think happened to Flo, Mr. Revell?"

He shrugged sadly. "It's likely she accidentally OD'd. Took a little too many pills with just a little too much gin. She wasn't a big person, you know. Wouldn't take much to be *too* much. But . . . with this Kennedy stuff going on? I'm not an idiot. *Of course* she could have been murdered."

"In that case, would you suspect someone involved in the assassination? Spooks or gangsters or Cubans?"

Oh my.

"I couldn't say, Mr. Heller. It's too terrible to think that that sweet woman, with so much talent and energy in her, could be gone. But I suppose . . ."

"You suppose?"

"Mr. Felton *does* have a lot to gain."

Could it be that simple? A jealous husband killing a rich wife to trade her faithlessness in on a pile of money? Did Florence Kilgore's passing have nothing to do with either Jack—Kennedy or Ruby?

Or had I run into that most unlikely of circumstances in this lunatic case—a genuinely accidental death?

CHAPTER 17

By day, the French Quarter—north of Canal Street, in the so-called "downtown" section of New Orleans—provided a quaint paradise for tourists. Awaiting them were cast-iron vines, flowers, cupids, and fruits adorning tall, cement-covered brick structures painted in light shades but with splashes of bright green via shutters and woodwork. Narrow streets were there to stroll, arrayed with antiques shops, tearooms, and art studios. Best of all, world-famous restaurants often served up their exquisite cuisine in courtyards amid banana trees, palms, and other semitropical flora, their shade still soothing in September temperatures in the 80s.

But at night, this heaven was replaced by an even more seductive hell. Those fabled restaurants—Antoine's, Brennan's, Arnaud's, the Two Sisters, and the rest—closed up early, as if New Orleans were some small roll-up-the-sidewalks Midwestern town; getting a real meal after nine P.M. was a trick here, but few cared. Tourists venturing into this friendly neon Hades were after the jazz, the booze, the girls; were eager to bump into gamblers and preachers, debutantes and streetwalkers, sailors and artists, bums and entrepreneurs.

From riverboat days on, the Vieux Carré had been a fever dream of throbbing rhythm, exotic color, and authentic Dixieland. Bourbon Street in particular remained a glimmering, cocksure concourse, where "No cover, no minimum" was the rule—that and minimum cover on the strippers at such flesh palaces as Casino Royale, Gunga Den, Club Slipper, and Von Ray's Texas Tornado.

The most popular and notorious such address was 228 Bourbon, between Bienville and Conti—the Sho-Bar, open twenty-four hours with the strippers absent only in the afternoon and early evening, replaced by a piano-accompanied girl singer. The modest three-story brick structure, with typical wrought-iron balconies on its upper floors (hotel rooms, often occupied by strippers during Sho-Bar engagements), shared the block with standbys like the Old Absinthe House and the 500 Club and new kids like the Hotsy Totsy and Bikini A Go Go, similar establishments all, but none offering the celebrated likes of Candy Barr, Sally Rand, Blaze Starr, and (this week's headliner) Jada of Carousel Club infamy.

Outside, pulsating neon beckoned and a canopied entrance bragged up star strippers, but the Sho-Bar interior disappointed. This drab, unimpressively appointed chapel of sleaze was crammed with postage-stamp plastic-top tables facing a modest stage with faded red curtains and a tarnished brass guardrail to keep back overenthusiastic ringsiders. Latin dance teams, tap dancers, and blue comedians were among the uninspiring "incidental acts," strictly *Ed Sullivan Show* rejects. What prevented a riot among customers was the girls, who delivered.

Right now a busty beehive blonde called Nikki Corvette, statuesque in a sheer black nightie over pasties and G-string, was displaying herself in various interesting ways on a red divan—allow that in a furniture store and you'd sell a shitload of divans. The four-man tuxedoed combo up there, taking up as little real estate as possible, was playing "When the Saints Go Marching In." Even in Beatlemania days, most of these clubs stuck with the area's traditional Dixieland.

The Colony back in Dallas kicked this place's ass, but the reputation and charisma of the French Quarter—and that name stripper talent—got them by.

The bar, with a few booths, was tucked under the balcony. I ordered a rum-and-Coke, and gave the bartender a five to let Janet know I was here. In five minutes, she was sitting with me in the farthest-back booth. She was in full stage makeup but still in street clothes—jeans and a bandana-style blue-and-white short-sleeve blouse with only her white high-heel pumps to give her away.

She reached across the table and clasped my hands with both of hers. "Oh, I'm so glad to see you, baby. I've missed you."

"You look great. Doing all right? Any . . . problems?"

She shook her head and the tower of red hair bobbled just a little; her makeup was typically over the top, green eye shadow, heavy eyebrows, lipstick as red as a candied apple—she was everything a man could want, but would never admit.

"You're carrying your little .22 in your purse?"

She nodded. "There hasn't been anything like trouble, Nate. Uncle Carlos was in a few nights ago and he talked to me, so friendly and sweet. You know I'm staying upstairs, right? I probably shouldn't. I mean, I'm sleeping with that little rod under my pillow."

"Rod" was such a silly old term. Yet there was nothing at all silly about her concern.

Her lips smiled, her eyes begged. "Why don't you bunk with me while you're in town, Nate?"

"What, two rods can live safer than one?"

"Don't make light."

"Why don't you come stay at the Roosevelt with me? That's one joint Marcello doesn't own."

She looked past me. "When I think of poor Rose, her . . . her skull crushed like a fuckin' melon. Jesus!" She shuddered.

Her hands were still clasping mine. I moved my hands around so I was clasping hers, and I squeezed. "Rose was a loose cannon, honey. She was a junkie and a flake. They know you have your head on your shoulders."

Her chin crinkled. "Well, it could be on the shoulder of a road getting squished, you know. And Flo Kilgore, *she* was no junkie whore."

"Not a whore, but maybe a . . . junkie of sorts."

"What do you mean?"

"She was addicted to pills and she drank too much. It may have been accidental. And that was Manhattan—all the other deaths have been in Texas, and maybe a couple in Louisiana. I'm going to look into those."

She gave me a smirk of a half smile. "You don't think Uncle Carlos has friends in New York?"

I didn't want to tell her that if Flo had been murdered, those responsible were likely CIA, not mob. That would spook her . . . so to speak.

"Flo may have been murdered," I said with a nod. "But there's no *question* that Rose was killed."

She shivered. "And *I* set up that interview with her for you and Miss Kilgore. Nate, you gotta do something about this. You have got to stop these fuckers."

I shifted subjects, slightly. "What about your friend Dave Ferrie? Is he coming tonight?"

She nodded. "I set it up for nine—it's almost that now. Like I said on the phone the other day, he's in here half the evenings anyway. Uncle Carlos lets him run a tab. And he can buy sailors drinks and try to get lucky. Rest of the time he's over at Dixie's Bar. That's for the gay set."

"What did you tell him?"

"Just that you were a friend of mine who asked to meet him. I told him you and Guy Banister were buddies back in Chicago, like you said."

Ferrie had worked for Banister, according to a reporter friend of mine on the *Times-Picayune.* Truth was, I'd always despised Banister, a toad of a man who had been Special Agent in Charge of the Chicago FBI office through much of the '40s and early '50s. But he'd been a heavy drinker whose erratic behavior got him fired. He'd gone on to be the New Orleans chief of police till he got bounced for the same reasons five or six years ago. In recent years he'd been running a PI agency.

"Listen," she said, pulling her hands gently free, "I have to get backstage to get ready. I'll spend a night or two with you at the Roosevelt, if you like. They got room service and my dump upstairs don't."

I smiled. "I'd like that. When do you get off? I'll take you out for something to eat."

"In this wacky town? Anyway, I got sets damn near all night. If you're an early riser in your old age, you could pick me up at five A.M. We could go to the poor boy stand on St. Claude—they're open twenty-four hours—or maybe beignets and café au lait at Café Du Monde?"

"That's worth a wake-up call. When's your last set?"

"Four."

"I'll come watch and then we'll go have poor boys or doughnuts or some damn thing. Then I'll take you back to the Roosevelt and sleep all day."

"Well," she said with a wicked glistening red smile, "we'll stay in *bed* all day, anyway. . . . There he is. There's your man."

She slid out of the booth and headed quickly off into the smoky darkness of the club, her bottom in those jeans more provocative than Nikki Corvette's bare one.

I glanced toward the customer who'd just entered, and was making a beeline toward me displaying a friendly smile, hand outstretched.

At first, in the dim lighting, he looked normal enough, a fairly big guy, around six feet, maybe two hundred pounds, his wide oval face home to large dark eyes, an anteater nose, a rather small thin-lipped mouth, and a pointed chin. He wore a rather jaunty golf cap and a long-sleeve white shirt with narrow dark tie and dark slacks.

Still seated in the booth, I looked up at him while we shook hands, his grip firm but clammy. This close, I could well understand why his appearance had been described more than once as bizarre—the cap rested on what appeared to be a red mohair wig, and Groucho-ish eyebrows had been fashioned out of strips of matching carpet. The effect was clownish.

"Nathan Heller, you are a famous man," he said, in a voice

whose nasal quality was offset somewhat by an authoritative manner. No Southern accent, more Midwestern.

"Not really," I said. "But that's kind of you. Sit, please."

On closer inspection, his clothing looked rumpled, slept-in, and he had the distinct bouquet of BO. What did this guy have against soap?

"I should be more clear," he said. "You're famous in the sense that you've been featured in some popular magazines. But in the circles I move in, you're a kind of hero."

"Really." My God, this son of a bitch stunk.

"You're the man who started it all."

"I am?"

He got a pixie-ish smile going, and his red-mohair eyebrows wiggled. "You were the midwife to . . ." And his whisper was barely audible over "Basin Street Blues," as Nikki Corvette bumped-and-ground. ". . . Mongoose."

Jesus, did every Tom, Harry, and dick know that little piece of history?

Well, maybe I could make hay out of it.

"I understand you've really done your bit," I said.

"Thank you, sir. That is much appreciated, sir."

"What can I buy you to drink?"

"They make a surprisingly good Ramos gin fizz here, considering the lowbrow nature of the establishment."

"Well, let's get you one, Dave . . . or do you prefer David?"

"Oh, I don't stand on ceremony. Make it David."

I tried to figure that one out while I waved over a waitress and ordered him his fizz. I declined getting a refill on my rum-and-Coke. This kook would require all my brain cells.

"So you knew Guy? What a guy!" He laughed at this would-be witticism. "How far back did you two hombres go?"

Hombres?

"All the way to the Dillinger shooting," I said. "He was there, you know. He was FBI, I was Chicago PD."

"Yes, he told me all about that fateful night. How his bullet brought Mr. Big Cock down!"

Okay, that was wrong in so many ways, starting with Banister not being one of the shooters, plus it hadn't really been Dillinger that night. But that's another story, and as for the size of Johnny D's dingus, I couldn't confirm or deny.

"You know, it was a tragic loss," he said, shaking his head, almost dislodging the cap. "For such a big man with a such a big heart to have that very heart attack him."

Banister was one of the as-yet-uninvestigated convenient assassination-related deaths that had occurred in Louisiana—in June of this year.

The waitress brought Ferrie his gin fizz and he thanked her, giving her a wink, getting a grimace in return.

"I admit I'm not aware," I said, "of what Guy did for the cause." Whatever the fuck the cause was. "You give me too much credit on Mongoose. As you say, I was just the midwife."

"But what a baby you brought into the world!" he said, toasting me.

I lifted my empty rum-and-Coke glass to him in return. "But Castro is still with us, I'm afraid."

"But someone *else* isn't."

Gosh, I wondered who he meant.

Then, leaning in conspiratorially, he made sure I knew: "Jack Kennedy was a nigger-loving traitor. Do you have any idea how many of our Cuban brothers he killed with his cowardice?"

So black people were niggers, but brown people were our brothers? I didn't bother trying to navigate the logic of that.

I just said, "No, David. *How* many were killed?"

"Too *goddamn* many! You know, I'm honored you want to get together. I didn't think a small fry like me would be on your radar."

"You're no small fry, David. You put a lot in motion. Ruby. Oswald."

He swallowed. He'd felt free enough tossing Mongoose around, but maybe those names were different. "Come on now, Nate . . . or do you prefer Nathan?"

"Nate's fine."

"Nate. Good. But loose lips sink ships, Nate. Don't forget that. Ships get sunk that way, yes they do."

"That's one of the reasons I wanted to talk to you, David. I was in Dallas last week, accompanying Flo Kilgore to a number of interviews with Kennedy witnesses—witnesses this Warren Commission has ignored or overlooked."

"She just *died.*"

"Yes."

"In New York, wasn't it?"

"That's right, but she was in Dallas all last week."

He was frowning in thought. Was he really unaware of what I'd just shared, or was he a better actor than he had any right to be? "Why would you *do* that? Help her in that way?"

"Well, first of all, she hired me. I'm a private eye, David, like you are. Your main client is Uncle Carlos, right?"

His smile was small because his mouth was small, but his beaming pride was big. "Yes. I do investigations for Mr. Marcello through his lawyer. But I'm also his private pilot. I was with Eastern Airlines, you know."

"No, I didn't know," I lied. My reporter pal had informed me that Ferrie had been fired by Eastern for "homosexual activity on the job." Prior to that, he'd been tossed out of a Catholic seminary for "emotional instability."

"But also," I went on, "I wanted to keep an eye on what the Kilgore woman found out. To make sure she didn't get . . . too close."

The big dark eyes under the red mohair strips turned to slits. Barely audible over a blaring Dixieland "Ain't She Sweet," he whispered, "You didn't . . . didn't liquidate Miss *What's My Line?*, did you?"

"No," I said. "But I found out something disturbing."

"What, man?"

"A lot of witnesses are dying."

"What do you mean?"

"I mean committing suicide or having traffic accidents or just plain old-fashioned getting shot."

"Could be coincidental," he said, but his wheels were turning. "Texas is a violent place. Lots of guns in Texas. Lots of spics and niggers there."

Said the brother of the Cubans.

"I don't think it's happenstance," I said. "I think it's a cleanup crew, David. I think loose ends are being clipped off. Well, I don't know about you, but I don't want to be one."

He smiled again. His teeth were too big for the little mouth. "Maybe that's true, but we're not loose ends. We're major players, Nate."

"Not as major as Uncles Carlos or Santo Trafficante. Or H. L. Hunt. Or Allen Dulles—the fired CIA chief on the Warren Commission?"

"I know who he is."

"Or Lyndon Johnson, either."

He had the expression of a guy viewing his own bad X-rays. "Uh, well, you're right. We're not *that* big, but I don't think . . ."

"David, could Guy's death have been murder?"

"What?"

"Heart attack–inducing or –simulating drugs are child's play for the CIA. Ever hear of Dr. Sidney Gottlieb? He's their number one Dr. Feelbad."

He was visibly nervous now. The confidence had drained from the nasal voice. "If you're right, this is terrible. What can we do? How can we assure the people in charge that we are reliable? I wouldn't betray the cause, Nate. I'm sure you wouldn't, either."

"Sometimes sacrifices have to be made. Look at Ruby. Look at Oswald."

He nodded. "That's true. And it's so sad. I was Lee's captain, you know, in the Civil Air Patrol? That's where I met up with him. I saw such potential in the boy. I recommended him."

"I'm sure he was grateful. And I'm a patriot, David, like you are, but I don't want to be the next sacrifice."

"My God, Nate, what do you suggest?"

"I want to meet with Uncle Carlos."

"What? Why?"

"He's a big fish. One of the biggest. I want to convince him that I'm trustworthy, and that I still have value to him. And I'll put in a good word for you, too, David."

He sipped some fizz and nodded, his mood brightening. "Well, I can arrange that. He's at Churchill Farms right now, so that's out—no phone out there. But I can get you a meeting tomorrow, probably, at his office at the Town and Country Motel."

"No. It has to be a public place. A neutral place. I don't want to become Yankee Gumbo, David. You do know what that is?"

"I know. I know." He looked around anxiously. "I'll see what I can do. See what I can do. Where are you staying, Nate?"

"The Roosevelt."

"I'll call you there, sometime tomorrow." He slipped out of the booth. Nikki was just finishing up to "Muskrat Ramble." He thrust his hand out again and I shook it.

He leaned close. "You're a good man, Nate. I appreciate you thinking of me in this tricky situation."

I was holding my breath, trying not to take in his BO. "Pleasure to meet you, too, David."

His confidence was back and he gave me a little military salute and headed out.

What a fucking lunatic.

I had wanted to size him up, and confirm a few theories, and I had. But what I mostly wanted was that sit-down with Uncle Carlos. I wanted to convince Marcello that I was not a threat. And try to determine whether he was behind the cleanup crew or whether a group of the Dealey Plaza boys had taken it upon themselves to tidy up, for their own benefit.

This was not to say settling scores was not on my mind. A penchant for revenge was perhaps not my best quality, but it was a trait

I was not likely to shed at this late stage of my existence. I would be sharing everything I knew with Bobby Kennedy—including every syllable of the Ruby interview. My capacity for remembering conversations damn near rivaled that James Bond gizmo Flo had recorded him on.

Eventually RFK would be in the White House, where he could deal with his brother's killers in a much better, more complete way than I ever could.

I sat through Janet's first set—her trademark "Hold That Tiger" routine was enough to put a smile on my face, as I thought about having Jada to myself in my room at the Roosevelt all day tomorrow, *jing jing jing*—and then I made my way out of the club and onto the sidewalk.

Funniest damn thing, a car pulled up at the curb looked exactly like the lime-green '64 Galaxie I'd rented at the airport. But I hadn't driven here, I'd walked over from the Roosevelt, and anyway there were a lot of Fords in the world.

"Your ride's here, Mr. Heller," intoned a mellow baritone, with just a tinge of Texas in it, and I turned to see Mac Wallace, his eyes half-lidded behind the heavy black-framed glasses, his smile more a smirk on his five-o'clock-shadow-smudgy face.

Then Ramon Rodriguez—one-half of the Chicago sniper team from last year, who I'd last seen almost running Sam and me down after that Beatles concert—sidled up beside me with a smile.

And a gun.

Muffled Dixieland from within the Sho-Bar provided background music as Wallace said softly, "Get in the backseat, Mr. Heller." His smile was awful, the smile of a man just drunk enough to be dangerous. "This may be New Orleans, but we're going to do this Chicago-style."

Close to me, digging the snout of a revolver into my side, the Cuban said, "Take you for a ride, *maricón*."

Somebody was behind the wheel, but I couldn't see him. I wondered for a moment if it was Ferrie—if so, I'd seriously misjudged him.

They looked like tourists, Wallace in a light-blue shirt jac, the Cuban in a straw fedora with a wide black band and a black-and-white geometric-pattern shirt, the driver in a tan-and-white plaid sport shirt. I was in a Crickteer suit, dark gray, not one of my tailored-for-shoulder-holster numbers.

Then the back door was opening and the nose of the gun in my side was nudging me, and if I cried out to the happy people on this noisy, neon-washed street, that gun would go off and I'd be the next dead witness. I had to let this play out.

I had to take the ride.

With the Cuban next to me in back, the driver glanced over his shoulder at us before pulling out into the slow, steady traffic of Bourbon Street. I realized he was no one I'd ever seen before, though he reminded me of somebody. He had a Gable-style mustache, and a hint of Latino in his heritage; but if I looked past that, he really, *really* reminded me of somebody.

Lee Harvey Oswald.

They cut over to Royal Street, just a block down from the raucous nightly party that was Bourbon Street, into an area where the ghosts of fashionable New Orleans of a century ago might be strolling right now, but hardly anybody else. On this sleeping street of closed curio and antiques shops, art galleries and fine restaurants, the Oswald look-alike pulled over and the Cuban dragged me out onto the sidewalk into the darkness under an overhanging balcony.

Wallace had gotten there ahead of us somehow, and was opening the trunk of the Galaxie—it was my rental, all right, lifted from the Roosevelt parking garage. My buddy Mac was tossing something in, something green and coiled like a snake, and a plump wad of cloth. Then he came over and grabbed me by an arm and yanked, and while I was off-balance, the Cuban swung the revolver, holding it by the barrel and cylinder I guess, because what caught the side of my head felt like the gun butt.

I went limp, though I wasn't out—Rodriguez had seen too many episodes of *Peter Gunn* maybe, figuring all it took was a blow on the head to guarantee unconsciousness. Had his blow landed right, I'd more likely been dead, but really it glanced off, leaving a wet bloody gouge. I knew I was better off in that trunk than in the Galaxie's backseat and I played like I really was knocked cold as Wallace dumped me in there and slammed the lid.

They hadn't bothered to tie my hands—Royal wasn't a busy street but it wasn't deserted. So they'd moved fast, and now we were moving, not so fast. Closed inside that trunk, I got as comfortable as I could, which meant positioning myself on my side, playing fetus. Traffic and other city noise lasted maybe fifteen minutes, and when the sound of the wheels changed to something smooth and humming, I knew where we were—going over the Huey P. Long Bridge.

My old buddy the Kingfish had spent upwards of thirteen mil on the thing—two lanes of US 90 on either side of double railroad tracks—but Huey hadn't lived to see it, missing by three months. From levee to levee, including railroad approaches, the monster was over four miles long. We were heading west into Jefferson Parish.

I had spent a lot of time in Louisiana on my two trips here in the '30s, but that had been over twenty-five years ago. Still, I didn't imagine much had changed. As we exited the bridge, with its notoriously tight lanes, we'd be heading into a landscape of dense swamps, oak-wooded lowlands, treacherous bayous, scattered settlements of poor whites and blacks, and an occasional modern sugar factory, as well as the ruins of old sugar refineries. The deeper into this territory we drove, the more chance I would become a heaping serving of Yankee Gumbo after all.

My fingers found what Wallace had tossed into the trunk ahead of me—a length of garden hose, about nine feet of the stuff, and a bath towel. I knew at once what they had in store for me. The hose, which was three-quarters of an inch in diameter, would easily run from the exhaust pipe of the Galaxie up to a slightly rolled-down window of the vehicle, where the towel could be stuffed to make a tighter seal, so the carbon monoxide could do its stuff. Looked like Mac Wallace figured I'd be getting despondent in this trunk and soon be ready to commit suicide, though my despondency would be strictly optional.

The car made a right turn onto a crunchy surface, a gravel or even more likely (considering where we were) crushed-shell road. The lane must have extended back under the bridge approach because I heard a rolling sound that might have been a car above me on cement. We went perhaps a mile farther and the car swung over a little and came to an abrupt stop, though the driver did not kill the engine. Car doors opened and closed.

When the trunk lid lifted, the Cuban in the straw fedora was smiling down at me and, with the nine millimeter tight in my hand—the one I'd tucked away behind the spare tire being unlicensed to carry in Louisiana—I fired three rounds into his face and each one found something to do, this one punching out an eye, that one dimpling his forehead, another shattering that smile like a brick through a window. He fell away fedora and all and I leapt out like a demented jack-in-the-box, and I could see Wallace, parked down a ways to the right on the other side of the road, leaning against the car he'd followed us here in, its motor running, his mouth hanging open with a cigarette in it so freshly lit he hadn't waved the match out yet.

But I could also see the Oswald look-alike on my right, too, but much closer, going for a gun in his waistband, and I gave him two rounds in the head, taking his skull apart and spraying brains and blood and bone into the night, his head going back just like physics had demanded of Jack Kennedy, and he did a backward pratfall, landing half on the crushed-shell road, half on the shoulder, in memory of Rose Cheramie.

I spun, with eight rounds left in the mag for Wallace and happy to give him every one, but he was already behind the wheel of his car, a red Chevy Corvair, which he swung around, tires stirring shells, the vehicle's nose toward me, rumbling right at me, headlights blinding, and I dove out of the way as he picked up speed, heading back toward the highway, spitting crushed shells, fishtailing.

With the Galaxie's engine still running (they'd hot-wired it), I was able to take off right after him, blinking away the half-blindness those headlights had caused. He didn't have much of a head start.

I tossed the nine millimeter temporarily on the rider's seat, steered with my left hand as I reached across to roll down the window with my right, then passed the nine millimeter to myself, from my right hand to my left, and half-leaned out of the vehicle Wild West–style as I ripped a shot off into the night. The sound was thunderous, echoing off the nearby river, filling the dark cathedral of the outdoors with reverberations.

After my shot, which missed both him and the vehicle, he began to weave, making a target that though big was erratic, and even with my thirteen-shot magazine, I didn't want to waste any more bullets. I would ram the son of a bitch. There, under a full moon that made spectral figures out of bordering cypress trees in their cloaks of Spanish moss, two vehicles sped down a narrow country road with the Mississippi an unseen but felt presence at our right, and the looming Huey P. Long Bridge up ahead.

I didn't want him to make it to that bridge. I didn't want him to make it back to New Orleans. I wanted him here, I wanted him now, in the swampy primeval darkness.

I was going a grinding one-hundred when I bumped his rear bumper and he tried to pick up speed but there wasn't anything left in the Corvair, and he looked back at me, his handsome bespectacled face turned hideous with hysteria, as if to beg for mercy, and this time when I rammed him, he lost control and I immediately took my foot off the pedal and watched him take off over the left shoulder and crash into the cement pillar of the bridge approach, the right front of the vehicle crumpling like a paper cup in a fist, with a tinkling of headlight glass adding delicate high notes to the discordant low-pitched music of crunching metal.

I pulled over, left it running, got out with the gun in my right hand, and walked slowly over to the Corvair, which had its right wheels off the ground, spinning, the exhaust puffing mightily into the night on the car's ride to nowhere. Night sounds were kicking back in, frogs, owls, nighthawks, crickets, a melancholy yet disinterested Greek chorus. I approached cautiously, though I could see him slumped behind the wheel, his head back, physics again, the windshield spiderwebbed where his skull had hit it, one lens of his black-framed glasses similarly veined.

He was breathing. Not quite unconscious. His face was smeared with blood and his forehead had a rip in it, showing bone. He looked at me with pain in his eyes. Somebody should do something to help him out.

I went back to the Galaxie and got the length of hose and the bath towel.

When I was rolling his window nearly (but not all) the way up, I noticed he had a package of Chesterfields in the breast pocket of his sport shirt. I relieved him of those. Then I rigged up the fake suicide. He seemed to be awake during the procedure, though he said nothing. I tried not to smile at him, but I just couldn't help myself.

I went back to the Galaxie and used the dashboard lighter to fire up a Chesterfield. I burned through three waiting for him to die. In the dankness near the river, though the night itself was cool and dry, with the ghostly trees and bushes gathered round, I might have been back on Guadalcanal, waiting for the Japs to make another *banzai* attack. Certainly I was in some kind of fucking jungle.

I pitched the last of the Chesties down the gravel-and-shell road. It would have been reckless to toss it into the brush. Funny thing, my first thought as I pulled out was to wonder if I had time to get back to the Roosevelt, clean up, and still meet Janet for beignets and café au lait. My wristwatch, easily visible in the moonlight, said it wasn't even midnight.

What was I going to do with all that time?

Then something came to me.

CHAPTER 18

Heading along US Highway 90 East, I almost missed the turnoff to Churchill Farms. I hadn't been the driver the one time I'd been there before. But my previous visit to the 6,400-acre swampland domain of Carlos Marcello had been nothing short of memorable, and my only real problem was spotting the turn at night. The moonlight helped.

For all of Marcello's visionary talk two years ago, about developing this property, nothing had changed. It still surprised me there was no gate, that this was not a private road. The lane remained a narrow strip of dust-generating rutted dirt, with barely enough shoulder on either side to allow cars going in opposite directions to make room for each other—not that I met any.

As I glided by in the Galaxie, the lights were on in the small, rustic-looking shrimp-packing plant with its Negro workers, one of Marcello's legitimate businesses. Otherwise, the full moon was providing all the illumination, lending an otherworldly beauty to the marshy landscape on my either side, untamed foliage shimmering in a gentle breeze, washed ivory. Dead cypress and living willows seemed to keep a watchful eye, like overseers in slave days.

The clearing came sooner than I remembered, the marshland making way as if Moses had parted it to take room for the barn-turned-farmhouse, its white paint job given a ghostly glow by the moon, several narrow downstairs windows burning yellow, the rest black (including those upstairs). It was almost one in the morning, after all. The red-painted shed off to the right had an abandoned look, no milling chickens and goats this time of night. Two cars were parked on the gravel apron beside the farmhouse—the familiar bronze Caddy and a sporty Dodge, a new model called Lancer, coincidentally also the Secret Service designation for President Kennedy. Had Carlos Marcello learned the meaning of irony after all?

Almost as if he were still perched there from my previous visit, Jack—Marcello's barber, chauffeur, and bodyguard, all in one tall, burly package—was sitting on the top step of the little cement porch, wearing a light-blue leisure suit, long legs angled in two directions as he smoked a cigarette, adding a little fog to an otherwise cloudless night. Well, anyway, he'd been sitting when I first entered the clearing. By the time I pulled up a few feet from the house, he was on his feet and approaching with a .38 revolver in his hand, calling, *"Guys! Guys!"*

They were out of the house before I was out of the car, two thugs in the kind of hats and sport shirts and slacks you wear on a golf course, if you're a fan of pastels, that is.

Hands high in the air, I said, loud, in a rush of words, "Jack, it's Nate Heller! Remember me? I have an emergency I need to talk to Uncle Carlos about."

The other two had slipped past Jack on their way toward me, also with guns in hand; but he told them, "Hold up!"

Then he moved through them like a cop through a crowd and planted himself, facing me, perhaps four feet away. His revolver in hand, but pointing down, he looked at me skeptically.

He wasn't exactly threatening as he said, "I remember you, Mr. Heller. But it's late and Mr. Marcello doesn't appreciate drop-in guests."

"It's an emergency, Jack. And I understand Uncle Carlos doesn't have a phone out here."

"That's right. This is where he gets away from it all. I will tell him you stopped by, and you can probably meet with him tomorrow at the Town and Country."

"It can't wait. You check with him."

"You call at the motel in the morning. I'll make sure you get an appointment."

"He's not going to like it, Jack, if you don't check with him. I said it was important."

He thought about that, but seemed about to say no, despite my insistence.

So I insisted some more: "There are some freshly dead business associates of his that he's going to want to know about. Right now."

Jack frowned. Then, very slowly, he nodded. "Okay. I'll wake the boss. You stay put."

He turned to go back inside, but paused on the way to whisper orders to the pair of fellow bodyguards. Then he glanced over his shoulder at me and gave me an almost smile. "Mr. Heller, this is unusual enough that I've instructed my friends to keep you covered. No offense is meant."

"None taken," I said.

One flunky, young and skinny in shades of green, including his wide-banded straw porkpie, stood facing me at my left, maybe six feet away; similarly positioned to my right was an older, beefier guy with pockmarks and a mustache and shades of yellow attire, including an Ivy League cap. Today's male fashions were definitely not doing thugs any favors. On the other hand, the green porkpie's Colt Python, a .357 Magnum, and his partner's Smith and Wesson .44, went a long way toward making up for it.

My nine-millimeter Browning was in its shoulder holster, by the way, a tight fit in a suit not cut for it. I also had a Colt Woodsman .22 stuck in my waistband, though concealed by my suit coat (one button buttoned), and a little Mauser .22 auto in my left-hand suit-coat pocket. These handguns had been retrieved from the late Rodriguez and the Oswald look-alike, when I'd returned to the scene to do a little of my own cleanup.

Not much had been necessary. I just wanted some extra firepower, if I was going midnight-calling on Uncle Carlos. And I did need to spend some time at the scene of Mac Wallace's tragic suicide, wiping off my fingerprints from a few surfaces—again, not many: the towel and garden hose, for example, were not conducive to prints. The window and its handle, however, were.

"Leo," the shades-of-green younger one said in a cornpone drawl, "I believe the old gent's heavy. Don't the old gent look heavy to you?"

He had noticed the bulge under my left arm.

"Good eye, Freddie boy," Leo said. "Give the man a frisk. You're gonna have to stand for a frisk, bud."

"No," I said.

They both looked at me like kids who just learned the truth about Santa Claus.

"Those weren't Jack's orders," I said, nothing confrontational in my tone. "Keep your distance and we'll stay friendly."

This seemed to offend Leo, though his irritation would have carried more weight if he hadn't been wearing that dumb cap. He growled, "What makes you think *Jack's* the one gives the orders around here?"

"Because I saw him give you orders. Don't overstep."

Leo frowned. "Frisk him, Freddie."

I laughed.

Freddie glared at me. "What's so funny?"

"It just sounded funny," I said with a shrug. "'Frisk him, Freddie.' Sounds like a British Invasion tune."

Hurt, Freddie put his Colt away in his own shoulder holster and said, "You gonna stand for a frisk, smart-ass, like Leo says."

When he stepped toward me, I shoved Freddie into Leo, and they both went down. I kicked Leo in the wrist and his .44 popped out and landed in the gravel a foot or so away.

By the time the door opened and Jack came back out, with Uncle Carlos right behind him—the five-foot criminal kingfish wearing a purple silk robe belted over white pajamas in his bare feet—they found me pointing the nine millimeter down at the two flunkies.

"What de fuck is *dis,* Heller?" Marcello demanded. "What *is* dis shit?"

The bullnecked, broad-shouldered little mob boss brushed past Jack and barreled down the steps in my direction. Walking on gravel in his bare feet caused him no more trouble than a Hindu fakir treading over hot coals.

"They got frisky," I said. "In the take-my-gun-off-me sense. Good evening, Uncle Carlos. Or is that good morning?"

"Let's hear it, Heller," Marcello demanded. He was frowning, making his dark wide-set eyes disappear into slits. His receding hairline gave several veins plenty of room to stand out his forehead.

"We shouldn't discuss it," I said, "in front of the children."

His nostrils flared. "Dis is *funny,* is it? You bargin' in on me, middle of the night? Roustin' my boys?"

"Apologies. Stressful evening." I gestured with my free hand, still training the nine millimeter on the two men down on the ground. "Jack, come over here, please."

Jack glanced at Marcello—he was at his boss's side now—and the Little Man, though sneering, nodded his permission.

With my free hand, I held my suit coat open, exposing the automatic in my waistband. "Take it," I told the hulking barber. "And get the little one out of my left suit-coat pocket, too."

He did so, then backed away, and displayed the weapons to Marcello, who seemed more confused than angry now.

I said, "I lifted that hardware off two dead men who tried to kill me tonight."

Again Jack glanced at his boss, looking for an explanation that Marcello didn't (or maybe couldn't) provide.

I put my nine millimeter away and the two flunkies on the ground looked at each other and then at their boss and the barber, too, not knowing what to make of my action or what to do about it.

"Go on, get up," I said, not harshly. "Leo, you can collect your .44. Just both of you, back off."

They did.

"This is a friendly call," I said to one and all, "but I'm not going to give up my gun. Too much shit has gone down tonight for me to take that kind of chance."

"And comin' out here like dis," Marcello said, his curiosity getting the better of his rage, *"ain't* takin' a chance?"

"Uncle Carlos, I am assuming," I said, not exactly telling the truth, "that you had nothing to do with the attempt on my life tonight. But I thought you should have the opportunity to deal with the mess I made, since this is your turf, and the dead men had ties to you."

"What *kinda* fuckin' ties, Heller?"

"They were involved in . . . helping you remove a stone from your shoe."

Livarsi 'na pietra di la scarpa!

His dark inverted-V eyebrows rose so high, they formed straight lines momentarily; the dimpled chin jutted out over his second, fleshy one. His dark eyes were moving with thought.

Then he summoned a somewhat convincing smile for me and gestured with his pudgy hands, saying, "Come have a chat wid me, Nate. You boys cool your heels, ya hear? Dis be a *friendly* chat."

Following his lead, I walked with Marcello over to where the clearing gave way to marsh. Where just two years before, he had painted pictures in the air of condominiums and shopping malls and theaters and stadiums. Right now the swamp stretched out in endless contradiction of that dream, the moonlight making silver highlights on the rippling water. Birds and bugs and frogs were singing their individual songs that somehow made a unified musical statement, as if to say they had been here before man and would be here after man.

"So, Nate, my frien' . . . what da fuck dis *about,* anyway?"

"Uncle Carlos, ever hear of a guy named Mac Wallace?"

He drew in some cool night air, then nodded as he let it out.

I asked, "You're aware that he was LBJ's man?"

The dark eyes squinted at me. *"Was?"*

"I killed him tonight."

"Did you now."

I might have just told him the score of a game he had nothing bet on.

But I elaborated: "Rigged up a suicide-and-car-crash combo that will have everybody guessing. On that crushed-shell lane under the Huey Long Bridge approach . . . Jefferson Parish side. It's right by the bridge, so it's gonna get noticed. But you may still have time to deal with the other two."

"What other two would dat be?"

"A Cuban named Rodriguez. The other I don't know by name . . . but he's the look-alike who went around Dallas, last November, advertising Lee Harvey's bad intentions."

He frowned and nodded and took me gently by the arm. We strolled back over to Leo and Freddie, to whom he had me give a more specific rundown on the corpses and their whereabouts. Then Marcello gave the pair quick but detailed instructions, getting a lot of nods in return, and soon they climbed in the Dodge Lancer and stirred gravel peeling out.

"Let's go in de house, Heller," Marcello said, through a forced smile, then led the way up the porch steps, pausing to say to his all-purpose bodyguard, "You keep watch out here, Jackie boy, hear?"

"Yes, sir," Jack said.

We did not sit in the kitchen this time listening to Connie Francis records. We did share drinks again, although this time I asked for rum and got it, with Uncle Carlos giving himself a healthy slug of Scotch, as before. This was the second floor of the renovated barn, the handsomely appointed conference room, its wood-paneled walls arrayed with framed aerial photographs of Marcello properties.

We sat at the long, polished-wood conference table, in two of ten executive-style black-leather chairs around it. My put-upon host was at the head of the table, which was only fitting. And for this one night, at least, I sat at his right hand.

"What da fuck happen t'night, Nate?" he asked. "Don't spare de damn details."

"It started at the Sho-Bar," I said. "I met with your man David Ferrie there."

I gave him the same routine I had Ferrie—that I'd been helping Flo Kilgore, just to keep an eye on what she was up to, but discovered witnesses were dying and had no desire to be the next target of a post-assassination cleanup crew.

"Dat homo ain't my 'man,'" Marcello said, meaning Ferrie, "but he sho nuff has his uses. Smart fella for a fourteen-karat queer—he's workin' on a cancer cure, can ya dig dat? Apartment's fulla lab rats, can ya picture dat?"

This struck me as an evasive response. He was talking about one thing while thinking about something else. I didn't want to give him time to scheme.

Pressing, I said, "Those three tonight, Uncle Carlos, who took me for a spin. We both know they were at Dealey Plaza."

"Lot of folks at de Plaza dat day."

"You weren't. You were in New Orleans, in court, beating the case Bobby Kennedy had against you."

"True dat. And David Ferrie, he sittin' next to me."

"Well, Wallace and the Cuban and 'Oswald,' they were in Dealey Plaza all right, each on a hit team, maybe the same one. Must have been at least three such teams, each with shooter, backup, wheelman."

Marcello just shrugged.

I said, "I'm assuming this team took it upon themselves to start disposing of witnesses. To protect their own asses."

"Dat make sense, sho nuff."

"This Warren Commission is a whitewash job, but it still doesn't hurt, discouraging citizens from sharing what they know. And you don't get more discouraged than dead."

"Dat's true."

"But with journalists like Flo Kilgore and Mark Lane and dozens of others digging into the case, Uncle Carlos, this thing is not going away. Killing the President of the United States is not just another contract kill."

"Nobody said dat it was."

"And this one had way too many players. Something this ambitious, it's hard to contain."

"You ain't wrong."

"I choose to believe that you didn't send those men to kill me tonight, Uncle Carlos. Or, for that matter, to kill Rose Cheramie or Hank Killam or Guy Banister or any of the others."

"Banister, he die of a heart attack. Dem others I never hear of."

"Fine. Maybe you didn't hear about that Rodriguez character, either, trying to run me down a few weeks ago. And almost killing my kid in the bargain? I'll give you the benefit of the doubt."

His upper lip curled back over feral teeth. "Ya know, Nate, I like you. I like you just fine. You got brains and nerve and I like dat. But you know what I don't like? Is fuckin' threats."

"We're just having a friendly drink in the wee hours," I said. "I figure it took about nine people, positioned around Dealey Plaza in high buildings and at that fence on that grassy slope, to help you and your powerful pals take that stone out of your shoe. Three of them died tonight, and some of the rest may already be dead. Frankly, I think maybe it would be helpful to you, to have all nine dead."

"Dere's a case could be made."

"At least one, I figure, is European. Hot-shot sniper from Corsica, and with your overseas connections, he was probably one of your contributions. Trafficante kicked in the Cubans, Giancana pitched in on Nicoletti, and maybe John Rosselli, who I figure for an organizational role. The spooks surely provided some top talent, not to mention fake Secret Service IDs and other goodies."

"Seem like you figure a lot, Heller."

"I really don't know all the details. All the players. I don't *want* to know. I just want to go back to Chicago and forget about it. And particularly forget I ever heard the words *Operation Mongoose.*"

The eyebrows hiked over the glasses, their inverted V's flattening out again. "Den . . . dis thing is *over* for you, Nate, t'night? Dat right?"

"It's over if you let it be over. I don't know if you sent out that cleanup crew, Uncle Carlos. I really don't. But I respectfully ask that you approach all your high-powered friends, who backed those high-powered rifles, and let them know that I am on the sidelines now. That, yes, I took offense when that Cuban tried to run me and my son down, and so I took the bastard out. And Mac Wallace, well him I encountered on another matter—he killed a client's husband—so I took him out, too."

"Pretty active ol' boy, dis Nate Heller."

"Maybe so. But it ends there. Ends here. Okay?"

That big puffy oval face had a friendly expression that I didn't like at all. "Not sure I know what kinda of powerful folks you mean, Nate . . . but, far as it goes, why sure. I spread de word. Glad to do it."

"I'm not fucking around, Uncle Carlos. You send the message to everybody from H. L. Hunt to your assorted spook buddies to Trafficante and Mooney and these various demented Cubans all the way up to the Oval Office. Anybody comes near me or my son, and this whole goddamn thing will unravel like a cheap sweater."

"My, my, Nate. Such colorful talk. Like one of dem private eyes on TV or in de paperbacks. Kind dat never gets killed."

"No, I can be killed. Anybody can be killed, Carlos. If history has taught us anything at all, that's it."

I reached under my arm and withdrew the nine millimeter and set it on the shiny wood next to my glass of rum.

"Why, for example, right now I am sitting in a room with Carlos Marcello. I talked my way in, and I could shoot my way out—you only have that barber of yours downstairs at the moment. And you would be dead. *Anybody* can be dead, Carlos. Ask Jack Kennedy."

His expression was blank, but it was taking him a lot of effort to keep it that way. For instance, he did not allow his eyes to drift anywhere near the gun by my hand.

"I know better than to get tough with a man like you, Uncle Carlos. I know not to threaten. Threats are such empty things. So here's a promise."

He frowned.

Time for the big lie.

I said, "The tape that Flo Kilgore made of Jack Ruby spilling every detail about Dallas has been duplicated a dozen times. Right now, it's in a dozen safety-deposit boxes all around the country. If anything happens to me, copies of that tape will go to Bobby Kennedy and the current attorney general and *The New York Times* and . . . well, you get the idea."

His eyes were wide and bulging, though his whole face frowned around them and veins were throbbing in his forehead again. "Dat's bullshit, man. Dere ain't no such tape."

Almost gently, I said, "There is. I might also mention that I have better than a hundred employees, coast to coast, most of whom are ex-cops, hard-asses who like their boss very much. Who would not respond well if he and/or his family were targeted again, and they will know, all of them, who to turn to for redress of their grievance."

He slammed a fist on the table and the glasses of Scotch and rum jumped, and so did the nine millimeter.

And so did I.

"Who da *fuck* you think you *talkin'* to, you Yankee sum of a bitch?"

"Not the cops or the FBI," I said easily, meeting his gaze. "And I could have gone to them tonight, and told them I'd been kidnapped, and that I fought back in self-defense against my captors."

"Dat don't fly! You kill *Wallace* t'night."

"No, he committed suicide after I chased him and he crashed into that abutment. He knew all his evil deeds had finally caught up with him, and took the coward's way out."

"Dat's what *you* say."

"That's what I would say to the cops and FBI, yeah. Also, that I'd been assisting Flo Kilgore in researching the assassination and this attempt on my life was the result. I would share all of my suspicions and observations, including the threat to the President's life you made to me in this house, two years ago."

Silence.

All around us were the framed aerial photographs of his properties, his empire, images of what he had to lose.

His face was stone but I could see his hands trembling. Had I frightened Carlos Marcello? Or was he about to explode in rage?

Finally he said, "What you want, Heller?"

I shook my head. "Nothing. Nothing but what I told you. Spread the word up and down the line—Nate Heller is out of this. If I die a natural death, those tapes are to be destroyed. Anything suspicious happens to me, the whole house of cards comes down . . . *capeesh*?"

I picked up the nine millimeter, and he flinched, just barely; then I tucked it back under my arm.

"Jack Ruby," he said, "he a damn looney tune. Nobody gonna believe what *dat* fool say."

"Maybe not. You can factor that in. But they bought it when he said he killed Oswald to spare Jackie and Caroline, remember."

He was shaking his head, trying to convince himself. "Dat TV woman, she didn't make no goddamn tape."

"No, she did." But he seemed fuzzy where Flo Kilgore was concerned, and I didn't think he was faking. I asked, "You didn't have anything to do with her death?"

"No. Hell no. I didn't send no goddamn cleanup crew, neither. Who need *dat* kind of attention?"

I was actually starting to believe him. "Okay, Uncle Carlos. I do apologize for the intrusion. Thanks for the drink."

He rose, puffing himself up some, making sure he still had his dignity, even if he was a squat little middle-aged wop in a silk purple robe, white pajamas, and bare feet. "You my guest, Heller. I walk you out."

I allowed him to do so. I followed him down the stairs and through the blandly furnished house and back into the moon-swept night. Frogs, insects, and night birds were still singing. Dark shapes were loping across the sky, darker shapes moving in the murky waters.

"You know, Nate," he said, quiet, his gruff voice just one small sound in a night of sounds, "if dat tape you talk about really *do* exist . . . you could sell it to me for a whole lotta loot."

"Uncle Carlos, I have loot. What I *can* use is a life-insurance policy. And, you know, at my age? That's not easy to get."

"You got dat right," he admitted.

"Anyway," I said with a shrug, "you could never be sure I gave you all the copies."

"Dere are ways."

"Like taking me over to Willswood Tavern and working me over with a blowtorch? Wouldn't do any good. I had other people salt those tapes around. I don't know even know where they are."

Marcello shrugged. "Dat's the neat thing about havin' a big organization. You can isolate yo' seff."

Maybe he meant "insulate," but I didn't correct him—I was his guest, after all.

With his barber-cum-bodyguard at his side, Uncle Carlos stood there watching me, a squat creature who happened to be the chief bullfrog of this particular swamp. I was just a fly who had maybe managed to put some distance between me and his darting tongue.

In the Galaxie, heading down the rutted road, I was shaking, something I could allow myself, now that I was out of Marcello's presence. I checked my watch. Just enough time to get back to the Roosevelt, clean up, and catch Janet's last set at the Sho-Bar. Beignets and café au lait were about all my jumpy stomach could stand right now.

There was one thing to attend to—I would have to ditch the Galaxie in the French Quarter, somewhere at least as deserted as Royal. I had rammed Mac Wallace, at high speed, and any decent criminology lab would likely find paint-chip transfer from one vehicle to another. Wallace had crashed nose first into that abutment, and any officer with any smarts would raise the question of damage to the Corvair's tail. Of course, that assumed cooperation between two parishes, Jefferson and Orleans, so maybe I didn't need to bother.

Still, after Janet and I returned, on foot, to the Roosevelt after the French Market, I best call the Galaxie in as stolen.

About halfway to the highway, I had to pull over to let the Lancer get narrowly by. The frowning faces of Leo and Freddie looked over at me; they were returning to Churchill Farms, to their boss, the Little Man. Almost certainly their trunk was crammed with a dead Cuban and a mustached corpse bearing a striking resemblance to a certain famous lone-nut assassin.

Maybe I was going to have fancy French doughnuts for breakfast, but I'd bet that swamp would be getting a heaping double helping of non-Yankee Louisiana Gumbo.

CHAPTER 19

The district attorney of Orleans Parish sat at a surprisingly small, uncluttered desk, though a table behind him was piled with law books, notebooks, files, yellow pads, and assorted other evidence that work went on in this office of dark wood paneling opulent enough to date back to Huey Long's era.

Or perhaps the desk seemed small because the man behind it was so big: Jim Garrison (that was the name on the door—not James) had stood to shake my hand, and I'd got a good intimidating look at the man. Six foot six, somewhat heavy-set, he cut an almost dapper figure in a light-blue three-piece suit with a dark-blue-red-and-white striped tie. He had handsome if slightly cow-eyed features with a high forehead and short, dark, well-barbered hair.

I was in one of several visitor's chairs across from him as he leaned back in a high-backed swivel chair and puffed on a pipe, its smoke nicely fragrant.

"Mr. Heller, I'm happy to report," he said, in a sonorous baritone, the words coming slowly yet distinctly, with only the faintest Southern accent, "that we have found your stolen rental car."

"Well, that's good news," I said. "Of course, your two investigators could have just told me that at my hotel."

He shrugged, as if that were of no import, but his eyes were hard and he seemed to blink only when he had to. "Well, there's some red tape to burn through. I hope to arrange it so you don't have to stay in town any longer than necessary."

Was I being asked to leave by the morning stage?

"Not sure I follow, Mr. Garrison."

Another shrug. "It's just with a stolen vehicle, you might expect to be involved with various legal formalities. But the car wasn't stolen from you, Mr. Heller—technically it was stolen from the rental company."

"Well, all right."

For this I'd been taken to the district attorney's office? Had the unlikely happened, and Orleans and Jefferson Parishes linked that Galaxie to the Mac Wallace fatality?

He swung halfway around to the table behind him and reached for an item, then swiveled back and tossed a *Life* magazine on the desktop. From 1958, it had Kim Novak on the cover posing as a pretty witch with a cat. I knew this issue well, because it also featured an article called "Chicago Private Eye Goes Hollywood."

"I had one of my people," he said with a tight, sleepy smile, "go pick this up at the library this morning."

It was only ten-thirty now. What the hell?

He laid the magazine out flat and flipped it to the article and the pictures of me, mostly with celebrity clients. "I was familiar with your name, Mr. Heller. Vaguely familiar, but familiar. This isn't the only article covering your . . . exploits."

"I don't really think of them as exploits."

He chuckled deep in his chest, but his eyes weren't laughing at all. "This meeting isn't really about your rental vehicle, Mr. Heller. That was in part a courtesy to you . . . to indeed tell you we'd found the car . . . but primarily as an excuse for you and me to have a friendly talk."

"Okay."

"One of my investigators spotted you last night at the Sho-Bar, talking to one of our more colorful citizens—Mr. David Ferrie.

And in Nawlins, Mr. Heller, being one of its most colorful citizens is something of an accomplishment."

"I'll bet." I shifted in my chair, which was wood and not near as comfy as the DA's padded leather number. "How is it a New Orleans cop would recognize me? That issue of *Life* hasn't been on the stands for some time."

"Oh, he didn't recognize you, Mr. Heller. And he wasn't a cop—he was one of my staff investigators. We keep a close eye on the Bourbon Street establishments. Our city depends on tourism, and B-girls running badger games only breeds ill will."

"Bourbon Street sells sin. That brings tourists."

"Oh, I'm no prude, Mr. Heller. Gracious, no. I got myself in a jam not long ago when I refused to prosecute an exotic dancer who had stepped over the line. . . . The girls are not allowed to touch their vaginas, you see."

"I assume you mean onstage. And I bet the boys aren't allowed to, either."

That got a genuine smile out of him and his eyes sparked. He rested his pipe in an ashtray, tenting his fingers on his vested belly as he rocked back. "I should explain how you caught my investigator's attention."

"Please do."

"Mr. Ferrie is an individual who we keep something of an eye on. He's a predatory pedophile, for one thing."

"Did your investigator think I was under eighteen?"

He ignored that. "My investigator noted you were in a rather . . . intense discussion with Mr. Ferrie, and he inquired of the manager of the establishment, Frank Ferrara, and *he* knew who you were. That's how your name came to my attention . . . that and this morning's report of a stolen car."

"So I got on your radar twice. But there's nothing to it."

"We brought Mr. Ferrie in," Garrison said, relighting his pipe, puffing it till its bowl's contents glowed orange, "just four days after the President's assassination."

The back of my neck prickled.

"We had a tip from an ex–CIA man that Ferrie—he's a pilot, you know, a disgraced one, fired by Eastern Airlines on moral grounds—had been hired to fly some of the assassins out of Dallas."

"Assassins?"

"There are those, Mr. Heller, who don't accept the government's lone gunman assessment. You think a man with a bolt-action rifle, with a loose telescopic sight and a tree in the way, could have done that crime alone?"

I shrugged. "Ferrie was in court in New Orleans on November twenty-second last year. With Carlos Marcello."

The DA of Orleans Parish surely knew all about Carlos Marcello. Hell, he was probably on Uncle Carlos's payroll . . . which meant I needed to take care with what I said.

"That was in the early afternoon," Garrison said, "and we understand Ferrie left for Texas by car later in the day. Frankly, all we did was pick Ferrie up, question him some, and hand him over to the FBI . . . who promptly sprung him."

"Maybe they didn't have anything on him."

"Well, we have since learned that Lee Harvey Oswald and Ferrie were in the Civil Air Patrol together . . . and Oswald was not yet eighteen, to pick up that thread again."

"What makes this your concern, Mr. Garrison?"

"It's my jurisdiction. Should I ignore the possibility that the men who planned the murder of the President did so right here in New Orleans? Understand, the extent to which Lee Harvey Oswald was involved in certain questionable activities locally is extremely interesting."

"I suppose so, but it doesn't have anything to do with me."

"What was your business with Ferrie at the Sho-Bar, Mr. Heller?"

"It's as you say, Mr. Garrison—it's *my* business."

The prosecutor pressed. "You must have known the man Ferrie used to work for . . . Guy Banister? He headed up the Chicago FBI a decade ago, I understand."

"I knew him. He was a drunk and a bigot."

"That's what got him fired as police chief down here. We understand also that he was active with the John Birch Society and collected and stored weapons at his address on Lafayette Street for anti-Castro Cuban exiles."

"Sounds about right."

"And here's another interesting fact—Lee Harvey Oswald was a frequent caller at Banister's office, and apparently worked out of there when he was distributing *pro*-Castro leaflets on Canal Street."

"Sounds like typical spook stuff."

"As well it might. Banister's address is in the thick of Intelligence Central here in New Orleans—offices of FBI, CIA, and Naval Intelligence, easy walking distance. Banister died the night before the Warren Commission interviewed Jack Ruby in his jail cell, by the way. What do you make of that, Mr. Heller?"

"Why should I make anything of it?"

He sat puffing on his pipe, leaning back, his manner casual, almost lazy, his eyes hard and alert. "You were on the rackets committee with John and Robert Kennedy."

"That's right. I don't remember that being mentioned in the *Life* article, though."

"I said I'd read about you elsewhere. So you knew Jack, and you know Bobby."

"I knew Jack a little. I worked for Bobby."

"Robert Kennedy's made public statements backing this lone assassin conclusion. Is that what he really thinks, Mr. Heller?"

"I can't speak for him."

"Well, you might mention to him that you and I spoke, and that I would be pleased to speak with him. That I have a strong feeling that New Orleans might be the key to his brother's murder."

"You do know he's not attorney general anymore, right?"

He nodded slowly in that irritating way wise men do.

"I don't think I have anything for you, Mr. Garrison. Am I free to go?"

"Certainly, Mr. Heller. Just leave your full contact information with my secretary, so we can deal with your rental car theft properly. You know there was some slight damage to it—I hope you picked up the optional insurance."

"I'm covered."

"Pleased to hear it."

At the door, I paused and turned to him. "What if I said I suspected significant mob involvement in the assassination?"

"I would not be surprised."

"Would it be a conflict of interest?"

The cow eyes tightened. "I'll choose not to take that as an insult, Mr. Heller."

"Fine. Then I'll say this. Never mind Bobby. You're in a unique position to get to bottom of this. You can subpoena people. A lot of the principal players involved hung around New Orleans. You can ask questions. You can do something."

He was sitting there, pulling on the pipe, rocking gently, thinking about that, when I went out.

Shep Shepherd had again managed the small miracle of putting an empty booth on either side of us in the VIP Room at the Chicago Playboy Club. We had enjoyed a late supper and were on to drinks, the hour approaching midnight. The CIA security chief was in a gray Brooks Brothers and I was in a gray Botany 500, the major difference being I had more color in my necktie. He was finishing up his third Gibson and I was downing my second vodka gimlet. The jazz combo was playing "What Kind of Fool Am I?"

"There's no way I can give you an absolute assurance," he said, "that the Company was blameless in the Kilgore matter."

"Not 'matter,' Shep. Murder."

"*Maybe* murder," he said with a gap-toothed smile, as inappropriate as it was boyish. "You said yourself it might have been accidental."

"Then where are the tapes?" I asked. "Her notes?"

"Who knows? As for murder, do you rule out the husband?"

"Not entirely. Frank Felton is a washed-up radio star, a failed producer, who single-handedly lost that breakfast show of theirs while Flo was away. Now he's inherited that town house, which is already on the market for two hundred grand, plus whatever insurance money and retirement funds come in."

"But you don't think he did it?"

"No. Somebody said to me, rightly, that Felton didn't have the balls. And I also think he still loved her."

His shrug accompanied a shake of the head. "Men have been known to kill women they loved. Perhaps more than any other kind. And then there's that young reporter from Indianapolis."

Our Bunny stopped by, bringing a fresh round; she was a golden blonde named Connie who'd been a Playmate last year.

"Mark Revell is no murderer," I said. "He's just a Midwestern kid with stars in his eyes. A nobody who likes to get next to somebodies. A fan. And basically a decent enough kid, if I read him right."

"So he's off the suspect list."

I sipped the gimlet. "Actually, no. There's a way he could be involved."

"How is that?"

"What if he were one of *your* assets?"

"My assets?"

"Well, the Company's. I mean, he's a reporter for an Indiana newspaper, but he globe-hops. Rome, Paris, London. Where does he get the money? Yeah, sometimes those junkets are paid for by movie studios, but not usually for a smaller market like Indianapolis. He was in a perfect position to do minor international courier jobs for Uncle Sam."

"This is getting a little far-fetched, Nate. Surely you can do better."

"Not so far-fetched. He denies having an affair with Flo, but she made it clear to me, and others, that she was sleeping with the kid. Why would he deny it? What better result for a star fucker than fucking a star?"

"Well, she was married."

"In a famously open relationship. I think the Company hired this kid to get close to her, to keep an eye on her developing Kennedy story. To seduce her, if necessary, to gain her trust. But here things get murky. What if Revell were asked to lift her assassination notes and her tapes, particularly the Ruby one? The kid worked with her, assisted her, and would know right where she kept such things."

"I'll bite. Suppose he did get that assignment. How would he pull it off?"

"With the Company's help. Dr. Gottlieb or one of your other resident mad scientists cooks up a mickey for Revell to slip Flo, which he does at the Regency piano bar, after the TV broadcast. She gets understandably woozy and he escorts her home. She flops onto her little bed in her office, going to sleep, while her protégé filches the JFK materials. But the mickey the kid has slipped her reacts badly with the booze and the Seconal already in her system—or maybe she wakes up and takes the Seconal, that's hard to say—and then? That's all she wrote. Literally."

"Even that would be an accidental death."

"Yeah, I guess. A manslaughter-ish kind of accident, though. Or . . . maybe Gottlieb or one of his cronies had given Revell something lethal to dose her drink with, almost certainly without the kid's knowledge. My little girl reporter had found out more on her own than the Warren Commission and all its investigators. So maybe it was decided that she had to go."

"She didn't do her investigating entirely on her own."

"No, Mark Lane was there for some of it, but he's already being discredited as a kook, despite his impressive credentials. But I was there, wasn't I? Which is why you happen to be in Chicago again, so soon, isn't it?"

A smile flickered on the boyish face. "Not necessarily. But there is a rumor that, uh . . . Flo Kilgore gave you a duplicate of the Ruby tape."

Looked like Uncle Carlos was spreading the word.

"Suppose she did?" I said. "What would it be worth to the Company for me *not* to come forward with it? To leave buried it and any copies I might have?"

"What *would* that be worth?"

The jazz combo started in on "I Wanna Be Around."

I said, "How about a simple assurance from those representing the country that I fought for? An assurance that my life, and my son's life—and my ex-wife's life, too, what the hell—are no longer on the line."

". . . That sounds reasonable."

"And I'll even throw in my own assurance that I have no intention of taking the assassination investigation any further. I was only sniffing around the edges, after all. I never even met Billie Sol Estes, let alone LBJ."

But others would pick up those threads. And I would in fact share what I'd discovered with Bobby Kennedy. Then there were the dozen signed statements in a dozen safety-deposit boxes scattered around the country, detailing that Jack Ruby interview, my substitute for the imaginary duplicate tapes with which I'd threatened Marcello.

"Of course," Shep said lightly, "this is all hypothetical."

"Of course."

"Hypothetically speaking, you would have a deal. Would you like to shake hands on it?"

"I don't think so. I'll also pass on signing anything in blood, if you don't mind." I slid out of the booth. I leaned in like a Bunny doing her trademark dip. "Don't contact me again, old buddy. We're done, you and I. I wish you and your family and Uncle Sam well. But we are done."

"All right, Nate. Consider yourself off the Christmas card list."

I straightened and nodded and was about to go when I felt his hand on my sleeve.

"One thing, Nate," he said, giving me that Bobby Morse smile. "Be aware that the Company is very grateful to you for your service in New Orleans."

"What service is that?"

"Why, tying off any number of inconvenient loose ends for us. . . . Oh, and I'll get the check."

The Warren Commission's final 889-page report was submitted to President Lyndon Baines Johnson on September 24, 1964, concluding that Lee Harvey Oswald acted alone in killing President John F. Kennedy (and wounding Texas governor John Connally). It also found that Jack Ruby acted alone killing Oswald.

Bobby Kennedy nearly lost his Senate bid, his grief and general disengagement in the process costing him dearly. But late in September, his opponent—the normally likable Senator Kenneth Keating—made a bid for the Jewish vote by accusing Bobby of settling a World War II–era case in favor of a company with Nazi ties. Supposedly RFK had done this just to please old Joe Kennedy, whose reputation as a Nazi appeaser still haunted the family. The charge infuriated Bobby, who before had considered Keating benign, and he struck back hard—he had lost one brother to a war, he reminded voters, and another to an assassin's bullet. It energized his campaign. He won in a landslide, and his path to the presidency seemed clear.

On October 5, 1966, Jack Ruby's conviction was overturned on technicalities and his death sentence set aside. Around this time, Ruby complained that a "mysterious visiting physician" had given him a series of injections; he also claimed to have received numerous chest X-rays, one lasting upwards of an hour. He succumbed to lung cancer on January 3, 1967, at Parkland Hospital, where both Jack Kennedy and Lee Oswald had died.

While I apparently removed one "cleanup crew," assassination witnesses continued to occasionally meet premature fates over the next few years. Albert Bogard, the car salesman who gave the Oswald look-alike a test-drive, committed suicide, in February 1966. Lee Bowers, the railroad towerman who saw unusual activity behind the Grassy Knoll fence, perished in a suspicious single-car accident, in August 1966. But most of those Flo and I interviewed survived—S. M. Holland, Mary Woodward, J. C. Price, among others. Witnesses who waited years, or in some cases decades, to come forward fared better.

Madeleine Brown did not go public about her long relationship with LBJ until 1997, revealing that her son Steven was sired by the late president. Steven, whose physical resemblance to his famous father was striking, filed a $10.5 million lawsuit against Lady Bird, Johnson's widow; but Steven died of cancer before the case was settled. Madeleine wrote a tell-all book that combined rapturous descriptions of lovemaking with Lyndon with revelations about her lover's cold-blooded role in the assassination, but the book did not receive widespread distribution or attention.

In 1970, Beverly Oliver came forward as the so-called "Babushka Lady" evident in photos and films of the Dealey Plaza tragedy, and published a memoir in 1994 that also received little attention. The 8 mm film she shot has never been found, though the House Assassinations Committee made the attempt.

Jim Garrison's investigation into the Kennedy assassination remains a source of controversy—Bobby Kennedy, initially supportive, later came to call the larger-than-life prosecutor a fraud. Bobby's reaction did not surprise me—Garrison's primary line of inquiry was CIA involvement, which might have brought Operation Mongoose to light, tarnishing JFK's memory and RFK's political future.

Garrison might have convicted David Ferrie as a JFK assassination conspirator, had the pederast pilot not died a mysterious suicide himself in 1967, leaving two unsigned notes (cause of death: a supposed brain hemorrhage). The crusading DA had to settle for tangential figure Clay Shaw, New Orleans business executive, who was acquitted in 1969, after the only criminal trial to grow out of the assassination to date. Notably, Garrison used his subpoena power to show the Zapruder film in public for the first time. His investigation inspired director Oliver Stone's 1991 film *JFK*, which fictionalized Garrison much as *The Untouchables* television series and movie did Eliot Ness. But Stone's film, as controversial as

Garrison himself, led to the passage of the President John F. Kennedy Assassination Records Collection Act of 1992 (the year of Garrison's death) and the formation of the US Assassination Records Review Board, making available to the public previously classified documents.

The groundbreaking work of Flo Kilgore and Mark Lane opened a floodgate of conspiracy research and theorizing, with a conspiracy cottage industry rising up to produce hundreds of books on the assassination, ranging from the ridiculous to the sublime. Defenders of the Warren Commission Report did their best to trivialize all such researchers into "conspiracy nuts," much like Lee Harvey Oswald himself had been deemed a crank with a gun. Even before Oliver Stone, however, the public remained largely skeptical of the Warren Commission.

In the wake of Watergate, and with the Zapruder film in wider circulation, the Gallup Poll reported that 81 percent of the American public considered the JFK assassination the result of a conspiracy. The House Select Committee on Assassinations (HSCA) was established in 1976 to investigate the assassinations of John F. Kennedy and Martin Luther King, Jr., and the shooting of Alabama governor George Wallace. The Committee issued its final report in 1978, concluding that a conspiracy was responsible for the assassination of JFK.

The two-year span of the House investigation sparked another round of witness deaths, some mysterious, others blatant.

Roger Craig, the former Dallas County sheriff deputy, continued to speak out about what he'd witnessed surrounding the assassination. Returning from a meeting with Jim Garrison, Craig was shot at, his head grazed. His car was forced off the road in 1973, resulting in a debilitating back injury that ended his law-enforcement career. In 1974, Craig answered a knock at his door and was struck by a shotgun blast, wounding his shoulder. In 1975, he died of a rifle wound in his father's home, a supposed suicide at thirty-nine.

A key Oswald associate, George De Mohrenschildt, was being sought by the House for testimony when he presumably blew off his own head with a shotgun, a shooting termed "very strange" by the Palm County, Florida, sheriff's office.

Mobsters called to testify at the House Assassination hearings had a particularly tough go of it. In 1975, Sam Giancana, while frying up peppers and sausages at home, was shot six times in the back of the head with a .22 automatic, and several more in the mouth—a mob message that a squealer had been silenced. In 1976, Johnny Rosselli turned up in an oil drum in a bay near Miami, strangled, shot, and dismembered. In 1977, Chuckie Nicoletti, sitting in his car in a suburban Chicago restaurant parking lot, was shot in the head three times, gangland-style, and the vehicle set afire.

No such abrupt fate awaited Carlos Marcello. While serving the last of several prison sentences, he suffered a series of strokes, became seriously disabled, and began showing signs of dementia. He lost the power of speech and any sense of who he was, finally reverting to infancy, dying in 1993.

Clint Peoples, promoted to Senior Captain in 1969, left the Rangers in 1974 and became US Marshal for the Northern District of Texas. Even after retiring, he continued to investigate Henry Marshall's murder, pressuring an imprisoned Billie Sol Estes to set the record straight. In 1983, a recently released Estes appeared before a grand jury and testified that LBJ has sent Mac Wallace to dispose of whistle-blower Marshall. With both Johnson and Wallace deceased—and the reputation of a US President to consider—the jury did not act upon these accusations; but they did officially change Henry Marshall's suicide to death by gunshot. Peoples, working to prove Mac Wallace's role in the assassination, died in an automobile accident in 1992, although his last words indicated he'd been run off the road.

In January 1971, Frank Felton was found dead in the same bed where his wife Flo had been found. At first called a heart attack, the death was deemed an intentional drug overdose—a real suicide in a case riddled with fake ones.

Mark Revell continued as the entertainment writer on the *Indianapolis News* into the early 1980s. He went on to work as a photographer of art studies, later receiving a master's degree in Christian Counseling from Jerry Falwell's Liberty University.

I saw Janet Adams a number of times in Chicago over the next ten years, though Jada's Carousel fame soon faded, just as her extreme sexpot style receded in the popular culture. We were never really an item but had a great time whenever we got together, though I was never tempted to become her fifth or sixth husband, or whatever number was next. She died in 1980, and some have made her death out as another mysterious one. It wasn't. Riding a motorcycle, she turned in front of a school bus, which was unable to stop. Nothing mysterious about that, just sad as hell.

LBJ stepped down from the presidency, a man defeated by Vietnam and the dire popularity polls it engendered. He seemed to be making way for Bobby Kennedy's candidacy. It's just possible Bobby had something on Lyndon that helped the President make that tough call. Undoubtedly Jack Kennedy's successor did some great things, but he was also a political animal capable of doing anything for power. Fighting depression, in poor health after severe heart problems, he died in 1973, two days after his second term would have ended.

No one from the House Committee approached me to testify, by the way, and I didn't come forward. Most of what I'd discovered was secondhand or old news by that point, and certain things I could not reveal, as there's no statute of limitations on murder. That's the reason this particular memoir could not be published until after my death.

On a less somber note, my son Sam did take over the family business. His flirtation with rock 'n' roll ended after he got kicked out of Gary Lewis and the Playboys when Jerry's kid signed a national recording contract. Like Jerry's kid, Sam wound up in Vietnam, much to my dismay, which is one of the reasons LBJ should be burning in Hell, and I don't mean Bourbon Street. Sam survived the experience, but like his old man, war left its mark.

In August 1966, in San Francisco's Candlestick Park, the Beatles gave their last live performance. The Colony Club closed its doors in April 1972. The Chicago Playboy Club, once the world's most popular nightspot, shut its doors in the summer of 1986. The Sho-Bar is still open for business in New Orleans (although in a different location).

In 1998, a Texas-based assassination research group presented evidence that a fingerprint, unidentified since its discovery in 1963, had at last been positively ID'd. The unknown print came from one of the boxes making up the so-called "sniper's nest" on the Texas School Book Depository's sixth floor. A certified fingerprint examiner, unaware of the context, made a fourteen-point match with a print from a long-suspected participant in the assassination—a print made when that suspect had been booked on a murder charge in 1951.

I can't tell you whether or not Lee Harvey Oswald ever knelt at that window in the book depository sniper's nest.

But Mac Wallace did.

I OWE THEM ONE

Despite its extensive basis in history, this is a work of fiction, and liberties have been taken with the facts, though as few as possible—and any blame for historical inaccuracies is my own, mitigated by the limitations of conflicting source material.

Ask Not is the third novel in the Nathan Heller JFK Trilogy, preceded by *Bye Bye, Baby* (2011) and *Target Lancer* (2012).

Most of the characters in this novel are real and appear under their true names, although all depictions herein must be viewed as fictionalized. Available research on the various individuals ranges from voluminous to scant. Whenever possible, actual interviews with the subjects have been used as the basis of dialogue scenes, although creative liberties have been taken.

Nathan Heller is, of course, a fictional character, as are the people he works with at the A-1 Detective Agency. In some cases, I have chosen not to use real names as an indication that either a surfeit of research is available on some minor historical figure, or that significant fictionalization has occurred. Joseph Plett, for example, has a real-life counterpart about whom little research was available beyond the details of his death and his association with Billie Sol Estes.

Flo Kilgore was introduced in *Bye Bye, Baby* as a composite of journalists Dorothy Kilgallen, Peter Hyams, James Bacon, and Florabel Muir, reflecting their respective roles in the investigation that followed Marilyn Monroe's death. Here Kilgallen is the sole historical counterpart for Kilgore, although the fictional character does not entirely parallel the real person (Kilgallen, for example, was a Catholic and married only once).

Kilgore's husband, Frank Felton, has a counterpart in Kilgallen's husband; and her assistant, Mark Revell, similarly has a real-life counterpart, although both characters should be viewed as fictional. Heller's theory regarding Flo's death has a basis in views expressed in Lee Israel's biography *Kilgallen* (1979) and the article "Who Killed Dorothy Kilgallen?" by Sara Jordan (*Midwest Today,* 2007), both of which also provided general Kilgallen background.

As far back as the first Nathan Heller novel, *True Detective* (1983), I have intended that my detective would one day delve into the Kennedy assassination. Long before I began writing professionally, I had a strong interest in the case, and vividly remember seeing on television Lee Harvey Oswald hustled around the station by Dallas police. My reaction as a teenager was that when Oswald said he was a patsy, he wasn't lying. I also saw Oswald shot by Jack Ruby when it aired live.

Generally I come to Heller novels with an open mind, following the research wherever it might lead; but I admit that where JFK's murder is concerned, I long ago formed my basic opinions about the case, based upon voluminous reading. Nonetheless, I was prepared to change my mind.

That did not happen. Prior to the writing of *Target Lancer,* my longtime research associate, George Hagenauer, and I devoured scores of books on the assassination, and in the year preceding the writing of *Ask Not* went through several more shelves of research works. The idea of doing a novel exploring the dead witnesses in the murder's wake sent me down several false trails—this book was extensively re-plotted perhaps seven times in the weeks leading up to the start, and several more during the writing itself.

As with *Target Lancer,* my original game plan here—to begin with the probable murder of Lt. Cmdr. William Pitzer as the case injecting Heller back into the Kennedy assassination (see *Without*

Smoking Gun, 2004, Kent Heiner)—was reluctantly discarded with the discovery of the Chicago aspect of the Billie Sol Estes "cleanup" suicides. Out of the fog enveloping the JFK tragedy emerged Malcolm "Mac" Wallace, and the final path for *Ask Not* revealed itself.

The greatest liberty I have taken here is time compression, particularly as it applies to Wallace, Kilgallen, and Cheramie. The latter two did not die until 1965, and Wallace's death—although fairly accurately portrayed here as a puzzling if satisfying mix of vehicular accident and carbon monoxide suicide—did not occur until 1971. For the sake of effective storytelling, I allowed Nate Heller to deal with Wallace in the compressed time frame presented here.

References for Wallace included *Blood, Money and Power* (2003), Barr McClellan; *LBJ: The Mastermind of the JFK Assassination* (2011), Phillip F. Nelson; *The Men on the Sixth Floor* (2010), Glen Sample and Mark Collom; and the seminal if controversial *A Texan Looks at Lyndon* (1964), J. Evetts Haley. Wallace is also a topic in Madeleine Duncan Brown's autobiography, *Texas in the Morning* (1997)—a decidedly weird book combining soft-core romance-novel sex with shocking political revelations. The Henry Marshall case and much more is dealt with in *Captain Clint Peoples, Texas Ranger* (1980) by James M. Day.

I make no pretense that this is a definitive work on the assassination—however based in fact, *Ask Not* is historical fiction on the one hand and, I hope, an entertaining, thought-provoking private eye thriller on the other. For the most part, I have limited Heller to gathering information uncovered by researchers during the era depicted, although this has not been a hard-and-fast rule. Nonetheless, there were countless moments when I omitted material because I did not feel Heller could logically obtain it in 1964.

As much as possible, I like to present Nate Heller in a role occupied by a real person (or persons) in history. For example, his participation in the formation of Operation Mongoose is based upon the real role played by private detective Robert Maheu, as detailed in his memoir, *Next to Hughes* (Robert Maheu and Richard

Hack, 1992). After stepping down as attorney general, Robert Kennedy indeed hired trusted investigators from his rackets committee days to quietly look into the assassination. Heller's initial visit to Carlos Marcello at the Town and Country Motel and Churchill Farms is based on real-life private eye Edward Becker's encounter with the Louisiana godfather, as described in *Mafia Kingfish* (1989) by John H. Davis and *The Grim Reapers* (1969) by Ed Reid. Davis is also a general source for the Marcello material in this novel.

My portrait of Jack Ruby was in particular influenced by *The Ruby Cover-Up* (1978) by Seth Kantor, the reporter who saw Ruby at Parkland Hospital shortly after the assassination. Also of help were *Jack Ruby* (1967, 1968) by Garry Wills and Ovid Demaris; *Jack Ruby's Girls* (1970) by Diana Hunter and Alice Anderson; and *Moment of Madness: The People Vs. Jack Ruby* (1968) by Elmer Gertz. *Nightmare in Dallas* (1994), Beverly Oliver's autobiography (written with Coke Buchanan), provided insights into both Ruby and Oliver herself. The book, while well-written, rather absurdly alternates between scenes of President and Mrs. Kennedy in the White House and nightclub singer Oliver at the Colony Club.

Helpful in shaping the portrait of Bobby Kennedy were *Brothers: The Hidden History of the Kennedy Years* (2007), David Talbot; *Robert Kennedy: His Life* (2000), Evan Thomas; and *RFK: A Candid Biography of Robert Kennedy* (1998), C. David Heymann.

Jim Garrison research included his own *A Heritage of Stone* (1970) and *On the Trail of the Assassins* (1988), as well as *A Farewell to Justice* (2007) by Joan Mellen. The last, despite a somewhat disjointed presentation, is a treasure trove of information on Garrison and his investigation.

Perhaps the best recent Kennedy assassination book, *JFK and the Unspeakable* (2008) by James W. Douglass, was enormously helpful here. Also, I am particularly indebted to *JFK: The Dead Witnesses* (1995) by Craig Roberts and John Armstrong.

The UK ITV series *The Men Who Killed Kennedy* (aired on the History Channel in the United States) explores many of the theories associated with the assassination, and I viewed all nine episodes, including "The Guilty Men," which deals with LBJ and Mac Wallace and was pulled by the History Channel after an outcry from Johnson's widow and surviving associates and defenders.

Numerous other Kennedy assassination books proved helpful, including *Betrayal in Dallas* (2011), Mark North; *Conspiracy* (1989 edition), Anthony Summers; *The Final Chapter on the Assassination of President John F. Kennedy* (2010), Craig I. Zirbel; *Head Shot: The Science Behind the JFK Assassination* (2010), G. Paul Chambers; *The JFK Assassination Debates: Lone Gunman Versus Conspiracy* (2006), Michael L. Kurtz; *Killing the Truth* (1993), Harrison Edward Livingstone; *Last Word: My Indictment of the CIA in the Murder of JFK* (2011), Mark Lane; *Legacy of Secrecy* (2009), Lamar Waldron with Thom Hartmann; *Murder from Within: Lyndon Johnson's Plot Against President Kennedy* (2011), Fred T. Newcomb and Perry Adams; *No More Silence: An Oral History of the Assassination of President Kennedy* (1998), Larry A. Sneed; *Rush to Judgment* (1966), Mark Lane; *To Kill a President* (2008), M. Wesley Swearingen; *Ultimate Sacrifice* (2005, 2006), Lamar Waldron with Thom Hartmann; *Who Shot JFK: A Guide to the Major Conspiracy Theories* (1993), Bob Callahan, illustrated by Mark Zingarelli; and *Who's Who in the JFK Assassination* (1993), Michael Benson. Please do not assume that my inclusion of a title here indicates wholesale endorsement of theories therein, just as their authors are not responsible for my interpretation of evidence I've fitted together from many sources.

Works consulted that specifically explore the organized crime aspect of the assassination include *Contract on America: The Mafia Murder of President John F. Kennedy* (1988), David E. Scheim; *The Plot to Kill the President* (1981, 1992), G. Robert Blakey and Richard N. Billings; and *The Kennedy Contract: The Mafia Plot to Assassinate the President* (1993), John H. Davis. Another key mob reference was *All-American Mafioso: The Johnny Rosselli Story* (1991) by Charles Rappleye and Ed Becker.

An indispensable tool—courtesy of George Hagenauer—was *Dallas Public and Private* (1964), Warren Leslie. The WPA Guides for Texas (1969 edition), Dallas (1942), Louisiana (1959 edition), and

New Orleans (1938) were also extremely helpful, as was *Historic Dallas Hotels* (2010), Sam Childers. *Fifty Years of the Playboy Bunny* (2010), Hugh Hefner, John Dant, and Josh Robertson, provided much of the Chicago Playboy Club reference, as did vintage issues of *Playboy,* which were also plumbed for advertising and fashion information. Vintage issues of the exotic dancer–dominated 1950's men's magazine *Cabaret* played a big role in my re-creation of the world of strip clubs in both Dallas and New Orleans.

Similarly useful was the film *Naughty Dallas* (1964), unearthed for DVD and download by Something Weird Video. The work of notorious low-budget Dallas filmmaker Larry Buchanan—an ad agency co-worker of Madeleine Brown's—*Naughty Dallas* features footage of a strip show headlining Jada, with exterior footage of the Carousel Club and interiors at the Colony Club.

General Chicago information and color was supplied by the following books: *Chicago Confidential* (1950), Jack Lait and Lee Mortimer; *Complete Guide to Chicago* (1954), Andrew Hepburn; and *The WPA Guide to Illinois* (1939).

The Internet has become an indispensable research tool, and it's difficult for me to believe that I wrote the Heller novels prior to the JFK Trilogy without its benefit. Small facts were checked dozens of times during a writing session—for example, the spelling of once common and now obscure products, the names of TV shows and popular music of the era, and the point at which slang terms entered general usage.

The following Web sites were helpful in the writing of *Ask Not* (names, not Web addresses, are given, since what might become of the Web addresses over time is unknown): 3525 Turtle Creek; The Beatles Bible; Billie Sol Estes: A Texas Legend; Bustout Burlesque; Con Artist Hall of Infamy; Dallas County Pioneer Association; JFK Assassination Debate—The Education Forum; French Quarter.com; *The Harvard Crimson;* History with Bill Zeman; The Kilgallen Files; MFF (the Mary Ferrell Foundation); MediaNOLA; *Midwest Today;* The Nostalgic Glass; Spartacus Educational; Texas Tiki; Travelgoat; and Unvisited Dallas. Also, Roger Craig and Madeleine

Brown interviews were found on YouTube. Wikipedia was frequently helpful, but used as a starting point for research and never the end game.

The following articles, found on the Internet, were utilized: "Beverly Oliver ('The Babushka Lady') Interview" by Gary James; "Dealey Plaza Revisited" by Helen Thompson; "Disappearing Witnesses" by Penn Jones, Jr.; "Jack Ruby: Dallas' Original J.R." by Josh Alan Friedman; "The Most Exciting Building in America" by Jim Key; "Rambling Rose" by Chris Mills; "When They Kill a President" by Roger Craig (unfinished autobiographical book); and "Yellow Roses" by Dave Reitzes.

My thanks to Gary Mack, curator of the Sixth Floor Museum at Dealey Plaza, for answering several research questions.

Billie Sol Estes, still living at this writing, offers an autobiography on his Web site. I paid forty dollars for this volume, directly to Estes, and never received it, my queries about its whereabouts going unanswered. Getting scammed by Billie Sol Estes seemed a fitting thing to experience during the writing of this novel, giving me far more satisfaction than actually receiving the book.

On the other hand, I ordered *Bond of Secrecy* (2008), E. Howard Hunt's biography, from its author, his son St. John Hunt, and soon received a signed manuscript-style copy. In a deathbed confession, the infamous spy fingers LBJ as a central figure in the Kennedy assassination. The book has been announced for more traditional publication, but at this writing is on hold.

My friend and longtime research associate, George Hagenauer, made many trips to Iowa for brainstorming sessions and research planning as we wrestled with handling this sprawling, often surrealistic subject. Thank you, George.

Thanks also to my friend and agent, Dominick Abel, who made sure this book happened; and my editor, James Frenkel, who gave Heller and me the chance to finally take on the JFK case.

As usual, the greatest thanks go to Barbara Collins—my wife, best friend, and valued writing collaborator—who was working on her draft of our next "Barbara Allan"–bylined novel while I was writing this one. Despite being caught up in her own book, she endured my constant opinion-seeking and need for a sounding board, and always had sharp suggestions to help me stop my head from spinning with research and find a steerable path.

On a number of occasions over the years, I have said in interviews and elsewhere that the Heller saga would conclude with the Kennedy assassination. For those who consider that bad news, I can reveal that Heller is contemplating a memoir about Robert Kennedy (dealing with both rackets committee days and RFK's assassination) as well as one on the murder of Martin Luther King, Jr. It's even possible that Heller will one day discuss a certain minor burglary at the Watergate Hotel.

ABOUT THE AUTHOR

MAX ALLAN COLLINS has earned an unprecedented nineteen Private Eye Writers of America Shamus Award nominations, winning for his Nathan Heller novels *True Detective* (1983) and *Stolen Away* (1991) and receiving the PWA life achievement award, the Eye, in 2007. In 2012, his Nathan Heller saga was honored with the PWA Hammer Award for making a major contribution to the private eye genre.

His graphic novel *Road to Perdition* (1998), the basis of the Academy Award–winning Tom Hanks film, was followed by two acclaimed prose sequels and several graphic novels. He has created a number of innovative suspense series, notably Quarry (the first hitman series) and Eliot Ness (covering the Untouchable's Cleveland years). He is completing a number of Mike Hammer novels begun by the late Mickey Spillane; his audio novel *The New Adventures of Mike Hammer: The Little Death* won the 2011 Audie for Best Original Work.

His many comics credits include the syndicated strip *Dick Tracy;* his own *Ms. Tree; Batman;* and *CSI: Crime Scene Investigation,* based on the TV series, for which he wrote ten bestselling novels. His tie-in books have appeared on the *USA TODAY* bestseller list nine times and the *New York Times* three. His movie novels include *Saving Private Ryan, Air Force One,* and *American Gangster,* which won the IAMTW Best Novel Scribe Award in 2008.

An independent filmmaker in the Midwest, Collins has written and directed four features, including the Lifetime movie *Mommy* (1996), and he scripted *The Expert,* a 1995 HBO World Premiere, and *The Last Lullaby* (2008), based on his novel *The Last Quarry.* His documentary *Mike Hammer's Mickey Spillane* (1998/2011) appears on the Criterion Collection DVD and Blu-ray of *Kiss Me Deadly.*

His play *Eliot Ness: An Untouchable Life* was nominated for an Edgar Award in 2004 by the Mystery Writers of America; a film version, written and directed by Collins, was released on DVD and appeared on PBS stations in 2009.

His other credits include film criticism, short fiction, songwriting, trading-card sets, and video games. His coffee-table book, *The History of Mystery,* was nominated for every major mystery award, and his *Men's Adventure Magazines* (with George Hagenauer) won the Anthony Award.